Dave Wragg really got into writing stories just as he finished his English GCSE, then took about twenty years to get back to it. In the meantime, he studied software engineering, worked in global shipping and technical consultancy, and once spent a year in the Foreign Office 'hiding in the basement'.

Dave lives in Hertfordshire with his wife, two small daughters, and two smaller cats.

THE BLACK HAWKS

DAVID WRAGG

Harper*Voyager*
An imprint of HarperCollins*Publishers* Ltd
1 London Bridge Street
London SE1 9GF

www.harpercollins.co.uk

First published by HarperCollins*Publishers* 2019
This paperback original edition 2019
1

A catalogue record for this book is
available from the British Library

ISBN: 978-0-00-833141-2

Set in Sabon by Palimpsest Book Production Ltd,
Falkirk, Stirlingshire

Printed and bound in the UK by CPI Group (UK) Ltd,
Croydon CR0 4YY

This book is produced from independently certified FSC™ paper
to ensure responsible forest management.

For more information visit: www.harpercollins.co.uk/green

For Sarah,
for everything

PART I

ONE

Chel ran. His feet slapped against the dusty pale stone of the winter palace ramparts, blood thumping at his temples and breath rasping his throat, while gulls wheeled above and the sleepless harbour bustled beneath. He rounded a corner, the yawning guards on the tower watching his progress with vague interest at best.

A mound of refuse lay stacked against the sea wall, a pile of ashen rags with a long stick propped beside it. Chel shifted to round it, teeth gritted, when the pile moved. It became abruptly man-shaped, and its stick swung out into his path. Before he could react, the stick smashed into his shin. He tumbled, arms outstretched, and sprawled head-first into the stones. A blast of pain tore up his shoulder.

Cursing and swearing vengeance, he tried to whirl, but his vision went purple and the combination of running, falling, and a pounding hangover sent him retching back into the dust. By the time the convulsions passed, the rag-pile man and his stick were gone, the ramparts empty.

'Thrice-damned pig-fucker!' Chel spat onto the ground, still leaning on one arm.

A pair of boots stepped to fill his vision, their laces intricately bound, the soft leather grime-free.

'I admit it, I did not expect to find you on the walls this time.'

He squinted up at the figure blotting the pink-flecked morning sky. 'Marekhi,' he coughed. 'Was just on my way to you.'

His liege's first sworn regarded him steadily. Her face was placid, her tone light. 'What did they challenge you with this time? A brandy cask? The barrel-dregs? Did you even make it back to the barracks?'

Chel coughed again by way of answer, wiped at his mouth as he pushed back on his haunches. His shoulder throbbed in time with his headache.

The slightest lip-curl marred Marekhi's flawless cheek, although her tone remained even. 'Lord Sokol will be expecting to see his festival robes at ten bells. You will be present, as will the robes, and you will look as though you belong.'

'Oh, he'll be up by then, will he?'

'Your odour will also be much improved. Am I understood, Master Chel?'

He sat back against the flagstones, no longer trying to stand. Her silhouette glowed golden in the morning light. 'Come on, Marekhi, where's your festival spirit?' he croaked.

'These petty defiances are a stain on our liege's name, Master Chel.' Her chin tilted. Her voice was quiet but carried clear over the sounds of the clamour of the port below. 'You are a man in sworn service to a lord who is a guest at this palace, and your deeds and . . . *presentation* are those of our liege. It's time you acted like it.'

'I can take a beating, if Sokol wishes to make me an example.'

'That should not be a point of pride,' she said, her voice steel-edged. 'You swore an oath. This behaviour shames your uncle and your family.'

'If my *step*-uncle wants the value of my service, he can earn it.'

'Boy, how much do you think your service is worth?'

For a moment she was snarling, then calm swept over her face. She turned and began striding away, boots clicking on the flagstones. 'Ten bells, Vedren Chel, with the robes,' she called over her shoulder. 'Obey, or don't. But attend to your stench.'

A breeze ruffled the palms in the courtyard, and they slapped together like a round of sarcastic applause. Chel caught a whiff of himself, recoiled, then nodded his thudding head in bitter acknowledgement.

'Fine.'

***

Chel bent over one of the stables' water-troughs, scooping handfuls of cool, musty water over his face. A palace horse watched him from the dark of its stable. Chel did his best to ignore it. He felt disapproved of enough already.

'You're up, Master Chel! Up-ish, at least.' A broad and beaming figure in a battered guardsman's uniform was at his elbow. 'Didn't think we'd be seeing you for a good while this morning.'

'Ungh,' Chel grunted, and wiped himself down with a horse blanket. 'Heali.'

'So,' the guardsman said, leaning forward, in a conspiratorial fashion. 'Did you win?'

Chel pressed one palm to his thudding temple. 'In a manner of speaking.'

Heali chuckled, a sound like marbles rattling. 'Can't say no to a challenge, can you, my boy?'

Chel grunted again and leaned back against the stable wall. The stable-yard churned with a gathering retinue, another of the minor lords assembling his host now that the campaigning season was drawing to a close. Chel watched the formation of their column with envious eyes. Within the hour, the column would be on the road, and its host would be back in their homes before winter hit.

'They're not staying for the festival, then,' Heali said with a nod to the milling horse. 'Any chance your lot . . .?'

Chel spat a wad of sticky dust. 'Sokol's so obsessed with rubbing up against royalty that he's hanging on for the court's arrival, and he's chummy enough with the grand duke that we'll not be kicked onto the road any time soon. I'm not that lucky.' He flicked away a spherical fly, hangover sweat mixed with trough water dripping from his brow. 'Five hells, how can you stand this heat?'

Heali chuckled again. 'How can you not, Master Chel? Thought you Andriz were the blooms of the desert?'

'Give it a rest, Heali. I grew up in the south. It's not that hot down there, not like this – by the harvest festivals we're usually a month or two into the rains.'

Heali cast a glance up at the pristine, punishingly cloudless sky. 'Doesn't look like rain any time soon, Master Chel. So happens, I was heading down to the kitchen to muster a bit of breakfast – care to join me? You look like a man in need of a feed.'

Chel's stomach hissed bile. His hangover agreed.

***

'Kitchen's closed.' A hard-faced woman in a smock barred the doorway.

'Closed? Nonsense, my jewel,' Heali replied. 'How could the kitchen be closed in a festival week? We're but days from the feast!'

The woman's eyes narrowed. She had a jaw like quarried stone and weathered hands to match. 'Off-limits, then. Especially to you, Heali, and whoever's riding your pocket today.' She flicked a sneer at Chel, who was quite offended. 'This is no time for your antics – we've got the Order of the Rose at our shoulders. Get your meat-fingers gone before the churchmen come looking at you too.'

The door slammed shut. Heali frowned at it, thick lips pursed. Chel frowned at Heali.

'My apologies, Master Chel, thought I'd be able to lend a hand to a brother in need. Come up looking a right pillock, eh?'

Chel gave no answer. His head hurt, and his palms and shoulder ached. His hunger had become a hot blade in his gut. He rubbed one hand over his eyes and started walking back toward the courtyard. Sokol's robes and the lowport beckoned, and he was in no fit state for it. 'I need to be going—'

'Heading out on an errand? Surely not on an empty stomach?'

Chel stopped in the courtyard archway, one foot in brilliant sunlight, squinting against the glare, already tired of the guardsman's manner. 'You're in luck, my boy,' Heali continued with a munificent smile, 'because your friend Heali knows where to get the best breakfast in all Denirnas Port.'

'You do?' At that, Chel perked up.

'Of course, my boy. Permit me to atone for my failing – I'll take you myself.'

'For the last time, Heali, stop calling me boy.'

'I mean no disrespect, Master Chel. You're still boyish from my end of the wick, that's all.' Heali raised a hand with a disarming grin. 'Come, let's take a wander. There's a little fellow in the lowport, does the most arresting grilled things.'

Chel gave a sour glance back down the gloomy hallway to the closed kitchen door. 'What do the Church care of festival preparations anyway?' he said.

A voice like the earth moving rumbled in the darkness behind them. Chel hadn't even realized there was a passageway there. 'Because the festival of King's Vintage is a lie, a sop to the masses to blot the vile truth from their eyes.'

He turned to find a gaunt figure looming over him, eyes mere hollows in the gloom, his dome of skull ringed by ragged grey locks. He carried a crate of earthenware oil lamps, clinking in time to his lurching steps. Heali sniffed. 'Lengthened your chain for the festival, did they, Mad Mercunin?'

'I know what they call me, Heali,' the cadaverous giant replied. 'Do you know what they call you?'

Heali laughed, but Chel detected an edge to it. 'Go on, sod off, you walking corpse. Go whisper your secrets to the cliff ducks.'

Mercunin shuffled away into the gloom, the crate heavy in his arms. 'Hey,' Chel called, 'what *is* the "vile truth"?'

The well-deep voice echoed from the stones as the porter slid into darkness. 'That the king is dead, and we shall all of us burn.'

Heali snorted. 'Take no heed of mad men, Master Chel,' he said, then walked out into the bustle of the courtyard, nodding for Chel to follow. With a bemused sigh he did, the old porter's words still rattling in his head.

***

'Is this place far?' Chel said as they wandered through the open palace gate, beneath the strutting statue of Grand Duke Reysel. A fresh streaking of bird shit adorned the statue; a pair of skivvies were doing their best to remove it. Duty guards nodded to Heali as they passed. 'I need to be back by ten bells.'

'And why's that, Master Chel?'

'Sokol will be expecting me to present him with his freshly arrived festival robes. Should have been here days ago, but you know what it's like this time of year.'

'I do indeed. Can't spend days on the walls without learning the motion of the ocean, eh?' Heali picked his way down the meandering ridge path, steering around the irregular mule traffic plodding uphill, festival loads stacked high.

Across the bay on the opposite ridge, the domes of the Academy glowed in the morning sun, safely nestled along the crest of the highport that towered over the harbour's eastern flank. In the handful of weeks he'd been in Denirnas, Chel hadn't made it as far as the highport, let alone the Academy. It looked pleasantly peaceful up there.

In the lowport, the summer's-end sun was well up, as was the seething press of peddlers, pilgrims and panhandlers. Everywhere was noise and movement, heat and humanity, and Chel's nausea came roaring back as he tried to follow Heali down the carved steps of the hill path into the town.

He kept one hand on his purse and the other on Heali's shoulder, buffeted by human tides.

They skirted a grim-faced servant tasked with scrubbing the latest Rau Rel graffiti from a pale wall, the words 'The Watcher sees all' disappearing beneath his brush. One of the palace guards watched over him; he nodded to Heali and moved aside as they passed. Chel shook his head. The partisans' graffiti would be back before they made it back to the palace. You couldn't go twenty strides in the port without seeing 'death to tyrants' or some reference to 'the Watcher' scrawled across walls; the only thing that varied was the spelling.

'Who keeps writing this stuff?' Chel muttered to Heali. Heali didn't respond.

Preachers' Plaza was already thick with idle folk circling the ranting box-clerics on their sea-crates, attending them or jeering them in equal measure. Chel took one look at the seething crowd and baulked; he could go no further. He almost cried with relief when Heali diverted from the main path, cutting round the plaza and between two of the low white buildings that blanketed the bluffs above the harbour. A narrow path led up to a flat roof, suddenly dim in the highport's shadow.

The shaded rooftop was still cool and mercifully removed from the madness below. A clutter of mismatched wooden furniture dotted it, tables and chairs arranged in haphazard fashion, some occupied by resting merchants and sea-folk. Silk pennants and throws hung from poles around the roof's edge, teased by the brisk ocean breeze, their sigils and symbols a mystery to Chel. A great clay oven dominated the hillside end, already smoking and sizzling, tended to by a small, wiry man.

Heali dumped himself in one of the chairs, nodded for Chel to join him and waved the little man over. Heali produced a purse from beneath his belt with a flourish, placing a stack of coins on the table that could pay for three breakfasts with change to spare. Chel made no comment.

The little man was beside him, asking him something with a cavalcade of syllables. Chel blinked back in incomprehension. The little man repeated his noises with practised patience.

Heali chuckled, marbles rattling again. 'Chicken or fish, Master Chel? I can recommend the fish.'

'Chicken.'

'Ha! Suit yourself.'

The little man nodded and scampered back to the oven, and a moment later the sizzling redoubled. Chel felt a surge of gratitude, although he declined the wine that was offered while they waited. He wasn't mad.

'Sure I can't tempt you?' Heali took a deep swig and smacked his lips, then topped up his mug. 'No such thing as a hangover at your age, young man. Splash of spiced wine and a sea breeze, see you right. Heali's little tip for you.'

Chel ignored him, his gaze on the flapping silk hangings at the roof's edge. 'Those Serican?'

Heali shot him an incredulous look, half smiling, anticipating a joke. 'No, Master Chel,' he said after a moment, the smile lingering. 'Not every piece of silk comes from Serica.'

Chel blushed at his ignorance, but at that moment the food arrived. Chel acknowledged that Heali had been right: it was excellent — spiced and fragrant and unfamiliar. He tore into it.

'So,' said the guardsman after a respectable number of chews, 'you've been enjoying festival week?' Chel only chewed. He could feel the food restoring him. 'Partial to a bit of brandy myself, as it happens. I was a young man once: every night defiance, every morning . . . regret . . .' Chel nodded along, half listening to Heali's words, until his platter was empty.

Hanging behind the oven was a wooden mask, taller than a man's head, carved with intricate detail and inlaid with a silvery metal. Its expression was unfriendly. Chel stared at it.

'What is that?'

'Battle-mask,' said a voice beside him. He turned to see a child looking back with wide, dark eyes. I must be hungover, he thought. That's the third person to get the drop on me this morning.

'A battle-mask?'

'My father was a famous warrior in our home. He has many masks.' The tone was even, the gaze level.

Chel shot a look at the wiry little man, as the girl started clearing plates. He was scrubbing the inside of the oven with something. 'He doesn't look like a famous warrior,' he said.

'That is why he would have killed you.'

Chel's eyebrows climbed. 'That a fact?'

The girl nodded, her contemptuous expression not far off the mask's. Chel squinted; he could see faded paint on it, yellow and maybe blue. 'The champions of the cantons were given masks if they won a great battle or defeated another champion in a duel. My father has six masks.'

'Cantons?' Chel blinked. 'You're *Norts*?'

She nodded, but her eyes flickered in disapproval at the term. 'Iokara.'

'I didn't think any Norts ever crossed the sea.'

'Then you should feel shame at your ignorance.' With that she turned and marched away, platters in hand, leaving Chel gawping in her wake. She reminded him strongly of his sister Sabina.

Heali was chuckling. 'Feisty lass, eh? His boy will be around here somewhere. He's even less forgiving.' He laughed again, and Chel's cheek twitched. 'Didn't think Norts crossed the sea. Not been around long, have you? How could you not know a mask? Everyone knows Norts fight in masks.'

'That's not what she . . . ah, forget it,' Chel sighed. His hangover had faded but his shoulder still ached. He looked back at the little man, who was running a sharp-stone over a gleaming steel carving-blade. He didn't let his gaze linger.

Heali was talking again, but Chel let the words wash over him. For the first time that morning, he felt vaguely human, and his eyes wandered over the spread of the lowport below, its ceaseless flurry. They had a good view down into the plaza from the rooftop. One of the preachers had attracted quite a crowd, although her proclamations were inaudible over the general clamour.

'. . . close chums, goes the word, but is theirs a harmonious affection? A bond of equals, or pals for the proles, as my old cousin would say? You've been with the good lord some time now, I'd wager, and . . .' Chel was half listening again, his attention drawn to something disturbing the crowds on the plaza's far side, perhaps a wagon trying to move through. People were definitely trying to get out of the way of something.

'. . . perhaps handle some of his correspondence?' Heali went on. 'See, there's always dissent, especially around a man with a title like the grand duke. Question is, should matters come to a head, which way would your liege be leaning? Now, Master Chel, as a young man who likes a nip, perhaps you'd—'

Movement on a rooftop overlooking the plaza caught Chel's eye.

'Sweet merciful Shepherd, it's that pig-fucking beggar! The one that tripped me on the wall. There, on that roof!'

He was off and running before Heali could stop him, pelting away and down the steep steps back to the lowport, chair tumbling in his wake. The shamble of rags had been unmistakable, the stick, the cloud of ash. He tore into the human press at the foot of the path, one eye on the rooftop on the far side of the plaza. The beggar couldn't have seen him, not from there, and even if he had, how fast could a shuffling old bastard leaning on a stick go?

The human tide at the plaza's edge seemed suddenly against him, as if the square were trying to empty itself in one go. Chel fought to get past, his eyes locked on the roof-line above, then with a curse changed tack. He rolled around the flood of traffic and into a side-alley, in dingy shade from the angled sun. Unimpeded at last, he drove his tired legs forward. The alley bent around toward the back of the plaza, and from there he'd have a direct line toward the crumbling rooftop where he'd seen the beggar. He just needed to find steps or a ladder, or—

Gaze still fixed on the bright sky overhead as he rounded the bend at full speed, he didn't see the figures in the alley's gloom. He crashed into them, sending one tumbling, crunching into dirt himself for the second time that morning. At least the robed man beneath him cushioned his fall. He was mumbling the world's fastest apology, already looking around for his target roof, when his cushion's companion whimpered, a small, pitiful sound in the claustrophobic stillness.

Eyes adjusting to the alley's shade, Chel looked from one to the other. The man he'd downed was back on his feet, clad in a dark, stained robe, a short, thick stick in his hand and a snarl on his face. Huddled against the far wall was the whimperer, a wild-haired woman, her face mud- and blood-darkened.

Chel swallowed, shifting back toward the pair. 'What's going on?'

The man's snarl widened. His head was shaved but for a dark tuft at its crest. Chel had seen hair like that around the port and assumed it was a fashion of sorts. 'Church business. Fuck off.'

'What kind of church business involves beating a woman in an alley?'

'The kind you don't get involved in.'

Chel set his jaw. He felt the fluttery canter of his heartbeat against his ribcage. 'I'm from the palace. I won't let you hurt her.'

The man's snarl became a grim smile. 'That, boy, would be a matter of opinion.' Chel braced for his swing, but instead the man bared his teeth and whistled through a dark gap at their centre. Chel heard the approaching thud of footsteps from the distant alley-mouth, the rhythmic jingling. He turned to see two more robed figures advancing, heads shaved but for the tuft, sticks in hand.

They passed through a musty shaft of morning light and their robes glowed a deep red, their steel necklaces gleaming.

Chel rubbed at his thudding temple. 'Oh, shit.'

***

The three robed men marched Chel and the bleeding woman out of the alley and shoved them into the sudden bright emptiness of the plaza, the sun's glare harsh against the whitewashed stone. Chel kept his feet, the woman collapsed to the dust beside him. She was draped in filthy rags, her visible skin scarred and blotchy, odd pale welts curled down her arms like vines.

'Shepherd's mercy, what is it now?'

A figure strode into view from behind a dark-wood cart that stood at the plaza's rough centre, its sides and rear caged with iron. She was slight and sharp-featured, her silver hair cropped close to the skull, and was swathed in robes of white and rich vermilion. A long, hook-headed staff tapped the stones in time with her steps. Chel recognized her immediately. He'd seen her at the winter palace, being treated by the servants with a deference that bordered on fear: Sister Vashenda of the Order of the Rose. No wonder the plaza had emptied so fast. Chel grimaced. A set-to with the Church on a hangover was about as far away from ideal as anything he could imagine.

'One of the heretics, Sister,' one of the tufts grunted. 'Fell short on her repentance.'

A sigh. 'And the other?'

'Interfered. Says he's from the palace.'

Her head tilted. 'Does he now?' She waved her free hand,

urgent, exasperated. 'Go, find the rest, get them to the croft. Clean this place up.'

The tufts departed, leaving Chel and the two women in the otherwise empty plaza, except for the cart. From the look of it, there were people inside, peering gloom-eyed from behind the cage bars. Chel swallowed.

Sister Vashenda was staring directly at him. 'Brother Hurkel,' she called toward the cart. 'Would you join us, please?'

The cart moved, shifting on its axle, then settled as its front lowered to the ground. The hulking figure that lumbered into view was clad in a rust-coloured tunic, a milk-skinned beast of a man with a shock of blond hair crowning a too-small head the colour of beetroot. An intricate steel necklace jangled at his beefy chest, and at his belt his stubby fingers rested on a short, heavy ball mace. Its head was stained dark.

'Yes, Sister?' the giant rumbled.

'Brother Hurkel, do you know this young man? He claims to be from the palace.'

'I do not, Sister. Perhaps he has hit his head. Perhaps he wishes to.'

Chel stood his ground. A sickly fire burned anew in his innards. 'I'm a sworn man in the service of a lord under the grand duke's aegis. I'm protected as his guest and servant.'

The sister walked toward him, her face curious, as if he were the most interesting turd she'd stepped in that day. She looked him up and down. Behind her, Hurkel had advanced, drowning them in his shadow. 'Do I know you, sand-flower?' Vashenda asked, eyes narrowed. 'Are you Sokol's brood?'

'By marriage, not blood,' he snapped, then cursed himself.

She offered a smile that contained not a jot of amity. Her teeth were so white. 'Between chosen people, a word of advice, perhaps?' She stepped close, a silver flower gleaming at her chest, bright in his eyes. 'Sand-flower or not, a lucky traveller keeps from the Rose's path,' she whispered, then clacked her teeth so hard in his ear he shied away, certain she'd bitten off his earlobe.

'Brother Hurkel,' she said, stepping away from him. 'How high does Lord Sokol rank?'

The beast-man waggled a slab hand, palm-down, his bottom lip protruding. 'Middling, if friendly with his grace the grand duke.'

'Of little consequence, then. Sand-flower, are you, perhaps, in need of some spiritual re-education at the croft? I doubt Lord Sokol will miss a "relative by marriage" for a few days, especially for the betterment of his eternal soul. Hmm?'

She was shaking her head slowly at him. Chel felt himself shaking his along with her.

'Good. Depart.' A brief, bright smile. She turned back to the rag-clad preacher, who had remained on her knees. 'Now, what have we here?'

The meat-pile growled. 'Heresy, Sister. Godlessness. Abomination.' His thick fingers tightened around his mace. Chel heard its wooden haft creak.

The box-preacher's head was up; Chel saw a fierce gaze, clear and defiant, that bore into the robed figures looming over her. When she spoke, her voice was cracked but strong. 'Your godless church is the abomination! Lo Vassad sits atop a festering dung-heap of corruption. Your type act not for the people, but for avarice, venality – how plush are your robes, false prelate.'

Sister Vashenda cocked her head and raised an eyebrow to her colleague, a hand to her mouth in mock-horror. 'Truly are evil days upon us, that such profanity be uttered before the Shepherd's humble servants. That the poor townspeople should have been so assailed.' She crouched in front of the kneeling box-preacher, lifting her chin with a finger, and trotted out her words with tired practice. 'Very well. Will you repent of your madness and ill-speech, and be welcomed back to the good Shepherd's mercy?'

'I will never bow to you, idolater. I have heard the voice of truth, felt the touch of the real Mother of the earth.' She rubbed at the odd scars on her arms, livid whorls shining in what sunlight escaped Hurkel. 'I have been chosen by the storm.'

Vashenda sighed. 'I will never understand you people.'

'You are dirt in the Mother's eyes! You are—'

'Yes, yes, dirt and damnation and such, very good.' Vashenda stepped away with a wave of her hand. 'Brother Hurkel, the heretic is yours. Have your fun, in God's name.'

A grin split Hurkel's beetroot face. He began to advance, the mace gripped in his meaty fist.

Vashenda's eyes fell on Chel. 'Sand-flower, you are still here.' When he said nothing, she continued, directing her attention away from whatever Hurkel was about to do. 'You know, people speculate on why the red confessors of the Brotherhood of the Twice-Blooded Thorn carry blunt tools on their divine business. Many believe that the Articles forbid the Shepherd's children from carrying weapons, or from spilling blood in divine service.'

Hurkel towered over the kneeling preacher, weighing the mace in his grip. He was chuckling to himself.

Vashenda gave a rueful smile. 'Nonsense, of course. God's will must be performed by whatever means necessary.'

Chel's heart was galloping in his chest. He looked from preacher to Hurkel and back again, light-headed, mouth dry.

'Sand-flower, what are you doing?' Vashenda's tone was low, warning, as he moved toward Hurkel. 'Sand-flower! Do not be foolish!' His breath coming in shallow gasps, fingers trembling, Chel stepped between Hurkel and the kneeling preacher, who was chanting something to herself in a low, urgent voice. He looked up into Hurkel's porcine eyes, staring back at him with a hot mix of incredulity and outrage.

'Sand-flower! Why in God's name must everyone . . .' Vashenda leaned her head against the crook of her staff, eyes clenched shut. 'I suppose we'll find out how much you'll be missed after all, you stupid boy.'

Chel didn't move. He couldn't. His gaze was locked on Hurkel. The enormous confessor was grinning again. Chel's vision was twitching in time with the thump of his pulse, a taste like burning at the back of his throat.

The distant peal of bells carried on the sea breeze, from somewhere out past the headland. They were joined by others, closer at the harbour's edge, then a moment later the plaza rang with the clang and jangle of churches, chapels and watchtowers.

Chel blinked. It couldn't yet be ten bells, surely?

Hurkel looked at Vashenda, who looked back at Hurkel, eyes narrowed, brows low. His expression matched hers. 'That's an alarm,' Vashenda said slowly. Hurkel grunted, his attention dragged away from Chel.

Shouts followed the bells. Suddenly the plaza was full of people again, running this way and that, their shouts and calls vying with the cacophony of bells.

Vashenda grimaced. 'We'll have to take the heretic's confession later. Brother Hurkel, put her in the cart with the others.'

Chel stood his ground. Already the plaza was thick with motion, the sound of the bells sporadically near-deafening. 'Leave her alone,' he shouted over the noise.

Someone was bellowing Vashenda's name from across the plaza, another red-robed, tufted type, his features animated with alarm. Vashenda exhaled in exasperation, then leaned forward and fixed Chel with a fearsome glare as the chaos enveloped them. 'This is not over, sand-flower. You may yet enjoy the chance to regret your choices.'

She growled at Hurkel and jerked her head for him to follow. Hurkel gestured at the cart, but she shook her head. 'They'll still be there when we come back.' The two of them stalked away, leaving the cart with its whimpering cargo locked at the plaza's centre. Chel felt his insides unclench as they passed from view. He needed to get back to the palace.

Heali was pushing his way through the crowd, his fleshy face waxy and pallid. 'God's breath, Master Chel. That's pushing your luck, even for someone of your blood.' He shook his head. 'Why would you get yourself involved in all that?'

Chel had stilled his breathing, although the light-headedness remained. 'You saw? I could have used some moral support there, Heali. Besides, I'm sworn. They couldn't have touched me.' I hope, he added to himself.

'I'm sure that knowledge would have been a comfort

once they had you strung up by your ankles in the croft. You want my advice, young man, you stay—'

'Beating the poor wasn't in any Article I ever heard.'

Heali gave a mirthless chuckle. 'Maybe you've not heard the new ones. They'll let anyone in these days, give some alley-boy a stick and a red robe and call him a confessor, I dunno, makes me question sometimes . . .' He tailed off. 'Stay out of their way, Master Chel, for your own sake. The Rose have a long memory and a longer reach.'

Chel only sniffed. His legs were trembling. He hoped Heali couldn't tell.

The wild-haired preacher's head emerged from beneath the rancid cart. 'They're gone,' Chel said, doing his best to look reassuring.

She clambered out and fixed him with her clear eyes. 'Mother bless you, child. You and your people shall be in her highest favour.'

'Er, if you say so.'

She turned and began working at the cage's bolt, trying to prise it open. Within, the sallow and frightened faces shrank back, more alarmed than ever. Interfering with the Rose's confessionals was simply not done.

'Hey,' Chel called after her. 'Hey! They'll be coming back, you don't want to hang around for that, right? This will make things worse!'

The preacher stopped for a moment, and looked out over the harbour as a briny gust from the coast blew dust around the plaza and the bells rang on around them. 'A great storm is coming,' she said, her eyes still on the harbour. 'The Mother has shown me. There will be a cleansing flood.'

He squinted out at the sea, still glittering in the morning sun, trying to work out what she saw; her words were all too close to Mercunin's earlier proclamation. 'You know, there's a porter up at the palace you should meet, you two would get on like a house on fire.'

Heali grabbed his arm, pulling him away. 'That's enough, Master Chel. You can't help the touched any more than you already have. We'd better get back up the hill.'

With one last look at the struggling preacher, they made for the palace.

TWO

What seemed like half the palace's population was crammed onto its white walls, jostling and bickering for a clear view of the bay. Above them, the lone, sad warning bell of the palace's solitary spire tolled in fitful answer to the jangling mass below.

'Can't see a bastard thing,' Heali muttered, squeezing around a gaggle of servants. He was a hand shorter than Chel, who didn't have much of a view himself. They laboured along the crowded battlements until at last they found a space between the chattering crowds.

'God's breath,' he whispered as Chel pressed in alongside.

The mid-morning sun, kept low in the northern sky over the sea by autumn's arrival, gleamed from the gentle waves of the bay. But where sea should have followed, the neck of the bay was blocked by a giant black vessel: long, wide and low, a floating fortress of dark wood and metal, its sails and oar banks crimson and gilded with silver. A pair of smaller vessels, just as dark, trailed it like ducklings. Chel guessed even the smallest would have rivalled the largest ship currently moored in the harbour. The main ship could have sailed over the grand duke's pleasure barge without scratching its hull.

They didn't seem to be advancing. The dark ships sat out to sea, riding the waves up and down in place, anchors dropped, while the terrified bells rang out around the bay. A small boat, black flag of truce fluttering from its prow, had dropped from the largest ship and was rowing into the bay beneath the watching eyes of the port's population, and the swivelling half-dozen giant skein-bows on the headland sea-fort. From the other direction came the duke's barges, moving to encircle it, the tin hats of crossbowmen glinting from their decks.

'What are they? Who are they?' Chel asked, his eyes not leaving the floating fortress. Adrenaline washed through him, refreshing the fearsome trembling that had only just left him from his encounter with Brother Hurkel.

Heali's brow was slick, his breath short. 'Norts, boy. The black ships of the Norts have come for us.'

Others were joining them, muttering and shouting filling the air as guardsmen jostled with servants and house staff, occasionally shunted aside by the arrival of someone with a title to wield. Their hubbub filled Chel's ears.

'Is it an invasion?'

'It's a blockade!'

'But if Denirnas Port is closed, it'll be nothing but river traffic ferried up from Sebemir! The north will starve!'

Chel nudged Heali. 'We're not enemies of the Norts. Are we?'

'I'm not much inclined to go down and ask them, Master Chel.'

In the port, the bells faltered, then one by one they

stopped. Perhaps the operators were now watching the scene in the bay, or piling their worldly goods onto a mule and making for the mountains. Two fluttering objects had risen from the main deck of the giant Nort vessel, like outsize birds with wings of spider-silk. They glimmered and glistened, borne aloft on the inland breeze, anchored by thin ropes or cables to the vessel beneath. The silk-birds soared up and over the little boat and the approaching barges, twinkling beneath as if they carried lanterns.

'What in hells do you suppose those are, Master Chel? Totems? Decorations?'

'If they're sails, they're very small and very far away.'

A further commotion ran through the crowd like a wave. 'Oh joy,' muttered Chel as he watched ducal guards pushing their way to the promontory. 'The grand duke and his entourage are here. I'm sure everything will be just fine now.'

'You sound a touch insincere, Master Chel.'

'Call me judgemental, but if three years in Sokol's service have taught me anything it's that the more skivvies, flunkies and lickspittles that surround a lord, the less contemplative their decisions.' And that's without counting his repellent offspring, he added to himself.

Robed notables scuttled in the duke's wash, hemmed by the brooding house-guards. Chel half expected to see Lord Sokol among them, but it was still early yet. He watched them bustle their bullish way through those already gathered, his lip curled. There was the duke's eldest, Count Esen, pushing an inattentive kitchen-waif from his path and almost off the ramparts; only the swift hands of a watching guardsman prevented her from falling. Count Esen only smirked.

Chel felt Heali's restraining hand on his arm.

He spat into the dust and sighed. 'At least that ghastly prick *actively* blackens his father's name.' He watched a pale, slumped figure come trudging after the other nobles. 'That little prince doesn't do a thrice-damned thing, just slopes along like a kicked dog after the rest of them.'

Heali chuckled. 'Tough job, being the ward of a grand duke. No doubt takes a lot out of him, weekly lectures at the Academy, the feasts and festivals.'

Chel froze. One last figure had come to join the ducal party: Sister Vashenda had stopped a way short of the promontory, looking out over the bay. Chel was rooted to the spot, sweat-slick, praying she didn't turn his way.

His prayers were for dust. As if sensing him, Sister Vashenda turned, and the sharp lines of her face locked rigid. She advanced, her hook-headed staff tapping the stone, signalling to her lackeys as she came. 'Sand-flower!' she called, her eyes burning. 'Impeding the work of God's messengers is a vile crime . . .'

Chel tried to stand his ground again, but his legs were shaking uncontrollably. He was safe here, surely, within the walls of the palace. A sworn man, a guest of the duke—

'. . . But the release of heretics is beyond contempt.'

'What? You mean . . . But that wasn't me!'

'There will be a reckoning, boy!'

Something had happened out in the bay. One of the seneschals gasped, 'Beneath a flag of truce no less!' Others around him shushed and jeered. The duke's barges had fired on the little Nort boat. Then the mutterings rose in pitch and urgency. 'What in hells!' a guardsman shrieked. Chel turned from the prelate and peered out over the jostling assemblage, toward the harbour.

'Sand-flower! Do not turn your back to me.' He heard Vashenda shout over the crowd. 'Brother Hurkel,' she called, 'take the Andriz!'

The floating silken birds were spewing flame. Streams of liquid fire poured from the sky, dousing the duke's barges. Screams filled the air as the flaming mass gushed over them, the men within scrabbling overboard as the flames roared up. Tin hats glinted on the waters of the bay, while gobbets of fire spat and hissed, burning on the surface.

'Witchfire!' came the cry along the battlements. Others joined it. People started to run, and at once the ramparts churned.

'Come hither, Andriz.' Chel turned to see Brother Hurkel come lumbering into view, his grin undiminished by the chaos around them. 'You're late for your lesson.'

'He means to take you, Master Chel, Norts be damned.' Heali was at Chel's shoulder. 'I'll stall him. Make for the sea-fort!'

Chel ran, the duke's roar to attack ringing over the thundering of his heart in his ears. He pelted off down the rampart, weaving in between hurrying guardsmen, servants and seneschals, all of whom had remembered urgent business elsewhere. Witchfire! he thought. Mercunin was right, we shall all of us burn. From behind him came Heali's bright wheedling. 'Ah, Brother Hurkel, if I might—'

'Fuck off, Heali,' was all Chel heard before the duke's signal drums rang out from the walls, loud over the sounds of the fleeing crowd. Ahead of him, the massive skein-bows cranked and turned, while ghastly burning smells were drifting over the palace, borne by the same wind that kept the silk-birds aloft.

Chel rounded a turret as great thrums filled the air. A

whistling volley of giant bolts, each as long as Chel was tall, soared out over the bay, blurs rippling through the air. He heard the distant eruptions of water and great tin booms like kettledrums where they found their mark. A ragged cheer rose from those guards still at the wall as the spray subsided.

Quickly, gasps and oaths replaced the cheer. Chel slowed, snatching a glance over the bay. The black ships remained, unsunk, bobbing on the gentle waves.

'Are they made of iron?' one of the guardsmen said, incredulous. 'How the fuck do they float?'

Something flew out from the black ship, something like a fireball, trailing bright flame and black smoke. The fireball shot over the water, faster than a skein-bolt, screaming like a demon. It smashed into the headland below the sea-fort, exploding in white and crimson flame and sending chunks of rock soaring into the air, stone splashing out into the bay.

Chel tumbled and skittered, his heart galloping up his throat in what felt like a desperate bid to escape. 'What in all the saints . . .?'

Another fireball launched from the black ship, then the turret ahead of him exploded. The blast showered flame and stone across the walls as the turret's skein-bow, arms burning, pitched over the collapsing battlement and dropped into the bay. A wall of choking smoke blew over the rampart, forcing Chel to hunch and gasp, while stone shards and pebbles rained down around him. From somewhere through the fog came the sound of Brother Hurkel's calls.

Chel wiped at his eyes and pushed himself to his feet as another explosion rocked the stone beneath him. 'Fuck. This.'

As smothering clouds of smoke and ash billowed over the walls, Chel ran.

* * *

He dropped from the wall above the stables. The palace was emptying, he couldn't see Sokol and his retinue, and their mounts were gone too. They must have cleared out at the first warning bells. How very Sokol. Chel took a long, ragged breath to try to calm his nerves. He had to get out before the Norts razed the entire port. There were still horses left, although not for much longer: already palace staff were tussling with liveried riders over the ownership and use of those that remained. Then, of course, there was Brother Hurkel and his companion confessors to consider. If witchfire hadn't put them off his trail, they may yet be lying in wait.

A narrow, two-wheeled cart stood just beside the stable arch, abandoned midway through unloading supplies for the kitchens from the look of it. It stood, facing the wrong way, a burly, bored-looking mule hitched before it. A dusty cloak lay across the driver's bench.

'Perfect.'

He jumped up to the cart and threw the cloak over himself. Sweating from the morning's heat, the strain of Hurkel's chase, the Nort attack and now cart-theft to boot, Chel geed the reins and drove the cart and mule forward, wheeling around the stables and toward the main courtyard and the outside world.

* * *

Chel couldn't keep his hands tight on the reins. They shook and slipped with his still-thumping heartbeats as well as with each rut on the road. He'd joined the main road out to the provinces, but all around him people surged, creating a long line back to the city. He could only hope that Vashenda and Hurkel had more to worry about than his escape.

A cloaked figure poked his head out from the crates in the back of the cart. 'Why are we slowing?'

'Argh! Who in hells are you?' Chel shrieked.

'We've been invaded! Invaded! They're going to kill us all! *Why aren't we going faster?*'

'Because this road is full of people, you plank. I'd rather not tip this thing and kill us and them before we get anywhere.'

Something about the way his companion stiffened when he'd called him a plank bothered Chel. 'Who *are* you? Why were you hiding in this cart?'

The figure pulled back his hood and looked up at him. Chel's insides congealed. He looked back at the pallid face of the hang-dog prince, the runt of the litter: Tarfel Merimonsun, Junior Prince of Vistirlar.

'Five bloody, blasted hells . . .'

'Why aren't we going faster?' shrieked the prince.

THREE

'Your highness! I'm so— I didn't realize. I was just trying to get out of the city and find my liege—'

'Immaterial! I'm commandeering you.'

'But—'

'Listen, peasant: whoever you're sworn to, whoever they're sworn to, totter high enough up the stack and they're all sworn to the crown. And who wears that?'

'Uh, your father?'

'Well, yes, but he's ill, isn't he? So while he recovers, the master of the Star Court is . . .?'

'Your brother, highness?'

'Exactly.'

'But he's not the one commandeering me.'

'Well, no, you gormless pleb, but that's why you're going to take me to him.'

'But your brother is in Omundi and that's days away – I'd be an oathbreaker! I have to be released, it doesn't work if I just walk away.'

'In my father's name, are all you provincials so thick-skulled? Your pestilent oath won't matter a gnat's fart once we reach my brother. The crown can supplant or dissolve inferior pledges, you homespun halfwit. You'll be released the moment my brother decrees it.'

Chel's hands went very still on the thin reins. The mule plodded on, making progress into the rough countryside. In Chel's mind, a second road was unfurling, one that led into a suddenly unconstrained future. For a moment he forgot his fear. 'Released from my oath?'

'In a heartbeat.'

'And what about a pardon for any unwitting offences against the Church?'

'Of course! My brother is on excellent terms with Primarch Vassad. Just get me to safety. And fast! This whole coast is unsafe. One of my brothers was murdered on the road by brigands, you know.'

Chel's mind was galloping ahead. The prince slapped at his arm.

'Do you dare defy a prince of the kingdom in a time of war? I'll have you e—'

'I'll take you, highness. I'll get you to safety, I swear it.'

'Well, about bloody time. There you go, you have a new oath already.'

Chel saw no sign of any of Sokol's band on the road. Images floated in his mind: silken birds pouring fire onto the water beneath, the screaming fireballs ripping across the bay and into the fort, the giant black ship, sitting implacable between frothing plumes. Already the memories were becoming unreal, too much to absorb, greasy moments slipping away into his subconscious.

He still felt a burn of shame at the thought of abandoning his sworn duty, despite the young prince's commands. He told himself that Sokol would no doubt be on the road east already, and that they'd likely catch him up, whereupon Prince Tarfel could explain the situation. Perhaps they'd all make the journey together, Sokol prideful of his new charge right up to the moment where Crown Prince Mendel dissolved Chel's oath before his eyes.

Chel and the prince went east, toward Omundi and the army.

***

The port was burning, great gouts of flame pouring from the sky like incandescent pillars. Whole buildings were reduced to rubble, the palace on the bluffs a blackened cadaver, the Academy opposite a scorching glare too bright to regard.

The city walls crumbled to ash as the entire sea lit with alchemical fire, washing like a wave over the port. He watched it rise before him, screaming silently, anchored to the spot in the ruin of the sea-fort. Heali's voice called to him, exhorting him to flee, but he remained rooted as the curtain of flame rose higher until it consumed the sky. There, at its centre, just before it fell upon him, he saw a tiny figure, dark against the blaze. It wore a snarling mask.

His head knocked against the crate behind him and with a gulp of air Chel woke. The reins were still in his hands, soaked through. Mortified, he tried to wipe away the worst of his slick sheen, while the mule plodded faithfully on. He felt in no hurry to sleep again.

It was a three-day trip to Omundi, rattling along the pitted dirt roads in the mule cart. The makeshift convoy moved as fast as it could, trying to put as much distance between themselves and the invading Norts as conditions allowed, the bulk of their contingent likewise seeking the safety of the League's armies.

They camped only briefly and stopped at few roadside shrines. Prince Tarfel made for a dreadful travelling companion: he insisted on hiding among the kitchen supplies in the back of the cart, where he alternated between gibbering panic, which was tiresome, and ostentatious boredom, which was worse. He was prone to bursting into song when under-occupied; his reedy tenor could at least carry a tune, but his limited repertoire ground down Chel's resolve as the journey wore on, to the extent that he considered teaching the prince some of the more rustic ditties favoured by Sokol's regulars. When not singing, the prince demanded explanations for everything they passed on the road, from the meaning of the plague quarantine markers to the frequency of the smoking char pits. The only sight to hush him was a rack of gibbets strung at a crossroads, the bodies dangling beneath shorn of noses and ears, the signs around their shredded necks clearly reading 'Rau Rel'. Otherwise, Chel kept his answers short. When a kingdom has been fighting the same war on itself for twenty years, there's little new to say, he thought to himself.

Chel tried to focus on the immediate future. He would ditch the prince with his brother, hop back on the cart and roll on south, cut east at the Lakes and be home ahead of the news of Denirnas Port's destruction. Away from the madness, away from murderous confessors and their lingering venom. By the time he arrived, he could shape the story of the Nort invasion to his choosing, his interactions with the prince, how he came to be reprieved from Sokol's pointless service, assuming Sokol had even survived.

Enough remained of the cart's contents to barter his way all the way back to Barva. He was going far away from all this. He was going home. All he had to worry about was what to say when he arrived. What to say to his sisters, what to say to his step-father. What to say to his mother. Chel bit his lip in contemplation. At least he'd have plenty of time to think.

'Look, the pennants, the pennants!'

Tarfel had roused himself and was pointing down into the river valley. Ahead of them, down the curve of the dusty road as it wound its way into the river valley, the bright walls of Omundi shone in the evening sun.

Spread like a dark blanket pocked with campfires before the walls, the armies of the Glorious League lay camped, the Church-blessed alliance of great Names and small, the crown-led instrument of divine unification. Siege engines stood idle in their earthworks, just out of bowshot, and Chel noted with distaste the rocky dam that had diverted the river's flow away from the city and down deep-cut channels in the earth. Little seemed to be happening.

Highest of all the pennants that fluttered at the centre of the camp was the white lion of Merimonsun, and Tarfel squealed with glee at its sight. 'Go there, go there!' Chel geed the mule down the slope toward the camp.

***

Whether or not the pickets at the camp's edge believed that the mule cart was an official royal conveyance, Tarfel's shrieking, princely entitlement and signet-waving had them escorted to the camp's centre in short order by nervous men-at-arms. An equally sceptical vizier bade them wait, still guarded, at the edge of a wide earth circle, ringed by the exotic tents of the great and good of the royal forces. Lions, pictorially speaking, were everywhere.

Overhead, a host of messenger-birds, doves and pigeons, seemed in constant circulation, teeming from the cotes stacked beside the grandest pavilion, coming and going in a ceaseless flutter of feathers. Panting foot messengers with grime-streaked faces came pelting past at regular intervals. All activity seemed centred on the pavilion, the hub for messages from hand and wing, a commotion of traffic in each direction at its entrance. Chel guessed that the news from Denirnas must have reached them by now. Beside the pavilion's flap, watching every item in and out, stood a tall, hooded figure, robed in white and vermilion and dusted with travel-muck.

Chel's heart thudded once and stopped, his pulse replaced with a sudden flooding lightness that spread over his skin. How had Vashenda got here ahead of them? His mouth was dry, tongue thick. Then his brain registered the difference of stance, of height, the curved sword belted beneath the robes, and he felt his heartbeat restart. It was not Vashenda. Another senior prelate, but not one who'd ordered him adjusted.

'Bear?' He was jolted out of his thoughts by a hand on his shoulder. 'Bear, is that you?'

'Five bastard hells, it can't be,' he whispered.

***

Chel and the prince turned to find a young woman standing behind them, excitement and trepidation surging over her face. Her straight hair was bound and shrouded in the fashion of the Star Court, and she gazed at them with eyes as grey as Chel's own.

Her face split in a wide grin and she threw her arms around him. 'I knew it was you!'

'Sab?' Chel reeled, carried backward by her momentum. 'How are you here? What are the chances? You look . . .'

She released him from her crushing grip. 'Taller? More dynamic? Matured like fine spiced wine?'

'Different.'

'It's been three years, Bear, near as matters. I wasn't going to stay small and grotty. You look the same, if dirtier. But what are you doing here?'

'I should ask likewise. Why aren't you at home?'

She arched an eyebrow. 'Why'd you think, Bear-of-Mine?'

Tarfel cleared his throat with a frown, and the girl grinned again. 'Aren't you going to introduce me to your friend?'

Chel sighed. 'May I present Sabina Chel of Barva, my little sister.'

Tarfel inclined his head, looking Sabina up and down. 'Not so little any more, eh?'

Frowning, Chel continued. 'Sab, this is His Royal Highness Tarfel Merimonsun, prince of the realm, youngest son of King Lubel.'

She'd already begun a bow of her own and she staggered at his words. 'You're friends with a fucking prince?' she hissed, head bent.

'Well, not friends exactly,' he said, experiencing several different flavours of mortification.

'Your brother was good enough to escort me here from Denirnas,' Tarfel said haughtily. 'Charmed, I'm sure.' He extended a grubby hand for her to kiss. To Chel, he murmured, 'Bear? You're not very bear-like, Chel.'

'It's, ah, a family thing.'

The sneering vizier reappeared, informing them that negotiations with the city had paused, if not concluded, and Prince Mendel had a moment for an audience with his brother. Tarfel swanned off after the man and into the grand pavilion. The robed prelate lingered outside, her hooded gaze swinging back across the Chel siblings, black eyes glittering within. Chel felt an unpleasant tingling as it swept over him, then the figure ducked beneath the flaps and was gone.

'Who is that? That prelate?'

Sab sniffed. 'Ah, Balise da Loran: "Lo Vassad's clenched fist". She's the Star's chief minister and a double-bastard.'

'Chief minister? She's a Church prelate!'

'She's also first sworn to Prince Thick, you know, after he had to start afresh. Many feathers in that cap.'

'Prince Thick?'

She gestured toward the pavilion. 'Mendel, the crown prince. Your new chum's big bro. The man's a haircut in boots. Pretty, though, even with the scars.'

He shook his head, baffled. 'So who's left at home, if you're here? Has everyone been sent away?'

'The twins are still there, Bear. They're too young to go anywhere yet.' She offered a sad smile. 'They'll look after Mum.'

'But why are you here? I mean, here, at Omundi?'

'You know, bit of this, bit of that. Making friends, keeping my eyes open.'

'Sab.'

'I'm travelling with the court. Can't you tell?' She twirled in her formal garb.

'As what?'

'As a lady-in-waiting, seconded to the entourage of our crown prince's intended. The Lady Latifah has about three dozen of us, so I just slot into the mass. Five hells, is that girl stupid: people call her Latifah the Dim, sometimes to her face, poor lamb. That was Prince Dunce's pick from the nobility's nubility. Shepherd's tits, imagine their children! They'll need breathing lessons!'

'How long in service? And when did you start cursing like a sergeant?'

'Are you interrogating me, Bear? Since the spring. Amiran thought it was time I made my way.'

'Of course he bloody did. You're far too young to be fending for yourself at court!'

'I'm not a duckling, Bear. I'm the same age you were when you set off on your travels. Speaking of which, where's Uncle Hanush? Is he with you?'

'Don't call him that. And no, he's not.' His cheeks coloured at the thought of Lord Sokol, and his clothes felt suddenly hot.

Sab narrowed her eyes. 'What's going on? How did you come to be escorting the little prince? Your last letter said you were spending the year burning farmers up north.'

'We did. Not burning farmers – well, some of them might have been. We were suppressing insurrections in the northeast all summer. Then Sokol decided we'd be wintering with Grand Duke Reysel at the winter palace in Denirnas, where they don't so much have winter as a cool spell between summers. Mostly we just seemed to chase people away from places.'

'And did you do much fighting? Are you a deadly swordsman yet? The finest blade in the provinces, slaying brigands and setting the ladies' hearts a-flutter?' She made swooning motions.

He shook his head, smiling. 'None whatsoever. I've been fetch-and-carryman to Sokol's fetch-and-carrymen since he took me in service. Even the dogsbodies give me errands.'

Sab shrugged. 'He did promise Mum he'd keep you safe. I bet you've learned some salty language from the soldiers, if nothing else.' She winked, then hugged him again. 'Oh, Bear, how I've missed you. Are you staying long?'

He said nothing for a moment. 'I don't think so.'

'Is Uncle Hanush still in Denirnas? Did he send you with the prince? We heard whispers, not long before you arrived, something about a fire at the port? I didn't pay it much heed, you know what expansive gossips the Star viziers can be, but seeing you here . . .'

Chel felt suddenly cold, his back prickled with sweat. He felt the muscle in his cheek twitch as images flitted through his mind, smoke and flame, half-dream and half-memory. With a scowl he drove the visions aside, rubbing at his temples with grimy knuckles.

'Something happened,' he said, teeth gritted. Focus on the future, he told himself. 'Listen, I've got things arranged. In exchange for getting Prince Tarfel here safe, he's going to have his brother dissolve my oath to Sokol, and then—'

'What? What did you say?'

'I've made a bargain with the prince.'

'To escape your oath? Bear!'

'The crown can supplant or dissolve inferior pledges, Sab, everyone knows that. It's law.'

'I don't care if it's law, an oath is an oath. It's your *duty*. It's the honour of the name our parents chose for us. That Dad chose.'

'Then it's as worthless as the oath! My sacred pledge pissed away on that waste of air? I've wasted years bringing him clothes while he hid from battles. I could be . . .' He threw up a hand in frustration. 'If I'm to be sworn into duty, let it at least be meaningful, or let me go home.'

Sab kept her voice low, but her gaze was searing. 'Does Uncle Hanush even know you're here?'

'Will you stop calling him that?'

'He's Amiran's brother.'

'And Amiran's our fucking father now? He sent me away, Sab. Now he's sent you away, too. Soon it'll just be—'

'A-hem.' The vizier was back. 'His highness the prince commands your attendance.'

'Which one?'

'You, boy.'

'No, which prince?'

If the vizier had been sneering before, now his expression could have curdled milk.

***

'Vedren Chel of Barva,' the vizier announced, contempt dripping from his voice, as he ushered Chel into the grand pavilion then withdrew.

'My brother's saviour!' Prince Mendel strode forward, grasping Chel's unresisting arm and pumping it, a warm smile beaming from his absurdly handsome face. Thick, golden hair like a mane crowned his head, matching a well-groomed beard. Chel found himself gazing into earnest, cornflower-blue eyes, creased with concern.

'Dear Tarfel was telling me of the horrors you saw at Denirnas when the Norts attacked, how you rescued him and carried him to safety.' Chel raised an eyebrow and nodded slowly, expression neutral. Tarfel avoided his eye.

'You must have been terrified. I know something of life and death situations myself,' the prince went on, one hand straying to a jagged scar that ran down one side of his face. It managed to follow the line of his jaw, if anything augmenting his already exemplary looks. 'But witchfire! God's breath . . .'

It seemed to Chel an ideal time to remind the princes of the agreement, in case such things had somehow slipped Tarfel's mind. He could stand his sister's disapproval — in time she would understand.

'Your highness, I—'

'I can only apologize that you had to face it alone. It's no secret that the siege is going badly – we should have broken Omundi long ago, and been with you well before festival week. I'm afraid it's the same as it was in Father's day – these wretched so-called "free cities" would rather starve themselves to death than rejoin the kingdom.' He shook his head, seeming genuinely rueful. 'We have . . .' Mendel went on, then tailed off, his beautiful face shifting to a frown. 'We have . . .'

A robed figure came gliding from the shadows of the pavilion's inner chamber behind the crown prince. Balise da Loran, still hooded, floated to Mendel's shoulder and bent to murmur into his ear. The light returned instantly to the prince's eyes.

'We have received more news from the port,' Mendel declared, as if the interruption had never occurred. Da Loran slid back into the shadows, to where a trestle stood at the pavilion's wall, piled with message scrolls and missives. Chel watched as she picked up one of the messages and cracked its seal.

'Yes, brother?' Tarfel was leaning forward, pained and

anxious. He was awfully pale in the lantern light. 'Have the Norts laid waste to all Denirnas?'

'No, dear Tarfel, indeed they have not. It seems Grand Duke Reysel may have overreacted to their initial overtures, and they made their point on the sea-fort in return. We'll have to add that to the reconstruction tally. For now, however, they seem content to sit in blockade, until their demands are met.'

'Demands? What are they demanding, brother?'

Behind them hung a giant embroidery of Mendel's late twin, Corvel, a golden sun framing his golden visage, white lions rampant each side. The embroidery bore the legend 'The Wise'. The twins had been known as 'The Wise' and 'The Fair' respectively – there was even a song about them – and from Chel's current vantage, Mendel was very fair indeed.

Balise da Loran was back at the crown prince's side, and to Chel's shock he seemed to be deferring to her. 'Their demands are unimportant,' came a gravelly and thickly accented voice from beneath the hood. 'Acknowledging them would be catastrophic.' She fixed Tarfel and Chel in turn with her hooded gaze, her face within lost in a void from which no light could escape. Mendel was looking at the floor. Chel kept his own eyes fixed on the crown prince; the prelate made his skin itch.

'The League's troops remain mired in the siege,' da Loran continued. 'Attempting to march everyone to Denirnas now – this close to the end of the campaigning season, with Omundi on the brink of collapse – risks an uprising in our own ranks. But we cannot show weakness in the face of this foreign provocation. We must hold firm, until we can marshal the forces to expel these godless savages.'

Mendel was nodding along, past the end of her words and into the silence beyond. After a moment, Tarfel said,

'Meaning what, brother?' forcing Mendel to look up again.

'Meaning—' da Loran began, but Tarfel cleared his throat, spots of colour on his waxy cheeks. Chel realized he was as unnerved by the prelate as he was.

'I'd say my brother can speak for himself in matters of state, wouldn't you?'

Da Loran stared very hard at the young prince, who seemed to lose an inch in height beneath her gaze. After a moment, she rumbled, 'Of course, your highness,' and turned her gaze to Mendel, who looked momentarily surprised. Da Loran muttered something, and the crown prince's eyes came alive.

'Meaning, Tarf my boy,' the crown prince proclaimed, refocused, 'that the festival celebrations in Denirnas must go ahead as planned. A symbolic gesture, true, but hugely significant. We will show the north that the crown of Vistirlar does not bow or flee in the face of heathen aggression. We stand tall. We celebrate the festival of our father in defiance of savage alchemy, and we show this fractured kingdom that we are not afraid.'

Chel listened with his brow crunched in rising incredulity. Tarfel seemed no less astonished. 'We do?'

'We do. And I can't think of a better representative of the crown to oversee the festival proceedings at Grand Duke Reysel's side.'

Nobody spoke for a moment, Tarfel slow to meet his brother's beaming gaze. A heartbeat later his pallid face became entirely bloodless.

'Brother! What the fuck?'

'Tarfel, language. You must be our avatar, little brother. You must bear witness to the splendour of the festival's events, first-hand.'

Tarfel's voice was very small. 'But they have witchfire . . .'

'Let them . . . Let them . . .' Mendel wasn't listening, 'Let them bob and rot in the harbour-mouth. Our people are resourceful, resilient. We will find ways to cope without sea trade. We can lump supplies over the hills from Sebemir's river docks, that should prevent total starvation.'

Tarfel looked to be gagging, unable to speak. Eventually he said, 'But you'll send reinforcements? The army, the League, some will be coming too? We're at war . . .'

Da Loran answered this time. 'The forces of the League are needed in the east. Omundi must fall.'

Tarfel had visibly slumped, his head slung from the sloping mound of his shoulders. Chel watched with a sort of vicarious horror. This plan seemed ludicrous, and he could not wait to be as far away from these people as possible. 'For how long?'

'While the campaigning season lasts, although I suppose at that point the League will be breaking up for winter.'

'But then you'll come? To the winter palace? You're expected . . .'

'It wouldn't be fair to leave Father on his own down south, would it? We'll send a couple of regiments, maybe a free company or two, but this is a battle the Norts cannot win, and they know it. They've spent what threat they have, and now they must sit and wait. They cannot break our resolve, our unity. Take heart, dear brother, they will be slinking back over the sea sooner or later – storm season in the north is but a couple of months away.'

'A couple of *months*?'

'Fear not, you won't be defenceless. Master Chel, I understand my brother made a promise to you?'

Chel swallowed. This was it.

'He did, your highness.'

'Good, very good. And who is your current liege?'

'Hanush Revazi, Lord Sokol.'

'Do I know him?' A quick look toward Balise. 'Not to worry.' A warm feeling began to creep over Chel. 'Would you mind kneeling?'

Chel knelt, almost unsteady, his hands trembling with anticipation. Mendel summoned a flunky with a clap of his hands.

'Right, you, vizier, get this down. Vedren Chel of Barva, by decree of the crown of Vistirlar, your oath is dissolved. All restitutions and so on through the usual whatsit and so forth – Balise knows this bit.' Chel bowed his head, a fluttering feeling in his chest. 'Ready with the next one? Splendid. Master Chel, your hand, please.'

The warm feeling vanished, replaced by a sudden tingling cold.

'I can't think of anyone better suited, dear Tarf. Now, Master Chel, if you wouldn't mind repeating the following . . .'

A short time later, and with very little fanfare, Chel found himself sworn into the service of Prince Tarfel Merimonsun of Vistirlar, under oath to serve, honour and protect. Especially protect. The whole thing felt oddly close to marriage. As he stood, he exchanged a glance with his new liege. Tarfel looked just as miserable as he felt. Back to Denirnas. Back to the Norts. Back to the Rose. Back to the muscular embrace of Brother Hurkel. Chel was reasonably certain he was going to vomit on the crown prince's gleaming boots.

Mendel clapped his hands again. 'There. You two will do wonderful things for the kingdom, I just know it.' He turned to the vizier, who had done little to mask his disdain during the proceedings. 'Now, please escort Prince Tarfel to the riders. At least, dear brother, you will have a proper escort for your return to Denirnas.'

Chel found himself marching out beside Tarfel. He swallowed down the rising bile, managing to hiss, 'You have to do something, highness! I was supposed to be released, not sent back to die!'

Tarfel returned his imploring stare with wet and haunted eyes. 'You heard my brother. This is the crown's will, and we will obey.'

Chel almost put a hand on his sleeve but thought better of it. 'This is the will of the Church! You saw what happened in there, that prelate was—'

'Enough, sworn man. I know what people say about my brother since his injury, but he is the crown's representative, and his commands are a royal decree. Now be silent!' The young prince looked to be on the verge of tears. Chel's own eyes were wild and giddy.

Outside the pavilion, a phalanx stood at the circle's edge, their robes shimmering in the light of the freshly lit torches. Tufted hair, rust-red robes, gleaming maces at their belts. The lead figure, of course, wore white and vermilion, if a little dusty from the trail, and was already in conversation with the hooded Balise. Vashenda had come to collect them. Chel felt like laughing, manic and loud. How could things be otherwise?

FOUR

'Welcome home, Master Chel! Back in time for the feast!' Heali fell in step alongside Chel, fleshy face all smiles. It was, Chel supposed, nice to encounter someone pleased to see him for a change.

A dozen Brothers of the Thorn, their robes the colour of blood in the evening sun, had flanked the crude carriage that passed for royal conveyance. Chel had been stationed on its back plate, bounced by every rut and divot, exhausted by the first hour on the road. He'd exchanged little more than a shocked sentence with his sister before they'd swept him away, but her confused and reproachful stare had stayed with him long after Omundi's broken valley dropped from view, along with her parting words.

'Duty isn't swearing to obey a person, Bear. It's about service to the kingdom, its people. It's about trying to make things better. Serve the people, Brother Bear. Make Father proud.'

He'd had no response for her.

Vashenda had ignored him on the road – which just

served to make his anxiety worse – with the exception of a pointed remark to the prince that he was at least properly guarded for his return voyage. 'Do you know what would happen if any harm came to you, highness?' she'd said. 'Do you know the trouble it would cause?'

With the sun sinking over the bay at their journey's end, the column was dispersing at the city gates, the body of their escort departing for the croft and taking the carriage with them. Vashenda remained, a harbinger, to supervise the prince's slow climb to the winter palace in person. Chel wondered if Hurkel lay up there in wait. The population of the refugees' shack-village at the foot of the outer walls had trickled back after the screaming exodus of the days before, but the port's fringes still looked strange and empty to Chel's eyes. Odd shapes dangled from the walls, indistinct in the gloom of the structures' shade, but his gut told him they were bodies. Bone-weary and ill-at-ease, part of him was glad when Heali appeared, unbidden, at his elbow, as what remained of the royal procession approached the gates.

'You survived then, Heali? What did I miss?'

The big man chuckled. 'A lot of bluster, Master Chel, then a lot of nothing. Norts calmed down a bit after making their point on the fort.'

'I heard.'

Heali leaned in close. 'Truth be told,' he said, his odour unimproved in the days since Chel had seen him last, 'the duke calmed down a fair stripe too. Think maybe he saw the merit of negotiation.'

'Perhaps the duke's a sensible man after all. Have they said what they want?'

Heali shrugged. 'They've declared a blockade, it seems.

Something about mistreatment of a citizen, or the return of stolen property . . . but what would a lowly guardsman know of international intrigue?'

'What indeed?'

'So now they just sit there, stopping up the bay. Nothing goes in or out. People in the port are going mad, whole place is . . .' he waved a frustrated hand '. . . constipated.'

They began to climb the winding trail to the palace. The black ships lurked at the edge of Chel's view, out at the harbour's fringe, huge and dark and implacable. Heali followed his gaze, looking pained. 'There have been some incidents. Place is swarming with refugees and pilgrims, watch can't control all the outsiders, their notions of justice.'

Chel thought of the little man and his oven, his stern-eyed little daughter, and felt suddenly sick. He didn't ask, afraid to hear the answer.

'Duke's insisting the festival is going ahead, ordered the folks to stay for the celebrations, but word's out that he's sent most of his own family south. Not sure most in the port can summon the enthusiasm.' He scratched himself. 'And you're quite the popular fellow, it seems.'

'Popular? What do you mean?' Chel was hoping for something positive, but Heali's words did nothing but stir queasiness in his gut.

'Had a few folks asking after you – you know the types, funny little haircuts, like to wear a lot of red. Don't worry, I told them you were long gone, although I wasn't expecting you to come riding back into port by return, was I?'

'Five bloody, blasted hells . . .'

'Still, word is you're the prince's man, now. Quite the

stroke of fortune, that; might even keep your ecclesiastical friends at bay. If you're lucky.' He raised a beetle-thick eyebrow. 'Makes you a connected fellow, though, wouldn't you say? An elevation like that could provide many opportunities. As it happens—'

They approached the palace gate, which stood wide open as ever. Chel blinked. 'What does it take to close this bastard? City's full of destitute and vigilantes, bay's full of heathen alchemists, the palace is piled with feast-food and lingering nobility and still nobody thinks to shut the fucking gate?' He threw up his hands. 'How in five hells am I going to protect that pointless prince if we can't even keep the door closed?'

Heali was looking at him through narrowed eyes, his gaze glittering in the light from the gate-side braziers. 'You expecting trouble, Master Chel?'

Chel tutted in irritation. 'No more than I have already. But two nights ago, I swore to give my life that Tarfel Merimonsun might keep his, and I'm thrice-damned if I'm giving it up to the first mask-wearing Nort or murderous Rau Rel partisan who wanders in off the fucking mountainside.'

The courtyard was eerily empty, devoid of its customary bustle. The minor damage from the preceding days had been patched and festival decorations were distastefully strung from every pillar and ledge, but unease permeated the atmosphere like a stink. No one from the palace was there to meet them. Chel wondered if Mercunin the ominous porter was still around.

Heali was still talking. '. . . fellow like you who walks beside a prince, he's got a certain *cachet*, might find certain *opportunities* . . .'

Vashenda had stopped ahead of them and was addressing the prince in the manner of a stern master to a hopeless pupil. She instructed him to wait, then swept around to face Chel and Heali. Heali muttered something and excused himself immediately. With the slightest frown, Vashenda moved off to confer with another robed figure. Chel and the prince were left alone at the edge of the deserted courtyard.

Tarfel affected a semblance of regal bearing as he surveyed the festival decorations. Chel tried to sound reassuring. 'Not what we were hoping for, highness. You were supposed to be safe with your brother by now, and I was supposed to be on my way home.'

'No, no, indeed.' For a moment the mask dropped, and Tarfel looked at him with wide, watery eyes. 'Vedren Chel – our bargain stands. We just have to wait it out until reinforcements arrive, until storm season, whatever it takes. Keep me alive, keep me safe through this, and I'll get you released. Again. Yes?'

Chel blinked. 'I swore to serve you and protect you, highness. I mean to keep that oath.'

'Of course, right you are. I'll release you at the end of all this, prince's word.'

Vashenda was back, a pair of guards at her heel; with a gesture she dismissed the prince in the direction of the residence, and the guards went with him. As Chel went to follow, she stepped in front.

'You,' Vashenda said, her silver scalp gleaming in the torchlight. 'With me.'

Chel realized he was clutching his sealed oath scroll in his sweating hand, held against his body like a talisman. She can't hurt me, he told himself. Not now I'm sworn to a prince. He swallowed, flicked a brief, troubled glance around the courtyard, and followed the good sister.

***

'Get in my way, put one foot out of line or release any more heretics back into the city and you will spend your final days learning new meanings of pain,' Vashenda said as they entered a small but plush bedchamber within the residence, adjoining a far grander set of rooms that Chel assumed belonged to the prince. 'Am I understood?'

Chel nodded. He could feel the sweat beading on his brow.

'Good. And thus let our understanding be reborn in the light of the Shepherd's mercy,' Vashenda continued, a sudden smile transforming her features into something even more terrifying. 'The past marches ever away, and we must watch the grass before us.' Chel wasn't sure if that was scripture or merely church-speak. 'You are now Prince Tarfel's man.'

Although phrased as a question, it wasn't delivered as such. He relaxed his sweaty grip on the oath scroll and nodded again.

'These will be your new chambers, at the prince's side. You will clean yourself, dress for the feast and await collection. You will attend the prince utterly, you will not leave his side.'

He nodded, too tired to do much more. At least he'd be able to collapse on the bed the moment the sister left; his legs were quivering beneath him.

Vashenda inclined her head, apparently satisfied. 'Then do not leave this room until they come for you.' She moved toward the door. He noted the bundle of sealed messages tucked into her robe; she looked in a hurry to deliver the last issuings from the pavilion at Omundi.

'Wait,' he called. 'I need to talk to Lord Sokol, or at least send him a message, or something. I need to tell him what happened.'

She raised an eyebrow. 'I would suggest the latter, lest you strain your voice. Lord Sokol and his retinue departed the same day you did.'

'What?' With the port's population looking so restored, he'd unconsciously assumed Sokol and his band had returned or remained.

Vashenda narrowed her eyes at his impertinence but continued. 'I believe he had urgent business to attend to in the southeast, quite unexpected I'm told. So unfortunate it should coincide with the arrival of our northern cousins in the bay.' She was entirely deadpan.

'But what about me? I should have been with him!'

The eyebrow raised again. 'Indeed, you should. And now you are the prince's man.' She walked through the doorway. 'Do not leave this room until they come for you.' The door closed with a clunk that sounded suitably final.

He flopped down on the bed. Sokol gone, fleeing home from the sound of it. And now Chel was anchored to a whelp of a prince, parked on a cliff-top, a beacon for belligerent Norts and their rains of witchfire and shrieking fireballs. If Hurkel didn't wander in and stave in his skull first.

A basin in the corner took care of the worst of the road-grime, and the clothes laid out on the bed fitted no worse than anything else he'd worn since he'd left Barva. They were absurd, of course: garish and gaudy, fine working on the details without any investment in comfort or utility. He guessed this was the uniform of the royal guard, perhaps even specific to the junior prince himself. He'd seen no one dressed in such ridiculous fashion anywhere near Prince Mendel. A belted scabbard completed the ensemble, and he was irked to find that the short blade sheathed within was an edgeless ornament.

And how, he muttered to himself, am I supposed to defend a prince with that?

The palace was deathly quiet, only occasional distant kitchen sounds echoing up from the grates. He saw no guards in the courtyard, or on the towers above. The place seemed deserted. An unease began to settle within the pit of his stomach. The situation seemed absurd. The Norts were still in the bay and Prince Mendel had no intention of granting their wishes. Surely they wouldn't simply sit and wait for the storms to wash them away? Why would the Norts not simply raze the rest of the port if they felt they were not being heard, and the rest of the north with it? And why would Mendel send his own brother back into the teeth of their alchemy for a mere festival?

No, not Mendel: Balise da Loran. And now Vashenda, another prelate, had ordered him to sit here and wait. Something untoward was happening, and he was at the centre of it. He should never have left the prince's side.

Dark clouds scudded overhead, the fat moon behind them shining through in scrappy patches, throwing slow-moving patterns over the tiled rooftops. He watched them flow and shift, eyes glazed, when movement in a moon-patch drew his eye. At last a guard had appeared, moving slowly along the rampart above the courtyard. Chel squinted. The figure was too ragged to be a guard. It shuffled forward, climbed over the wall and dropped to the roof below. As it dropped, Chel saw a long staff in its hand and its ash-streaked and tattered robes. Chel's heart stopped in his chest. It was the man from days ago, the beggar who had tripped him, who had landed him in the mess with the Rose in the first place. An intruder inside the walls.

'Pig-fucker!'

Chel almost tore the door from its hinges as he raced from the room.

***

He pounded through the empty, darkened hallways of the residence, making for the main courtyard. The winter palace had more hidden corners than he'd given it credit for, and his fuddled brain was struggling to process navigation as well as haste.

A large figure stepped from the darkness into his path and he careered into it, sending them both sprawling.

'Easy there, Master Chel! What's the commotion?'

'Heali?' Chel knelt, dazed. 'What the . . . Are you lying in wait for me or something? Where is everyone else?'

Heali dusted himself off as he got back to his feet. His clothes looked different, but it was hard to tell how. 'Why, attending to duties, Master Chel, as I assume you are too. But as it happens, glad to run into you, a stroke of fortune, you might say—'

'Not now, Heali.'

His dark eyes were narrow in the distant torchlight. 'Something amiss, Master Chel?'

Chel shook his head, then looked past the heavyset guardsman into the courtyard. The main gate still stood open. A single sentry leaned against it, looking to all the world asleep. 'Just look at this place! Guards missing from their posts, the gate hanging open, and I've seen an intruder climbing over the wall.'

'Someone's inside the palace? One person?'

'Not just anyone, Heali. Something is going on! We need to rally the remaining guards, close the gate, secure the duke and his remaining family, the prince, everyone.'

'You absolutely certain, Master Chel?'

'I know what I saw, Heali. I'm heading for the walls. Maybe we can still catch him. Are you coming?'

Heali muttered something in reply, but Chel was already sprinting for the stairs. Somewhere a distant bell was ringing.

FIVE

'There's fire down in the city!' Chel squinted in the darkness. The ramparts were deserted on either side, a cold wind blowing in from the sea. 'What in five hells is going on?'

Heali was still a few steps behind him, wheezing from the climb. 'God's balls, boy, let me catch a breath.'

Another bell was ringing somewhere closer, down in the port. Chel darted along the ramparts. Beneath them, the gate was still open, but he hoped to see men rushing to close it at any moment.

'He was there when I saw him, moon-side. Come on, he can't have—'

Two riders galloped through the courtyard, fast enough to throw sparks from their horses' shoes on the stones, then through the gate and onto the hillside. Chel stared after them. He watched them thunder down the winding trail toward the port below, heading for the city's south gate. Beyond them, he saw a line of torches, bobbing in formation, making slow progress up the hill from the direction of the fires. The riders slowed as they approached the torches, came to a momentary stop, then accelerated again, disappearing into the darkness that pooled at the valley bottom. The torches bobbed on, continuing their climb.

'What in hells was th—' He turned to find Heali standing right behind him. The guardsman's avuncular face had lost its habitual joviality.

'Heali? You all right?'

He shook his head, features dark. 'I'm sorry, my boy,' he said, and Chel felt the chill of sweat on his back return. 'I misjudged you.'

Chel took a step backward, part of his exhausted brain trying to recall how many paces from the edge of the rampart he'd stood. 'Misjudged me how? What's going on?'

'I thought we'd be able to come to terms, Master Chel. I thought I'd be able to keep you clear. I was wrong. It's a shame, truly.'

Chel took another backward step. His fingers were trembling, his voice hoarse. 'What do you mean, Heali? The fuck are you talking about?'

'You were supposed to be lucky.'

He saw the dull moonlight glint from the knife in the guardsman's hand. Heali advanced, fleshy mouth a grim line. Chel's back foot scraped over the rampart's edge, emptiness beneath his heel. He met Heali's dispassionate gaze.

'Why?' he whispered.

Heali offered a remorseful sigh.

'You're the goat.'

He jabbed forward. The knife caught Chel in the ribs, scraping along one of the ornate buckles and scoring a gash along his flank. He felt only the bump of impact, no pain, then the hot rush at his side. Heali tried to pull back the knife for another stab, but it had snagged in the excessive folds of Chel's fancy dress.

Chel unfroze. He grabbed Heali's knife-hand with his own, forcing the blade away from his body before it could carve him again. With his other hand he swung a wild punch at the guardsman's head, glancing the meat of his cheek and making him curse. Heali warded a second flailing blow, then with both hands tore the knife clear of Chel's uniform. Chel scrabbled backward, away from the drop, until his shoulders met the hard stone of the wall.

Heali put a finger to his cheek, probing for damage, then shook his head again. 'Enough, boy.'

Heali took half a step when something dark smashed over his head, staggering him forward, shards of the object showering the ramparts. He turned in surprise as a figure at the top of the stairway lobbed another dark shape. It thumped into Heali's face and bounced off, shattering on the stones at his feet in a dark splatter-mark. Chel squinted in the half-light. It looked like the remains of a lamp-oil jug from the kitchens.

Heali had recovered enough to take a step toward the figure, which stood with a crate at its feet and a grease-light in its hand. Too late, Heali realized what had doused him. He turned back toward Chel as the grease-light arced through the air, trying to outrun the flame that flared at his feet and leapt for his legs. Screaming, the big guardsman stumbled and flailed, flames surging up his body, then one foot missed the rampart and he was gone, a puddle of amber flame left fluttering on the stones.

Chel heard the impact on the courtyard below, then nothing more. One hand clutched to his injured side, he made wobbly progress to the rampart's edge and peered down. A dark shape lay sprawled below, unmoving, small yellow flames flickering at its edges. He shivered, and felt the pain, hot and fresh, as well as a sudden urge to both vomit and piss himself.

Three guardsmen ran into the courtyard, gave the sprawled and burning shape a cursory glance, then ran straight through the gate and out into the night.

He turned to find Mercunin, the cadaverous porter, looming over him, his grease-light back in his hand. The man's hollow eyes were pools of shadow, even with the light so close.

'Thank you,' Chel said, trying to stop his teeth chattering. 'I . . . You . . . Thank you.'

The twin voids gave nothing away. 'We shall all of us burn,' the man intoned in his earthen rumble, and Chel thought his rictus mouth twitched upward at the words. Then Mercunin was stalking over the deserted ramparts as the fire-pool guttered and died. He collected his crate and vanished down the steps, clinking. Plenty of oil jugs remained.

Chel risked another look at Heali's broken form, shivered and winced, then stumbled to the wall. The line of torches was almost at the gate. He could see the glimmer of steel in their dancing light.

Armed men were about to storm the palace, the guards had fled, and still the gate stood open.

***

By the time he'd lurched his way down to the courtyard, he could hear the thud of marching feet on the dusty road outside. The guards and sentries were long gone, and Chel realized he had no idea what, if any, mechanism operated the gate. Throwing his shoulder against the gate's heavy wood achieved little more than forcing more blood from his abdomen. He didn't have time to figure it out; the men were moments from the palace. No palace bells rang, no guards had come running. He was on his own.

He risked a quick look through the archway. The armed column made its way up the incline, maybe two dozen figures. They sported pikes and torches, and Chel spotted axes and knives at their belts. Their clothing was dark but motley. His eyes darted to their heads.

Each man sported a shaven head, save for a tuft of hair at its crest. Chel's eyes widened. The men were confessors.

They halted before the gate, then at a signal each raised something to his face and affixed it. Wooden masks. Chel jerked his head back, breathing hard. The masks were crude, rough-made things, nothing like the fine-wrought snarling mask the little Nort in the lowport had displayed. Confessors were disguising themselves as Norts? Nothing here added up. He had to raise the alarm.

Skirting Heali's still-smouldering corpse, he drove his aching body toward the palace interior.

***

Chel burst through the open archway and stumbled into the western hall, which had been dressed for the festival. A few people drifted between its elegant columns as Chel looked around, wheezing, singed and bleeding. The smell of smoke carried into here as well: something was burning within the palace, but no one seemed to be doing anything about it.

The handful of nobles who had chosen – or been forced – to stay rather than flee after the Nort attack looked up in shock at Chel's entrance, as did the skeleton crew of servants, minstrels and feast entertainers who surrounded them. Ignoring their ire, Chel made for the grand duke and the remainder of his family at the high table, where they were surrounded by half a dozen or so of his preening house guard.

'We're under attack,' Chel croaked, his voice scratched and hoarse. 'Take shelter!'

'Who in five hells are you?' boomed the duke. He had remained seated. Beside him sat his strutting son Count Esen, who was staring at Chel with the same expression as he might a coil of catshit, and beside him his hairy cousin, Morara.

Chel tried to bow, wincing at the pain in his side. 'Vedren Chel of Barva, sworn to Prince Tarfel, your grace.'

All heads turned to the far end of the table, where Prince Tarfel, scrubbed pink and draped in lace, was seated, flinching at the sound of his name. He looked up at Chel, his expression shifting from surprised confusion to embarrassment.

'Well, Merimonsun?' bellowed the duke. 'Is this one of yours?'

The little prince flushed from head to foot. 'Well, as you say, your grace, in fact—'

'Answer me, boy!'

'Yes, yes, he's my sworn man. First sworn. Only, really, I've not—'

Chel looked from one to the other, almost bursting with frustration. 'Please, your grace! We don't have much time – armed men are entering the palace as we speak.'

Some of the nobles started to rise, panic flushing their plump features.

The duke raised a thick eyebrow and tweaked his pointed beard. 'Then where are the alarms, Chel of Barva? Where are the palace guard? Where is my commander to tell me of this emergency?'

Chel looked around. The commander of the palace guard was entirely absent. This did not reassure him.

Count Esen leaned forward, handsome features locked in a sneer. 'Have this dog beaten, Father. He's clearly drunk, and likely lost a wager to send him here. These provincial irregulars are notorious for it.'

Chel locked eyes with the young count. The noble's eyes glittered with mocking challenge. Fuck you, Chel thought back. I'm trying to save your life, you abject halfwit.

He said nothing.

'I can smell burning!' a noble shouted. She looked young and earnest. 'And there's a bell! In the distance!'

Chel looked back to the duke, ignoring his son. 'Please, your grace. I saw not a guard between here and the city gate – I've just run straight in here unchallenged. I can't tell you where everybody is, only that soldiers are inside the palace right now. We must take refuge!'

The duke looked at him through narrowed eyes, then around the room, gauging the rising panic in the hall. Several of the nobles had begun to chatter among themselves, despite the duke calling for quiet, and members of one family, including the girl who had noticed the smell of smoke, were already making for one of the doors out of the hall.

'Remain in your seats!' the duke bellowed. They ignored him, and a moment later had disappeared down one of the narrow hallways that led toward the main wing of the palace. Others were rising, the servants already making for the kitchen exit, the minstrels in hot pursuit. The duke remained seated, glowering at Chel, and growled for his own men to stay put.

Chel looked to the prince, who was likewise unmoved. 'Please, your highness, we need to—'

Screams silenced the hall. From the first passageway, a bloodied noble came stumbling back into the room, slick hands clutching at a savage rent in his midriff. 'Norts!' he shrieked, then collapsed. He did not move again.

At last the duke was on his feet. 'Bar the doors! Bar every fucking door in this hall!'

***

The duke's guards moved quickly, rushing to the doorways and slamming them shut, then dragging festival tables in front. Screams and hammering came from beyond more than one. Then they moved to the storm-shutters, hauling closed the wide windows that had offered such a charming view out over lower terraces and the western sea beyond. Few nobles remained in the hall, besides Chel and guards: the duke himself, his son Esen and nephew Morara, and Prince Tarfel. Wherever the others had fled to, Chel hoped they were safe. Somehow, he doubted it.

The duke was breathing hard, his face flushed and gleaming. 'Norts in the palace. Shepherd's eye, we're doomed.'

'Charge them, Father!' Count Esen was at his father's side. An ornate, slim-bladed dagger had appeared in his hand. 'Drive these dogs back into the sea!'

The duke waved him away. 'You, prince's man. How many did you see?'

Chel swallowed. His side was beginning to throb. 'At least twenty, your grace. But they weren't coming from the sea, they came up the hill path from the city gates.' He shot Count Esen a look of challenge. 'And they're not Norts at all. They're in disguise.'

The duke shook his head. 'Norts, partisans, it's piss in a gale. Assassins are in my palace, murdering my guests. We'll either have to fight our way out, or dig in here until reinforcements arrive.'

The eyes of the hall fell on the wide archway beyond Chel. There was no door, only a long hallway to the eventual doorway between them and the water gardens.

Chel turned to the duke, one hand still clasped to his side. 'Keep yourself, the prince and your family safe. I'll do my best to hold them off or draw them away.'

The duke stared at him, thick brows lowered. 'You'll need luck indeed to see off a score, Chel of Barva.' He turned to the prince, who was cowering behind the table. 'Quite the sworn man you have here, Merimonsun.'

The prince whimpered something. Chel met his helpless gaze, nodded, and set off.

He hurried down the hallway, trying not to limp; already his side felt like it was seizing up. The garden doors were bigger and heavier than he'd realized. His breath coming in serrated gasps, his side burning, Chel drove the one door closed, then the other. From down the hallway came the crash of silverware and the groan of wood on stone as the duke's guards upended tables to barricade the archway.

Chel slid his edgeless half-sword between the overlarge handles, then, when the sword wobbled and flapped in its setting, he braced his body against the doors and gripped the handles tight. A slim gap remained between the solid wooden panels, and he peered through it, anxious to catch a glimpse of the column's progress. He had the most narrowly angled of views across the area beyond the doors, a vaguely circular courtyard ringed by colonnaded walkways. He could see the edges of the flickering light of their coming attackers, hear their clanking footsteps on the smooth stone beyond.

Someone screamed. He pressed his eye to the gap, but the doors' thickness blocked his angle. He saw blurs of dark arrows flash through the sliver of night, before a swirl of what looked like orange briar shot past his narrow viewport. The torchlight jumped and swung, the shadows on the surrounding walls flailing in concert. Further shouts and cries followed, along with the clatter of metal and whump of fearsome impact.

Chel considered opening the doors a crack. He needed reinforcements.

The doors smashed inward, hurling him backward onto the flagstones, jarring his bones and knocking the back of his head against the stone. Reeling and cursing, Chel looked back at the doors. His edgeless sword lay bent on the dark stone. Over it, framed in the doorway by torchlight and the flames that licked from the opposite windows, stood a towering silhouette, its outline blurred as its loose robes swayed around it.

Chel squinted.

His eyes fell on the long staff in the figure's hand. His eyes widened.

'The pig-fucker!'

The man before him was tall and broad, his former hunched

shuffle discarded. Grey, lank hair hung from his head, his features indistinct in the flickering torchlight. He swung the staff around his body, thumping it into a meaty palm.

'Come again, little man?' His voice was deep and clear, its accent mild but vaguely northern.

He scrabbled forward, snatching the half-sword from the floor. 'You're the pig-fucking beggar. You have caused me nothing but trouble since you tripped me.'

The beggar shook his head. 'Get out of my way.' He started to move forward.

Chel pushed himself to his feet. 'No.'

The beggar paused. Chel stood half a head shorter than him, holding the bent, blunt blade before him like a religious artefact. 'What?'

'I won't get out of your way.'

The beggar looked past him to the hallway's end, where oil lamps glimmered behind upturned tables. Irritation darkened his shadowed features. Behind him, the noise was peaking, the sounds of metal on metal and metal on flesh reaching a crescendo. Flames licked higher from the palace buildings.

The long staff swung before Chel was ready, sweeping his legs out from under him. Again he thumped back against the stones, the staff's other end bouncing savagely from his wounded abdomen. He hissed and spat, curled double on the cold stone floor.

Muttering, the beggar set off past his prone form, tapping the staff as he went.

Chel's hand gripped the man's ankle, and he stumbled. He whirled around, grimy robes sending up a cloud of ash, and kicked Chel's hand away from his foot. Chel felt his fingers bend too much.

'Just *fuck off*, will you, boy?'

The beggar made it almost to the barricade when Chel landed on his back, bloodied and screaming, flailing one-handed at the beggar's head.

'I won't let you hurt the prince!'

The pair stumbled forward into the piled furniture, colliding with one end of a badly balanced long table and crashing in a tumble of blood, ash and wood-splinters.

In the shuttered darkness of the hall, Chel staggered to his feet, blood streaming from a new gash in his forehead. He gripped a broken chair leg, ignoring the splinters in his palm, and swung at the beggar's head as he rose. He missed, thumping the wood against the man's shoulder and earning an enraged bellow in return.

The beggar scrabbled for his staff but Chel was faster, even with blood in his eyes. He landed one foot on the long wooden pole before the beggar could lift it and took another swing at the man's reaching form. The beggar swivelled, dodging the blow then driving a fist into Chel's midriff. A second hit followed, connecting with his slackened jaw and sending him sideways.

Chel pushed himself to his knees as the beggar snatched up his staff. 'Stay down, boy,' the man snarled.

Chel lunged forward, planting his shoulder into the man and driving him backward against the polished stone of the wall. The beggar's surprise was short-lived. Thick arms wrapped around Chel's neck and shoulders, and a moment later the beggar twisted and Chel found himself slammed into the stonework himself, his cheek grated like cheese. His right arm was jammed back against him, the joint screaming against its limits as he struggled.

'Nine hells, boy, why won't you lie down?' The rough voice in his ear mixed rage with bafflement.

'I won't . . . let you . . . hurt the prince,' he managed.

'God's dancing balls, boy!' The arms that pinned him swung him from the wall, out to face the ruin of the feast. 'I'm no danger to your fucking prince!'

He strained, gasping in the beggar's relentless hold, before his eyes made sense of the scene before him. The men of the duke's guard lay face-down at the foot of the steps to the high table, their throats cut, swords still in their scabbards. Grand Duke Reysel himself lay sprawled over the high table, his ample belly slashed and stabbed with dozens of gory wounds. Behind the table, blood-streaked knife in hand, stood Count Esen Basar. He was grinning. Around his neck hung a makeshift Nort mask.

'We started without you, couldn't risk . . .' The count's grin froze as he registered the beggar gripping Chel. 'You're not one of mine,' he said, eyes widening. Something was rattling at one of the shutters. 'Morara! Now! Do it now!'

'The prince—' Chel began, when an upturned table clattered sideways across the hall. The count's hairy cousin Morara kicked another chair aside as he closed on a cringing royal shape in a darkened corner. Chel writhed in the beggar's grip, struggling to free himself, before kicking at the man's shin.

The beggar bellowed and snarled. 'Fuck *this*!' He wrenched Chel's arm around, grinding the bone from its socket, then flung his stricken form against the wall. Chel's battered forehead clunked against the stone and he slumped sideways, his vision blurring.

From his new vantage point on the hall floor, events took on a certain fuzzy, dreamlike quality. He saw the beggar move away from him with what seemed leisurely ease, although part of his brain was still registering the sickening damage to his shoulder and the latest blow to his head. He watched as the beggar slammed his staff against the closest storm shutter, sending it arcing open to the night beyond. Something flew in from the wide window, a man-shaped darkness, and piled straight into Count Morara. The count went from standing to screaming in a heap of bloody pain as gleaming blades rose and fell in the dancing amber light.

Chel watched this as numbness flooded from his ruined shoulder across his body. He watched Count Esen back away from the beggar, then throw his knife at him. The beggar caught it and threw it back. The flying blade carved the handsome count's cheek wide open, and screeching, he ran. He fled like a panicked doe, fast and fleet, around the room's edge, over Chel's slumped form and out through the collapsed barricade before anyone could grab him.

'Now *that's* a fucking shame,' Chel tried to say, then the blackness overcame him.

PART II

SIX

Every part of Chel's body hurt, from the scrapes to his face through to his burning side and battered middle, down to the sour and aching muscles of his legs. His right arm was strapped across his body, bound tight, and its shoulder throbbed with menace. Hot blood pounded against his temples like a three-day hangover. He was very thirsty.

He reeked of smoke, sweat and mule, and vague memories from the previous night floated through his wobbling mind. Flames, mostly, and blood. Firm hands, rough on his battered body, dragging him. Harsh voices and pain. The counts. The grand duke. The prince. Faces and shapes, unfamiliar, large and small. A mule. Bells.

He opened his eyes.

He was in a cramped store-room of sorts, piled with sacks and crates, with odd-pitching wooden walls. The only dim light came from a grille somewhere above, along with muted shouts and the occasional distant bell. The building around them seemed unsteady, as if it were shiftly slightly in a strong breeze. Someone beside him was snoring.

It was Tarfel, nestled beside him on a bed of lumpy sacks, still in the remains of his evening finery, soot-streaked and ragged. The prince stirred and whimpered in his sleep. He had a graze on his cheek, a nascent bruise beneath it, but looked otherwise unharmed. Chel guessed that the dark spatters on the prince's silken shirt were from elsewhere. Chel wondered if he should let the prince sleep. He looked so pale and feeble, his mousy hair flopped over his scrawny features, his fringe puffed up on every out-breath.

Chel pushed himself to his feet and looked down at his own ruined clothes. The voluminous outer layers had been ripped away, leaving him in a dark snug tunic and trousers. He lifted his shirt to find the gash at his side bandaged, the skin around the dressing clear of crusted blood. Someone had cleaned his wounds and bound them, then left him here with the prince. That had to be a good omen. He tried to wring recollections from his brain. A woman's voice, perhaps?

He glanced around, ignoring the complaints of his grumbling neck and shoulder. A glimmer of light along the base of one wall revealed a door. Chel tried the handle with his good hand. It was resolutely locked. With a sinking feeling, he returned to the prince.

'Your highness? Prince Tarfel?'

Tarfel stirred, then rolled over. 'I won't!' the prince said with remarkable clarity, and Chel blinked. 'I won't go! I don't need lessons from those horrid old men.'

He mumbled on with decreasing coherence, before finishing with a half-garbled demand for the servants to bring fresh pillows. Chel blew the hair out of his eyes and pinched the bridge of his nose with his good hand. 'Prince Tarfel!'

A rolling snore echoed around the store-room. Chel prodded the prince with a foot. He got no response.

Shouts echoed overhead, followed by thumps and clunks in the structure around them, then the whole building lurched into motion, rocking gently as it went. After a moment of unsteadiness, Chel collapsed onto a sack beside the prince. Of course it was a bloody boat. No smell of brine, no great lurching waves. They weren't at sea. They must be on the river, and that had to mean Sebemir. The only questions were: where were they going, and who were they with?

Tarfel at last lifted his head, blinking in the gloom.

'Whatever is going on?' the prince said after a moment of dark, creaking quiet.

'We're on a boat, highness,' Chel replied. 'I think we've been kidnapped.'

'Oh,' the prince said. Then, after a moment, 'What?'

'Do you remember, highness? Someone tried to kill you last night, and someone else tried to kill me. Heali . . .' Chel shook his head, numb at the memory. 'The guards were gone, the Watch Commander with them, and those people in the palace weren't Norts. Esen Basar killed his father, and I think he was trying to kill both of us. He had . . . he had a Nort mask, a pretend one. And . . . that pig-fucking beggar saved us.' His shoulder pulsed at the memory. 'But he ripped my arm out, and dragged us over the hills to what must be Sebemir, and now we're locked in a cupboard on a riverboat. So I think it's safe to assume that we're still in trouble.'

'Oh,' the prince said. Then, after a moment, '*What?*'

***

For a time, Chel slept. He woke to the sound of raised voices beyond the door. The sky visible through the grille still offered the crimson streaks of sunset. It could not have been long. The prince was snoring again beside him, and Chel nudged him with his good arm.

'Voices.'

Tarfel stirred and sat up. His bruise had darkened.

'Who do you think they are?' Chel said. 'Those that took us.'

'Oh, they'll be mercenaries,' the prince said with a grimace.

'Not Rau Rel?'

'Of course not, partisans would have murdered me immediately. You know, "death to tyrants" and all that nonsense.' The prince shifted uncomfortably. 'I imagine I'm to be ransomed. Question is, who would have the gall to order my abduction?'

'Well, considering we've just seen Grand Duke Reysel murdered by his own son, perhaps the usual rules don't apply right now, highness?'

The prince put one hand on his weak chin. 'A little patricide isn't uncommon, especially among northern Names. Notoriously emotional bunch, prone to hysteria.'

'Morara and Esen meant to kill you, too, highness, and make it look like the Norts were responsible. Unless . . . Unless . . .' Chel had told no one of the confessors beneath the Nort masks, but he had announced in front of Count Esen that he knew that the Norts were false. Had he doomed all those present in doing so? Was this his fault?

Tarfel ignored him. 'Exactly, and now I'm kidnapped! Who would dare hold the kingdom to ransom?'

'I'm not convinced that our kidnappers and your

would-be assassins were working toward the same ends, highness.' Seeing as one lot seem to have murdered the other.

'Since Father's Wars of Unity ended – the first time, at least – a few outposts of resistance to his rule have lingered: the southern territories, of course, the so-called free cities of the North, that grubby lot in the south-west . . . But none of them would risk bringing down the fury of the crown by stealing a prince.'

'Are you *sure* it wasn't the Rau Rel?'

'Don't be absurd. A gaggle of mud-farmers have no coin for mercenaries, even barely competent ones. Mud-farmers, dissidents, disgraced minor nobility, barely a name to their, er, name.' He rubbed at his elbow, bruised from impact on a vegetable sack. 'This was one of our continental rivals. They were imperial colonies when the Taneru ruled, and now witness their impudence. They shall pay for this, the moment I am freed. I shall not forget this insult.'

Chel nodded, turning away and rolling his eyes. 'Of course, highness.'

Tarfel's pout froze, gradually replaced by a faraway, fearful look. 'Our bargain stands, doesn't it? Chel? See me to safety, I'll see you released.'

'On my oath, highness. And if it's really mercenaries on the other side of the door, maybe we can make them a better offer.'

Chel crept forward, feeling every ache of the damage the previous twenty-four hours had wrought on him, and pressed his ear to the door.

***

'. . . cutting it fine, boss. Any finer we'd have been wafers.' A rumbling, gentle voice. Peeved.

'Not my choice. We had a run-in with some of our friends of the cloth.' Chel remembered that voice: the beggar's growl. He rubbed his good hand over his strapped shoulder and bared his teeth. So that was his kidnapper after all.

'Ah, hells. I thought we'd be rid of the pricks at least.'

'They had freelancers. Half a dozen horse-archers. Mawn if I'm any judge – and I am. They butchered some local militia they must have taken to be us.'

'Twelve hells, boss, Mawn this far east?'

'Forget it. We're alive, and back on track. Despite enough cock-ups to leave a convent smiling.'

'Ah, don't be blaming me again, man!' A reedy voice with a strong accent. Somewhere over the southern waters, Clyden most likely. 'Told you before, friend Spider was covering while I took care of business. It's not my fault I get tummy trouble, I'm delicate downstairs. You know, come to think it, could be a waterborne parasite from that last crossing. You ask me, it's a wonder that we're not laid low more frequently, given how often—'

'Stop eating half-pickled fucking fish for breakfast, Lemon!'

'I wasn't the only one dropping bollocks out there, man! If Loveless could hold back on fucken every pretty thing she lays eyes on, we'd—'

Chel heard the creak and thump of the outer door.

'We were just talking about you,' the beggar said.

'Nothing good, I hope,' came the reply. 'She's aboard, by the way. In case you were worried.'

'Not for a moment.'

'No doubt. She wants a word. Or equivalent.' The newcomer chuckled at that, for no clear reason.

Chel heard the beggar growl at the others and stomp away, then the groan of the door in his wake. All seemed quiet. He shifted, trying to catch something, when the bolt thunked and the door flew open. He pitched forward into an aching heap on the boards of the hold.

A sinewy, shaven-headed man with an aquiline nose and an abundance of earrings stood over him, a nasty grin on his face. He wore a tight, sleeveless tunic, exposing arms marked with a fearsome quantity of company tattoos. 'Hello there, fuck-nuts. Having a good snoop, were we? Hear anything good?' He rolled him over with the toe of his boot.

Chel said nothing for a moment, feeling his body throb beneath the pressure of the boot. Two other figures were in the low room, but he was struggling to make them out from where he was pinned. 'Only,' he said after a moment, his voice cracked, 'that the little one should eat less fish.'

The bald man bellowed a laugh at that, as did the woman behind him.

'Little one? Little? I'd wear your balls for earrings if you had any, chum,' came the Clydish voice. 'I've got a fucken name.'

Chel spread his good hand, still prone. The bald man's foot hadn't moved. 'We've not been introduced.'

The man laughed again and removed his boot, then reached down with a muscular hand and dragged Chel upward until he was sitting against the wall. 'Fair's fair, now. Tell the sand-crab your names, boys and girls.' He added under his breath, 'Not like it'll make much difference in the long run.'

A woman stepped forward from the gloom. She was the most striking woman Chel had ever seen: maybe a hand shorter than him, with a short shock of hair, alchemical blue, and a jawline so strong it could have been sculpted from marble. She kept one loose hand on the hilt of a short sword that hung from her hip. He had to wrench his gaze away from her, worried she'd think him simple.

'Well, you've met the Spider here,' she nodded at the bald man. Spider leered at him. Her accent was soft but distinct, something foreign but eroded to little more than uncommon vowels. 'And the large and amiable gentleman back there is Foss.'

Behind her, a shape shifted against the wall, something Chel had at first glance taken to be a pile of sacks. He was enormous: big hands, big face, wide around the middle. He looked like a small hill. His hair was tied back in a thick bundle of dark braids, and his curly black beard boasted two streaks of grey at the corners of his chin. He offered Chel an awkward smile.

'I go by Loveless,' the blue-haired woman went on, 'and this fine specimen of Clydish stock is Lemon.'

The final figure bowed her head in acknowledgement. She was small and wiry, her pale skin splashed copper with freckles. A mountain of orange hair bounced above a face that was round-eyed and squarish. She still looked irked.

Tarfel shuffled out of the store's darkness beside and above him. 'Why are you called Lemon?'

'Because she's round and bitter,' Loveless said with a straight face.

'I'm not fucken round!'

The laughter that filled the room met a sharp end when

Spider rounded on the captives, his mirth vanished. 'Now that's enough about us. Who the fuck are you?'

'I am Tarfel Merimonsun, Prince of—'

'Oh, do shut up, princeling,' Loveless said. 'We know who you are, you blithering pillock. Why do you think you're here?'

'About that,' Chel said, still sitting against the wall. His shoulder pulsed. He wondered if it had been Loveless who strapped him the night before. Perhaps it had been Lemon. Or maybe the other one they'd referred to?

'The Spider asked you a question, Andriz piss-pot.' Spider was still very close to him, and Chel could see the top of a freakish knife jutting from his belt. 'Who are you, and what the fuck are you doing here?'

'Vedren Chel, of Barva. I'm sworn to the prince.'

'Chel?' Loveless said. 'What does that mean?'

'I'm not sure it means anything. Do names always mean something?'

'Oh, dear little scab-face, names mean *everything*.'

Lemon had wandered closer. 'Got any nicknames? Any monikers or *noms de guerre*?'

'Any what?'

'Ah, come on, man. All our *noms* are *de guerre* these days. What do other people call you?'

Chel thought of the various names he'd been called over the last few years. 'Chel.'

Tarfel pushed back into the conversation. He looked vexed at being excluded. 'His sister calls him "Bear"!'

That got more sniggering. 'You don't look much like a fucking bear,' Spider said. 'More like a shit-eating rat. Are there rat-bears?'

'I think there are in Tokemia,' Lemon said.

Chel swung his sore head toward the prince. 'Thank you, highness.'

Tarfel had the decency to look abashed, then a thought crossed his features before Chel's eyes. 'You're not Rau Rel, are you?' the prince said to the room.

More laughter. 'No, princeling,' Loveless said. 'We're mercenaries.'

Delight spread across Tarfel's face. 'See, Chel? Which company?'

The mercenaries exchanged cautious looks.

'Black Hawk Company,' Lemon said after a slight hesitation.

'I've not heard of that one. How many strong are you? Two thousand? Five?'

Lemon looked around the room. 'The second one.'

'Five thousand?'

Lemon coughed. 'Aye, well, we're an incipient venture. Up-starting, if you will. Old hands, new pennant.'

'Could I, by any chance, make you an offer?' the prince said.

'Only if you offer to fuck off back into that store and stay quiet until Kurtemir.'

Chel saw the big man, Foss, stiffen at that. He guessed that their destination was not intended to be divulged.

Spider was back at his ear, and this time the knife was in his hand. 'The Spider notes with disappointment that you still haven't answered his question. Why are you here, sand-crab rat-bear?'

Chel's mouth felt suddenly dry, and he swallowed. 'If you don't know, I sure as snake-shit can't tell you.'

'He's here because I want him here.' No one had heard the door open this time, but there the old beggar stood, head ducked below the low lintel. He walked slowly into the hold and into the light. His rag-bundle clothes were streaked in grime: dust, soot, blood and who knew what else, his hair hanging in great ashen strings before his face. 'Get to your duties. We're not away clean yet.'

Foss gave him a sharp glance. 'The river dock closed as we left it,' he said in a low voice. 'A sail?'

'Not yet,' the beggar said, then turned to the rest of the hold. 'Was I mumbling? Get to it! Not you, Lemon – you'll be keeping our friends company for now.' Lemon started to protest, but he held up a hand. 'You need the practice. The rest of you, out.'

As the other mercenaries shuffled out, the beggar marched to a water basin in the corner of the hold. He reached down and dragged his rotten clothes over his head, discarding layers of rags at his feet, then leaned forward and dunked his head. Chel watched through narrowed eyes as he splashed the water over himself, washing away coats of filth, then stood again, water cascading over his bared torso. Chel's good hand was back on his ruined shoulder. Who was this brutal old bastard who had done him such damage?

The man before him had jet-black hair and skin the colour of sand, and was nowhere near as aged as Chel had thought. His body was sharp-edged and thickly muscled, and criss-crossed with more scarring and tattoos than Chel had ever seen on a single human. His upper arms cascaded with markings, some no doubt Free Company, but none Chel could distinguish or recognize. What kind of man could serve in that many companies anyway? An alarming collection of knives belted at the man's waist glittered in the lantern light.

The beggar turned back to the hold, and at last Chel

saw his face in the dim light. He was prow-faced, his nose a sharp, brutal beak, his dark and heavy features following in its wake. He seemed surprised that Chel and Tarfel were still there. He looked like a furious eagle.

He pinned Chel with a glare. 'Got something you want to call me?' Then he grinned, short and sharp. 'Lemon! Get those fuckers locked away.' With that, he scooped up a shirt and strode for the door.

A moment later the hold was empty, but for the disconsolate, muttering Lemon. 'Aye, right. Practice, is it? Fuck's sake, like I had any fucken alternative. Would he have me shit my breeches on duty? I ask you.'

Tarfel had already wandered back into the store in anticipation of being bolted away. Lemon checked over Chel's bandages and strapping, while he lay piled where Spider had left him.

'The tall one,' Chel said. 'With the nose. He's the brains?'

'The brains? Maybe the spleen, or wherever bile comes from. Right, you'll live. Now get yourself back in there, wee bear, or ancestors-take-me I'll fuck you right up with a hammer.'

Chel looked up at her. Buried in the matted fur and leather of Lemon's outfit was an array of ironmongery, small hammers, axes and picks. 'Are you a miner?'

She half smiled. 'Once, maybe. In a sense.'

'It doesn't work, you know.' It was Tarfel, from within the store's gloom. 'Your name, I mean.'

'Oh aye?'

'Lemons. They're not bitter, they're sour. That's different.'

'You're telling fucken me! I've been telling those half-wits forever! Oh, but it's all "Ah Lemon, what's the difference, you're a shite-heap either way".'

Chel sensed an opening. Lemon seemed grateful to have someone to talk to. 'They don't sound like they're very nice to you.'

Lemon frowned. 'Are you joking? They're the best bunch of bastards I ever rode with. Not that they know the value of an education, mind.'

'You're educated?'

'I may not have attended a fancy *Hacademy*, but knowledge is power, wee bear, as the powerful know. Like me.' She jabbed a thumb at herself. 'For example, these folk we saw earlier today.'

'Who? The prince and I didn't really—'

'Hush and listen, this could save your life some day.'

'Oh?'

'Aye, "oh". See, thing is, most people, they don't get hit by arrows much.'

'That so?'

'Indeedy. So, if and when they do, they don't know what to do. They think that's it, and they should just keel over, curl up their toes, back to the ancestors.'

'Whereas . . .?'

'Ah, you can fight on with an arrow in you! You can fight on with a dozen, like a fucken pin-cushion. I knew a fella, a Clydish man, mark you, not like one of you northern piss-sheets, fought on with sixteen arrows, two spears and a sword in him. Carried on for hours, cracking heads and ripping limbs.'

'And he lived?'

'Well, no, but he didn't lie down and die at the first blow, did he?'

'So what's the big secret? If you're hit by an arrow, don't die?'

'Aye. That's the secret: don't die. Now budge your skinny arse, before I help you along.' She gave a meaningful wave with a fat-headed hammer, and Chel began to drag himself back into the store. The door closed behind them, and Lemon bolted it.

'Hey, Lemon?'

'What do you want, bugger-bear?'

'What about the big guy? He got any names?'

'Oh, Rennic? Hundreds. More than the rest of us combined.'

'And what do you call him?'

'We call him boss.'

SEVEN

Chel and the prince sat in the stuffy gloom of the barge store, surrounded by vegetables.

'Why did you antagonize them?'

'Sorry, highness?'

'You were riling them up, Chel. I'll be ransomed in Kurtemir – ghastly place, but accessible at least – and until then all you have to do is be quiet and meek. I'm assuming you'll be included in any arrangement, of course, but I can't see why you wouldn't.'

'Thank you, highness.'

'Didn't they teach you manners, etiquette, *politesse*? Where was it you grew up?'

'Barva.'

'And they taught you nothing of diplomacy, of catching more flies with honey than vinegar? It's simple, Chel: it's important for people to like you, or they won't do what you want.'

'Nobody does what I want anyway, highness.'

A moment of relative silence passed. Chel lay back against

bumpy sacks, feeling the soft advance of sleep, lulled by the barge's gentle rock and the river's wash. Even the dull agonies that racked his body couldn't stave it off. 'Highness, when the Norts attacked, you were down in the stables . . . Why were you hiding in the mule cart? Why not just take one of the horses if you wanted to flee?'

'Oh, that's simple enough. I can't ride.'

Chel blinked in the darkness, long and slow. 'You can't ride?' How could a prince not ride?

'No, never learned. Mendel promised to teach me, but well, the brigands, his injury, Corvel's death, et cetera. You know. Anyway, why do all your insults revolve around intercourse with animals?'

'Highness?'

'It's always "pig-sucking this", "horse-stroking that" with you. Is there something I should know?'

Chel coughed, shifting against the scratchy bulk behind him, feeling throbbing aches all over. 'I suppose I picked it up from Lord Sokol's regulars. Most were from the fields, I imagine that sort of thing came up a lot.'

'I'd like you to cut it out, Chel. You're sworn to a prince now, and such vocabulary is . . .'

'Unseemly?'

'I can see we understand each other, Chel. Chel?'

He was already asleep.

* * *

Somewhere in the small hours, hazy dream images slipped away: Heali falling over and over, the knife glinting in his hand, while soft yellow flames licked at a slumped form on the stones below. Chel rubbed his eyes and winced. The prince was snoring beside him on the floor of the store, their legs pressed in the gaps between crates and barrels. The darkness was near-absolute, only a sliver of indigo starlight lighting the boards where they lay. The starlight moved, and Chel turned his head to look up at the deck grille above them. A shape blocked most of it. A man-shape.

'Your highness?' The voice was low, whisper-soft. The barge creaked and flexed around them, the sound of the river's wash now dominant, and Chel had to strain to hear. 'Are you there?'

Chel nudged the prince, who woke after a couple of shunts. Chel motioned to keep quiet, then upward at the grille.

'Highness?' came the voice again.

'Who's there?' Tarfel said in as soft a voice as he could manage.

'A loyal servant, highness. Here to rescue you.'

'How many are you? We're well-kept.'

'There's a boat coming, but we must be ready for it. I've opened the hatch on this side – unbolt it on yours and I'll raise it.'

Tarfel and Chel exchanged glances. The prince was beaming in the gloom. One-handed, Chel clambered onto a barrel, then reached up and ground open the lower latch on the grille. Slowly, the man above them levered it out, and a wider swathe of starlight flooded the hold.

The man's arm thrust down into the gap. 'Highness, your hand. Quickly, please.'

Tarfel went to climb for it, but Chel shook his head in the gloom. *Let me check.* The prince nodded, twitching with impatience. Chel steadied himself, then reached up to take the man's outstretched hand. It was cold to touch, and rough, but it gripped him with an iron strength and dragged upward. Chel braced his feet against the wall of the store, hoping its creaks would be covered by the noise of the barge's passage.

As soon as his head and good shoulder crested the hatch in the deck, he found himself looking up at the face of their rescuer. He was rangy, shaven-headed, a single gold earring glinting in the starlight. His eyes widened as the light caught Chel's face.

'Who the fuck are you?'

Still Chel dangled in his grip, one-armed, his toes braced against the wall below the hatch. 'I'm s—'

His gaze caught the knife in the man's other hand, wheeled back to strike.

The man's eyes followed his, then they locked stares. Without a word the man thrust forward with the blade, and Chel did the only thing he could think of. He drove back with his legs, pushing away from the wall, and yanked the man into the hatch after him.

His attacker slammed his head on the lip of the opening as he fell, and for a split-second Chel congratulated himself before his own thumping impact, spread across a splintering crate and a sack of something solid. The man fell straight onto him like a dead weight, crushing the air from his lungs, the knife vanishing into the darkness.

'Chel? Chel? What's happening?' Tarfel's voice was urgent and timorous in his ear.

He tried to answer, but his abdomen was in spasm and he could barely breathe, let alone speak. Instead he honked in what air he could and wrestled his good arm free. The man was moaning and stirring, and Chel swung feeble, one-armed punches past his head.

'Hoy, what's going on in there?' It sounded like Lemon on the other side of the door. 'Don't make me come in and sort you out, you pestilent pissants.'

Tarfel looked at Chel with fearful eyes. He did his best to look reassuring while gasping like a harpooned seal and jabbed a finger toward the door with what he hoped was encouragement.

'Get Lemon?' the prince said.

'Get . . . Lemon . . .' Chel croaked.

The man crushing his lungs shook his head and pushed himself up, and for a moment Chel managed a real inward breath. Then he couldn't tell which bangs were Tarfel thumping on the door and which were the assassin landing punches into his sides as he flailed his good arm and struggled beneath the man's weight.

Light burst brilliantly across the store as the door to the hold flew open. Lemon stood framed in the doorway, a small, wiry silhouette, an orange halo around her head.

'Right, yon fucker!'

The weight lifted from Chel's chest as the man struggled to his feet. Something whistled through the air and connected with the assassin's head with a dull clunk. Lemon strode through the door and over Chel's prone form and punched the reeling man in the throat as he staggered. He collapsed to the floor, gasping, and Lemon crunched her knee into his face. The assassin slumped, passed out on the floor.

'Where'd this shite-box come from?'

Chel's own breathing was barely under control, and he felt like the room was spinning even as he lay beside the broken would-be assassin. He managed to wave his good arm toward the empty hatch above.

'He said he was here to rescue me,' Tarfel said from his hiding place in the opposite corner.

'Aye, right. Course he was.' She stooped to reclaim her hammer.

'He said there's a boat coming.'

'Ah, ancestors' piss-wine! Now I have to wake everybody up.'

Lemon turned and marched back to the doorway, then paused. 'Stay here, dullards. For all that is sweet in this shitty world, do not fucken wander off again. Yes?'

Tarfel nodded. Chel managed a groan. Lemon disappeared into the flickering light of the hold, then a moment later a coil of rope came whistling through the door and thumped down onto the boards. 'And tie that fucker up!'

***

By the time Chel had recovered his feet and spat a bloody mouthful into a corner, Tarfel had made a decent fist of tying up their attacker. Not being a natural knotsman, he'd gone for quantity over quality, and thick balls of contorted rope jutted from the man's constricted limbs. He'd also found the man's knife, which he presented to Chel with great solemnity. Uncertain of what to do with it, Chel took it in his good hand and tucked it in his belt as he'd seen others do. He hoped he could keep his balance and avoid falling on it, which seemed the most likely prospect at that point.

Sounds filtered down through the open hatch. Cries and clangs and thumps.

'Someone's fighting,' Tarfel said.

Chel nodded. 'More than likely. Let's go, highness.'

'What do you mean, let's go? The Clydish oaf said to stay here!'

Chel chewed something salty around his mouth. He could feel his face swelling up again. 'She did. But all we know at the moment is that people are trying to kill us, or maybe just me to get to you, and that we're in the hands of mercenaries employed by interfering foreigners. That doesn't strike me as people we should be bending over backward to keep alongside, highness.'

'But what good is going up there?'

'Up there,' Chel said, 'is a boat. And if we time it right, we can be away before anyone knows we're missing, leave these bastards to sort things out between themselves. All we need to do is get to shore. We're still well north of the lake – this part of the world must be teeming with folk loyal to the crown. So, I say again: let's go, your highness.'

This time, Tarfel followed.

They crept through the empty hold and up onto the lower deck. The moon was lost behind drifting clouds but the stars were bright, and the scattered forms of bodies lay clear across the planking. Three on the lower deck, another over the rail on the fore tower. The sound of combat came from over their heads, the aft upper deck. Chel ignored it. He had seen what he was looking for.

'There, grapples!'

He limped forward, feeling every wound and trauma as he crossed the deck with the prince in his wake. A rope ladder dangled from rusty hooks from the barge's high rail, and Chel peered over the side. There on the slick water below bobbed a long, narrow rowboat, tied against the side.

There was someone in it.

The figure below gave a cry and raised the crossbow in its grip, its projecting bolt-head gleaming in a sudden burst of moonlight. Chel floundered, too shocked to react.

Something whistled past his face, close enough to flutter his hair, and he assumed the bolt had fired and missed. Yet still he could see it in the crossbow below him, even as its owner wobbled. He refocused. Something long and dark was projecting from the top of the figure's head. Something fletched. Another black arrow swished down toward the boat, thudding into the crossbow wielder. The crossbow clattered against the boat's hull.

Strong hands gripped him and pulled him back from the rail. He looked around to see Foss, the braided hulk, steering him back toward the hold. Spatters of blood shone on his face in the starlight. Tarfel was already walking ahead of them, unprompted.

Lemon stood in the hold's low doorway. 'Aye, right, fancied a spot of night air, did you? Wankers.' She shot an uneasy look up at the upper deck as they reached her. 'I won't mention this if you don't, but get the fuck back below and maybe we'll all still be breathing come sun-up, eh? Good lads!'

***

Chel was dozing, exhausted, his head against the door, when he heard the clump of boots on the boards beyond. Shivering awake, he strained an ear to catch Rennic in low conversation with a gruff-voiced woman he took to be the barge's captain.

'—him aboard in Sebemir, with three more flimsies,' he heard the captain saying. 'Nowt peculiar with any, some of the crew knew 'em. Or of 'em, least.' He heard her stamp a foot in frustration. 'Peasy fucker shanked my helm.' A pause. 'If any's left when you spit him out, I'll take a bite myself.'

Chel didn't hear Rennic's reply, but a moment later one set of heavy boots stomped out of earshot. He slid over from the door, mindful of his earlier eavesdropping tumble, and was gratified when it was yanked open a moment later.

Rennic stood in the doorway, head ducked, more than filling the frame. He reached in, past Chel and the blinking prince, and grabbed the bound legs of their would-be assassin. He dragged the man's slumped and mumbling form over the grimy floor and into the hold. He did not shut the door after him.

Chel and Tarfel peered into the lamp-lit hold. A single chair stood at its centre, and without apparent effort Rennic hoisted the man up onto it, leaving him lolling with the barge's rise and fall on the water. In the gloom beyond the lamp, Chel made out the huge, implacable form of Foss, arms folded, standing against the wall. Beside him leaned Loveless, and in the corner Lemon squatted, apparently cleaning her ironmongery with a rag. Spider was beside the door, picking his teeth with the point of his curved knife. All looked unharmed, if a little bloody.

Rennic looked around. 'Any water to hand?'

Loveless stepped forward. 'Allow me.' She slapped the man hard across the face. 'Wake up, shit-head!'

Rennic gave her a long look, eyes narrowed.

'What? Look, he's awake. Now keep out of the way.'

The man was blinking, his eyes darting around the hold. A moment later he struggled against his bonds, but only briefly. Tarfel's knots were good enough, and the man had taken in enough of his situation to realize that even freed of his ropes he'd remain in a tight spot.

Loveless leaned back against a barrel a few feet away from the bound man, her manner relaxed.

'So,' she said.

The man looked up. A carpet of dried blood had crusted down one side of his face, and his features looked misshapen from swelling and hammer-induced realignment. His breathing was harsh, each breath in a nasty, rattling wheeze.

'You might as well kill me now,' the man said. 'I've got nothing for you.'

Loveless smiled at that, a wolfish smile on her winsome face. A pale, narrow scar, forked like lightning, marked one side of her face from temple to cheek. 'We both know that isn't true, chum.'

'Beat me all you want. You get nothing.'

'Why would I beat you?'

The man blinked flecks of dried blood from his eyes. He looked confused. 'To get me to talk?'

Loveless leaned forward. 'Come on, we're all professionals here, chum. No need to pretend that torture is worthwhile.' She stood and began to walk around the bound man in a slow circle. 'Sure, it can make the person doing the torturing feel better, and assure clients that, well, Something is being Done, but the trouble is . . .' She stopped behind the man, who looked increasingly uneasy, and laid a gentle hand on his shoulder. '. . . You just can't trust the information, can you?'

'So you're not going to kill me?'

Loveless's face was impassive. 'Oh, we're definitely going to kill you.' The man sagged. 'If we didn't, the captain of this vessel most certainly would. And she'd be far less civilized about it. But. The good news, chum, is that we're not going to torture or beat you first.'

The assassin was still blinking. A rusty tear trickled down his swollen cheek. 'Then get the fuck on with it! Why are you talking to me?'

'Because I think you want to help us.'

'Do I fuck. You're going to kill me.'

'It was the people who placed you on this barge who did that. This is just inevitability working its way through.'

'What?'

Loveless swung around the man, a hand on each of his shoulders. She moved with grace and menace. 'What brought you to us, chum?'

'Stop calling me that.'

'Was it coin? It's no good to you now, either way.' Loveless tilted her head. 'Or was it threat? They have something of yours, or someone? Forced you?' She leaned forward, so close that the man jerked his head back. 'No, you're not the sort, are you, chum? And we can discount loyalty – those unfortunates whose organs are soaking the decks outside weren't any company I've ever seen, nor was there a sworn among them. And you're no man of the Shepherd, are you, so I think we can discount the holy calling.'

She stood. 'Coin it was, then. And where is that coin now? Did it even reach you?'

The man in the chair seemed about to sob.

'Nothing up front and sent to your death. No family, no friends to collect on your behalf. Not that they'd pay, would they? We both know that. What do you think your reward was going to be, had things gone your way tonight? Silver or steel? The type to pay a man to kill a prince aren't the type to leave a killer alive to spend his fee.'

'He's not a fucking prince!' the man spat. His cheek ran with rusty wash.

'Is that so? Then why all this trouble?'

'Because people can't go around saying they're princes!'

'Was he doing that? How did you hear?'

'They told me. Well, they told Varint, and she told me.'

'And who is Varint?'

The man blinked again. 'She was in the boat.'

'Ah. That's a shame. What did Varint tell you?'

'That some little piss-prick was going around calling himself a prince, and he needed ending. They said he might be going south on a boat, so we was to get aboard as flimsies at Sebemir and keep watch.'

'And then?'

'If we saw anything, we signal shore. Varint had riders going up and down the river paths.'

'Why the boat? Why not just stab him and hide?'

The man didn't answer, and Loveless leaned in close. 'Why the boat of comrades, chum? Why come aboard?'

'Because any fucker that took him aboard was a traitor, and they should be sliced along with him,' he spat.

'So you were going to kill everyone.'

The man stared off into the middle distance. 'Yeah. Traitors got it coming. Varint said we could keep the barge.'

Loveless nodded. 'An attractive offer. Who did Varint say had hired you?'

The man shrugged.

'You can do better than that. What kind of person did Varint talk to?'

'The kind that don't like being spoken of.'

'You're forgetting, chum. You're already dead, remember? What do you have to fear from unseen others now?'

The man started blinking again, and Loveless put a hand back on his shoulder. 'Come now, it'll be over soon. Everyone you had loyalty to is gone now, and those who remain were happy enough to see your blood spread for nothing. Who hired Varint?'

'. . . Church. Red confessors.'

Loveless stood up straight again. 'Thank you, chum, you've been very helpful.'

'Why do you keep calling me that!'

Her voice was utterly expressionless. 'Because it's what gets fed to fish. Foss, would you see this arsehole out?'

The dark shape detached itself from the pool of shadows by the wall and strode forward. Without ceremony, Foss squatted and scooped the squawking man onto his shoulder, then thumped out through the doorway. Chel heard the man's cries grow in pitch, before a final shriek, and a moment later, a splash. Foss reappeared in the doorway shortly afterward, stone-faced.

Loveless acknowledged his return, then shook her head and blew out her cheeks. 'What a prick,' she muttered.

Spider chuckled. 'Should have let me dose him, could have had him dancing a jig while he sang his little heart out.' Rennic rolled his eyes as Spider slouched from the room, still chuckling to himself.

'I will tell you what, I do not care to have that wanker along,' Lemon muttered from her corner as the door closed.

'Shut your yap, Lemon,' Rennic growled in response. 'He comes with the job, which is more than you've managed.'

Loveless sloped forward and reclined in the chair, after

dusting off the worst of the former assassin's leavings. 'Well, that confirms a few things. Where does this leave us?'

Rennic leaned back against the wall, his mouth a hard line. 'Unchanged. We knew they were following us, and now we know how. If luck holds, we've cleared all who had sight of our cargo.'

'And if not?'

'We'll skip that one when it falls.'

Lemon looked up again. 'You know, a word of thanks wouldn't go amiss. If I'd not roused you pillocks, that bastard and his pals would have carved us hither and yon.'

Rennic nodded, his eyes twinkling in the light. 'Yeah? And who got *you* up, Lem?'

'Woke myself,' came the hot reply. 'Close duty, it was. On hand to deal with situation in yonder store.' She waved her hammer toward the open door where Chel and Tarfel huddled, peering out. The eyes of the room turned on them. Tarfel shrank straight back into the shadows.

Rennic walked toward the doorway, eyes fixed on Chel. Chel stood up, good hand on the frame, every muscle in his body united in complaint.

'How the fuck are you still upright, scab-face?' Rennic said, his head tilted. 'Didn't you head-butt that fucker unconscious and drop through the deck?'

'Something like that.'

Rennic grinned, sharp and wolfish. 'Maybe I'm not such a bad judge of character after all.' He leaned in close, his voice low. 'But understand this: you're here because I want you here, and I want you here for him.' He nodded toward the prince. 'This may come as a shock, but I want to keep young Prince Fuck-face alive and well, and that's more than can be said for most folk you'll meet. So I would be most grateful if you would do me the considerable favour of not trying to run off again. Do you understand me? Just nod if you do, it's been a long day.'

Chel managed a nod.

'Good. Now back in your box. We've got a long way to go and I'm tired as shit of looking at you.'

He shunted Chel back with a palm, and Chel collapsed onto his sack-bed. The door closed and bolted and he and the prince were once again in darkness. Chel flopped back and looked up at the distant patch of stars. The grille was back over the hatch. That seemed about right.

EIGHT

In the morning, they were let out for good behaviour. Chel shuffled into the hold with tender steps, his entire body racked with aches and jolts. Lemon checked his dressings again and worked his strapped arm at the elbow. She muttered constantly as she worked, before finishing with a 'No big moves for at least a week – you'll have to train the other hand,' then departed with a mucky chuckle.

Tarfel was munching on some kind of radish. 'I'll admit,' he said between crunches, 'this could be worse.'

Chel surveyed the now-deserted hold. Its doorway to the deck lay open and unguarded. His shoulder throbbed and his face itched. 'We've been locked in a box on a riverboat for hours, while people have taken turns in trying to kill us, highness.'

'But they haven't, have they? Killed us, I mean. If they really had it in for us, they'd have done it by now. Karaman of Tawal was set upon in Lauwei, dragged off his horse in the street. They stabbed him up so much he was dead before he hit the ground. So I heard, anyway. All I need to do is sit tight until we reach Kurtemir, then it's a quick ransom and off to the nearest palace. You'll be a free man, I can start plotting my royal revenge.'

Chel shook his head. 'I wouldn't put anything past this lot. Don't confuse the absence of immediate cruelty with kindness, highness.'

Tarfel nodded, mouth full of radish. 'I'll try not to.'

***

The vessel in daylight was revealed as a low, wide-bodied barge, a smuggler's crate. The crew avoided them all, for the most part. They were professionally unobservant. The Black Hawk Company were dotted around the vessel, which was making steady progress up the wide, curving river, past countless churning watermills, small riverboats with oars and poles, toll points and ferries. Chel and Tarfel were allowed the run of the deck in the dazzling morning sun. The rocky red shore was several hundred yards away on either side, and Chel doubted he'd get very far if he tried to swim one-armed. He glanced at Tarfel, who was wandering around the upper deck looking relaxed, almost cheerful, as if performing a royal inspection. Chel doubted the prince could swim either. He couldn't even ride. How could a prince not ride?

Chel wandered along the vessel's edge, his good hand on the high rail, his eyes on the distant shore. Drifting around a cluster of barrels he almost trod on Spider. He and a dark, hollow-eyed girl of about Chel's own age were sitting in the shade of the barrels, almost comatose. Dried pods crunched beneath Chel's feet, and Spider's eyes snapped open. He snaked out a claw-like hand and grabbed the front of Chel's shirt, dragging him forward and down to his level.

'You.' Spider's eyes were bloodshot, unfocused.

'Me,' Chel said. His heart was already beating faster.

'You.'

Spider smiled then, a dreamy, inward smile, and his grip relaxed as his eyes closed and his head lolled back against the barrels. Chel backed away, tasting sour adrenaline, then skirted around to the far side of the barge, as far away as possible from the barrels and their occupants. He bumped into Tarfel, coming the other way. The prince was singing, and for a moment Chel flashed back to their trip in the mule cart to Omundi. It all seemed a very long time ago. It must have been all of five days.

The princed finished off the final lines of 'Red Runs the River' with a beatific smile, took a breath, then launched into the opening of 'The Ballad of the White Widow'. Chel liked this one; it was reasonably new.

Lemon came racing across the deck, waving her hands and making a hissing noise. Chel and Tarfel turned to watch her approach, the prince pausing his singing. 'Everything all right?'

'Just, ancestors . . .' She put her hands on her knees, took a couple of long breaths. 'Just don't sing that one, yes?'

'Whyever not?'

She waved a hand and blew orange fronds from her face. 'Just . . . anything else, all right?'

The prince shrugged, turned and sauntered away across the deck, the reedy strains of 'Blessed are the Liberators' going with him. Chel hovered.

'What's the problem with that song?'

Lemon stood, her breathing back under control, and shook her head. 'Boss-man doesn't like it. And you'd be voyaging on the right side of prudent to skirt his ire, given we're all trapped on this wee boat together. Last time he heard a minstrel sing it, he threw a chair at his head.'

'All . . . right . . .' Chel nodded, no less puzzled. 'Hey, who's that girl? The one over with Spider. A bit . . . thousand-yard stare.'

'She's the Fly.'

'Oh, that's convenient.'

'Not really. He always calls them that.'

'Them?'

But Lemon was already walking away, leaving Chel alone on the deck. He clambered, painfully, up the short ladder to the forecastle, where he found Loveless in the shadow of the mast, apparently in conversation with herself.

'Keep on south, I suppose,' she said. She was leaning back against the prow, beside a tall stack of crates, looking off toward the distant shore. 'What would you do?'

She paused, then shrugged. 'Well, you know me. Whatever works.'

Chel heard no reply, but Loveless snorted with laughter. Then she saw him.

'Are you lost, bear cub?'

He wanted to turn and run. 'Who are you talking to?' he said instead.

She arched an eyebrow. 'Wouldn't you like to know?'

A shout came from the barge's stern. It sounded like '*Sail!*'

Loveless's eyes narrowed. 'Go and see what that is.'

Chel went.

***

He found Rennic and Foss already on the rear deck, staring out over the rail at the pale wash of water that trailed them. Neither looked over as he approached.

'What's going on?' he said.

'How far back?' Rennic said to Foss.

The man-mountain tipped his head from side to side, his bundled braids swaying. 'Half a day, maybe?'

'Any chance it's local?'

Foss shook his head. 'They closed the port, boss, and the river with it. That one has a dispensation.'

Rennic grimaced. 'How long until they catch us?'

Again, Foss looked uncertain. 'Depends on the currents and the wind. But she'll be faster than us, no doubt. We chose this one for profile, not for speed.'

'How long?'

'Two days. Three at most.'

'Fucking hells. We'll be lucky even to reach the lake mouth in that time.' He gripped the rail, knuckles white. Chel squinted in the early orange sunlight. He thought he could make out a pale smear at the distant curve of the glittering river. It might have been a sail, he supposed.

***

Lemon roused them sometime in the small hours of their third night aboard the barge. Chel and Tarfel were still confined to the store, but they'd at least been allowed a couple of bedrolls and some blankets and had carved out a snug corner each among the sacks and barrels.

She led them up onto the rear deck without speaking, and the humourless glitter of lamp light in her eyes made her silence contagious. There stood the rest of the company:

Foss and Loveless by the tiller, gazing out over the lightless waters that lapped in their wake; Spider and his dead-eyed companion, looking at least more alert than Chel had seen since they pushed off; and Rennic, in low conversation with the captain, a hard-faced woman in her middle years, her thick, silver-black braids gleaming in the low deck light.

'What's happening?' Tarfel whispered to Chel as they came to a stop by the top of the stairs. He could offer no reply. The night air was chill, the rippling sky overhead thick with dark veins of moonless cloud, and he found himself stuffing his good hand beneath his bandages to try to keep his fingers warm. The dwindling heat of the northern autumnal days was long gone by this hour, and the cool breeze blowing along the river left him shivering.

Rennic looked over at them. His sharp features were exaggerated by the deep shadows cast by the fluttering lanterns, and for a moment he looked truly monstrous. 'Gather your shit,' he said. 'We're going ashore.'

Chel turned toward the barge's prow. They were still half a day or more from the lake, although he was sure he could see the amber glow of the lights of Kurtemir on the distant horizon. Then he looked back, beyond the figures at the rail. There, now only a few hundred yards behind, the forelights of the chasing vessel shimmered in the midnight fog.

'They're going to catch us,' he said.

'Not if we're not here. Now get your shit.'

Tarfel looked panicked. 'But we don't have anything!'

'Good. The boat's tied at the rail. While the mist holds, come on.'

They were bundled swiftly down the rope ladder to the long, narrow vessel that had brought their would-be assassins, still tied at the barge's flank. Spider and the Fly went first, squeezing around the bundles of supplies that were already packed along the boat's centre. Lemon and Foss sandwiched Chel and the prince, no doubt to keep them from any rash action, and finally Loveless and Rennic descended. Rennic looked up and back, gave a signal of acknowledgement, and Loveless began to cast off.

'What about them?' Chel said, his eyes on the handful of crew up on the decks. The water seemed so much louder in the boat that he had to raise his voice.

Rennic didn't look at him. 'They'll be fine.'

'If we're pursued, they're at risk.'

'They know what they're doing. Now shut your mouth.' He looked around in frustration. 'We need to be away. Where in hells is she?'

Chel frowned. Loveless had untied them, and they had begun to drift on the rising waves of the barge's wash. Everyone he expected was already aboard.

A shadow detached itself from the great dark shape of the barge that loomed over them, then with a hissing sound it spooled itself down the loose rope that dangled from the rail until it was only a foot from the waterline. A moment's flexion, then the shadow pushed itself away from the barge's hull and out over the water, arcing around. As it passed over the boat, the shadow detached itself and dropped onto them. The boat bucked and rocked as the shadow landed with a thump, then unfolded itself between Rennic and Loveless at the rear of the vessel.

'God's breath!' Tarfel shrieked. 'Who's that?'

'Keep your voice down,' Lemon said, and cuffed the prince around the head.

'A fucking show-off, that's who,' said Loveless, before clamping an affectionate arm around the new arrival. A patch of starlight revealed their latecomer to be a spare-framed woman, her shaven head gleaming almost blue. Chel spotted an unstrung bow poking up from her back, along with the dark-fletched arrows he'd seen thumping into the last occupant of their current vessel. She grinned at Loveless, then made a series of curious gestures with her fingers. Loveless laughed and said, 'Would I bollocks.'

'Voices down, eh?' Lemon growled again, then she and Foss slid their paddles over the side and they began their slow voyage through the mist to the shore.

***

'I don't understand,' Tarfel said, slapping water from his boots on the rough loose stone of the river bank. 'How is this any faster? It'll take much longer to get to Kurtemir if we're walking, surely?'

'We're not going to Kurtemir,' Rennic said. 'Not any more.'

'But . . . Well, where are we going then?'

Rennic pointed. Not upriver, toward the lake, but inland, and upward. Giant black shapes blotted the western horizon, little more than jagged crests of darkness against the predawn bruise of the sky.

Tarfel followed his finger. 'We're going toward the mountains?'

'No. We're going over them.'

'What? Are you mad? There are savages up there, wild animals, storms!' The prince was almost screaming, and

Chel stepped between him and Lemon before a cuff arrived. 'Well, clearly you are mad – you kidnapped a prince of the realm, for God's sake – but . . . but . . .'

'Oh, don't worry.' Rennic stepped close to them both, his hard face expressionless in the gloom. 'Safer to cross at the Low Passes than stay on the river. I hope those noble legs of yours were bred for climbing. Now grab a pack and get moving.'

'I won't, you can't make me! There are rules.'

'Is. That. So.'

'Just take me to any of the Names, hells, anyone with a pennant, a castle and an oath.'

Chel pursed his lips. Grand Duke Reysel had been a Name, and his own son had offed him. Would any other Name be safe?

'Thrice-damn it,' Tarfel went on, 'I'm a prince and I'm worth a fortune.'

'From where I'm standing, you're neither.'

'*What?*'

Loveless slung one of the supply packs onto her back. 'See, that's the funny thing, princeling,' she said.

Tarfel looked befuddled. 'What is?'

'Well,' she said, 'you're only a prince, as it were, because people agree you are.'

'Nonsense. I'm a prince because my father is the king.'

'Right. And people agreed he was.'

'Nothing of the sort! He's the heir of the true king of Vistirlar. My grandfather Akko reunited the provinces, reforged the kingdom.'

'That's the thing, though, isn't it? We can all look back on it and talk about true kingy-ness, but you ask Old Man Rennic here about which of half a dozen company men or

Horvaun warlords might have sat on the throne in those days, he'll tell you some stories.'

Rennic grunted. 'Not that old.'

Loveless scooped up another pack and pressed it against Tarfel's midriff. 'Here. And here's where we have our current predicament. 'Cos you might have missed this part, but word's been spreading of your princely demise at Denirnas in the Nort attack.'

Tarfel shuffled the pack onto his back, almost unconsciously. 'But that's no issue. I'm alive! People will be pleased to see me!'

Loveless raised an eyebrow, stretching the forked scar at her temple. 'No one is ever truly pleased to see a prince, you can take my word for it.' She reached out and steered him around, toward the dark spread of the woods that fringed the top of the bank. Already the rest of the company were shuffling through the darkness toward them. Chel picked up a sack with his good hand and slung it over his shoulder with a wince, then followed.

'But your true problem is this, o princeling,' Loveless continued as she began to walk. She had one hand on Tarfel's lower back, herding him forward. 'A dead prince is no longer one that anyone need concern themselves with, and it clearly suits someone's agenda that you become such. To wit, you might not personally be dead, but the popular conception of Tarfel Merimonsun, Prince of Vistirlar, has passed on. And once no one agrees you're a prince any more, well . . . you're not a prince any more.'

'I don't understand.'

'I'm sure you will soon.'

'Why bother ransoming me, then? Why not just let me go?'

She smiled, stunning, chilling. 'Don't worry, princeling. You're still valuable to someone. Someone with the heft to make you matter again.'

***

They made it through the woods into the foothills by dawn, the pale light in the north-eastern sky barely troubling the persistent darkness of the clouds. They were higher still when they saw the column of thick black smoke rising behind them, down in the valley. From the next rise, they saw the angry scarlet and orange flames roaring at the choking column's base, before the ravaged hulk of the barge cracked and split and sank into the river, sending thick white clouds up after the black.

Rennic avoided Chel's eye. 'Keep moving. We don't stop until dusk.'

***

The going was hard, especially an arm down. It was no surprise that the mercenaries were far hardier than Chel or the prince, capable of keeping an even, untroubled pace over the steep and broken ground as they wound their way higher. Whenever Chel or Tarfel lagged, one or two of Rennic's crew would appear behind them with a firm nudge or grip on an elbow to drag them forward. The cuffs weren't frequent. They didn't need to be.

When not stumbling, sweating and feeling like his legs were aflame, Chel kept an eye out for the new woman, the silent late arrival. Already he was thinking back to the one-sided conversation he'd seen with Loveless. Had this woman been on the barge with them for three days without him seeing her? He thought of the arrows from above that had saved him from being on the wrong end of the boatman's crossbow. If that was the case, he was glad of it.

He struggled to see her most of the time as they climbed through the trees, and not just because he spent most of the time with his eyes on his feet, blinking away sweat. The day was cool and clouded, at least. He saw the shaven-headed woman only sporadically, appearing at Rennic's side for a moment, or walking beside Loveless for a few paces. Then she was off again, ahead, around, above, he couldn't tell. The woman moved like a mountain creature, sure-footed, and eerily silent. Chel couldn't shake the feeling that she was all around him, watching and laughing a silent laugh at his floundering.

'Who's that?' he said to Lemon.

'Whisper.'

'Sorry, who's that?' he whispered.

'Oh, you're a right funny fucker, aren't you?'

Chel continued in uncertain silence.

Despite his decree, Rennic allowed them an hour of rest at the day's peak. Spare rations were shared, and both Tarfel and Chel collapsed against the hard, red earth of the slope and slept. Spider kicked them awake after what seemed like a moment, but the sun had moved into the north-western clouds and already the day was cooling. 'Plenty miles to go,' he said with his nasty grin. Spider, like the others, seemed unaffected by the climb. Even the Fly seemed no more blank than usual. Only Lemon gave voice to complaint, a steady stream of muttering and grumbles floating from her direction as she marched. Yet her pace never dropped, and while she seemed a little pinker when they stopped, she was up and off again the moment they resumed.

Chel staggered after, trying to force his aching legs back into motion. He watched Lemon's boots stomp along in front of him and let the sound of her utterances lull him into a steady rhythm.

'Oh aye, right, into the mountains we go. No bother there. Not like there's fucken wolves and bears and whatnot. Always fucken wolves. Wildlife, shitehawks all. If I see a fucken wolf I'm gonna brain it with a fucken hammer and wear its flat head like a fucken hat. No fucken wolf better come near me. Lemon the wolf-hammer, that's what they call me. Too fucken right, wolfy, just you try it. Just you show me your little wolfy teeth. I'll have your fucken tail to clean my arse.'

'Lemon, please, hush,' Foss sighed from a few paces over.

'No,' said Lemon.

NINE

They trekked onward, winding through coarse red rock and dense moss-green forest toward the pass. When Chel's strength failed, Foss and Lemon propped him up and helped him on. When Tarfel collapsed, exhausted, Foss slung him over his shoulder like Chel's supply sack and continued his climb. By the middle of the third day, Chel saw the brilliant snow-carpeted peaks looming above, cloaked in drifting wisps of cloud. The air around them was chill and thin and worries of a frozen death from exposure superseded fear of their unseen pursuers.

Rennic drove them on at a brutal pace, his belief unwavering that the aggressors who had torched the barge were mere hours behind them. Every cracked twig became an assassin's approach, every distant howl the advance of a hunting dog. Eventually, Chel tired of the constant tension, fatigue numbing his panic away. He could only be on edge for so long, and if they were caught, well, he'd either survive or he wouldn't. The most bothersome thing about dying, he'd decided, was that his family would never know that he had, let alone where.

They came to a halt in the lee of a sheer rock face, pitted and weathered by the ages. The escarpment continued a few hundred strides in each direction, and above it lay a snow-covered plateau. By the time Chel and Tarfel brought their aching forms level with the others, Rennic was already in conference with Foss, Loveless and the silent woman, Whisper. Various gestures were made toward the summit of the cliff, and nods exchanged.

'Spider!'

The ever-snarling man strode over, leaving his vacant companion sitting with her back to a boulder. Spider himself looked none too pleased by their surroundings and climate. He was wearing sleeves for the first time since Chel had met him.

'Up there. See it?'

He nodded. Rennic handed him a thick bundle of rope.

'Then away you go.'

Spider bared his teeth, then threw the coiled rope over his shoulder. He took a step back from the rock face, surveying it for a moment, then sprang up and forward, arms extended. He caught on a prominent chunk of rock with both hands, his feet moving up the rock face alongside his body, then he swung over and up with one extended hand, lodging in some near-invisible hold. Another extension and draw, and he was ten feet above them. He moved with extraordinary speed and power, his movements precise, and made no show of exertion or discomfort on the frigid, brittle rock.

Loveless saw Chel's gaze. 'Told you, cub. It's all in the names.'

***

'What is this place?' Chel surveyed the bare interior of the dwelling, running his good hand around his battered midriff after being hauled up on the rope. Behind him, Foss and Rennic were pulling up Tarfel while Lemon bellowed encouragement from below. Spider and the Fly were already in the next chamber, from the sound of things enjoying more of their seed pods. He had no idea where Whisper was.

'Trapper's hut, probably,' Loveless said, stacking their supplies against the bare stone of the mountain that composed one wall. 'This is a popular route. Good lookout spot, but not much for defence.' She peered through a gap in the logs laid on the plateau side. 'Keep the weather off, give you a good view for hunting downslope in the summer, but that's about it.'

A shrieking mass of Tarfel was slung in from the cliff-side.

'Bit big for a hut,' Chel said, conscious of his proximity to Loveless. He tried not to look at her too much. He found himself all too readily mesmerized by her looks.

'Maybe the local lord liked to bring a party up here, stick some bolts in passing wildlife from relative safety. Maybe the trapper had a good buyer for his pelts and a bit of coin to spend on his hide. I'm not here to explain the world to you, cub.'

'But how did you know it was here?'

'Easy to spot from below, but hard to get to; easy to get to from above, but hard to spot. Occasionally there's an upside to having Rennic's friend Spider along after all, it seems.'

Lemon, Rennic and Foss stomped in from outside, kicking snow from their boots. 'Aye, right,' said Lemon, rubbing her hands together, 'let's get a fucken fire on and warm this place up, eh?'

'No fire.' Rennic's voice was hard, but his tone softened when Lemon threw up her hands in outrage. 'You know what could be out there. We can't take the chance. Let's be grateful for shelter for a night, and the fact this place is stuffed with pelts. I'm sure they can spare a few for a band of needy travellers.'

Thick furs, grey and brown, were dug out and distributed. Watches were set, dressings changed. Chel and the prince were sent to the second room and buried under warm animal skin, where they slept like the dead.

***

Loveless leaned back against the barge's rail, eyes closed, her face golden in the warm sun. He stepped closer, chest curdling with anticipation.

'Who are you talking to?'

She smiled, eyes still closed. 'Wouldn't you like to know?'

He took another step, and he could see beyond her, over the battlements. Beneath them, the lowport burned orange, great plumes of black smoke choking the sky.

She was next to him, close, too close.

'I'm sorry, my boy,' she said, and he felt his feet slipping on the rough stone. 'It's a shame, truly.'

'Why?' he said, as Heali towered over him, a long knife gleaming in his hand.

'Who needs a one-armed Andriz?'

He couldn't move, both arms strapped against his body. He was tipping backward, feet stuck, but Heali's outstretched hand closed toward his face. Bright yellow flames rolled over the arm, and Heali's body fluttered with glowing, smokeless fire.

'You were supposed to be lucky.'

The hand covered his eyes, his nose, his mouth, his face. Everything was black, and the flames burned cold, so cold. He tried to struggle, but he was bound tight, and crushed, he fell.

***

A freezing hand was clamped over his mouth, another pressed against his bandaged shoulder. Chel's eyes snapped open to find the Fly's wide black eyes looking back, her face bathed in the slats of silvery moonlight that penetrated the hut's timber. Still sluggish and addled from his dream, he simply stared at her, immobile. She raised one finger to her lips and nodded to her right. There in the darkness, Spider crouched, his breath fogging in little clouds. He was not smiling.

Chel felt suddenly very cold.

The Fly clambered over with a light touch, to where Tarfel lay snoring beside him in a relative mountain of furs. Through bleary eyes he watched her wake the prince the same way she'd woken him, straddled with her cold, cold fingers over his mouth. Spider watched from the corner, silent and still.

Once both were awake and wrapped in covering furs against the frigid night, the Fly led them to the far corner of the hut, where the open doorway led to the crisp expanse of snowy plateau, gleaming silver and bright in moonlight, dotted with dark boulders. Spider followed behind them, his very presence an unspoken threat. Tarfel didn't even try to speak.

'Time to get you out of here, your highness,' the Fly said to the prince, her voice low and rasping. Chel wasn't sure he'd ever heard her speak before.

Tarfel looked baffled, bordering on panicked. 'What? Now?'

'You're off to be ransomed.'

'Oh. Jolly good, then. Ah, the others?'

'We're the advance party. They'll catch up.'

Chel looked past them to the snow-draped plateau. It looked wide, open and freezing. 'But—'

Spider put a hand on his arm, the grip too tight to be friendly. 'Cram it, rat-bear. You're not here to talk or think. Just do as you're told like a good little servant.'

Three packs were already waiting by the door. This had been planned. Chel wondered if Spider and the Fly were supposed to be on watch, and whether the rest of Rennic's band lay sleeping, oblivious, in the first chamber. He wondered what would happen when the hawk-faced man discovered them gone.

Spider and the Fly shouldered two of the packs, then levered the third onto the prince's back. Chel looked around for his sack, but the Fly shook her head. 'We'll be moving fast. Now, outside.'

A moment later they stood a few paces beyond the door, in the shadow of a large boulder, shivering beneath their furs, their breath almost frozen in the air. The trapper's hut was a rising bump in the snowscape behind them, nestled under several feet of snow; their exit was a dark rectangle in the pure white. The escarpment dropped away a few strides beyond them, a hard line in the silver moonlight.

'Your pack is twisted. Here, let me give you a hand, highness,' Spider said as he moved behind Tarfel, steering the muddled, compliant prince around so he faced the boulder and Spider could access the pack in question. Chel watched them from a few paces away, his good arm rubbing his body over the furs in a futile attempt to warm himself. The dream lingered like the cold in his bones.

He turned at the creak and crump of the snow crust beside him. The Fly was at his shoulder, her eyes on the glittering plateau and the creased upright terrain beyond it.

'Where are we going?' he said.

She didn't respond. Instead, she turned to face him, stepping in close as she did so.

Close, too close.

Who needs a one-armed Andriz?

Without thinking, he shoved her away with his good hand. She stumbled backward, feet catching in the deep snow, the trapper's skinning knife in her hand flashing bright in the moonlight and her pack flapping from her shoulder. She hit the snow with a whump and a muffled curse, a few paces out from the shadow of the boulder, a blot on the gleaming snow. Chel heard Spider grunt in surprise behind him, and he realized he was trapped between them, one-handed and unarmed. The Fly began to climb back to her feet.

Something whistled through the air, swishing through the night's stillness. The Fly staggered and dropped back to her knees with a gasp. Another whistle followed, and something connected with the Fly's hunched form with a fleshy thud. This time she cried out, a screech of shock and pain. The snow beside her splattered dark.

It's Whisper, Chel thought, transfixed, his tongue electric in his mouth. She's rescuing me, just like on the barge. Another arrow flashed past, out from the plateau's far side. It glanced off the boulder beside him and slapped into the snow at his feet. Its shaft was pale, its fletching bright. These were not the same arrows as he'd seen on the barge. These were not Whisper's arrows.

'Inside!' Spider grabbed his shoulder and dragged Chel and the prince back toward the hut. Spider hurled them inside then ducked under the door, slinging his pack into a corner and crouching beside them. 'Not a word,' he hissed. 'Not a fucking word, or you're cut in your sleep, fuck the ransom.'

Tarfel nodded, mute, while Chel lay flat on his back, staring out at the plateau. The Fly was a dark mound against the pure whiteness, a shadow flooding the snow around her, its white crust staining black.

Spider bounded for the first chamber, bellowing of ambush and attack, without a backward look. His erstwhile partner lay curled out on the plateau, her low, haunting moans the only thing Chel could hear. She sounded like a dying animal, keening and growling and gurgling. He watched, horrified, wondering all the while if he was responsible, if he should have done something different. But then, she had been about to stab him . . .

Another arrow flashed through the night, slamming into the Fly's twitching form. She cried again, less in rage and more in pleading. The next arrow quivered as it drove into her side.

'Stop! Leave her alone!' He was at the door, screaming into the night. Only the biting chill at his cheeks told him he was crying. An answering arrow skimmed the boulder in a flash of sparks, then disappeared into the deep snow on the hut's roof.

'The fuck are you doing?' Lemon was behind him, her arms around his shaking form, hauling him back from the doorway. 'Don't give them anything else to aim at, you bellend!'

She pulled him back into the hut and toward the first chamber. He couldn't take his eyes off the Fly. She was crawling, arms outstretched, dragging herself back toward her pack and the boulder, the snow around her now a black mass. Another arrow hit her just before he was dragged out of sight, and he heard her cry.

'Spiiii-deerrrr . . .'

The first chamber was chaotic but warmer, lit by a solitary candle in Foss's bulky hand. Tarfel was already there, huddled against the wall, trying to cloak himself in a mountain of furs. The mercenaries were in varying states of readiness, from Spider and Foss, fully dressed, weapons in hand, to Rennic and Loveless, who were half-naked, rising from the same fur-bed in the opposite corner. Chel barely processed their shared bedding, but he felt something hot lurch in his chest. Nobody else seemed to notice or remark on it, and there were more pressing concerns.

Behind him, Lemon was buckling straps and rummaging in a bag of what sounded like iron bars. 'Where's Whisper?' he said, his voice cracked.

'Probably out scouting the path ahead. Usually is.'

'Doesn't she sleep?'

Lemon stopped, then withdrew a long, slim hammer with a hooked bill from her bag. 'Her? Not often.' She offered a mirthless grin. 'Didn't you hear? Sleep's the curse of the young, wee bear.'

Rennic's clothes and boots were on, his face dark and furious in the candlelight. He fixed Spider with a glare. 'What do we know?'

Spider grimaced, his teeth long. 'Fly's down. Out on the plateau. Archers, short-bow. Half a dozen, top tier.' He crunched his teeth together. 'Sadistic fucks.'

Rennic and Foss exchanged glances. 'Sounds like our Mawn friends from Sebemir. Hot fuck, they're tenacious.'

A low, bestial howl split the night. Chel shivered, and Foss made the sign of the crook and muttered prayers. Rennic sucked air through his teeth and looked back to Spider. 'Can we reach her?'

Every muscle in his body rigid, Spider shook his head.

'What in nine hells was she doing that far out on the plateau?'

Spider's gaze sought Chel, pinned him to the log wall.

'Just taking a piss.'

The gaze dared him to disagree. Chel kept silent.

Rennic growled. 'Grab gear. We probably have a moment or two before those pricks tire of their game and start thinking about burning us out. The snow won't hold them long.'

Something hissed on the roof, and thick drops of water throbbed past the gaps in the log wall. 'Fucken *hells!*' Lemon shouted.

Loveless was by the entrance, urging them out. 'Away we go, boys and girls, right now. Grab your packs and sacks, back down the rope before we're roasted meat.'

Chel stumbled back into the second chamber, eyes fixed on his supply sack by his discarded fur pile. As his hand closed around it, his resolve failed, and he looked out through the doorway into the frigid night.

The Fly lay still, a dozen arrows jutting from her body like pins in a cushion, pale steam rising from the snow around her. He stared at her for too long, blinking freezing tears. She and Spider were going to kill him. The knife had been in her hand. He had only pushed her. But still it felt wrong. Still he felt culpable.

You were supposed to be lucky.

Another thump on the roof was followed by a familiar hiss. Chel shouldered the sack and fled from the room.

* * *

It happened fast. Rennic and Loveless went first, whizzing down the rope out of sight before Lemon grabbed the prince and wrapped herself around him and the rope. Then they too were gone, and Foss stooped to sling Chel over his shoulder before they made the drop. The night air bit again, the wind harsh along the escarpment's sheer face, and as they descended Chel looked back and up at the hatch. Spider stood framed in it, his gaze fixed on Chel, eyes burning with hate and a long knife in his hand. For a moment Chel thought he might cut the rope while they were still on it, but instead he watched them all the way down. Then the rope dropped, and Spider, now lost in the darkness above, began to clamber down the rock face.

Whisper met them at the bottom. She and Rennic traded hand signals for low words in the moonlight, and she pointed out two bodies behind one of the scattered boulders along the trail, one stuck with the broken shaft of a dark arrow.

Chel flexed his toes in his freezing boots, willing the

feeling back into them. He felt groggy and lightheaded, and overcome with melancholy. 'What now?' he said to Foss.

'Now, my friend, we run.'

TEN

For hours, they pounded through the deep snow in the moonlight, weaving in and out of dark clusters of tall trees, trying to stay out of the open. Chel and Tarfel struggled along with the others, the snow sucking at their legs, the thin, chill air stinging their skin and freezing every stream from eyes, nose and mouth. Three days of climbing the mountains and half a night of sleep had left them both exhausted, and only the terror of murderous pursuit kept them going.

With the first fronds of light twinkling in the north-eastern sky, Tarfel caught his foot on a snow-covered rock and crashed head-first into a drift. Chel stumbled over him, ostensibly trying to help, but instead grateful for the chance to collapse one-armed onto the soft snow. He lay face-down, panting into whiteness, his cheeks so numb he no longer felt their burning. There he waited for death.

'Get up, prolapse!' Lemon stood over them, Foss at her elbow. 'Fuckers'll be on us pronto. Not like we're hard to track in this white shite.'

'I can't go on. Let me die here.' It was Tarfel's voice, but the words could have been Chel's.

'Oh, aye, I'd love to, but then we wouldn't get paid, and this whole affair would have been rather a waste of everyone's time and effort, yes?' She hauled them over, leaving them snow-dusted and staring at the dark foliage above.

Rennic's thumping footsteps drew close. 'Fuck's the problem?'

'Princeling wants to die here. The wee bear seems on board.'

Chel expected an explosion. Instead, the hawk-faced man took a long breath, surveying their wooded surroundings. They were in a shallow, sloping gully, thickly wooded on either side and dotted with the same black projecting rocks that littered the mountains.

'Good a place as any. Dawn's coming, be quick.'

Chel sat up. His heart thumped on in his chest, a little faster at Rennic's words. He bit back the desire to ask what was happening, hating the gormless inquisitor he'd become. If I still had two working arms, he told himself, I'd never have ended up like this.

He met Rennic's granite-hard gaze. No, said his inner voice, you'd likely have been dead for a week.

'Get up,' the big man said, and Chel did.

The crew arrayed themselves around the gully, concealed behind trees and rocks. Spider and Whisper disappeared vertically, clambering up into the snow-drenched trees and out of sight. Again, Lemon was left to babysit Chel and the prince. They were sent to the top of the slope to lurk behind a ridge and a low ring of boulders, leaving enough obvious tracks on their way up for the whole group. There they waited, traitorous breath fogging in hot columns through their trembling fingers.

'You know,' Chel whispered to Lemon, 'you could just let me and the prince go. We're off on the quiet, you're no longer pursued, everyone's happy.'

She gave him a look of incredulous horror.

'Are you fucken cracked, man? Think our friendly chasers'll take our word that we've sent you on your merry way? And what of our payment for the job? 'Sides, you'd get yourselves murdered by wolves or snow or something inside twenty paces. No, wee bear, we're rather, you might say, committed to our current venture, eh?'

Tarfel saw them first, his stifled squeak alerting Chel and Lemon to their hunters' arrival. A handful of figures had appeared at the gully's distant base, their forms indistinct against the grey of the snow in the predawn light. They moved swiftly, without stealth, their attention on the deep tracks they followed and the landscape surrounding them.

Chel clenched inwardly, pressing himself against the frosty rock beneath him. It was one thing for faceless shapes to shoot arrows at you in the dark. It was another to see your would-be murderers approaching with such casual menace. They carried crossbows, heavy in their arms, and maces and axes hung from their belts.

The figures closed on them, advancing up the gully, fanning out as they did so. Chel counted five. In a few moments more they found the churned snow where Chel and Tarfel had fallen, the criss-crossed footprints where the crew had made their preparations. The foremost was now ten paces from Rennic's hiding place. Chel could see him, crouched against a dark trunk, his long staff pressed against the bark. He had tied back his hair and was utterly still.

'The fuck is this?' one said. Her accent was eastern, wetlands. Not a local, then. Looking nervous, she levered back the arms of her crossbow with a grunt.

'Which way did they go?' This one sounded local. 'Where are those Mawn-buggers when you need 'em, eh?'

The lead man stood. 'Looks like upward. But guards up, could be they left a— Uff—'

'A what?'

The lead man was swaying on his feet. Chel could see the surprise on his face as he looked down to see the long black shaft protruding upward from his chest. Chel thought of Lemon's words. Would the man know he didn't have to lie down and die?

It was academic a moment later. A second arrow hit the man in the upper chest, sticking up above his cloaked shoulder and sending a hot jet of blood over his face. The man shrieked and stumbled backward, gesturing upward in his incoherence, his crossbow fallen from his hands. The other four crouched and cursed, their bows flashing upward at the treetops, searching for the arrows' origin.

Then everything happened at once. A man-shaped rage ball dropped from the branches above them, crumpling the man at the back to the ground and spraying arterial gore in frenzied arcs. Another arrow flashed out of the trees, splitting the eye socket of the non-local woman. She screamed and fired her crossbow, driving its bolt into the fleshy thigh of the man next to her. As he spun and cursed, Rennic and Loveless exploded from the trees on either side, covering the distance faster than the remaining man could react. Two sharp blows from Rennic's staff drove him from his feet into the snow, a third left him unconscious. Loveless, meanwhile, delivered one killing strike after another, first impaling the man with the wounded thigh on her beautiful sword, then slicing open the neck of the half-blinded woman. They dropped to the snow in succession, the gruesome pink mess at their feet enfolding them like a lover's arms.

Rennic knelt and drew a knife from his belt across the unconscious man's throat, then stood, leaning on his staff, breathing heavily. Loveless tried to clean her sword on an unbloodied scrap of fabric, but one was proving hard to come by. Spider continued stabbing the victim beneath him, his breath coming in halting gasps, his teeth gritted. He was slick with blood from neck to knee in the early light, a true vision of nightmares.

Rennic grinned and wiped something dark from his bearded cheek. 'Good work. Now let's get back on it before—'

A bright arrow splintered the staff beside his face, showering him with needle-shards of wood.

'Fuck-sticks!'

Around them branches bucked and rippled as shafts ripped through the foliage. Chel saw flashes ripping through the upper limbs, arcing toward where Whisper hid.

'Down!'

The crew ducked, Chel slithering down the cold stone of the rocks that lined the ridge. Beside him, Lemon hissed. 'Sly fucks ambushed our ambush!'

Heart thumping, Chel risked a swift peek over the rock. Whisper had clambered down from her tree and was ducked behind a meaty trunk while arrows thunked against its side. She looked peeved. Rennic and Loveless looked similarly pinned down, and Spider lay among the corpses. He was so soaked with blood it was impossible to tell whether he was hit or merely playing dead. Chel suspected the latter.

'What do we do?'

Lemon flicked a gaze over the rocks, then over at Foss who crouched behind a snow-covered thicket along the ridge-line. 'Aye, right. Keep our heads down, let them think they're flanking the folks below, then Fossy and I spring the jaws.'

'What about—'

'*You* stay here, wee bear, and keep yourself and Prince Gobshite well from sight. Yes? You wander off, you'll get your both selves skinned.' She fished a short, wide-bladed hatchet and an anvil-headed hammer from her collection. From down the slope, Chel heard something splinter and Rennic's answering curse.

The chill dawn breeze blew over them from beyond the ridge, and brought with it a faint, delicate jingling. Something familiar about it nagged at Chel, and he turned away from the rocks for a clue as to what bothered him.

Two human shapes loomed up over the low ring of boulders, one very much bigger than the other. They were clad in furs and hunting gear, but even in the early light Chel recognized the rust-coloured robes beneath.

'Hurkel,' he said, throat cracked.

'Whassat?' Lemon looked over, then turned to follow his frozen gaze. 'Aye, fuck! Fossy!'

Tarfel's shriek carried over the woods, sending hardy birds bolting from the trees at their periphery.

The blond giant dropped from the outer boulder into the ring with a thud, crushing the snow beneath, then extended one arm, pointing. He was grinning. Behind him, the other confessor made more hesitant progress, sliding down the rock with his mace brandished like a ward.

'Kneel, heretics!' Hurkel roared. 'Beg for the Shepherd's mercy, that you may be spared eternal damnation!'

'Stick it up your bollocks,' Lemon replied, and hurled the short axe at the oncoming giant. He watched it all the way, then juked aside. The axe whistled past his beefy arm and split the face of the robed man behind him, who collapsed unconscious without a sound, thin sprays of blood fountaining from either side of the buried axe-head.

Hurkel reached Lemon in three strides, catching the haft of the hammer she swung at him. He towered over her, grinning all the while, as she strained to free the hammer from his grasp, then lashed a kick at his knee. Hurkel grunted, then punched her with his free hand. Lemon wobbled, and as her grip sagged Hurkel wrapped a hand over her face and began to squeeze.

Chel rolled across the snow. His good hand closed around the second confessor's discarded mace, and he struggled up onto one knee behind the giant.

Mustering all his strength on his weaker side, he smashed the mace against Hurkel's knee. This time, the confessor bellowed and staggered. He flung Lemon's limp form aside and rounded on Chel, favouring his other leg.

His close-set eyes widened in surprise, then his grin expanded. 'Sand-crab! How the Shepherd smiles on loyal servants. I'd thought the chance to dispatch you on your downward journey was long gone.'

Chel pushed himself to his feet and raised the mace, alarmed by its tremble in his hand. 'Come on then, you great white prick.'

Hurkel punched him in the face. It had been a good few days since he'd last taken a blow, and most of his superficial injuries, especially the rough scabs on his face, had been healing up well. Hurkel's fist rattled the teeth in his jaw, fractured his cheek and split his lip wide. He felt his brain move in his skull, and his vision was at once a mass of yellow and purple. He became only latterly aware that he was falling backward, then snow crunched beneath him and the pain bloom began as his nerves caught up with the damage.

Hurkel laughed, then looked around, searching for the prince, who was scuttling up the rocks away from him. Chel blew bloody spittle from his ripped mouth and tried to sit up. 'Is that it, you rancid rat-fucker?'

Hurkel turned back. 'Oh, sand-crab, you are thrice-damned and corrupted. You are beyond the Shepherd's love.' He raised a boot to stamp on Chel's head, wincing at the movement.

Foss launched himself from the top of the rocks, landing on Hurkel's back and sending him staggering. The boot crashed to the snow beside Chel's ear, close enough for flecks of snow to spray his ravaged cheek. The two spun and struggled, Foss's arms wrapped around Hurkel's neck and chest, the blond giant's ponderous arms flailing up at him, before Hurkel hooked an arm and pivoted, throwing Foss over his shoulder. It should have slammed him helpless to the ground, but Foss twisted as he was turned and got his feet beneath him, landing almost upright. He dropped immediately into a wrestler's pose: knees bent, palms down, one arm extended, the other close to the body.

Hurkel nodded his head from one side to the other, as if considering, then assumed much the same pose. Even half-crouched, he still had half a head on Foss. The man with the braids might have been the biggest of Rennic's crew in bulk and strength, but Hurkel looked capable of devouring him.

'So shall the faithless betray the love of their maker,' Hurkel said, 'but the faithful shall be blessed with weapons of righteousness, and see the damned riven beneath their feet.'

'The virtue of the believer shall shine from deeds, not proclamations,' Foss replied.

The two circled, exchanging the odd half-slap blow, each keeping their distance, then Foss drove forward with his shoulder low, wrapping his arms around Hurkel's massive thighs and heaving upward. Hurkel staggered backward, but Foss couldn't get him all the way over and Hurkel began to rain blows down on him, laughing with increasing mania. The confessor reached down and wrapped his arms around Foss's torso, then with a grunt levered his legs up off the ground until Foss was thrashing in mid-air.

Lying prone, Chel slammed the mace against Hurkel's knee. When Hurkel staggered, he swung again, catching him a glancing blow on the kneecap. Hurkel roared and dropped Foss, snatching at the mace as Chel tried for another blow. He grabbed it and yanked it from Chel's weakened grip, but before he could do much with it, Foss crunched his other knee with Lemon's hammer.

The giant howled, clutched his knee and pitched sideways, unable to support his hefty bodyweight. As he fell, Foss scrambled to his feet and pounded the side of his trailing leg for good measure. He reached down and jerked the mace away from the curled and moaning Hurkel, then helped Chel to sit up. 'Watch him,' he said, pressing the mace back into Chel's palm. 'If he moves, hit him again.' Chel immediately thumped the mace against Hurkel's battered leg.

Foss called over the rocks. 'Boss? We have the churchman.'

An arrow skittered off the boulder beside him and clattered down into the snow.

Rennic's voice came echoing back. 'Hear that, Mawnish travellers? We have your paymaster. Your engagement is ended.'

For a moment, the wood was still. Then a woman's accented voice rang out. 'Rennic? That you?'

Chel risked standing to look over the ring of stone. Rennic and the others were much where he'd last seen them, although Whisper had moved two trees over and Spider had crawled into thick undergrowth. Rennic was standing, his back still pressed to a tree trunk, staring at the brightly fletched arrow that was jammed in the top of his staff.

'Grassi?' he called. 'Grassi of the Mawn, are you out there?'

Again silence, and then: 'Black flag?' came the woman's voice.

'Black flag,' Rennic said, and at a stroke the tension dissipated. Rennic, Loveless and Whisper stood and moved out from their tree cover, Spider climbed to his feet, sheathing a long knife at his blood-soaked belt. Three dark forms materialized out of the trees, one of them only feet from where Spider had lain. Chel had no idea which of them had had the advantage.

Chel passed the mace to Foss. Hurkel began to move, and Foss hit him again.

One of the dark forms advanced on Rennic. She was barely two-thirds of his height, clad in dark furs and leather, her abdomen wrapped with armoured scales and a short bow at her shoulder. She grinned when Rennic stepped to meet her, a playful grin tinged with a hint of malice.

'Didn't know we hunt old men,' she said.

Rennic's smile was tight but genuine. 'The fuck you doing out this way?'

'You didn't hear? More uprisings down south. Double coin at least, cold as shit down there.'

'So why are you up here, with these god-bothering arseholes?'

She shrugged. 'Detour. You know Grassi, if money good, service good.'

'You were paid up front?'

She nodded. 'Not imbecile, Rennic.'

'And we can end it here?'

'Normal day, no chance. Today, feel, uh, charitable. But—' she jerked a slim finger in the direction of the circle of boulders. 'Make sure he dead. This damage to reputation, Rennic. Always complete contract.' Around them, the other Mawn were retrieving their arrows, yanking them from trunks and branches, completely indifferent to the watching mercenaries. Grassi grinned again. 'Fortunately, we not go back to Sebemir. We go south. Always where the action is.'

'Always.' Rennic nodded and offered a small smile in return.

'We not the only ones taking contracts from the Rose, Rennic. Nobody else going to give you a pass like Grassi.'

'Don't I know it. Good to see you, Grassi.'

'Good to see you, Rennic.' She reached up and ran a hand down his cheek with great affection, then turned and stomped back into the woods. Her two companions joined her, then another two before all five were lost among the thickening woods.

'That's it? That's fucking it?' Spider was up beside Rennic, the long knife back in his hand. 'Those animal fucks killed the Fly! They butchered her!'

Rennic didn't look at him. 'And they could have done

the same to us. They haven't. Let's be grateful for that much, and take this no further.'

Spider started to speak again, but Rennic was already slogging up the slope. 'Perhaps you might enjoy a word with Brother Hurkel, Spider. To take your mind off things.'

Loveless fell in beside him. 'So that was Grassi of the Mawn, eh?'

Rennic grunted.

'She's pretty. Little, but pretty.'

Rennic didn't reply.

'I liked her armour. Very flash. Hey, don't you have some like that?'

They reached the rocks where Chel waited, good hand on the cold stone, one side of his face pulsing with waves of pain. He could feel the swelling already, his lip fat and bloody, one eye half-closed.

'Hells, look at you, boy. The fuck happened up here? Where's Lemon?'

'Don't call me boy,' Chel slurred through throbbing lips.

Tarfel was crouched over Lemon's stirring form. 'I think she's all right,' the prince said. 'She's instructing me to eat my own genitals.'

***

With one knee shattered, Hurkel hunched like a wounded bear at the centre of the stone ring. He muttered scripture in a monotone through gritted teeth, eyes fixed on the muddy slush before him. The crew kept their distance, conscious his muscular arms still had speed and reach. Dawn had broken, the yellow morning sun scraping at the peaks behind them. Downslope, the gully was a mess of churned and vivid pink.

Rennic leaned against one of the stones opposite the stricken confessor. 'So. Brother Hurkel.'

Hurkel ignored him, rocking gently as he murmured.

'Foss, what's he reciting?'

'It's the Article of Resolve. He thinks he's going to be a martyr.'

'Hey, Hurkel!' Rennic prodded him with his splintered staff. Hurkel snarled and snatched its end, before Foss thumped him with the mace again and he released it with a growl.

'Thrice-damned you are, every man, whore and faithless sand-crab among you,' Hurkel said. 'The flames of nine hells shall ravage your bleached bones for eternity, while your souls scream for salvation that will never come. You are beyond redemption.'

Rennic stared at him for a moment, hand on his chin, then stood. 'You know what? Fuck this ape.' He reached for a knife from his belt. Hurkel resumed his incantations with greater urgency, eyes closed, face raised to the sky and hands clasped.

Loveless put a hand on Rennic's arm, and he deferred to her. She took a step forward, still keeping her distance. 'Been with the Brotherhood of the Twice-Blooded Thorn long, Brother Hurkel?' she said.

'Demons take you, whore.'

'That's a yes, is it? Since you were a tiny meat-stack, I'd guess. Orphan? Foundling? Backstreet accident to some poor Horvaun working girl?'

'God turns his back to painted harlots, vile whores, accursed street-rats.'

'Brother Hurkel, that just isn't true. Your god preaches love for everyone, especially the lost and unfortunate. I'm sure Foss here could quote you an apposite Article.'

Foss nodded, but remained silent.

'You'll not speak of God. You know nothing of his will!'

'I suspect I know about as much as you do, Brother Hurkel.'

He clenched his teeth then spat at her, a gobbet of something landing on the muddied snow beside her boots. She pursed her lips. 'Quite the charmer, aren't we, Brother Hurkel? I bet the ladies can't keep their hands off you. Oh, forgive me, you took a vow, didn't you? First to the Rose, then when you, let's say, *bloomed* into this vision of even-tempered manhood before us, I bet the Thorn couldn't wait to sweep you into their bosom.'

Loveless took a small step closer. 'You can't bear it, can you, Hurkel? You can't bear to see the pretty girls enjoying themselves, enjoying other boys, enjoying each other. You can't stand it. That they can't stand you. Your mother rejected you, the serving girls in the monastery shrieked and hid from you, and now every woman who claps her eyes on your grisly mug runs a mile.'

'Shut your vile mouth, trollop!'

'Never was a vow of celibacy so unnecessary.'

He lunged for her then, thrusting forward on one hand with the other outstretched. She danced aside, whipping the short silver sword from its scabbard at her belt. She held it before her face, looking along the flat of the blade at the snarling confessor. 'Please, Brother Hurkel. Make me do it.'

Hurkel's face was the colour of rotten beetroot. 'That's a fine blade. I'm going to fuck you with it.'

She raised an eyebrow. 'And you seemed like such a nice boy.'

He lunged again, fast and unstoppable. Loveless swayed and the sword moved in a blur, hissing through the air. Hurkel's hand gripped Loveless's jacket. His hand was no longer attached to his arm.

Hurkel began to shriek as the reality of his mutilation dawned. Thick, bright blood pumped from the stump at his wrist, pooling on the ruined snow beneath him.

'For God's sake, Loveless, look at this mess. Now one of us will have to touch him,' Rennic sighed.

'You will die unlamented and alone, Brother Hurkel, and as your life leaves you, you will realize that you are alone with your god, and that he knows you for what you are. Shorn of pomp and sacrament, you are a transparent nothing. A robed void. A tiny, wasted existence.' Loveless brushed his severed hand from her clothes, then kicked it along the ground at him.

'Fuck off and die, Brother Hurkel.'

Something howled in the distance, and Whisper gestured to Rennic.

'Wolves?'

Foss looked at the carnage that surrounded them. 'What could possibly have attracted them?'

'Packs and sacks, Black Hawk Company! We're away from here right now.'

Lemon struggled to her feet at the edge of the circle. 'Aye, right, wolves, is it? I'll tell you what I'll do to any fucken wolfy comes near me. I'll . . .' She wobbled and sat down again.

'Foss, carry her, please.'

'You know,' came Lemon's voice as Foss hoisted her, 'I've got this idea for a better kind of crossbow . . .'

The crew grabbed the remainder of their supplies. Chel wasn't sure where his supply sack was. He suspected it was in the blood-soaked grime beneath Hurkel. It had his food rations and a small knife. He hoped he'd cope without them.

'What about him?' he said to Rennic as the crew began to move off over the ridge.

Rennic didn't look back. 'Fuck him. Let the wolves have him. Come on, Fossy! You can pray for them later.'

Foss had his head bowed, his hands clasped as he stood at the peak of the ridge. The effect was marred only slightly by Lemon's groggy form slung over his shoulder. He shook his head then turned to follow.

As howls echoed from the peaks, the Black Hawk Company left the crimson stone circle and Brother Hurkel, whimpering and trying to stop the blood, behind them.

ELEVEN

Chel pressed handfuls of snow to his face as he trudged, trying to numb the throbbing. His adrenaline had drained away and the exhaustion of the night, and the preceding week, was sapping at his steps. He walked between Foss and Tarfel, hoping one or the other would catch him if he fell. Presumably Foss.

'Why did you pray?'

Tarfel had hardly spoken since they'd left the trapper's hut for the second time. Foss nodded at the prince's question, taking a long breath through his nose.

'For their departing souls.'

'But they were trying to kill you. All of us, really.' Chel thought of the Fly, and his own lingering guilt.

Foss gave a half-smile, a little crack of white on one side of his mouth. 'They were still people, and they still died before their time.'

'And that man on the boat? You threw him in the water.'

Foss looked a little uneasy. 'I may have loosened his bonds before he went overboard.'

'But what if he couldn't swim?'

'Sometimes, princeling, you have to trust in God's mercy.'

Something stirred in Chel's memory, and he spoke almost without meaning to. 'My father once said that every premature death is a tragedy, no matter the circumstances. Even if someone was a bad seed, like Hurkel, the tragedy was that they couldn't be saved.' He blushed, suddenly conscious of the attention of the group.

Foss nodded. 'Your father a churchman?'

'No. Well, yes. I . . .' His father had claimed he'd intended to join the Church, but it hadn't been God's plan after all. He'd certainly brought sacrament and faith to his duty as a minor lord. Chel's chest tightened at the thought of the cost of his father's devotion. 'I don't want to talk about it.'

Foss's eyes were gentle. 'Suit yourself, friend. We all have our intimates.'

'I had an intimate once,' Lemon said from Foss's back. 'Gave me terrible gas, it did. Burned with a blue flame.'

'You,' Foss said, levering her down to the ground, 'sound much recovered. On your feet.'

'Bah. You're only saying that because of the smell.'

Chel started to find Loveless keeping easy pace beside him. She looked placid, although a thin arc of what he guessed was Hurkel's blood stained her cheek below the scar. She said nothing for a time, walking in comfortable silence, then as they crossed a bright snowfield, she spoke.

'You're a dutiful sort, aren't you, cub?'

'I, uh . . .'

'We know what you did at the palace. What you've done since. You're dedicated. Loyal. Where does that come from?'

'Come from?'

'Is it from your father? Is he a dedicated sort?'

'He . . .' More memories swamped him. His father's smiling, open face, his impassioned words, all blurred by time. The great locked door, the coughing beyond. The black wagon that came in the moonlight. Chel felt his throat close, tears stinging the corners of his eyes. 'He's dead.'

'I'm sorry, cub.'

'He was dedicated.'

'I'm sure he was. And you want to make him proud, don't you?'

Chel stopped, his aching legs grateful. 'Do you always do this?'

She stopped with him, her head tilted on one side, blue hair gleaming in the morning light. 'Do what?'

'Analyse people. Pick them apart. Like with that man on the boat. Like with Hurkel.'

She snorted. 'That fucker required bugger-all analysis, cub. I've seen his type infesting the Rose for years.'

'His type?'

'Bullies and frustrated sex-pests. The insecure and power-hungry.'

'Sex-pests?'

'It's always about sex, cub. Deep down. You think any man who gives a damn about himself takes a vow of celibacy? Either they have no intention of keeping it, or they thought themselves a lost cause to begin with. And when people deny their nature, they've taken a step down a dark road.'

'And what's their nature?'

'Humans are sexual creatures, cub. We rather need to be, don't we? Propagation of the species and all?' She stretched her arms high and wide, and Chel watched and tingled.

'I suppose so.'

'But pretending things are otherwise, no matter how fierce or how grandly, don't make them so, cub.'

Rennic's angry shout from ahead set them moving again, Chel wincing with every step.

'It's always about sex. Shepherd knows how much of human history has been steered by some central figure's urge to fuck someone or something.' She nodded at Tarfel, who walked a few paces ahead of them. 'You know how the wars of the provinces began?'

'The reunification? It was a holy mission, wasn't it? The schism, the corruption of the old church, the rebel provinces who wouldn't abandon their discredited faith . . .' Even as he spoke, he found his own words ludicrous, trailing off in the face of her wry smile. 'Fine, how did the wars begin?'

'Oh, Old Man Rennic can tell you that some day. But rest assured, it has sex at the very heart of it. It always does.'

Tarfel had stopped to let them catch up. 'What are you talking about?'

'History,' Loveless said with a straight face.

'Oh. Did you notice those ruins back there? They were Taneru, late empire. They were big on circles of things in remote places.' Then: 'Where did you get your sword?'

She laughed. 'That one's not for telling, princeling. As the Foss says, we all have our intimates.'

'I had an intimate once,' came Lemon's voice from beside them.

'Lemon, hush,' said Foss.

***

They made it to late afternoon before the weaker members of the party could go no further. By then, despite the applications of snow, Chel's face had swollen to what Lemon considered hilarious proportions. The crew made camp in the cleft of a rocky runnel, steep stone to their backs and a clear view over the surrounding woods that covered the mountainside beneath the snow. To Lemon's roaring approval, Rennic and Whisper allowed a fire, and a moment later she was scampering around gathering wood, barking at Tarfel to assist.

Chel slumped against a fallen trunk. Whisper, Rennic and Loveless stood at the runnel's edge, conversing in the ruby light of the setting sun. Whisper had led since they'd left the clearing, ranging over the snowscape without apparent difficulty or fatigue. It was hard to read her mood, but Chel thought she looked unsettled. Rennic wore his perpetual scowl, which helped little, but Loveless seemed expressionless, distant. Chel wondered if she was thinking back to her encounter with Hurkel. He'd barely processed the day's events himself; the Fly's keening death beneath the starlight seemed altogether like something from a dream.

'How's the face?'

Foss knelt beside him, surveying his damaged visage with professional care. 'Still rotten!' Lemon called from the fire, and Foss shook his head with a half-smile.

Chel pushed a gentle finger against his cheek and hissed. 'Not good.'

'Go easy on the snow, friend. You don't want frostbite on top of the rest. The lip will heal fast – lots of blood-flow there – and your cheek will repair in time, but you might be a bit lopsided once it settles down.'

Chel tried to grimace, but it hurt too much, and Foss gave a gentle laugh. 'Nothing wrong with a bit of lopsidedness, my friend. Here, look.' He pushed the side of his nose, and it went completely flat across his face. He released it and it sprang back.

'What the . . . What happened?'

'Years of bad choices. Rest up now. You did well today.' He clapped a hand on Chel's good shoulder and stood. Chel afforded himself a smile of satisfaction.

'Aye, right, my go.' Lemon appeared next to him, one of her satchels open on the snow before her, rummaging for fresh dressings. 'Let's get those wounds looked at.'

'What about yours?' Lemon had a pattern of dark bruises staining her face, the result of Hurkel's crushing grip. He wondered what damage she had taken from the punch. She gave no sign of pain or discomfort.

'Ah, bollocks to that, bear-man. Nothing that fat bastard could do to me I haven't already done myself. Now, let's see how that arm's doing.'

He let her strip his bandage, shivering in the chill air as she moved his damaged arm around, testing its range of movement. As Lemon worried at him, Chel looked over at the grumpy conference at the stream's edge and said, 'What are they talking about?'

'Well, I couldn't say for certain, but it's probably relating to the fact we're miles from where we're supposed to be, down on manpower, we've lost or abandoned a load of supplies and the seasonal storms will be breaking any day. Now hold still while I— Sweet mercy!'

The arm did not smell good.

'You're going to need to start using this again now,' Lemon said, nose wrinkled from its flaky stink. 'Or you'll be a shrivelled cripple-bear for years to come. Just elbow down for now, we'll get to the shoulder in another couple of weeks. Make sure you can see your hand at all times. And give it a fucken wash!'

'How do you know all this?'

'Like I said, an education. A real one.' She began to re-sling his upper arm, leaving the elbow free.

Chel watched Whisper say something in her hand-language to Rennic and Loveless, then stalk off into the woods, her bow in her hand. She seemed to leave only the faintest impressions in the snow.

'Does she ever talk?'

Lemon followed his gaze. 'Oh aye, she talks plenty. Right gobby, she is.'

'But, you know, with her mouth?'

Lemon said nothing.

'Why doesn't she speak? What's her story?'

Lemon finished the sling and began to pack up her satchel. 'A person's story is their own, wee bear. You want it, you ask them, and if they want to, they'll tell you. And if they don't, they won't, and you'll have to go on living your bear-life.'

'So I'm supposed to ask her?'

'Yep.'

'But I won't understand the answer!'

'Aye, right. Well, that would be your problem.'

Chel frowned. 'Then what's your story, Lemon?'

'Aha, clever Trevor. I'll tell you this much, if only for persistence: I'm from over the waters, south-easterly, originally.'

Chel sighed. 'Say it isn't so.'

Lemon grinned. 'I know, shocking, eh? Most folks is stunned by that revelation.'

Whisper reappeared, two braces of mountain wildlife dripping blood from her grip. She passed them to Foss and

Spider, who set about plucking and dressing the meat, then setting it over the now-roaring fire. The crew ate in exhausted silence as the sun dropped below the peaked horizon, their bedrolls already laid as close to the fire as safety would allow.

'What happened back there, Chel?' Tarfel was right beside him, pale hands to the fire. 'What did they want, do you think? That church fellow and his hirelings.'

'I think they wanted you, highness.'

'How flattering. Although their manners were rather rough, eh?'

'I think they're trying to finish what they tried at the winter palace, highness. We're loose ends, and they're looking to trim us.'

'But who? Who wants me trimmed?'

Chel bit at his thumb. He hardly dared voice his fears. 'Someone with the command of some senior prelates.' Someone at the top of the Church. That could only mean Primarch Vassad. He thought of Balise da Loran, the messages at the League's camp, how she'd plucked the correspondence from Prince Mendel's table. He thought of his sister, travelling with the court. Travelling at the prelate's mercy.

'Are you all right, Chel? You look unwell.'

'I was thinking . . . that I left my sister with the Star Court. I worry for her safety.'

'I worry about Mendel, ever more so since the attack those years ago, since our brother Corvel died. He was the same age as I am now, you know? Mendel was lucky to escape with his life.'

Chel nodded, offered a sad smile. Of course he knew. Everyone did.

'Who do you think they're taking us to, highness?'

'What did the blue girl say? Someone who can bring me back from the dead? Let's hope it's not another stalwart of the cloth . . .'

Despite the dispatch of their pursuers, Rennic ordered a two-man watch overnight. Chel and Tarfel were excused, for which Chel was both relieved and a little insulted. Spider was paired with Foss, and Chel made sure his and Tarfel's bedrolls were on Foss's side of the fire. He watched Spider from the corner of his eye, but the bald man never looked at him, never repeated his threat from the night before. He didn't need to.

'This is no surprise,' Rennic said as they finished their meal in the twilight, 'but we're not where we're supposed to be. After that fuck-up, we've gone further off course. We don't have the time to retrace, even assuming we wouldn't run into more red bastards.' Those around the campfire nodded, including Tarfel, to Chel's wry amusement.

'We were aiming for Lizard Pass. That's shot now. New plan is to cut all the way to the High Passes, get up, round and down before the storms hit.'

Mutters and tuts filled the air. 'That's Nanaki territory,' Foss said.

'I know.'

'They're . . . unpredictable.'

'I know.'

'Especially with people who look like him.' Foss nodded to Tarfel, who looked blank.

Chel spoke up, his defensive instincts prickled. 'What's the Nanaki's problem with the prince?'

'Come on,' Lemon said, 'milky skin, yellowish hair? Looks like a fucken Horvaun to them.'

'They're not fans of the Horvaun?'

'Aye, no – who do you think drove their people out of the southern coastlands, eh?'

'Reavers did? I didn't know that.'

'Not like they were welcomed elsewhere, was it? Hence their remote habitat and general lack of amity.'

'What about you? You've got pale skin.'

'Aye, fuck off, wee bear. The noble Clyde is friend to all.'

Rennic offered a grim smile in the firelight. 'We'll just have to keep the princeling's ugly mug under wraps, won't we? Besides, this late in the year, they'll all have moved beneath the snow-line. We should have a clear run.' He stood. 'Make the most of those bones. We're on half-rations until further notice. Whisp and I have first watch.' He turned to walk away.

'Wait, no circle, boss? We lost—'

'Not from me. Ask Spider what he wants.' With that he strode away.

'Spider? Want me to—'

'Fuck off, fatso. All your weepy gibbering won't make a sloppy shit of difference. She's good and dead either way.' Spider glared after Rennic, then stalked off into the twilight in the opposite direction. Chel watched him go with a mixture of relief and lingering unease.

'Ignore him, Fossy, friend Spider's taking his lack of vengeance a little personally, I'd hazard.'

'I realize, but—'

'And could have been a little more perilous for us if boss-man hadn't met his wee friend among the Mawn, eh? Those buggers don't take prisoners – or leave survivors.'

'Not true,' said Loveless, gaze distant.

'Oh aye? You know better, Ell?'

'They take prisoners all right.' Loveless spoke with a cold detachment that Chel found unsettling. 'They use them. On their recruits. On their children.'

'Use them how?' Even Lemon sounded unnerved.

'They whip the kids up into a frenzy, then give them a blade and set them on their prisoners. Over and over, chanting, wailing, cheered on by all around them. They're promised all the delights of adult existence as a reward – booze, sex, adulation, independence. So they stab, and they keep stabbing, until it's normal, natural, wonderful. Then they wheel in another.' She paused, pulling her knees up to her chest and wrapping her arms around them, speaking only to the crackling fire. 'They train their children to exalt in the act of killing.'

Nobody spoke. Lemon slowly replaced the stopper on a wine-skin. Somewhere distant an animal screeched.

'And tomorrow it's the High Passes on half-rations. Twelve hells,' Foss sighed, and those around the fire sighed with him.

'Twelve hells? There's only five, right?' Chel said.

'It's nine,' Loveless said, preparing her bedroll, her reverie passed. 'The Foss is double-counting.'

'Nonsense, friend, it's twelve.'

'You're all correct, really,' Tarfel said, his voice quiet. The company turned to look at him. He cleared his throat. 'Different churches have counted the hells according to different scales, but even within the New Church—'

'True Church,' Foss corrected.

'—there's disagreement between the Articles over the precise number. All that's certain is that it's more than one.'

Loveless arched an eyebrow. 'And how do you know that, princeling?'

Lemon chuckled. 'Didn't you hear? Yon princeling has *hattended* the *Hacademy*.'

Tarfel coloured and looked at his feet.

'Anyway,' Lemon continued. 'Doesn't matter, right? It's all the same old, same old.'

'How can you say that, Lem?' Foss looked more animated than Chel had seen previously. 'The hell of usury is very different from that of infanticide or simony.'

Loveless jammed another branch onto the fire. 'Funny how these old priests have such a clear and vivid picture of the punishments on offer for whatever they've decided doesn't suit the Church that week. No wonder the hell count keeps rising.'

'Aye, right,' Lemon said over the top of Foss's objections. 'Not real, though, are they? I mean, hells as physical places, like.'

Foss's expression had darkened. 'You're saying there are no hells, Lemon?'

'Aye, no, they're a whatsit, metaphor. Like, the concept of eternal punishment, it's a . . . a . . . metaphysical construct, so it is.'

'What in His name are you talking about, Lemon?'

'Aye, never mind. Night night.'

* * *

Chel slept as close to the fire as he dared, on the hard, moist ground where the snow had melted. Tarfel was a lump beside him, Loveless a sighing bundle beyond. Spider lay opposite, his gaunt features exaggerated by the lick of flames, sneering even in sleep. Chel slept fitfully, struggling to find comfort. He woke in the death of night, the frigid air chilling his marrow, stinging his swollen face like a slap. Spider crouched beyond the subdued fire, glittering eyes fixed on Chel and a long, curved blade swaying in his hand. Chel blinked long and slow, the rest of his mind some way behind his eyes. A moment later, when they snapped open with grim unease pricking his innards, Spider was gone.

It took him a long time to go back to sleep.

TWELVE

'Get up! On your feet!'

Sharp pain in his shoulder dragged him from sleep. Rennic stood over him, firm hand on his weak shoulder. Around him, the world was white.

'Move your hide, boy, or you'll die on this mountain.' With that, the big man was gone, vanished into the blankness that surrounded them.

Chel struggled to his feet. The fire still burned, reduced to ember glow, but the mountainside had been transformed. The air was the colour of the snow, the horizon and surroundings impossible to discern. Delicate flakes drifted through the air, settling with a feathery touch on his shoulders.

Foss loomed out of the white, a dark tower. 'Come, friend, stow your roll and grab your prince.'

'What time is it?'

'Dawn. Or what should be.'

'What's the rush? We can't travel in this, you can't see a thrice-damned thing!'

'We can't stay out in the open.'

'It's hardly snowing. We get far worse down south.'

'Not this, friend, but what follows.'

'And what follows?'

'Aye, fuck, what's the yapping?' Lemon was beside them. 'Let's get a wiggle on, tubers.'

She dragged them on, scooping up Tarfel as they went.

'What's happening?' the prince asked. His hair was dusted with snowflakes, and for a moment in the dazzling white he almost looked like his brother.

'Storm's coming, princey. One that might kick the arse clean off us.'

'Oh. Oh dear.'

* * *

Whisper was off, bounding into the haze as the others stumbled along in her wake. Chel concentrated on his feet, his weakened hand clinging to the bundled bedroll pressed against his body. Nobody spoke, not even Lemon, although the light snow continued to drift on a gentle breeze. The dread suffused them. Every time the wind picked up, Chel felt the others around him tense.

They slogged for hours, although time was lost to them. From instinct more than a reading of the swirling grey-white, Chel guessed it was noon before they paused, sheltering beneath a thick cluster of trees at the apex of what might once have been a goat-trail.

'Are we nearly there yet?' Loveless said with a giggle, bent double as she recovered her breath.

Rennic's face was grim. The snow that stuck to it made him look like the broken old beggar that Chel had first sighted in Denirnas, and he shivered.

'Ah, come on, it's not that cold,' Lemon said from beside him. She produced a smattering of rations from one of her sacks, handing out salted meat and now well-dried bread. Whisper took hers with a nod, then vanished into the darkness beyond the trees. Chel realized he'd never seen her eat.

'Why doesn't she eat with everyone else?' Tarfel asked, looking after her. 'Is she hoarding?'

'Ever tried eating in polite company without a tongue, princeling?' Loveless wasn't smiling.

Tarfel looked blank. 'No?'

'Let me know if you'd like to try it.'

They chewed in silence, while around them the snow thickened, and the trees creaked in the wind.

***

'We're close now.' Rennic was leaning hard on his staff, hair blowing across his face. The snow on the ground had reached Lemon's knees. 'We'd see them if it weren't for this piss-licking cloud.'

'Which are we going for?' Even Foss was flagging. The dull burning in Chel's legs was by now an old friend.

'Whichever we can.'

They were halfway across a steep, open slope when Chel heard the prince stumble. He turned back, wading through the snow in the direction of the fallen prince, reaching him just before Lemon who was bringing up the rear. Between them, they levered him upright, frost-dusted and spluttering.

'Aye, come on, princey, we're falling behi—'

It was like being hit by a wall of ice. The gust blasted them sideways, whipping them with frozen shards, howling in their ears like demons. Tarfel shrieked and wailed, and all three landed back in the snow. Then it passed, leaving a strange void in its wake, a moment of eerie silence in the white before the sounds of the – invisible – world returned. From somewhere down the valley, Chel heard the wind come howling again.

The glare shifted, and Chel saw shapes ahead, little more than dark smears. 'Come on,' he urged, heaving himself upright. 'We can't risk getting separated.' He called away to the others but the growing wind swallowed his cries. At least they had stopped to wait. Lemon was up, her orange halo festooned, arms beneath the re-fallen prince.

'Give me a hand with this, will you, wee bear?'

They drag-stumbled along the slope, making for the shapes, as the wind rose again and scoured them with waves of ice crystals. Chel was rasped and numb, no longer able to feel the stinging of his exposed skin, his toes a memory. He snatched a glance over his shoulder, toward the shapes, into the teeth of the storm.

'Shit.'

The shapes were trees. They'd lost the others.

'Shit.'

***

'Ancestors' grace,' Lemon whispered, looking down at her blue-tinged hands. 'That fucken smarts.'

They huddled closer against the ancient, scarred tree trunk, shivering and shedding ice. Somewhere down-valley, the wind howled again.

'Is the storm over?' Tarfel said, his skin the colour of the snow.

'Don't know, princey.'

'Where are the others?'

'Don't know, princey.'

'What are we going to do?'

Lemon turned to Chel. 'How do you stop yourself just punching him all the time?'

The howling came again, and Lemon froze. Chel read her expression. 'That's not the wind, is it?'

Lemon shook her head. 'It is not, no.'

Tarfel looked panicked. 'What? What is it?'

When Lemon didn't answer, Chel met the prince's gaze. 'Wolves.'

'Oh dear. Oh dear, oh dear, oh dear.'

'Still, there's one piece of good news,' Lemon said, cracking a bloody grin. 'If them wolfy bastards are coming out to play, that's probably it for this shitehawk storm.'

'Oh,' Tarfel said, his expression brightening. 'Well, that's something.'

'Aye, right. Ain't it just.'

Chel squinted at the drifting haze beyond the trees. The baying echoed from the slopes around them, but it was getting louder. 'I think the fog's lifting. How far away do you think they are?'

Lemon was rummaging in one of her sacks, grim-faced. 'Hard to say. Maybe close enough to get wind of us.'

'Maybe they've found Hurkel and his friends.' For a moment, the image filled his mind of wolves tearing into the stricken confessor, and he felt his stomach lurch. He couldn't be sure if it was horror or guilt. 'We can fight them off, right? You're the champion wolf-slayer.'

She coughed. 'Aye, right, well . . . There might have been a little, to use an *Hacademy* expression, hyperbole.'

Chel paused. 'Hyperbole?'

'A touch of old-fashioned exaggeration, if you prefer.'

'You made it up? You've never killed a wolf?'

'Oh, fuck off, pal. I've smashed in more living things than you've eaten, and that's a fact. Just not, uh, your actual wolf.' She wiped at her nose, then pulled a short, fat blade from her bag. 'Fuck-all good these'll do us, wee bear. By the time friend wolfy is close enough to jam one of these in his guts, he'll likely be enjoying a good munch on your gullet.'

She replaced the knife in the bag and went back to rummaging, muttering as she went. 'To think I left Clyden for this. Eaten by a fucken dog with a hairstyle.' She paused her delving, looked momentarily wistful. 'Go out, see the world. Return in triumph at the completion of your tour. Seemed pretty straightforward.' She shook her head at Chel's blank look. 'We have a Clydish word, *tourist*. You might consider me a tourist. Ancestors, you people know absolutely nothing.'

'We can't stay here. The fog's lifting; if we move fast we can find the others' tracks. We have to assume they're looking for us already.'

'Aye, if the wolfy bastards didn't get them first.'

A little voice at the edge of his mind interjected: Why are you in such a hurry to chase after the mercenaries who kidnapped you? Why not make a run for it with the prince? Break for freedom?

'Shut up,' he said aloud.

'Eh?'

'Nothing. Let's go.'

THIRTEEN

Chel, Lemon and Tarfel slogged along the edge of the woods, searching for tracks. An improvised spear – one of Lemon's knives lashed to a broken branch – dangled from Chel's weak hand, the shoulder above it now pulsing with a vengeful ache. It could join the queue, as far as he was concerned. Nearly every part of his body ached or throbbed, each crunching step through the ice-littered snow jolting fresh pain through his body. The exertion kept him warm though, he thought, watching his gasping breaths fogging past his eyes. It might not have quelled the giddy lightness in his ribcage, but it had stopped his hands shaking.

The mist that had smothered the mountainside was breaking and lifting, and the opposing forests and peaks began to show through the meandering chunks of cloud. The trio followed the churned snow at the wood's edge, now clearing in the grizzly light, around the curve of the slope and upward. Chel squinted through the trees into the distance, conscious that at any moment the wolves might catch their scent and come for them.

The wind favoured them. They climbed on.

'I'll be buggered,' Lemon said, stumbling to a halt. Tarfel almost went into the back of her. Ahead, visible as the haze dissolved, the wooded slope reached a barren apex at the shoulder of two great peaks. A towering marker stone, snow-shod and strung with woven pennants, marked the junction. 'The High Passes. One of them, at least.'

'Do you think they made it?' Chel asked. He realized he was tingling with hope. The only upside to losing the others was not having to worry about Spider shanking him while he slept.

Lemon shrugged. 'Let's go and look.'

'You know,' said Tarfel, catching his breath. 'I'm quite offended they didn't come back to find us. I'm supposed to be ransomed, remember?'

They wandered out from the drooping canopy toward the pass. The trees split away from the high rocks, leaving the path upward flanked by dark woods, battered and lumped with snow.

'I'm sure they meant to,' Chel said. 'Maybe they still do. They might have lost their bearings.'

'Come on, wee flowers,' Lemon said. 'Once we're over the pass it's downhill all the way.'

Tarfel made a small, squeaking noise.

'Highness? Are you all right?'

In the darkness of the woods beyond them, half a dozen pairs of yellow eyes glinted. More eyes lurked within the woods opposite.

'Aye, this is a fucken joke all right. Wolfy bastards have flanked us!'

Chel gripped his spear in both hands and backed toward

the others. Lemon, too, had a knife on a stick. Tarfel merely gibbered.

Chel risked a look over his shoulder. 'We're thirty paces away. We could run for the pass.'

'Aye, then what? There's no magic gate up there, wee bear. Just more fucken mountain. Stay close, move slow.'

Tarfel broke from his whimpering. 'They're not attacking. Maybe they're afraid of us.'

'I doubt it,' Chel said, but the prince was right. The wolves hadn't left the cover of the trees. The three humans backed slowly up the slope, weapons extended, watching the wolves. The eyes followed them, tracking their progress from the darkened woods.

'What are they waiting for? A hunting horn?'

Tarfel was looking up the slope. 'We're nearly there! I think I can see—'

The first wolf broke cover, bounding from the trees over the snow with disturbing speed. Others followed, springing from either side like the jaws of a trap.

'Run!'

Barks and yips filled the air, rich with excitement and anticipation. The marker stone was fifteen steep paces away, each slogging step a battle in its own right.

'Fuckers have herded us,' Lemon snarled between gasps. 'Teased us into the open . . . for the babies to hunt!'

Chel heard the soft crunch of animal steps approaching his side and swiped with the spear. A small wolf danced away, keeping its pace, running parallel but out of reach.

'We're being . . . used for . . . training?'

'Aye, bad as the fucken Mawn!'

The ground flattened as the stone approached. Lemon spun and lashed out with her knife-stick, scoring the muzzle of a wolf who got too close. She was off and running before it could leap.

Tarfel was a few steps ahead, arms flailing as he ran. 'There's wood here! We can use it for . . . something!'

A broken pole lay beside the marker, a torn section of boards jutting up from it. A structure must have once stood there, perhaps a hut, but it had been long collapsed with age.

'No time for a fire, princey!'

The wolves were paces behind, keeping out of reach of the knives. Beyond the marker, the landscape opened out; the peaks fell away either side, and Chel saw the range falling to what he guessed was the south-west. A huge, silver lake lay far beneath them, at the base of a ringing throng of sloping crests.

'We could make shields?' Tarfel lurched toward the boards, trying to drag them clear of the snow piled against them. 'Help me! Quickly!'

Lemon took another swing at a closing wolf, but it bounced away unharmed. It looked like it was grinning. 'Are you fucken cracked, princey? There's a dozen of the shites!'

The wolves were circling, hemming them in around the marker. They hadn't yet blocked the drop-off that led toward the lake. Chel ran to the prince's side, yanking at the wood with his good arm. He'd had an idea.

'Good man, Chel! Glad someone agrees.'

The boards came free in a shower of loosened snow, a torn section of nailed wood a few feet square, the broken post along one edge. Chel slammed it flat with one foot, then swapped his spear to his good hand. It looked solid and square. It was worth a try.

'Lemon! Can you clear a path?'

'You what?'

'There!' He jabbed the spear toward the drop-off, then tossed it to Lemon.

She caught it with her free hand. 'Aye, for what it's worth!' Darting around them, she made for the lake-side edge, swiping the spear at encroaching wolves. Those behind began to close, snarls locked, growls deepening.

'Chel? What are you doing? I can't pick up our shield.'

'Help me push, highness.'

'Come again?'

'Push!'

Good hand outstretched and weak hand flapping at his side, Chel ground the section of boards forward over the snow. The thick post at its prow churned and bounced, carving a wide, shallow furrow as they began to move. Tarfel dropped alongside him, pushing with two hands as they gathered speed toward where Lemon stood.

'What are we doing, Chel?'

'We're going to ride out of here.'

'Oh, super.'

Chel gritted his teeth and pushed, feet slipping and scuffing against the yielding snow beneath. He could hear the wolves behind them, gaining in confidence, padding ever closer even as Lemon bawled and slashed at them. He snatched a backward look. The line of wolves was mere paces behind them, their jaws wide.

'Er, Chel?'

He looked around to see Lemon directly in their path, driving wolves from before her. She turned at the rushing sound of the approaching boards, and her eyes widened. The post whacked into her ankles, knocking her backward onto the board. She thumped down between Chel and

Tarfel's hands, momentarily slowing their progress. Their aggressor down, the wolves came lolloping forward.

'What the fuck are you doing?'

'Either push or stab something!'

'Right-o!'

She righted herself on the board as Chel and Tarfel grunted back up to speed. The ground was beginning to slope downhill, and the movement was becoming easier. Lemon sat up, the improvised spear in one hand and her broken knife-stick in the other. She hurled the half-spear at an onrushing wolf, sending it yowling from their path.

'Er, Chel, what happens next?'

Lemon spun on the board, rising to her knees to fish a slim axe from her pack and heave it at the wolves who now followed them at a run. Her target was almost beside Tarfel, jaws apart, ready to snap at his trailing legs. The axe scythed into its flank and it stumbled, tumbling into a grey ball as it lost its pursuit.

The incline was sharp enough that the board was beginning to pull away from Chel's grip. He looked up from the broken boards to see the drop-off opening before them. It looked almost vertical, and a moment of numbing doubt struck at his chest.

Then something snarled at his side, and jaws tore at his boot. Lemon lunged past, jabbing with the spear, and the pressure on his leg was gone before he'd even felt pain. His doubt vanished.

'Highness, get aboard and hold on!'

He dragged himself forward, scrabbling with burning legs onto the wood beside Lemon. Tarfel did likewise, curling into a ball with a tight grip on the front-post. The board was moving fast now, still accelerating, and with a lurch they slid over the lip of the drop-off and the chill air began to tear at them as their stomachs tried to leave through their mouths.

The world became a blur of flying snow and rushing air, and Chel had to close his eyes against the torrent. They flew down the mountainside, carving a wide, flat trail as they bounced off humps and sailed over dips. Lone trees flashed past, the occasional black rock peeking through the snowy blanket. Every bump and shudder wrenched at the boards beneath them, every uneven impact threatening to smash their carriage apart and grind them to wolf-paste on the unforgiving terrain.

At length the incline began to relax, and their impossible pace slowed. The jumps and judders diminished, although the splintering creaks beneath them were ever more ominous. It took Chel a moment to realize that the high-pitched squealing he'd been hearing was Tarfel, not the sound of the air being ripped from their lungs.

'Are they still there?'

Lemon was facing backward, lying as close to flat on the board as she could as they whooshed over the snow. She peered out from her snow-matted fountain of hair. 'Looks like the fluffy bastards gave us up. Ha!'

Chel uncurled, his fingers numb and his entire body smashed and frozen. The wind still whipped at them as they travelled downslope, their speed decreased but still uncomfortably fast. The sparse trees of the drop-off were getting thicker as they approached the silver lake.

'We need to slow,' he said, grasping around for something to jam into the rushing snow. His spear was gone, his sack was gone. Everything was gone, abandoned or shaken free in their flight.

'Lemon, have you—' Something caught his eye ahead, before the trees. Was that a person? 'What's—'

The board bucked beneath them as they sailed up and over a half-submerged boulder. For a moment, they floated in space, thrown up from both board and ground, then they crashed to earth. The board flipped and smashed down onto them, splitting on impact, half torn away. The thick post bounced on, pinwheeling and spraying splinters across the snow, before sliding to a final halt some way short of the woods.

Chel sucked a painful breath into his battered lungs. Brushing away snow and splinters, he pushed himself up to his knees. Broken wood littered the snowscape around where Lemon and the prince had landed.

Lemon sat up, spitting snow. 'Fucken *hells*!'

Chel moved toward Tarfel. He was alive and unbroken, but a savage gash at his hairline had already begun to pump a steady flow of bright blood down one side of his face. He tried to blink the drops away, eyes shocked and distant.

'That was rather exciting.'

Chel tried to tend to the wound with handfuls of snow, swiftly calling for Lemon. 'Down south, when it snows . . . Sometimes the children slide down hills on wood.'

'How tremendous.'

A distant howl echoed from the peaks above them. It sounded mournful. Lemon bustled over, lamenting her lost pack and equipment. Everything had been shaken free in the descent, their gear scattered across the deep snow of the mountainside two miles above. 'Fucken disaster, man. Fucken disaster.' She looked up at the howl. 'Oh, fuck off, wolfy. We'd have smashed you little furry bastards to bits if we hadn't let you get away.'

Chel wiped a sliver of blood from the re-opened split in his lip. 'At least we're alive.'

She sat back on the snow and sighed. 'Aye, right. We need food, water and shelter, boys, or we're nine kinds of buggered come nightfall. Assuming friend wolfy doesn't decide it's worth the effort to come down here after us, seeing as we seem to have lost all our FUCKEN WEAPONS.'

'You never know,' Tarfel said brightly, blood streaming down his pallid face. 'Maybe we'll find someone.'

Chel looked around, the hair pricking at the back of his neck. A lone figure stood at the edge of the woods, unmoving, exactly where he'd seen it before the crash. He scanned the fringe of trunks, and at once he saw the rest, another five or six figures, lurking at the wood's edge.

'Or maybe someone has found us,' he said, his tone leaden.

***

The woman before them was of indeterminate age, her walnut skin as creased as her features, her steel-grey hair tightly braided, woven with the same small animal bones that decorated the simple tunic beneath her furs. The spear she was waving in their faces, however, seemed anything but friendly. The other figures shuffled over the snow behind her, moving easily on wide rings of bone bound with straps of hide. They carried spears and bows of horn, and their faces betrayed nothing.

'Oh, shitty ball-cakes,' Lemon said. 'It's the fucken Nanaki.'

'And we were having such a pleasant day,' Chel sighed.

The woman jerked her spear again, making it clear she

wanted them to stand. Lemon clambered up, then turned to pull Tarfel to his feet. 'Keep your fucken face out of sight, princey,' she hissed. 'Golden boys like you don't go down well in these parts, remember?'

Tarfel looked up at her, his face crusted with thick streaks of darkening blood. 'How?'

Lemon grinned. 'Perfect, princey, perfect. Never change. And don't, for the love of mercy, wash.'

Tarfel gave her a blank look, then slowly returned her smile. 'All right.'

They began to wade through the biting snow again, prodded by Nanaki spears. Chel plodded beside Lemon, shielding Tarfel. He glanced at the spears that lingered at their elbows, keeping them slogging forward through the thick snow, and kept his voice low.

'They don't look too friendly. How much trouble are we in?'

'Ah, well, that depends. If they're devoted followers of tradition, we'll be dandy. Nanaki custom demands that they take in strangers and show great hospitality – enemies of the people notwithstanding.'

'And if they're non-traditional?'

'Then they will probably eat us.'

'*What*?'

The woman with the spear grunted, and they fell silent. Moments later the dark forest swallowed them. Even the birdsong seemed lost in the wood's oppressive muffling, nothing left to hear but the crunch of their footsteps and the sound of rasping breath.

'They're *cannibals*?' Chel whispered.

'Aye, well, rumours abound.'

'What sort of rumours?'

'The sort that abound.'

'Sometimes, Lemon, I don't think you know as much as you maintain.'

'Aye, well. Don't come running to me if one of these fuckers chews your legs off.'

They slogged through the frigid gloom, encircled by the sure-footed Nanaki, until cold light glimmered through the trunks, and, with great reluctance, the woods opened onto the lake shore. Encircled by leaden shingle, the watery expanse gleamed silver beneath the grey sky, its placid surface occasionally rippled by distant gusts. Dull tongues of ice already lurked at its fringes.

A cluster of huts perched at the lake's edge, small dwellings huddled around a larger, central structure with a conical roof, a handful of wooden piers jutting from the clump into the lake on blackened legs; the water beneath was thick with murky ice. A narrow ribbon of smoke rose from the open roof of the central building and into the pale sky.

A tall figure, if a little hunched, his bald head uncovered despite the thick furs cloaking his torso, stood before the hut ring, ankle-deep in churned snow. His earrings glinted in the pearly light.

'Ah, Spider, you bollocks!' Lemon cried on seeing him, but Chel felt only the mountain's cold sting.

'Five hells,' he whispered, stopping short. Spider had betrayed them again, this time to a bunch of bone-covered cannibals no less. Tarfel stumbled into the back of him and the two collapsed into the snow, to the irritated shouts of the Nanaki around them. Unfriendly hands hauled them upright, Lemon's among them, and they were shunted onward without ceremony.

'Fuck you playing at, wee bear? On with you!'

Chel trudged, lead-legged, shorn of hope. Lemon didn't know what he did, what had happened that night on the plateau. Spider would take no chances with them this time, that much was certain. There was no way Chel and Lemon could overpower them, especially after the battering they'd taken. Chel ached from cracked face to frozen, exhausted legs, had no weapons to speak of, and barely one good arm. His ankle throbbed where the wolf had snagged it. Regardless, he steeled himself as they approached Spider and the foremost hut. Its doorway was dark, covered by a hanging of thick hide.

Spider grinned, pointed and nasty. 'There you are. We was getting worried. Now get inside, you arseholes.'

Lemon was already bounding up the steps to the doorway, Tarfel a step behind. Chel couldn't summon the strength to catch them. He caught Spider's gaze.

'You too, rat-bear,' he said. 'Catch your death out here.'

He held back the hide as the others entered. Chel felt the eyes of Spider and the Nanaki on him, and fists balled, he dragged himself up the steps to the doorway. Spider was right behind him, his voice low in his ear. 'Missed you, rat-bear. So glad the wolves didn't finish you off.'

'I was supposed to be lucky,' Chel whispered to himself.

Spider shoved him inside.

FOURTEEN

The air within the hut was warm and close, swirling with steam in the distant, flickering torchlight. Struggling to adjust his eyes and keep up with the others, Chel shouldered aside another thick hide hanging and stumbled into a wide, low space, warmer and brighter than the first, walled with earth-packed tree trunks. At the centre of the building lay a crackling fire-pit, the conical roof above it open to the slate-grey sky. Low tables ringed the fire, and one of them was well attended.

'You're late again, Lemon,' Rennic called from the table. He held a clay cup in his hand and looked as cheerful as Chel had ever seen him. Foss, Whisper and Loveless sat around him. Their expressions blossomed with relief at the sight of the stragglers. 'I'm going to have to dock your share at this rate. At least now we can start drinking properly.'

'Stick it up your bollocks, boss,' Lemon said with a delighted grin, striding over to the table. Tarfel bounded after her, beaming, while Chel dragged himself after them.

Relief flooded him, but it didn't wash away all of the unease. Anxiety lingered like a faithful hound.

He slumped down on the floor beside the others, feeling every jarring impact across his battered body. 'What are you doing here?' he said, the fire's warmth prickling at his frozen fingers. 'What are we doing here? What's going on?'

Loveless cocked an eyebrow at him, then slid a clay cup across the table. 'Shut up and have a drink, cub.'

'What is it?'

'Tea.'

Whatever was in the cup made his eyes water and tasted of burning.

'That is *not* tea.'

'They call it god-piss.' She was smiling, and he smiled back.

'That's . . . a better name for it.'

He managed three more swallows before the warm floor claimed him, and he passed out beside the table on a pile of furs.

***

When he woke, the patch of sky above the fire-pit was black, but if anything the hall was warmer. Joints of meat sizzled on spits over the flames. Nanaki had joined them, sitting at the other tables around the fire, watching them with hard, indifferent eyes. Chel counted maybe a dozen of them, including the bone-woman who'd jabbed her spear at him. Not as many as he'd expected given the size and number of the huts. This couldn't be all of them. The hall looked like it could seat three times that many and still offer generous elbow-room.

Tarfel lay at his back, snoring gently. Chel envied his peace.

'Ah, our wolf-slayer is awake!' Foss's rich voice greeted him as he sat up with a wince. 'Lemon claims you fashioned a siege engine from driftwood and crushed a dozen beasts.'

Chel looked at Lemon, who was sniggering behind her hand. Several empty clay cups lay on the table before them. 'Something like that,' he said, sliding off his boot to inspect the damage to his ankle. The wolf's bite hadn't broken the skin, but he had a sharp pattern of livid indentations as a reminder.

'God's balls, boy, but your feet reek.' Rennic wasn't looking at him, but the wave of his hand made his meaning clear. 'Lemon, wash him up.'

Lemon made a 'why me' face but slid out from under the table and to her feet. 'Come on, wee bear. There's some hot water this way. Hottish, anyway.'

He took her extended hand and she pulled him upright. Despite, or perhaps because of, the nap, everything seemed to hurt more than before. His shoulder and cheek were in direct competition to throb the most. At his feet, Tarfel stirred and made to follow them. Rennic's hand clamped around his shoulder, pinning him to the earth.

'Not you, princeling. We need to keep you muddy, remember? The Nanaki have a ritual vendetta against the Horvaun, they will kill you on sight. We don't want that, do we?'

Tarfel shook his head, watery eyes suddenly fearful, and settled back down against the furs. He was shivering, despite the fire's warmth.

Lemon led Chel toward a wooden trench of water at the hall's far wall, evidently the source of the steam that had permeated the atmosphere when they'd arrived. Murky lukewarm water lay within, large, fire-baked stones at its bottom. After days of little but half-melted snow as a cleanser, Chel wasn't complaining.

'See, they were coming back for us,' Lemon said, unconcerned by his attention or lack thereof. 'Nanaki found the others up at the pass, brought them downslope. Happens that friend Spider can pass a smattering of Nanaki lingo, managed to express to them that others in our party were left mountainward. They were on the way back up when we met them on our way down.'

Chel blinked. 'And they're friendly?'

She shrugged. 'Looking traditional thus far, wee bear. Thus far.'

She helped him lever off his filthy clothes and shoulder-strapping, then waved away his feeble, one-armed washing attempts. She sponged his grimy torso and crusted wounds, holding his damaged arm gently out to the side. Chel was suddenly conscious of the intimacy of her actions, and the potential eyes of a dozen Nanaki and Rennic's crew on them. Lemon seemed indifferent, and he tried to relax, stiffening only when her washcloth rode over his fresher traumas.

Lemon rinsed the cloth, then leaned in close to dab at the dried blood on his face. 'When we saw the huts,' she said, her tone conversational but voice low, 'you got a look in your eye. Like a bunny looking to bolt. Put the wind right up me, you did, wee bear.' Another rinse, another dab, her face inches from his own. 'Mind conveying what got you so puffed?'

He said nothing, but she caught his glance. Spider sat at the table's end, the far side from where Tarfel lay. For that at least, Chel was grateful. Spider looked cheerful and relaxed; Chel was not.

'Aye, right, I see. Now what's little old Spider done to you, wee bear?'

Chel averted his eyes, looking down at the pinking scar across his abdomen that Heali had left him. He pursed his lips, winced, then sighed. Lemon was the closest thing he had to a friend in his odd new life. But he had no way of knowing how deep her loyalties to the rest of the company ran.

'That night in the trapper's den,' he said, his voice barely a murmur. 'The night the Mawn . . . the Fly died.' He concentrated on the earth by his feet, the patterns made by the splashes of grimy water. 'We were out on the plateau, Prince Tarfel and me. Spider was going to take the prince away, leave the rest of you, claim the ransom for himself. The Fly was about to stab me when . . . when they shot her.'

He met Lemon's gaze. Her eyes were pale, steady and serious. 'He told me not to tell anyone. He said he'd kill me.'

She nodded, then made a show of stowing the cloth and cloaking him in a loose hide. 'That was good advice, wee bear. I'd suggest you stick to it.'

He frowned, eyes questioning. 'But—'

'Listen, and close. You're not dead yet, are you? Believe me, if the Spider chose to make you dead, you'd be dead, luck of the sand-flowers or no. At the moment, you've given him no reason to doubt you, eh? *So keep it that way.*'

'But aren't you—'

'Hush it, bearling. No whispered chats, no sidelong looks, you understand. Give him nothing. From now on, you and friend Spider are, well, best of friends.' She piled his clothes onto his extended arm. 'Give him nothing. And maybe we'll both still be breathing come the end of all things.'

With that, she strode away and back to the table. With the greatest effort, Chel wrenched his gaze away from the back of the shaven head that waited there.

***

A little later, cleaner but no less battered, Chel sat back down at the table with Rennic and the Black Hawk Company. He did not look at Spider. Whisper slid a wooden platter of food toward him, some of the roasted meat as well as what he guessed to be lake fish, some kind of root vegetable and local berries. He stared hard at the hunks of roasted meat, then shot Lemon a look.

Foss burst out laughing. 'My friend, don't tell me the orange one has filled your head with tales of Nanaki cannibalism?'

Chel said nothing, but his cheeks burned as the rest of the table joined in the laughter. From the number of empty cups and jugs, they'd enjoyed as much liquid refreshment as solid while he'd slept and washed. Even Whisper flashed him a grin, although she didn't appear to be eating.

'Shepherd's piss-pot, boy, it's goat,' Rennic said, grabbing a chunk from the platter and taking a greasy bite. Still he didn't look at him, and Chel wondered if he should take offence. His eyes flicked to Spider, then immediately away. Spider's grin seemed no nastier than usual.

'Don't call me boy,' he said, to himself if no one else, then helped himself to fish and vegetables.

'Stroke of luck this, right, aye?' Lemon was saying at

the table's far end. 'Finding a welcoming Nanaki sept still kicking around this close to winter. Not to mention one of then turning up my pack.' She patted the returned bundle at her feet.

'Maybe our bear cub is lucky after all,' Loveless said. Her speech was slurring, her eyes glassy. 'Good for bear. Good for us.'

'Luck or otherwise,' Rennic said, 'we can be grateful. We can leave in the morning, get below the snow-line before we meet the others.'

'Others?' Chel still had a mouthful of fish. It tasted of nothing.

Rennic turned to him at last. His eyes burned beneath his dark brows, although his gaze was fractured, its focus diluted by booze. 'We're to meet reinforcements. Spider sent a runner ahead. We'll be back on track in a few days.'

A couple of the Nanaki had struck up some music, one strumming a gut-strung instrument of some description, the other tubbing along on a trio of small hide drums. The Nanaki he saw struck Chel as wrong for a family group. Where were the children, or the old people? The youngest members of the sept looked a year or two older than him, the eldest probably the spear-toting woman who now lurked at the back of the hall, watching over them with her flinty glare. Chel suspected she was no older than Rennic. He knew little of Nanaki society, but this lot barely scratched two generations, and seemed too few in number to occupy the complex of huts.

Nodding along to their inexpert rendition, Chel gave a mental shrug. Perhaps they'd sent the young and the old below the snow-line already and were intending to follow once the lake froze. It seemed extreme, but people did extreme things for family, didn't they?

'I'm saying it don't matter how fancy you are, how much gold you got, you can't escape the Spider.'

Chel's attention snapped back to the table. Spider had a finger like a knife-blade on the table, gaze intent. For a moment, Chel thought he meant him.

Foss shook his head, lips pursed. 'What about lords in their castles?'

'Piece of piss. Up the walls, in through the bedchamber window, gheeeeoooooik.' Spider drew the finger across his corded throat.

'Come on, friend. Guards, sheer walls, moats. You can't lay siege on your own.'

'Fucker's got to come outside some time, right?'

Whisper made a series of gestures, and Spider nodded. ''Xactly. Bowshot from a rooftop, fuck, use a crossbow if you're a worthless shit-heap like Lemon—'

'Hoy, fuck off!'

'—put some wood and steel in the fucker's head.'

Foss shook his head again. 'I've seen men travel the road, armoured caravan, bodyguards pressed so close they couldn't tell one fart from another. You'd have to be hell of a shot to squeeze one through there on a windy day.'

Whisper twiddled her fingers, and Foss nodded. 'Present company excepted, my friend.'

Spider's grin was more snarl than smile. 'Where there's a will.' The grin deepened. 'Plague beggar.'

Lemon blinked. 'You what?'

'Find some dying plague fucker, not too far gone o' course, but riddled with white pox or black. Promise his family coin on the event of his passing – shit, if the mark's that heavy, there should be plenty to spare. Then, your man shuffles through the crowd, unarmed and non-threatening, like, then coughs his plague guts over the mark. Sure, the guards will get him, but you'll get your mark. Takes patience, but the deed's done.'

Foss wrinkled his nose in distaste. 'You don't strike me as the patient type, Spider.'

'You'd be surprised by what type I am, fat boy.'

'And what about,' Rennic's voice, heavy with alcohol, carried over the table, 'if your target never leaves his citadel, uses loyal proxies for field-work, and has a network of spies and informers watching for any hint of plot against him? Not to mention a private army of fanatical foot soldiers, all in the service of our good Shepherd.'

Tarfel's bloodied brow was creased. 'You're talking about Primarch Vassad?'

Rennic swung his glare at the prince. 'Am I? You tell me, princeling.'

'Easy,' Spider said, voice raised and dark eyes fixed on Rennic. 'Hunt and kill the proxies. Hunt and kill the figure-heads. Stick to the shadows. Get something they want. Draw them out. And trust no one.' He sat back. 'Every fucker's got to come out eventually. And when they do, the Spider is ready.'

Loveless was leaning on one hand, eyes half-closed. 'You do think a lot of yourself, don't you, Spider?'

'I've brought down fucking kingdoms, me,' Spider hissed, nostrils flared. 'You fuckers have *no* idea who I am. Especially you, Beaky.' He pushed himself to his feet and strode away.

Loveless chuckled. 'Now that's true enough. That terrible prick could be anyone. If that's all the talking done . . .'

She moved to stand, one hand on the table to steady herself. 'It's time to move on to the entertainment.'

She turned to the two Nanaki working at the instruments, offering a dazzling smile. 'Boys, got any dancing music?' They stopped playing and gave her a blank look, unsure but eager. Chel felt his jaw clench when he saw how they looked at her, perhaps seeing his own desires made flesh. She sighed at their incomprehension and turned back to the table.

'Which of you hapless bastards fancies banging out a tune? I *need* to dance.'

Foss put up his hands in apology, and Whisper shook her head with a smile. Rennic didn't even acknowledge the question. 'More of a percussive specialist, me,' Lemon said. 'Not one for plucking.'

Loveless twisted her mouth in mock-disappointment. 'And I could really use a good plucker.'

Chel clenched his jaw, feeling hot under his damp clothes. Even with two good arms he'd have had nothing musical to offer.

Tarfel coughed, a small sound among the hubbub. 'I can play,' he said.

They turned to him, Loveless tilting her head to one side, lips parted in excitement. 'That right, princeling? You can be my plucker?'

Tarfel peered past her, ignoring the pendulous innuendo, to look at the gut-strung flat-box across the Nanaki's knees. 'I could have a go. I've had a bit of training.'

'He's *hattended* the *Hacademy!*' Lemon called, then belched. 'Pardon.'

Loveless marched to the prince, hauled him upright, then led him across the hall to the musicians. Despite her evident inebriation, she moved with confidence, without lurch or stagger. She pointed at the string-player, then jerked her thumb aside. 'Move it, handsome.'

Baffled but keen to please, the Nanaki stood and proffered the instrument to Loveless. She stepped aside, and Tarfel emerged from her shadow to take the Nanaki's place. He sat down cross-legged, settling the instrument across his knees, then ran his finger over the strings. The hall fell silent, as all eyes, Nanaki and other, turned to see what the hooded, blood- and dirt-covered stranger would do.

The exception was Spider, who stood in one corner, bare-armed with his back to the rest of the room, in low conversation with two of the younger Nanaki women. When one turned to see what had drawn her companions' attention, Spider reached out a hand to her chin and turned her head back toward him. His touch was gentle, but the message was as clear as it was menacing. Chel broke his gaze away before Spider saw him. Lemon's words loomed large in his mind.

Tarfel struck up, his first tentative plucks becoming a rudimentary melody. It wasn't one Chel recognized, although its basic tune sounded like a child's song, or perhaps the under-theme of a church rondel. The prince hit a fair few duff notes as he began, learning the instrument's tone as he went, matching his expectations to its sound, and without any clear moment of change, he began playing with two hands, plucking with one and strumming with the other. The music changed with his playing, acquiring a texture and pace, its initial melody now sure and strong, played with urgency and variation.

'I'll be a feathered shitehawk,' Lemon said. 'Yon princey's a minstrel!'

Rennic glowered. 'I *hate* fucking minstrels.'

'Then you should probably take a break from it,' Lemon said, then fell sideways in giggles.

Rennic spat on the earth and stood. 'I'm going for a piss.'

Loveless was grinning, swaying in time to the tempo. 'Now this is more like it! Whisp, old girl, take those drums off this young man so I can dance with him!' She twirled her hands, beckoning to the two former musicians.

With a smile and a roll of her eyes, Whisper stood on lean legs and picked her way over to the drummer. He handed over the little drums without protest, anxious to join his fellow as he approached Loveless for the dance, and a moment later Whisper was seated beside the prince, slapping at the drums in supporting beat, enriching here and there with a flourish of fingers.

Loveless danced with her eyes closed. Chel watched, fascinated and ashamed, absorbed in the poise of her movements, even after three flagons of Nanaki god-piss. The two young Nanaki, lean and muscled and overpoweringly *masculine*, moved in close to her, attempting to match or mirror her movements. Their competition was obvious, and Chel hated them. Loveless, on the other hand, half opened her eyes, smiling at each in turn. She never once missed a step, even as Tarfel and Whisper upped the tempo.

Lemon poured more spirit into their cups, although Foss shook his head. Several brimming jugs remained. 'Grandfather's withered ball-sack, that girl would fuck a fencepost if you drew a cock on it.'

Chel's voice was louder than he'd intended. 'You think?'

Lemon paused, placing the jug back down on the table with the over-precision of the steaming drunk.

'Am I right in thinking,' she said, 'that you're after a tumble, wee bear?'

Chel said nothing. His mouth no longer worked. He could feel blood pounding against the new skin of his lip.

Lemon leaned forward, pushing her face close to his. 'Weeell, I'm game if you are. Shall we go? Reckon most of the outer huts are empty, if a little chilly on the arse.'

He stared at her, sweat at his back, panic churning his innards. He stared at her square, freckled face, her squarish, upturned nose, her wide, round, blue-green eyes, her pursed, cheeky lips. He'd never really thought of her in terms of attraction, but when he took a moment to—

She burst out laughing. 'Aye, right, thought not!' She chuckled to herself, then her expression softened as she looked back to where Loveless danced, swarmed by the Nanaki men. 'Don't fret, wee bear, you'd not be the first to be drawn, like . . . like . . .'

'Moths to flame,' Foss said from across the table, his tone sombre.

'Flies to shite, more like. Anyroad, you should count yourself lucky – you're not really her cut of cloth.'

Chel bristled. 'And what's that?'

'Aye, you know. Young, dumb, full of c—'

Foss cleared his throat.

'Pretty,' Lemon finished, eyes glassy. 'Still, take heart. Two out of three ain't bad.'

Chel frowned. 'Are you saying I'm stupid? Or that I'm ugly?'

Lemon and Foss merely grinned at each other.

'Sod off, the pair of you.' He forced himself to his feet with his good hand. His legs had begun to ache more than ever in his brief rest. 'I'm going for a piss, too.'

'Don't piss on the boss,' Lemon said as he turned to stagger away.

'Or crush any wolves,' Foss said. Chel waved a hand at them in irritation.

'Hey, bear, seriously,' Lemon said, the mockery dropped from her tone, and he turned back toward them, feeling every thump of his pulse around his battered body.

'What?'

'She'd break you in half.'

'Oh, shut up, Lemon.'

'No!'

He limped away, feeling a strange mixture of embarrassment and pride. For the first time in months, maybe longer, he felt like he had friends.

***

As Chel hobbled around the dance floor's edge, Tarfel finished the piece with a flourish, then looked up from his cowl with a breathless grin. Beside him, Whisper gave the prince's playing an approving nod. Chel diverted, limping over to them.

'You know, Chel,' the prince said, wiping the sweat that beaded on his bloodied brow with the back of one hand, 'it's really quite a sophisticated instrument, all things considered. You know, for savages.'

His forehead was streaked copper in the firelight, his pale skin showing through muddy. With an apologetic grimace, Chel reached out and tweaked the prince's cowl forward. 'Best be careful, highness. Vendettas and all that.'

Tarfel blinked, then nodded. He'd evidently enjoyed some

of the Nanaki spirit too. 'Right you are, Chel, right you are.'

'You play very well, highness.'

Tarfel bit at his lip. 'It was one of my mother's great passions. She used to play all the time in her tower, or so I'm told. She died birthing me – did you know that, Chel? I suppose most people do. Not many musicians in the family though, on Father's side at least. Mendel played a bit here and there, but since Corvel . . . Well, I've not seen him pick up an instrument. We used to be so close, you know, the two of us, Mendel and me. Corvel was always off learning, training in matters of state. No time to play with little brothers, quite understandable of course. But Mendel, he had time, we did everything together . . .'

Tarfel tailed off, his eyes suddenly tearful. Chel stood awkwardly before him, his need to urinate increasingly urgent, unable to interrupt the emotional prince, watching with a mixture of genuine sympathy and extreme discomfort. 'We're friends, aren't we, Chel? You're my sworn man, I shouldn't be addressing you by your family name all the time. You may not have a title, but you need a better address.'

'Er, Vedren, highness?'

'Vedren? Vedren . . . Vedren it is. Thank you, Vedren.'

'Thank you, highness.'

A hand on Chel's good shoulder shoved him sideways, and Loveless's face jutted past him. 'Hoy, golden boy! Less yap, more slap, yes?' She was sheened in sweat, the blue crest of hair plastered to one side of her head, and her eyes had the faraway look of a poppy-fiend. Chel shivered at her proximity.

Alarmed, Tarfel nodded, then set his hands back on the

gut strings and began to play. 'Faster!' Loveless cried, and as Whisper joined his accelerating melody with a syncopated beat, Loveless gave a roar of approval and slapped Chel across the buttocks, then slid back to her waiting dance partners, eager to resume their barely disguised mating ritual.

Dazed, Chel watched her go. His eye caught Foss and Lemon sitting at their table beyond the improvised dance floor, grins wider than ever. Foss raised his cup and winked.

***

Chel was reaching for the hide when it swung aside and Rennic ducked back into the hall. He noticed Chel and his outstretched hand and grunted, letting the hide fall closed behind him. Chel stood, uncertain, throat dry and conscious of his overfull bladder.

'Lemon,' Rennic said, then paused. His voice was rough as shale. 'Lemon says you kept them alive out there.'

Chel said nothing.

Rennic sniffed. 'Keep it up. Better you don't make a fool of me.' He moved to push past.

'Wait,' Chel said, almost putting his hand on the bigger man before reconsidering. Rennic's stare was colder than the lake ice. 'Why did you bring me, when you took the prince? Why am I here?'

Rennic was silent for a moment, rocking on his heels. It occurred to Chel that there was a good chance he was utterly drunk. At length he put his hand on Chel's good shoulder and leaned in. He smelled of sweat, leather and raw booze.

'What you're looking for,' he rasped, 'is out there.' He

pointed through the hide. Chel followed his gesture, frowning with concentration. 'Follow the tracks to the line of trees, you'll know it by the smell.' He barked a laugh and clapped Chel on the wrong shoulder. 'Go write your name in the snow, boy.'

Then he was past, thumping across the earthen floor toward the others. Chel winced and rubbed his throbbing shoulder, then shoved his way through the hide.

The darkness beyond was familiar if momentarily drowning. Chel stood, breathing hard in the sudden cold, waiting to see the vapour form before his eyes. One hand on the coarse timber wall, he made his unsteady way toward the glimmering patch of moonlight at the end of the passage. As he neared it, voices reached him, so close he nearly gasped.

It took him a moment to parse what he heard, unsure of the language or speakers. A man's voice, low, indistinct, its tone merry if insistent. A woman's tinkling laugh, then a word spoken slowly, its enunciation heavy, unfamiliar, foreign.

'Smoi-daa?'

The man's voice again, the word repeated in low tones.

'Spoi-daa?'

Spider. Chel gritted his teeth. 'Shit.' He began to back away, back down the passageway. There was another door on the other side. The voices followed him as he went, each of his halting steps as delicate and muffled as he could make it.

'Fur-loi? Somo Fur-loi?'

Chel heard it then, Spider's throaty chuckle, his voice clear in the bitter night. 'Yes, darlin'. You can be my Fly.'

Chel limped faster.

FIFTEEN

The cold slapped and stung his skin, despite his cloak of Nanaki spirit. The night was overcast, the moon a pale, watery smear lost behind billows of fat silver cloud, but the ubiquitous snow reflected enough meagre light for Chel to stagger to the trees and relieve himself. Lazy flakes drifted around him as he considered trying to write his name, then thought better of it.

Refreshed but shivering, he turned back toward the huts, making for the outer door. As he approached the wafting hide, he heard their voices within: Spider's flint-edged rumble, the Nanaki girl's thick laughter. They were in the outer chamber, blocking his way back inside. He hovered a moment, teeth on the edge of chattering as the warmth flooded from his body into the bitter night air, then scowled. Sod it, there were other entrances.

He trudged around the outer hut ring, hands shoved beneath his arms, the snow crust crunching beneath his feet as the lead-coloured lake filled his view. It seemed utterly flat in the feeble moonlight, immobile, lifeless, thick growths of ice encroaching from the shoreline like grasping fingers. Drifts of blown snow had dusted the ice like dandruff.

A figure strode into view in a sudden blaze of mellow light from the interior, darkened as soon as the hide flapped shut behind it. Blinking in the returned gloom, Chel watched the figure march from the hut down to a creaking jetty, travelling a well-worn path in the snow. The figure wore thick furs and moved easily over the slippery boards: one of their hosts.

Something made Chel pause. He couldn't explain why – he had every reason to be where he was, after all – but he felt the urge to hide, to stay unseen. The Nanaki paced to the end of the jetty, knelt, and began pulling up a rope that dangled down into the frigid water below. A moment's inspection of whatever was at its end, then it fell back with a splash, and the Nanaki pulled up another. Chel pressed himself gingerly against the outer wall, keeping to the moon-shadow. Fishing lines? Traps of some sort?

The figure pulled up several more ropes, letting a few drop back into the water, keeping the rest and untying whatever lay at their ends. Then the figure was up, the items bundled in its arms, making confident progress back down the jetty toward the waiting huts. Chel ducked back around the wall, breathing into his hand to try to mask the vapour. Another flash of mellow brilliance, and he was alone in the moonlight.

He was shivering, his teeth rattling in his jaw, fingers numb, and he knew it wasn't all from cold. Lemon's words echoed around his head, and he couldn't fight the curiosity, the *need to know*. His steps on the slick and groaning jetty were slow, cautious, his eyes on the knotted ropes at its end, body tensed against another sudden wash of light from behind. His breath felt raw in his throat.

The ropes were dark, soaked and half-frozen, stiff and sharp against his palms. The first he tried didn't move, its end locked into the ice chunks lurking below the jetty. Heavy pulls on the next revealed a dark lump of ice, heaved into the moonlight, a solid frozen block. He let it slide back into the water.

The third rope came more easily, less wet-frozen than the others. He pulled a knotted bundle out from the frigid depths, heavier still as it left the icy water, his shoulder screaming from the effort. With gasps of exertion and pain, he hauled the bundle up onto the jetty, levering it onto the wooden boards as he flopped down beside. He felt completely numb.

He picked at the knotted rope with his good hand, teasing at the contents beneath. Something hide-wrapped lay beneath the rope, tightly parcelled. He tweaked back the hide to reveal pale stacks, half-pickled by the ice-water, dark blotches like cut ends. He worked at the sodden rope, wishing he had a knife or lever. A length slipped at last and the hide fell away, and he saw the jagged edges, the protruding bone. It was meat. Preserving meat.

Chel paused, breathing hoarse, willing his failing fingers back to life. He could kick the bundle off the jetty and be back by the fire in the space of another twenty breaths. All he had to do was stand. He could feel the cold oozing into him from the jetty floor, creeping up through his legs, gnawing at him. All he had to do was stand.

He yanked at the rope again, and the loop came free. He stared at what lay beneath, throat closed, breath frozen, then rolled onto his hands and knees and began to vomit into the black water below.

Beside him on the jetty, pale and shrivelled in the wavering moonlight, stretched the clawing fingers of a human hand.

***

Whisper drew back the hide curtain as he was reaching for it, his good hand trembling, skin pale from more than just cold. She gave him a genial nod, then her eyes narrowed as she took in his wild expression, brow sweat and caked trickles of vomit at his chin.

Her hand moved fast in the gloom, but her expression was easy to read. *What's wrong?* She mimed drinking, then heaving, and raised an eyebrow. Over her shoulder, Tarfel was winding down his latest rendition, unaccompanied, while Loveless swung arms with one of the Nanaki bulls.

Chel shook his head. His voice was cracked, his throat still dry and resentful from retching. 'Bodies,' he managed.

Whisper's eyes narrowed further, one hand moving to the hilt of the long knife at her belt. Her bow and quiver lay by the table in the hall, along with most of their weaponry. She gestured with the other hand. *Where?*

'In the lake.' He swallowed hard, fighting down revulsion. 'Cut as meat.'

Her expression didn't change, but the knuckles on the knife hilt gleamed pale in the murk.

'Have to warn the others.' Already his mind was racing away, past the terror of eating their own and onto becoming prey himself. Was this why there were no children or old people among the Nanaki band? They'd all been slaughtered already? Is that why they'd taken them in?

Whisper nodded, casting a quick look over her shoulder. The Nanaki matriarch remained at the back of the hall, wavering in the haze of smoke and steam and sweat, the creases of her eyes impossible to read. Her bone spear remained in her hand.

Whisper motioned downward. *Wait here.* She turned back to the room as Tarfel struck up the first chords of his next number. The notes were immediately familiar to Chel.

'Oh, shit,' he whispered. His eyes flicked to Rennic, whose broad back obscured the rest of his view of the crew's low table. 'Not that song! Stop him!'

Whisper turned back in confusion, and Tarfel began to sing.

'O they told of her beauty,
The maiden of stars,
But cometh the—'

A clay jug smashed against his head.

Yelping and reeling, the prince flailed at his head, showering the earthen floor with shards of pottery and splatters of fiery spirit. Rennic was on his feet, swaying slightly, one hand still extended and the slow-dawning realization of a mistake crossing his face. Tarfel rubbed at his eyes and face, wailing and flinching, the cowl pulled from his head and the crust of old blood run from his face in slick rivulets. His milk-white skin shone in the firelight.

The Nanaki moved fastest. Before Lemon or Foss could rise from the table, the matriarch had barked a command and weapons of bone and steel were inches from their throats. The two men dancing with Loveless pulled their daggers without hesitation, one of them gripping her around the waist while the other danced around her kicks to press his knife to her cheek. Rennic was surrounded by three Nanaki, their spears extended, while two more registered Whisper's presence by the doorway and hurtled toward her. Only Tarfel was left unattended, but he seemed more concerned with brushing clay from his hair and mewling. He looked on the verge of tears.

Rennic stared around the chamber. 'Uh . . . black flag?'

Whisper fixed Chel with a stare and made a scuttling gesture with one hand against her body, before shoving him back into the darkness and turning to face her oncoming assailants. The hide curtain swung shut, muffling the shouting beyond.

Spider.

Find Spider.

His mouth still sour with bile, heart thumping against his ribs and glossy sweat cooling on his brow, Chel stood frozen in the darkness. Shouts carried through the curtain, the clatter of metal. At any moment, the hanging would be ripped aside, and a bone-tipped spear would drive into his torso. His meat. Ready to be bled, dressed and carved.

Find Spider.

Of course it had to be Spider. Bloody, bloody Spider.

He snorted, swallowed, then turned and bolted for the snow beyond.

***

The tracks to the hut were easy to follow.

'Spider?'

The hanging moved aside. Spider filled the doorway, close and gnarled and suddenly much bigger than Chel remembered. He was stripped to the waist, the scattered moonlight gleaming from his shaven dome and knots of muscle. He said nothing, staring at Chel with cold, black eyes.

'Listen, I know we're not . . . that is, we've . . .' Chel swallowed, tried again. 'There's trouble,' he blurted, trying to keep his voice low, mindful of Spider's likely company in the chilled, darkened hut. 'They found out about the prince. They've pulled weapons, surrounded the others. Whisper sent me to get you – you're the only one who can talk to them!'

Spider tilted his head back, dark eyes glittering in the moonlight. 'Where's the little prince?'

'They've got him. I think they mean to hurt him . . .'

Spider breathed long and hard through his narrow nose. 'Stay here.'

He disappeared back into the hut.

Chel stood alone in the cold, wondering if his shivers came from temperature or adrenaline, expecting to hear the crunch of footsteps on snow at any moment as the Nanaki butchers came up the slope to finish the job.

He heard a sound from the hut, something like a sigh, then a moment later Spider ducked through the doorway, dressed and bristling with knives. He grunted and gestured toward the central building.

'Move it, shit-rat.' He stepped in close, a hooked knife in his hand without seeming to travel from his belt. 'If that fucking prince dies, then all this arse-grief will be for nothing, and the Spider has come too far to get nothing. The Spider might be tempted to push your eyeballs out the back of your head by way of compensation.'

'Um. Understood.' Chel nodded. He could cross that bridge when he came to it. Spider was already loping toward the main entrance; Chel hurried after.

'What about your, uh, friend?'

'What friend?' Spider didn't even look round. 'Who

fucked up? Was it Beaky? Never could keep his piss straight after two jugs.'

'They're cannibals. Truly. They've got a load of butchered bodies freezing on ropes in the lake.' He was amazed by how easily he could say it.

Spider didn't blink.

'And?'

***

Spider moved over the snow like a sure-footed beast, low on all fours, leaving shallow impressions compared with the deep, rutted tracks that had led from the entrance. Chel laboured after, trying to keep up while limping against the thick drifts, his breath great silver plumes in the milky light. He did his best to outline the situation in the hall as he went.

'What's your steel?' Spider said as they closed on the central hut.

'Come again?'

'What are you carrying?' Spider stopped, turning to Chel with incredulity mixing with his existing disgust. 'What are you armed with, rat-bear?'

Chel spread his hands, as much as his strapped shoulder would allow. 'I don't have anything.'

'God's fucking cock-pus.'

'It's not my fault – I've been disarmed since Denirnas, and even before then, uh . . .'

'What? What kind of fucking bodyguard are you?'

'I only took the oath just before your lot snatched me and the prince.'

Spider's eyes were glittering coals. His hand moved in a

blur, faster than Chel could register, and Chel found a knife at his chest. With a flick Spider reversed it, and Chel found himself taking the hilt with his good hand, while a sudden surge of adrenaline fizzed cold in his gut. The blade was long and narrow, a stabber, not a slasher. It was very cold, and heavier than it had looked.

'Keep that close, rat-shit. The Spider will be taking it back later, one way or another.'

Spider reached the outer doorway and crouched beside it. Chel waded up beside him and did likewise. 'How many of them are there? A dozen?'

'Fourteen,' Spider said, then considered. 'Thirteen.'

Chel opened his mouth, then said nothing.

'They'll know we're loose,' Spider said. He had a hooked blade in each hand, and slow steam floated in wisps from his bald head. 'They'll be looking. Are you ready?'

Chel nodded. His options were limited.

'There are two entries to the hall, one at each end. The Spider will take the one closer to Prince Fuck-face, you the other. They'll be off their guard at our arrival, maybe we can talk them down, maybe not. Whatever goes down, you're following up with that dagger – stick it in as many of them as your shit little rat arms can manage, aim for the soft places. Eyes, ears, neck, tits, cock, you name it. Jam up some fucker's arsehole and he's out of the fight, yes? None of your lordly pissing around here, understand?'

Chel nodded again, hoping his distaste wasn't too obvious.

'The Spider takes the prince, you get those other useless fuckers out of there. Their weapons are by the table, yes? Head that way, sling them over. They won't be expecting a rat-faced cripple to spray steel, so that's in your favour. Yes?'

'No.'

'The fuck you say, rat-boy?'

'I'm taking the prince.'

'Did you hit your head?'

'Think about it. You can talk to the Nanaki, they know you. If there's a bloodless solution to this, it's you convincing them that all's well, that Tarfel's not worth any trouble.' He tried not to think of the lake meat, or Spider's absent friend in the hut. Bloodless seemed a remote outcome. 'Either way, they won't be expecting me, like you said. You make the big entrance, see if they're open to negotiation, hold their attention. I can grab the prince and get him to safety before anything, uh, untoward happens. That's what matters, right? The prince being safe. Like you said, he dies, this was all for nothing.' And I spend eternity in an unmarked grave in these mountains, assuming I'm not digested first.

Spider considered. To Chel's eye he was weighing probabilities, and it felt like an awful lot rode on which way Spider's scales would tip. After a moment, he grimaced. 'Fine. The Spider should make the big entrance. You'd only fuck it up.' He twirled the knives, one after the other. 'But you come back, rat-boy. Get that bleached weasel out in the woods and come back, give a signal, wave your little rat arms. You think about running, you will not be getting far.' Spider's gaze was a darkness from which there was no escape.

Chel swallowed. 'Of course—'

Spider's hand went over his mouth, rough and cold and salty. He shuddered and tried to move away, but Spider's eyes were on the doorway. He whipped his hand away, the curved blade reappearing as it moved, then stood silently, pressed against the doorway's edge. Chel pulled back from him, his own dagger cold and strange in his off-handed grip. He fixed his eyes on the heavy hide, watching its every curl and ripple in the breeze.

All was still, no sound but the rolling bustle of wind in the forest around them, and the pounding of blood in Chel's ears.

The hanging moved aside.

The Nanaki was half out of the door, his spear leading proud, when Spider rolled over him like a boulder. One hand clamped over his mouth, Spider's legs wrapped around his arms and body, and they tumbled into the snow before the Nanaki could cry out. One hooked blade rose and fell, rose and fell, and blood sprayed into the churned drift. Spider locked the man tight, crushing his struggles and convulsions, his protests only gurgles as the life flooded from him into the mush beneath. His movements slowed, then stopped altogether. Spider stood, wiping his blade and brushing himself down.

'Twelve.' He hawked and spat a fat gobbet onto the cooling body at his feet. 'Fancy sticking him with your blade, get the feel of it?'

Chel took three attempts to shake his head.

So much for bloodless.

***

The scene in the hall was little changed, as Spider peeled back a wisp of hide covering from the inner doorway and they peered in. Lemon and Foss had been moved away from their weapons, and joined by Whisper, who sported a fresh cut across the top of her chest. One of the Nanaki was bandaging his hand in the corner. Loveless remained pinned between the two young studs, steaming with booze and fury. Rennic stood at the hall's centre, his hands raised in supplication, still trying to surmount the language barrier. The Nanaki matriarch looked unmoved, although Chel found her expression as hard to read as ever.

Tarfel had remained where he was, curled in a ball and whimpering beside the instruments, his back to the wall. Despite the fuss over his heritage, he seemed at the bottom of everyone's priorities. Chel nodded toward him.

'I can reach him from here, if you draw their attention to the far end.'

'The Spider will draw plenty, don't you worry, rat-bear.'

'Uh-huh.' What had his mother said about people who refer to themselves in the third person? He'd forgotten her exact words, but the essence had been: wankers.

Spider was away, scuttling back through the darkness like his namesake. Chel waited at the doorway, counting his ragged breaths, feeling the weight of the dagger in his hand. It was still grave-cold, his fingers offering little warmth in the circumstances. He peeked into the hall again. The fire crackled away at the hall's centre, yet somehow its amiable heat now repelled him, its association with the butchered human-meat too close.

The far hanging flapped aside, and Spider strode into the room. The Nanaki fell into uproar, weapons brandished, threats made clear despite the foreign tongue. Two Nanaki nocked arrows to their short bone bows, swivelling to face the new threat. Spider's hands were up and empty, his tone conciliatory, his eyes glittering in the firelight. Tarfel sat alone and forgotten. Chel moved.

He kept low against the wall, retracing the steps he'd

followed on his way out such a short time before. He skirted an upturned table, closing on the prince, sweat prickling along his back from more than the fire's heat. His ankle throbbed and yowled with every hunched step, but he pushed on with gritted teeth. A gentle tap on the prince's cloaked shoulder was all he could risk, his darting eyes on the figures beyond, Spider's low, placatory words against the aggressive barks of the Nanaki present. How long before they realized that at least one of their number would not be returning?

Tarfel turned. His head was sticky with dribbled spirit and dried blood, his hair matted and lumpen against his scalp. His eyes widened as he registered Chel, and his lips parted to speak. Chel shook his head with fury, jamming his good hand forward to still the prince's mouth. The pommel of the dagger mashed into the prince's lips and he recoiled with a gasp, Chel's mortified grimace scant mollification. Chel watched a single tear roll down the prince's filthy cheek, gnawing his fist in mute apology.

A swift glance suggested no one had heard the gasp over the central dispute. Chel beckoned with his weak hand, head inclined toward the doorway, and the prince nodded, eyes wet and wide. They crawled at a gallop, Chel not risking a look back, his pulsing heart pressing against his gorge so hard he feared his eyes would burst from his skull. He ushered Tarfel past him at the doorway, through the dark passageway beyond, and out into the stinging cold of the night.

'Vedren!' the prince said as the starlit night welcomed them. Chel gestured on, aiming for the line of dark forest at the head of the slope. 'Why did you hit me?'

'I'm so sorry, highness. It was an accident,' he managed, breath coming hard. 'We need to keep moving.'

'Why is the snow so dirty? What's this by the door?'

'Come on!' Chel grabbed the prince by the arm and dragged him into the woods.

***

They climbed into a snow-draped thicket that offered a narrow, fractured view of the huts below. Chel tried to calm his breathing as he peered back down the slope, scanning for any movement. The lake beyond was a pewter slab, the odd sliver of moonlight that slipped the gloomy cloud glinting from its sullen surface. His fingers and toes were long since numb to the cold, his limbs beginning to stiffen and seize.

'Vedren?' The prince's voice was meek in the darkness, almost buried in the whispering creak of the surrounding forest.

'Highness?'

'They were really going to kill me, weren't they?'

'I don't know, highness. They certainly didn't seem best pleased to see you.'

'Why do they hate me? Why would they want to kill me just for how I look?'

Chel bit his lip. It hardly felt the time for a diversion into ethno-politics, and the Horvaun reaver purges that had driven the Nanaki into the remotest parts of these mountains.

'I need to get back, highness. We can talk later.' He rose to his feet, cursing every battered bone in his body.

'What? What are you talking about! You can't go back! You can't leave me here! I command you!'

'I'm sorry, highness. I must.'

'But, but, it's cold! There are wolves! What if the Nanaki murder you like the others? Why don't we just run, right now? The two of us?' Tarfel spread his pale palms in the darkness. 'After all, what do we know about those people, these kidnappers, assuming they're not dead already? You know, I don't think they're planning to ransom me at all.' His voice rose in pitch. 'They've not been very nice to me and I don't see why you should risk your life helping them when for all we know they're planning to cut our throats as soon as they get us to wherever it is they're dragging us!'

Chel nodded. 'And that's why I have to go back. Without them, we'll not last a day out here. Certainly not with the Nanaki hunting us.' And certainly not if Spider survives and comes after us, either. I prefer my eyeballs on the inside of my skull.

'They're not your friends, Vedren. They're mercenaries, hired by my enemies – by *our* enemies.'

'I know, highness. I still have to go back.'

'You are refusing a royal command. I am . . . displeased!'

'Take this, highness.' Chel held out the dagger, hilt first.

'What? I can't fight off a horde of Nanaki if they come for me.'

Chel nodded.

'It's not for them.'

Tarfel's indignation vanished, and he suddenly seemed very small in the moonlight.

'Oh.'

SIXTEEN

Chel collected the sticky bone spear from the doorway and crept inside, feeling every hunched step pulsing along his body. He needed a long rest. And a bath. And something to eat that wasn't cannibal cuisine.

He peered around the hide and into the hall. Spider remained closest to the matriarch, his empty palms still front and centre, his words loud and insistent. He'd had little luck convincing the Nanaki to stand down, but he'd stalled violence for a time at least; surly grunts from the matriarch punctuated his broken appeals. All were congregated on the far side of the fire, and Chel crept behind the closest low table, hefting the spear in his good hand. He had a low opinion of his hand's coordination, but his experience with the wolves had taught him that sometimes it's enough just to have a sharp thing on the end of a stick to hold out in front of you.

Foss, Lemon and Whisper were herded together and surrounded by at least three Nanaki hunters. Rennic had another three around him, and Spider had two, plus the matriarch and what looked like her bodyguard, paying him close attention. Loveless was almost his side of the fire, still held fast by her erstwhile dance partners, her face dark as a thunderstorm. The crew's packs and equipment lay piled and propped at the edge of their original table, now only a few paces from where Chel hid. He squinted. Their odds were not good. He needed a plan.

Spider tried negotiation again, rattling out another burst of syllables in the unfamiliar Nanaki tongue. The matriarch snarled, spat and jabbed a gnarled finger at Tarfel's former resting place by the instruments. She was midway through her point, whatever it was, when her dark eyes flicked to where she pointed, and she tailed off. The creases around her eyes stretched then scrunched, and Chel tensed. He still had no plan.

'Rat-bear!' Spider roared, his eyes darting around the room. 'This is the time!'

Chel still had no plan.

The room erupted into multi-lingual shouting and the clatter of shifting weapons.

'Rat-bear!'

Chel still had no plan.

Spider's hands dropped to his waist, and the Nanaki surged toward him.

Chel drove himself upward and hurled the spear with his good arm, realising he was screaming as he did so. The weapon flew from his hand, arcing through the air and passing well wide of any of the Nanaki. It whistled through the group, touching nothing, before glancing against the wooden wall and clattering to the floor.

Chel paid it no heed. He'd kept moving, his eyes alone on the equipment by the table. Spider, too, had been unfazed by the spear's sudden arrival, and from the corner of his eye Chel saw crimson sprays erupt as Spider slipped the spears of the approaching hunters and tore at them with his hooked blades. The eyes of the rest of the hall were still on the bouncing spear, the gurgled shrieks of the stricken hunters melding into the background chaos.

Chel's hand closed on the scabbard propped against the table, and he spun and flung it across the hall, offering a small prayer to the Shepherd that Loveless had been watching.

She had been watching.

What followed was a tumbling cascade of violence. As the Nanaki reacted too slowly to the carnage in their midst, Loveless caught the hilt of her blade with an extended hand. She flicked the scabbard away as she turned against the man holding her, twisting in a scything motion that ended with her elegant sword hacked into his neck. He fell away, screeching and clawing at his rupture, and she kicked off his collapsing form to drive her blade through the lung of his companion as he lurched to intercede.

Spider leapt from his first victims toward the Nanaki surrounding Foss, Lemon and Whisper, while Loveless advanced on those around Rennic with a dark fire burning in her eyes. The hunters beyond had realized the danger, but they turned too late to confront the new threats at their perimeter. Foss erupted, his thick arms wrapped around the heads of two of his former captors before they could bring their spears around. Lemon darted between them, grabbing the bone tips of their weapons as they struggled, crushed and blinded, and guiding their wild thrusts into each other's gut.

Whisper had sprung from the reach of the hunter who

swiped at her with a cleaver, hopping up onto a table then away as he slashed after her with clumsy strokes. Chel, inured to further horror, lofted an axe toward her, possibly one of Lemon's. It crunched into the table between her and the hunter. For a moment, both stared at it, then as the Nanaki charged forward to cut off Whisper's reach, he jerked sideways then downward as a bone-tipped spear burst from his sternum. He collapsed, gasping and gurgling, revealing Lemon behind him. She gave a thumbs up, then swung on.

At the hall's far side, Rennic stood with a broken spear in his hand, hot blood running from cuts to his cheek and chest and a comatose hunter at his feet. Two more Nanaki closed on him, their aggression tempered by the havoc in the hall, the shouts and screams of their compatriots. One turned as Loveless arrived with fury, the hunter's skull almost split in two by the venomous blow. The remaining hunter cursed and whimpered, then turned to run. Rennic ran him through with his broken half-spear.

Close movement caught Chel's eye, a burst of motion in the firelight. The matriarch was sprinting toward him, pacing a clear path through the carnage, murder in the dark creases of her eyes. Chel was the only thing between her and the doorway. He stood, weaponless, as she bore down on him, the long spear in her hand level with his gut.

He ground his heels into the earth. 'Come on then, you crusty old fucker. Come on!'

Her eyes widened, and she stumbled on a loose hammer from Lemon's pack. Chel watched the gleaming spear-tip as it lurched toward him, pushing himself aside as it whistled past. For a moment he locked stares with the matriarch, then he grabbed her jacket with his good hand and smashed his forehead against her nose as hard as he could.

The pain was excruciating, bright blooms across his broken face, purple explosions before his eyes even as his sight went dark. He blinked hard, fighting back tears of shock and pain, feeling the woman sag in his grip as he swayed on his feet. His vision cleared enough to see another swing of the spear coming at him, half-hearted, and he leaned into the matriarch as the weapon flapped against his back, then drove his knee into her abdomen.

She collapsed into the dirt, and to his shame he kicked her on the ground, jaw clenched, spittle flecking his lips.

The hall was quiet, aside from the groans and gurgles of the injured. Spider strode up to him, knelt and without ceremony carved open the matriarch's throat. Chel wobbled, the reality of the situation, and his actions within it, flooding into him as the adrenaline departed. He considered vomiting again.

'I'm impressed, rat-bear.' Spider said, wiping his blade on Chel's shoulder. 'Now where's my fucking knife?'

'Sod your knife,' Rennic said, looming behind him, glassy-eyed and bloody. 'Where's that bastard prince?'

***

By the time Chel returned to the hall with the shivering Tarfel in tow, the Black Hawk Company had rolled the Nanaki bodies over to the far end and out of the doorway into the cold. Foss and Lemon were at work turning the bloodied earth where they'd fallen, a well-intentioned if futile endeavour; the floor of the hut would likely be forever marred. Tarfel sat straight down by the fire as Rennic stoked it. He did not look at Chel.

'We should bury them,' Chel said, his eyes fixed on a

trailing foot that jutted beyond the hanging hide. Rennic shot him a fierce glare. 'They'll draw the wolves, if nothing else.'

'We should burn them,' Loveless said from at his elbow. She was no less bloody than Rennic, although little of it seemed to be hers, but her clothing was torn and she smouldered with quiet rage. Her scabbarded sword was back at her side. 'We should torch these miserable fuckers, and this whole sick fucking graveyard with them.'

Spider picked at his teeth with the point of the now-returned knife. He met Chel's questioning look and leered. 'Passed on your findings, vis-à-vis dinner.'

Chel looked around the hall. None of the others seemed to have voided their stomachs at the news, or at least if they had they'd cleaned it up with the bodies. The tables that hadn't been overturned or forcibly cleared during the earlier carnage now stood empty, as did the spit over the fire. At least there had been fish.

'We'll burn them,' Rennic said. 'But not tonight.'

Whisper ducked through the hide behind them and strode over, her fingers and hands twirling their signal dance. Chel tried to parse the movements, hoping to discern meaning, but these were not the obvious mimes she'd offered earlier. Each shape was distinct, one- or two-handed, hanging for an instant before the next followed. He gave up and flicked back to the reactions of the others. Rennic and Loveless were attentive, but Spider wore a scowl. They made fleeting eye contact, and for that moment they shared a mutual frustration at their incomprehension. Then Spider turned his head and spat by his boot, and their connection was over. Chel hoped it was a positive sign.

'Well, that figures,' Loveless said as Whisper's hands

stilled. She slumped back onto a table, her righteous fury draining.

Rennic nodded. 'Should have fucking seen it. Too late in the year. I said it was too late in the year.' He turned to Spider. 'This is your mess, Spider. You let us sit here, drinking and eating, in the company of *fucking monsters*.'

Spider sprang forward, the pointy blade tight in his grip. 'And that's where you'd have fucking died, Beaky, if the Spider hadn't swooped in and cut you fuckers to safety. Where's the fucking thanks there?'

'A situation entirely of your making! We trusted your judgement and that fucking pile of human waste over there is the result.'

'And who tipped these fuckers off to the princeling's tribe? Strikes me you should be showing a little more gratitude, Beaky, for even having a job in the first place. Not like anyone else will work with you, is it? You should be *giving thanks* for scraps from the Spider.'

Rennic waved a contemptuous hand and strode away, and Whisper followed. Spider stalked off in the other direction, knife clenched beneath white knuckles. Chel stood beside the table, looking from one to the other. He felt completely lost.

From the table, Loveless tilted her head his way. Her scar shone livid in the firelight. 'Those body parts you found, cub, in the lake. They're Nanaki too.'

Chel grimaced. 'So they did eat their own. Was that why there were no very old or young?'

'Not exactly. Whisper reckons different sept. Probably the original owners of this place.'

Chel sat down on the table beside her. He felt nothing at their proximity. 'Fuck.'

'Fuck indeed, cub. This bunch were probably outcasts already, waited until the first of the snows then came raiding as the other septs moved downslope. Looks like they were planning to wait out the winter here, piled high with family meat. Until we came dancing into their laps.'

'Fuck,' Chel repeated. 'Think they would have attacked us anyway? Even if they hadn't seen the prince?' Tarfel sat cross-legged before the fire, cloak wrapped twice around him. He was pouting and avoiding Chel's eye.

Loveless tilted her hand: *maybe, maybe not*. 'Risky for them either way. Bunch of armed strangers, not much coin, and Lemon is wretched stringy. May have been planning to wait until we were good and shit-faced, or fully comatose, then take care of us in the quiet of the night. Cannibal cocks.' She spat in the direction of the corpses. 'So perhaps golden boy did us a favour after all. Once they saw his complexion, they showed their true colours.'

Chel was quiet for a moment, face scrunched in reflection. 'Why does Rennic hate that song so much?'

She turned to look at him, a surprised frown creasing her brow. 'You would have to ask him that,' she said, holding his gaze for a moment. Then she looked away, staring into the fire, and Chel realized that was all he'd get.

'Fucken cannibals, man!' Lemon strode over, one of the jugs of spirit, somehow unscathed, dangling from her hand. 'Fucken honest-to-ancestors cannibals, like I said. Not that any of you wankers believed me, eh?'

Chel spread his hands. 'I believed you.'

'Aye, right, but only 'cos you're almost as gap-skulled credulous as Prince Gormless over there!' She thumped down on the table between them, shunting them further apart, then proffered the jug to each in turn. 'No? Bollocks to you. It's the perfect time for more drinking. Ugh, wee bear, you smell of sick.'

Returning, Rennic kicked out some turned earth and shunted a table aside from the fire. 'Listen up, pustules. This has been a catastrophe, and I expect you to be offering up some prayers of thanks to your creator of choice that you live and are, in most senses, whole. We cannot afford another fuck-up like this, as at the very least I will run out of words to describe the depths of incompetence.'

'Aye, fair play, boss, this was just bad luck, eh?'

Rennic pointed his glare at Chel, who shrank against the table. 'Oh, there's no such thing, Lemon. Now get to sleep. Tomorrow we burn this fucking place to the ground, and the ghouls with it, and we go on our way and never speak of this again. First watch is Spider, first watch of Spider is Foss.'

From somewhere beyond came Spider's snarling retort, but Rennic ignored it. He swept his gaze around the shattered hall, blood-streaked and quivering with suppressed fury.

'Tomorrow is another day. And if it's anything like today I'll kill the fucking lot of you myself.'

SEVENTEEN

They were three days below the snow-line, tracking the path of a white-frothing river, when they saw the riders coming the other way. Four figures on horseback, another on foot, leading a train of well-laden ponies, picking their way up the hard-packed slope. Whisper signalled and the crew spread across the gritty landscape, ducking behind bleached crags and boulders. Foss and Lemon took their customary positions around Chel and the sullen prince, pushed below an outcrop toward the back of the group.

There they lay in tense and uncomfortable silence, listening for the echoing crunch of hooves on loosened stone, hearing only the whine of the wind through the narrow valley, the rolling whisper of the scrubby trees. From his vantage, pressed against the dusty ground, Chel could see Rennic in one direction, crouched and ready at the trail's edge, his thick black hair tied back from his eyes; in the other direction lay Loveless, her sword still sheathed but her fingers flexing on its fine hilt.

The sounds of horse were ever louder. The riders were nearly on them.

'River of shit, you call this an ambush?'

The voice came from behind them. Chel spun over, feeling the dull protest of his still-weak shoulder, to see a tall, muscular figure standing upslope, silhouetted by the dim midday sun. He struck a casual pose, a long, bladed spear resting across his shoulders, his arms dangling over its shaft.

'How the fucken—' Lemon was scrabbling to her feet, grabbing for handfuls of ironmongery, as Foss rose beside her like a wave. The new man took two lithe steps down the slope, swivelling and bumping the butt of his spear into Lemon's chest as she tried to stand. She thumped back down against the rock, almost crushing Tarfel.

'Arsehole!'

'Simmer down, orange midget.'

Foss took a step toward him, his arms spread wide, and the man ducked and reversed his spear, sweeping the blade around in a wide arc that stopped an inch from Foss's bearded chin. 'Same for you, man-mountain, unless you'd rather end the day a foot shorter.'

Foss remained immobile, neither advancing nor flinching, but the wide whites of his eyes told their own story. Chel pushed himself up on his elbows, squinting against the sun's hazy glare.

'That's enough, Dalim.'

The woman's voice carried up from the trail, and Chel poked his head over the outcrop to see that the horses had reached them. One of the four was riderless, presumably that of the man above them. The lead rider, the speaker, was a grave-faced woman close to Rennic's age, great streaks of white braided into her thick, dark hair. Mail glinted beneath her riding leathers, and a curved sword was strapped at her saddle. 'You've made your point.'

Dalim waited a moment longer, then swung the spear around. He twirled it around his arm then across his back, before grounding it at his feet with a flourish.

'Prick,' Lemon said, rising to her feet with a short axe in her hand.

'Stand down, Lemon.' It was Rennic, who had emerged from his position and was approaching the riders with no great concern. Spider was two steps ahead of him.

Dalim smirked as he made his unhurried way back toward the horses. 'Lemon? What a perfect name for something sour and pissy.'

'I will eat your fucken guts, pal!'

'Lemon!'

Dalim was already past them, striding easily toward where Rennic and Spider were converging on the lead rider. He was lean and handsome, his dark hair short and braided tight. He spread his arms wide as he approached, spear gleaming in the dull light. 'The Spider of Karvik, and . . . is that . . . Gar Rennic, as I live and breathe! Spear of the South! The Eastern Eagle! I thought you'd be off waging some doomed rebellion down in the plague-lands.'

'And I thought you'd be face-down in a ditch somewhere, Dalim, fucked inside-out by passing boar. Life is full of disappointments.'

Dalim's smirk faltered a little at that, then recovered when he saw Loveless emerging from the rocks on the far side. 'And what is this gorgeous creature that dazzles my humble eyes? My darling, you must crave the company of a real man, after your travels with this bunch of festering shit-balls.'

She didn't even look at him as she walked past. 'Piss off, Dalim. You stink like a hen-house rapist.'

His mouth pressed tight, muscles pulsing at the corners of his square jaw. He looked about to respond when the lead rider spoke.

'This is not what was agreed. Your messages have been nonsensical, but we expected you in Kurtemir.' Her voice was calm, serious, her face grave. 'I am pleased we have located you, but you must understand our confusion. You may deliver your full report once we are off this slope, but I expect some manner of explanation.'

She was addressing Spider and Rennic both, but Spider stepped to one side. 'Old Beaky can fill you in, Palo.'

Rennic was leaning on his splintered staff. 'We have something for you, Palo. The messages didn't lie.'

'Enough to warrant the dereliction of your contract?'

'You can judge that for yourself. Princeling, get over here!'

Tarfel appeared, half dragged into view by Foss. He looked sullen, petulant, and was still not speaking to Chel after the horrors of the Nanaki outcasts.

'Shepherd's shit-stack,' Dalim said, eyes wide. 'Is that one of Lubel's spawn?'

Palo, the lead rider, stared hard at Tarfel. 'Young man, what is your name?'

Tarfel stared at the ground, pouting. After weeks on the road, he'd changed from the doughy, pale thing that Chel had first seen at Denirnas. His paunch had gone, devoured by hard rations and daily exertion, and exposure to the sun had darkened his pasty skin and lightened his hair. He was still a slumped, stunted thing, but it was no longer so impossible to believe that he could be related to the dashing, handsome, damaged Prince Mendel. Still, since Chel had refused his command to escape, he had retreated to a permanent sulk for the duration of their descent.

'Tell her your name, princeling.'

'Tarfel.'

'Your full fucking name, or so help me I will slap a chin onto you.'

'Tarfel Merimonsun! Tarfel Merimonsun, called Tarfel the Young, Prince of Vistirlar, third heir to Great King Lubel the First, himself called Lubel the Joiner, son of Akko the F—'

'Thank you, your highness, that is enough.' Palo gazed down at Tarfel from her mount with eyes that were neither warm nor unkind. 'I am pleased to make your acquaintance. My name is Ayla Palo.'

'Never heard of you,' Tarfel muttered toward the rocky ground.

Rennic's hand went back, but Palo stilled him with a gesture. 'I look forward to conversing with you further on our return. For now, we should be away and off this mountainside before we encounter anything untoward.'

Dalim whistled, appraising Tarfel. 'Expected the runt to be fatter.'

'Shepherd's crotch, Dalim,' Loveless called, 'he's not one of your cock-piglets.'

'Palo, wait,' Rennic said. He was staring at the horseless member of the new arrivals, a slender type in travelling furs, half-obscured by Palo's horse. 'Is that our runner?'

Palo nodded. The figure took a step forward, revealing a clean-cheeked Nanaki, barely more than a youth: the runner that Spider had dispatched before affairs at the lake had escalated. Chel blinked. Until that point, he'd given no thought to how the riders had found them.

'Huh,' he said. 'Surprised he went ahead at all. Given, you know . . .'

Beside him, Lemon shrugged. 'Mayhap friend Spider is more persuasive than we credit.'

Rennic looked to Palo for assent, then approached the boy. 'Do you understand me?'

The Nanaki returned a slow nod, his face pinched in effort. Rennic puffed air from his nose. 'You beat my best guess by half a day.' Rennic reached out and spilled a jangle of small coins into the delighted Nanaki's cupped hands. 'Now here's where we part ways. You'll want to get back to your people.'

Chel frowned. It seemed hardly fair to send the boy back into the mountains when Rennic knew full well the rest of his sept were burned to ash. He looked to Lemon, but she'd turned her head away. Foss had found a patch of loose grey dirt that warranted close inspection. A cold feeling began to grow in Chel's gut.

Rennic clapped the youth across the shoulders, steering him up the trail and away from the horses. 'Your god go with you,' he said.

The arm around the Nanaki's shoulders swivelled and clamped over his mouth, and as the boy's eyes went wide two quick cuts at his neck opened his arteries. Rennic held him tight as he thrashed and kicked, his movements spasmodic and desperate. His eyes flicked and darted, unable to see what had happened even as hot life drained from him. At last, his frantic gaze fixed on Chel, locking him with a silent plea. Chel could not break away, feeling every thudding heartbeat against his ears with conspirator's guilt. It took him a good few breaths to realize that the boy's eyes were glassy, his movements stilled.

It was not the first time Chel had seen someone die, but it was the first time he'd stared into their eyes as they did so. The cold in his gut had become a leaden nausea, a thick, heavy thing that blistered like a bog, sending tendrils of bile up the back of his throat, teasing him to gag. Sweat coated his skin.

'Aye, fuck, man,' Lemon said.

'What the fuck did he do that for?' Chel's throat was thick, his voice cracked.

Foss stirred. 'You know the tale of Murendi the Righteous?'

Chel nodded, his mouth tight. 'Yeah, survived the murder of her clan by bandits, grew up, trained in the desert, took her revenge years later . . .'

The big man nodded. His deep eyes were sad. 'Can't risk another Murendi.'

'But we're not bandits!'

Foss sighed, his hands instinctively making the sign of the crook. 'I'm sure that would depend on who you ask.'

Rennic released the boy, and his lifeless body slumped to the rocky ground and rolled off the trail. Rennic wiped his knife and turned to walk away. Spider knelt over the corpse for a moment, then stood with a jingle as he pocketed the coins.

Rennic turned back. 'The fuck are you doing, animal?'

'Get fucked, Beaky. Weren't me who dumped coin on him then opened him to the winds.'

Chel wiped the clammy sheen from his brow with his weak hand. 'We should bury him.' His voice was trembling at the edges, but he hoped it wasn't enough to show. 'We can't leave him out like this.'

Lemon cleared her throat. 'Aye, right, but generally, like,

the hunting types are more into burning than burying. Less for the animals to dig up, see?'

'Then we should burn him.'

Rennic looked up the slope. He looked haggard and bloody, but the ferocity of his gaze was undimmed. 'You want to build this whelp a pyre, sand-crab, you go right ahead. But you might remember that had things been different, he would have delighted in our slaughter on that mountaintop and would no doubt have feasted on our sweets with the rest of his happy sept.' He spat off to one side. 'I'll not apologize to the likes of you for doing what must be done, when no one else has the stomach for it. So think on that while you gather your pyre-wood, one-armed and whimpering, mourning the loss of a cannibal pirate who has probably gnawed on the bones of more children than you've seen summers.'

Spider nodded with a sneer. The two of them returned to the horses and Palo, who had remained stone-faced throughout.

'Who is that?' she said as they approached.

'New boy,' Rennic said before Spider could speak, and Chel felt vaguely warm.

'Andriz, eh? Hot shit, how'd you wind up with this misty shower of piss?' Dalim had come bounding back up the slope, even as the others were descending. 'Nothing good will come of travelling with these cast-iron pissants, luck of the sand-flowers be damned. They don't call me Dalim the Perspicacious for nothing.'

Loveless looked back over her shoulder. 'No, they call you Dalim the Slug-Tugger.'

Dalim flashed back a mirthless smile. 'She wants me, that one,' he said, his voice low. 'I won't let her get a sniff, that's why she's such a *dick* about everything.'

Chel nodded, face impassive. 'Uh-huh.'

'What's your name, sand-flower?'

'Chel.'

'And how do you come to be travelling with this reeking failure collective, Chel the Andriz?'

Chel looked around. His prayer over the boy's body complete, Foss had joined Lemon and the others, steering Tarfel as he went, and Chel found himself alone with Dalim on the slope. Loveless tossed a glance back at them and waved an arm.

'Get a move on, cub!'

Chel offered Dalim a gesture of apology and started to pick his way down the trail.

'Just lucky, I suppose.'

* * *

Tarfel stood before Palo, squinting up at her with Loveless at his back. The rider looked down on him with steady eyes, then swept one leg over her saddle and slid to the ground, keeping the reins in her hand. These she offered to Tarfel.

'Your highness.'

'Thank you, but I prefer to walk.'

Palo's eyebrows rose a fraction, the closest thing to a reaction Chel had seen in the time he'd been aware of her. Irked at the prince's peevishness and still giddy from Rennic's inclusive dismissal, he called out, 'He doesn't even know how to ride!'

At the heart of a circle of vocal expressions of amused, derisive astonishment, Tarfel turned back to Chel. His shattered look of betrayal stilled any residual excitement Chel felt, the warm feeling expunged and supplanted by the cold of misjudgement.

'As his highness wishes,' Palo said, and slung herself back onto the horse. The general mirth fell away beneath the sweep of her humourless stare. 'We should be on our way.'

They trudged away down the trail as a column, while high above, circling buzzards gathered against silver-veined clouds.

***

'Would you rather be a tarantula, or a hairless cat?'

Lemon had returned to one of her old favourites as she and Foss marched alongside the pack ponies. Chel walked in their footsteps, listening but holding his peace. Tarfel was ahead of them, almost striding, keeping pace between the lead riders and Rennic and Spider, who seemed in competition to establish ownership over the prince.

'What's a tarantula?'

'Great big fucken spider, hairier than your mam's arsehole.'

'Please, Lemon.'

'Go on, choose!'

'The cat, then. Spiders are disgusting creatures—' All three of them flicked their glances to their eponymous colleague, who remained out of earshot. '—with disgusting habits. Even a hairless cat has poise.'

'Aye, right, and you're all about poise, big man. Your turn.'

'Hmm. Would you rather be . . . a king, or a warlord?'

'What kind of warlord?'

'One of the Horvaun. You know: dreadstone fortress, reaver army, swathes of blood tithes, temples to demon gods.'

'Piece of piss, man. Warlord every time. I bet they have some mega-feasts.'

'But you'd be illegitimate in God's eyes. You'd have no support from the Church, no Shepherd's grace.'

'Hells, man, when were those last the same thing?'

They fell quiet, and Chel heard snatches of the conversation at the head of the column. '. . . has made the most of events in the north, after Omundi's fall,' Palo was saying. 'A royal decree, issued, of course, with the blessing of the Holy Church.'

'A royal decree? From Lubel?'

'In name only, as ever. Lubel lies yet inert, and the oaf Mendel delights in his instruction by Primarch Vassad's pet prelate.' Chel thought once more of his sister, prayed she had somehow escaped da Loran's attention. 'The decree demands new levies, a banding together to repel the foreign invaders. Even the Free Companies must contribute.'

'They mean to march on the Norts?' Rennic sounded sceptical.

'It is doubtful; their blockade seems, on the face of it, genuine. But the structures are in place for a massing of forces. The workshops and forges in Roniaman are frenzied. Black Rock teems. Come the thaw, the kingdom will be on a war footing once again.'

'He'll never keep the Names together. It will dissolve. Too many agendas.'

'Perhaps.'

'So we can look forward to another two decades of spite-fighting, or Vassad rolls a giant force over the Territories and the last of the free cities then finally crowns himself? Is there a third option?'

Palo's voice was quiet but clear.

'We perform our duty.'

Chel's skin prickled at her words.

PART III

EIGHTEEN

Sea salt laced the breeze by the time they slowed their pace. The stockade ahead of them girdled the crest of a cliff overlooking the churning grey expanse of the western sea, the ordered plantation at its walls in stark contrast to the half-cultivated scrubland that surrounded it. While they'd seen the odd goatherd on their descent, Palo had swung them well wide of what might have been considered civilization on this side of the mountains. Abandoned villages, broken walls and ruins had littered the landscape. The structure before them now was the first inhabited building of any size they'd encountered since the huts by the lake. A handful of guards lurked on the walls, their longbows starkly outlined against the ashen sky. No pennant flew overhead.

'Where are we?' Chel asked.

Whisper walked closest, her loping stride curtailed to keep pace with the remaining ponies. She gestured, more in hope than expectation.

'Water . . . Top?'

'Wavecrest,' Foss said from ahead. He looked relieved. 'Not far now.'

The guards waved them through. Inside, low stone structures with flat roofs surrounded a wide courtyard; a few rows of olive and skeletal cherry trees stretched away downslope within the walls. Gulls circled overhead, and a stiff breeze blew over them from the cliff-top. Palo walked her horse to a hewn-timber stable block, followed by Dalim and his henchmen, where they dismounted and gave their reins to a waiting groom.

Figures had emerged from the largest of the stone buildings, heading across the courtyard as Palo walked bandy-legged toward them. A youngish woman, perhaps a year or two younger than Loveless, led the group, her pregnant belly swaying as she strode. She carried a small child against one hip, while four others of varying ages orbited her. Two men and three women followed, their clothes thick and worn, their faces similar. Their expressions suggested muted surprise.

'Bouncing ball-bags,' Lemon muttered. 'Are all those babbies hers?'

Foss chuckled. 'Not much else to do out in the middle of nowhere, perhaps?'

Palo and the younger woman embraced, then began talking in a dialect that Chel gave up trying to follow. Gestures and sharp looks followed in their direction, especially toward Tarfel who remained stiff between Rennic and Spider. Chel hadn't shared a word with the prince since the mountainside, but Tarfel's sharp and jealous looks in his direction as he'd walked with the mercenaries had been impossible to miss.

The conversation at the courtyard's centre ceased, and the

pregnant woman turned toward them, a broad smile on her face. Chel realized with surprise that Palo was deferring to her. He began to wonder exactly who these people were.

'Friends,' the woman said. Her accent was thick, unfamiliar but clear. The toddler at her hip was grinning in parallel. 'You are welcome to our home. Rest yourselves. We will prepare water and food.'

'Aye, right,' Lemon said, her voice low. 'About time someone did something nice for us.'

Chel gave a rueful nod. 'Let's hope nobody tries to eat us this time.'

***

'Right, let's see how she fares. You've had long enough now.'

The last of the strapping was off, and after soaking his arm in a wooden tub of hot water, Chel's shoulder was back beneath Lemon's bony grip. She held his spindly arm with firm, cold fingers, moving it slowly one way, then the other, testing the movement and his response. Her mountain of hair was tied back from her face, which was still streaked with travel dust. Apparently, she'd not yet found time for a wash herself.

'How long have you been an— Ah!'

'Stop moaning.'

He blinked fresh tears from his eyes. The sudden sharpness of the pain had almost floored him. '—an independent contractor?' he finished.

'A freelancer?' She wrinkled her nose in thought, the freckles dancing. 'Hard to say exactly, as – ah, still your whining – I'm not sure where I'd draw the line. It's not like

I woke up one day and said to myself, "Today I shall become a mercenary, thank you, world." You know what it's like, when you're just doing something on the side while you make your plans, keep you ticking over, like, and then, well . . . Girl's got to eat, eh?'

Chel nodded. He had no idea what she meant. His shoulder was pulsing like an angry star. The wind blew in cold over the cliff-top, autumnal and gusty, making him shiver.

Lemon sat back and puffed out her cheeks. 'Well, you've made a right fucken mess of this, wee bear. Told you not to dick it about, didn't I?'

'What? What's wrong? Won't it heal?'

'Oh aye, it'll heal all right, but the joint's going to be weak, brittle. You'll need to behave yourself, do nothing silly, and we both know that's asking too much of you, isn't it?'

He flapped his mouth in protest.

'Aye, it'll probably ache in cold weather or when there's rain coming or some such shite. My congratulations, wee bear, on your first old man's hurt. It will no doubt be the first of many. Assuming your luck holds.'

She stood and turned to walk away.

'Wait! What do I do now?'

She cocked her head. 'Now? Get some clothes on and get Fossy to teach you how to get some strength back in that wanking claw of yours. My bit's done.' She shook out her hair, sending a cloud of dust and twig fragments into the air. 'Got to be some fucken booze in this slice of paradise.'

* * *

Foss was sitting in a shaft of narrow autumn sunlight between the thick roots of a great round tree at the courtyard's edge, his braids splayed over his shoulders and a carpet of fallen leaves beneath him. Loveless and Whisper sat close by; Whisper was shaving her head with a narrow, curved blade of fearsome sharpness.

'Wise to come to me, my friend.'

'It was Lemon's suggestion.'

'Then doubly so. Best not to anger the little orange one.' He ignored the shout from the courtyard's far side. 'Let your friend Foss show you some simple movements. It's going to take time, and repetition. Do you have the will, and do you have the patience?'

The smile on his face vanished. His eyes were dark and unblinking. Chel felt suddenly exposed, inadequate. Sweat prickled on his back. 'Well, I—'

Foss grinned again, breaking the spell. 'We'll see how you go, friend. Nobody's perfect, eh?'

Foss took him through a series of repetitive motions, some with a branch in his hand, most with the support of the other arm, while Chel grunted and sweated and swore through what should have been trivial endeavours. Whisper and Loveless watched, a mixture of amusement and sympathy on their faces, exchanging half-audible quips at his expense. Soon he was doubled over, feeling ready to vomit.

'It's no use. This arm is ruined. Lemon told me as much,' he gasped.

Foss chuckled. 'Really, my friend, have a little faith. Once I had an injury much like yours. And now . . .' He reached up one slab of hand, then the other, and gripped the branch above him. The tree creaked as he hauled himself upward, braids flying loose. Chel felt something stir behind him and looked down to see the stockade's children had appeared. Their gazes fell on the man heaving himself slowly up and down from the branch, their faces clouded in confusion. Then, as one, they ran forward and grabbed hold of Foss's clothes and legs, dangling from him as he pulled himself away from the ground.

'Hey! Ho! Where did you come from?'

Still, Foss pulled himself upward, as the hanging children shrieked and giggled. Chel found himself laughing as well, their mirth infectious, and Foss seemed to see the funny side as he dragged four extra little people up and down from the tree.

Chel looked over to Whisper and Loveless to share the laughter. Whisper was watching the scene with a sad smile, her eyes misty with private melancholy, while Loveless was staring at the children with obvious discomfort. She shifted to her feet, then strode away, her eyes averted. As she passed, she muttered something about alchemy, and then she was halfway across the courtyard.

'Fuck's this?' Rennic was beside him, silent in his approach, his hawk face clouded with the customary displeasure he wore like a favoured hat. Foss shooed away the giggling children and sat back down, coughing and self-conscious. Whisper barely acknowledged his presence.

'We were—'

'Don't care. Where's Loveless?'

Chel tried not to answer too quickly. 'She wandered off, said something about regents.'

'Reagents,' Foss corrected gently.

Rennic bared his teeth and nodded. It didn't seem to surprise him, and it certainly didn't please him. 'Lemon?'

'Hunting for booze.'

The air had taken on the nip of evening, the redoubled sea-wind whispering through the grove behind them, sending the lingering foliage dancing. Rennic's expression chilled the atmosphere a little further. He motioned to Whisper.

'Would you mind retrieving our illustrious colleagues?'

She blinked, her reverie dissipating, then the familiar, dispassionate professionalism returned. She nodded, and with loping strides set off across the courtyard.

Chel watched her go, scanning the open ground and the buildings around them. There was no sign of Spider. Palo and the others were somewhere inside the big house, while Dalim was sparring with his two confederates, twirling a long, plain staff as they took turns to swing training blades at him. His gloating laughter carried over the sound of the wind in the trees. 'Where's the prince? Where's Tarfel?'

Rennic didn't look at him. 'Inside.'

'Is he safe?'

'If he keeps his mouth shut.'

Chel opened his mouth to speak, then said nothing.

Whisper reappeared, Lemon slinking behind her. She had washed her face, but her expression suggested she'd found nothing to drink. Rennic turned as they approached.

'Loveless?'

'Indisposed,' Lemon said, her tone acid.

'Very well. Pay attention, fuckers. For all that fulsome ham-slapper's blithering—' he waved a hand in Dalim's direction, '—he's right about one thing. We have been lax, these past few weeks. We have been sloppy and weak. We have lost one of our number, Spider's hire or no. We have fucked up, and hard. That meat-pile confessor, white wolves, cannibal outcasts. That fucking princeling would be six times dead already, the rest of you not far behind, were it not for the boy.'

Chel shivered with adrenaline, a warm glow spreading out from his chest. He didn't even mind being called boy.

'This ends now. I will not have my company's fate teetering on the contributions of an amateur, a whelp, an invalid. This fucker can't swing a punch, he can't use a sword, hold a shield, shoot a bow . . . Nine hells, he can't even carry his share of pack-weight. *Don't you fucking smirk at me, Lemon, this is on you more than anyone.*'

The warm glow faded.

'We have been face-down in a shit-swamp of our own making. Now it's time to get the fuck up.'

'Meaning what, boss?'

'Meaning drill. Rigour and training, starting tomorrow, for as long as we billet here. We have lost our edge, and we either hone ourselves sharp again, or we die in ignominy. If the Black Hawk Company is ever going to be . . .' A cluster of figures emerged from the big house, and Rennic acknowledged their summons. 'We start at dawn,' he spat, then turned and walked away.

Chel released a long-held breath. 'Why's he so angry?'

Lemon sat down beside Foss with a sigh. 'He always gets like this when a job finishes. You know, twitchy. High-strung.'

Foss nodded. 'Likes to know where the next meal's coming from, I suppose.'

Whisper gestured, and Foss put up his hands. 'Not that he doesn't have a point, indeed.'

'Did he mean it? About me?'

Whisper pivoted a hand. *Maybe, maybe not.*

Lemon grinned. 'Suits his purpose to give us a bollocking now, but aye, right, why not? You've done us all right, wee bear. For a damned foreigner.'

Chel returned the grin, then his expression clouded.

'Wait, what do you mean, the job's finished?'

'I hear you dribbling pricks are in danger of doing some training tomorrow.'

It was Dalim, the long staff laid across his shoulders and a smirk on his clean-lined face.

'Didn't your mam ever tell you it's rude to eavesdrop, Dalim? Did you even have a mam, or did you just hatch out of a heap of cow-shite?'

Dalim swung the staff off his shoulders and twirled it in a figure of eight around his head before striking it at his heel.

'We saw that one already,' Foss said.

'I seem to find myself lacking a decent sparring partner,' Dalim said, brushing his fingernails against his jerkin. Chel looked beyond to see his henchmen and former sparring partners sitting beside a brazier in the lee of the stables, looking none too energetic. One was wrapping a bandage around his head. 'Shame the Eagle has flounced, he's decent with a pole. Any of you feeble featherweights up for a beating?'

One dark arch of eyebrow raised, he surveyed the group. Foss shook his head with a humourless smile while Lemon flicked Vs; Whisper didn't even look at him. 'What about you, Chel the Andriz? I could strap an arm if you feel it would make it a fair match. Hells, I could even wear a blindfold. What do you think? Still too much man for you, sand-flower?' Dalim's finger jabbed at his chest.

'Thanks, but I don't want to get my hand dirty.'

Dalim's face curdled in disgust. 'I stand corrected, Chel the Andriz. You're well suited to this bunch, just another reeking failure on the rank pile.'

Chel bristled. 'You keep hinting at things, Dalim. Perhaps you should put some meat on your words.'

Dalim narrowed his eyes, then smirked. 'You don't know, do you? You don't know who this liquid shit lake are.'

'I know enough.'

'If you knew enough, Chel the Andriz, you'd have no hunger for fail-meat.'

'God's bollocks, Dalim, you'd fuck the sound of your own voice if you could pin it long enough.' Loveless was a few paces away, advancing on them with a sharp and hungry expression. The diminishing sun cast a pale, yellow light across the courtyard, its twinkling shafts drifting through the rolling silver clouds as if through a prism. Even in the weakening light, it was clear her hair was no longer blue. A crest of violet now adorned her head, her fingertips stained a matching hue.

She caught Chel's stare and flashed him a flat, fleeting smile. 'Time for a change.'

'Matches your eyes,' he said, and her smile returned for another instant.

Dalim wasn't smiling, but neither did he look displeased. 'Loveless, my merry belle. Are you so anxious to feel the pounding of my weapon?' He waggled the staff to hammer home his innuendo.

Loveless pursed her lips. 'All I see is a little prick with a little stick. And I've little interest in child's games.' She drew the gleaming short sword from its dull leather scabbard, the blade glittering in the light of the newly lit braziers sparking around the courtyard.

'If we do this, we do it properly. Fetch your blade, and your balls if you can find them.'

Dalim stood and stared at the sword-point, unwavering in her extended grip. For a moment it looked like he might concede, but instead he raised his gaze to hers.

'You're a singular piece, Loveless. Wait here.'

He moved quickly off into the dusk in the direction of the stables. Loveless began to circle her arms, one at a time, loosening her shoulders, then flexing her neck and back.

Foss stirred beneath the tree. 'Are you sure this is wise, my friend? Given the boss's words a moment ago—'

She frowned without looking at him. 'Not now, Mother. I need to concentrate.'

She was dipping her chin to her shins when Dalim reappeared, unwrapping the leather that bound the blade of his spear. Chel shuffled around to Lemon and Whisper.

'Does she do this sort of thing a lot?'

Whisper tilted her palm again.

'Is she going to win?'

Unsurprisingly, the palm waggled again. Chel sighed and tried to sit back against the tree, but his nerves kept him upright and fidgeting.

Dalim untied the final cord. 'Fancy little knife you've got there, precious. Loot a tomb, did you?'

He threw off the skin that covered the blade, revealing a weapon no less fine and fearsome than Loveless's. The last red rays of sunlight cast the inlaid metal crimson as fresh blood.

'You give yourself away, Dalim. Where'd you dig that relic up?'

Chel tapped Lemon's arm. 'What do you call one of those? A spear with a blade like that?'

Her eyes remained fixed ahead. 'Glaive.'

'Glaive. Right. Thanks.'

Its cutting edge freed, Dalim whipped the weapon around him in a lethal circle, twirling and spinning as he pivoted on one foot, then the other. He finished on one leg, the other foot bent to his knee, the glaive thrust forward with the tip of its blade swaying six inches from his adversary's face.

Loveless puffed the leading crest of fringe from her eyes. 'Are we going to fight or fuck about?'

Dalim hauled back the glaive, swivelled and bounced, then cricked his neck. 'First blood?'

'To the death.'

Dalim's eyes widened and he took half a step back. Loveless grinned.

'Just messing. First blood it is.'

'If you're lucky, you'll still be pretty when this is over.'

'And if you're lucky, I'll hand you back your bollocks.'

Dalim moved with lightning speed, closing the distance between them in two strides, the glaive travelling upward in an arc as he moved. Chel gasped as the blade swished through the air, whipping past Loveless's face as she darted aside. Dalim swivelled, twisting the thrust sideways and dragging the glaive across and into her body.

'Fucking hells,' Chel said, his voice a strained whisper. 'He'll kill her!'

Steel clashed, and Loveless rolled back in a ball, the short blade held before her. She staggered to her feet, woozy and disorientated, as Dalim skipped around her. He twirled the glaive as he moved, swaying with each bounding step, then lashing out with the blade with sudden ferocity.

Loveless parried, throwing the sword into the glaive's

path. Twice, three times she blocked his blows, skittering backward with increasing desperation.

'We said first blood,' Dalim said as he feinted a swing with the blade, 'but we never said how much.' He ducked a clumsy swipe from Loveless and jabbed the butt of the haft back into her midriff in return. She tumbled backward, the sword clattering from her grip, and scrambled onto her hands and knees. Dalim pranced across, moving between her and her fallen sword, the glaive slapping at the ground before her questing fingers.

Chel looked around in alarm. 'We have to do something! He might really hurt her.' His words got no response. He became aware of more people around them, the occupants of the compound gathering in the torchlight to investigate the commotion, transfixed by the brutal duel.

'You know,' Dalim said, his entire face a smirk, 'some say that it's against the Shepherd's teachings to strike an unarmed foe.' He rested his foot on the sword. 'Myself, I don't subscribe.'

He levered his toe beneath the blade, then flicked it up, catching the hilt with his off-hand.

'Maybe I'll keep th—'

Chel looked at Foss. *Was Foss smiling? Why was Foss smiling?*

Loveless drove forward, springing from the ground like a gazelle. Dalim saw the movement, but one-handed could only flail with his weapon at her approach. Before he could drop the sword she was on him, inside the sweep of the glaive, one hand catching the haft as it passed. She twisted, guiding the weapon around her, spinning into Dalim's body and delivering a crunching elbow to the centre of his face.

He stumbled back with a howl, dropping the sword and

clutching at his nose. Loveless swung down, catching the falling sword with a dancer's grace and driving her opposite heel into Dalim's midriff. He grunted and lurched back, at last regaining control of the glaive and snapping it around with viper speed. Loveless was already away, the sword returned to her hand but held loose at her waist, and as Dalim charged forward with wild strokes she ducked and swerved away from each, fluid as spring water.

Chel's mouth was gaping.

Loveless swayed to one side as the glaive drove forward, then slapped it away with contempt as Dalim tried to swing the blade around. 'Hey, Dalim,' she said.

He growled and swung again, the glaive tearing at the air. She danced away, aside, and parried.

'Dalim.'

Another clang of steel.

'Dalim.'

'*What?*'

She reached up and tapped her nose, then waggled her eyebrows. His assault paused, Dalim reached up to his own nose. His finger came away sticky. A small trickle of blood was leaking from one nostril.

'You lose, fuck-stick.'

'You cannot be . . . You fucking sea-cow! You played me?' He was as incredulous as he was irate.

'Like a one-stringed lute.'

'What is happening here?' Palo's voice wasn't loud, but every one of them stiffened. Chel turned to see her standing at the head of a small group that included Spider, Tarfel and Rennic. Rennic radiated a cold, silent fury, which seemed to be directed more at Loveless than anyone else. She blew him a kiss.

Dalim wiped his nose with his forearm, leaving a dark streak. 'Training, comrade. A friendly wager.'

'And what were the stakes?'

Dalim paused, mouth half-open.

'Loser digs out the latrines,' Loveless said without missing a beat.

Palo nodded. 'Then let us end this matter here. I cannot think of a good reason why we would leave perfectly serviceable training weapons aside when sparring. I'm sure this oversight will not happen again.'

Loveless and Dalim nodded, as did those around Chel.

'Good.' Palo seemed satisfied. 'We'll gather to eat shortly, where we'll have much to discuss, I'm sure. Please make sure you're clean and presentable for our hosts. Thank you.'

With a few coughs and shuffled feet, the group began to disperse. With angry snuffling, Dalim retrieved the leather covering for his glaive and turned toward the stables.

'Dalim?' Palo inclined her head.

'Comrade?'

'The latrines are over there.'

Dalim's dark and handsome eyes flicked to Loveless and back, as the muscles of his jaw worked in the glowing light of the braziers. She kept her expression neutral.

'My mistake, comrade.'

He shouldered the glaive and set off the other way. Loveless watched him go, waiting to see if he shot her another look. He didn't. Chel stepped forward, but Rennic was already beside her.

'I thought we'd agreed to keep away from that oily little shit?'

'I never agreed to that.'

'Indeed, I believe you missed our gathering earlier.

Attending to your appearance?' He flicked a hand at her newly coloured hair.

She raised an eyebrow. 'A girl has to look good to feel good, boss.'

He snorted. 'Does she fuck. Lemon's living proof.' She turned to go, but he put a hand on her shoulder. 'I'm serious. It's bad news to incur the wrath of the small-minded, and that fucker has the wit of a beetle. He's going to hold a grudge.'

'I'll just have to live with that.'

'Easy thing to say . . .'

'Anything else you need to add? You heard Lady Palo, it's time to wash up and brush up.'

Rennic took in a deep breath through his hatchet nose. 'Go on. Fuck off.'

She did so.

Chel stepped beside Rennic, watching her walking away in the twilight. 'Is she all right?' he said.

'Fucked if I know,' the big man said, then turned his gaze to Chel. 'But I'm not going after her.'

* * *

Chel rounded the corner to the low wooden structure where the stockade's residents heated water, arms tucked against the evening's growing chill. Something moved in the shadows ahead of him, something hunched. He heard retching.

'Are you all right?'

The figure sat back with a resigned sigh. The light from the courtyard's braziers illuminated a shock of violet hair. Chel hurried forward.

'Loveless? What's wrong?'

She looked none too pleased to see him as she wiped spittle from her chin. Her skin was pallid, waxy from a thin layer of sweat. She waved a hand in dismissal, affecting imperious indifference.

'I'm fine.'

He crouched down beside her. 'Are you hurt?'

She maintained her glare a moment longer, then her expression broke and she sat back against the wooden structure, eyes distant. 'Hells, he was fast,' she whispered, one hand rubbing her midriff.

'I thought you were toying with him?'

She rolled her eyes. 'Had to make him think that, didn't I? Him and everyone else.' She sighed again, wincing, then pulled her shirt up around her ribs. Even in the low and flickering light, the ugly welt spreading across the base of her sternum was clear, dark fronds of bruise creeping up beneath the strapping that bound her chest. A gleam of blood had beaded at its centre.

'Fuck me,' she said. 'Looks like he won after all.' She locked eyes with Chel. 'You tell no one of this, yes, cub?'

He nodded, rigid with intent. 'No one.'

'Good.' She pulled down the shirt. 'Now let's give ourselves a rinse, eh? We should look simply sparkling for our generous hosts.'

NINETEEN

The main chamber of the large stone house was low-ceilinged and hot from half a dozen iron braziers that lined its walls. Chel and Loveless arrived to find the others already seated around a T-shaped table, lit by candles in wide-based holders. Other tables stood empty against the room's far side, stacked against the wall; the house was accustomed to hosting larger gatherings. The food laid out on the main table wasn't plentiful, but it looked more appetizing than trail rations. Chel felt a sudden hunger on seeing the golden crusts of small loaves shining in the candlelight.

Their late entry went unremarked as one of the residents of the stockade ushered them through. It was hard to tell if the man was servant, family member or vassal. Everyone they'd seen deferred to both Palo and the pregnant young woman, but Chel could determine no specific social order to their deference.

Tarfel was sitting to the left of Palo and her friend, looking sweaty and confused in the room's heat. Chel realized he'd not seen the prince since they arrived at the stockade. He'd either washed or been cleaned, and he was dressed in the closest thing to formal wear that Chel imagined was available. He did not make eye contact, but the seat beyond him was empty. Of the young woman's many children, there was no sign.

Dalim sat to Palo's right, his nose swollen and expression petulant. His hands looked red and well-scrubbed, and he looked away as Loveless sashayed past the table and plonked herself down next to Rennic. Chel made toward the empty seat beside Tarfel, when Spider strode in from a side entrance and sat himself proudly next to the prince. Chel hovered a moment, then sat down next to Foss, who winked at his approach. He caught Lemon's eye as he settled on the bench, and she gave him a questioning look. He returned it, his eyes on the flattened cables of red hair that were plastered to the side of her head. Her eyes flicked up, then back to him, and her expression darkened. Either side of him Whisper grinned and Foss chuckled.

'Don't say a fucken word, wee bear. Not one fucken word. A Clyde's tresses are her own concern.'

The pregnant woman at the table's head stood and the room fell silent. She once more bade them welcome and introduced herself as Erdi. After signalling for the remainder of the food to be brought, she excused herself and swayed out of the room, leaving them to eat. Chel watched the actions of the others at the head table carefully, anxious not to transgress any social mores. Palo began eating as soon as Erdi was through the doorway, and Chel relaxed.

Lemon had watched the woman go with a frown of deep suspicion. 'Where's she off to, then? Too good to eat with we riffraff?'

Whisper rolled her eyes and put a finger to her lips.

Foss tore off a hunk of bread and began to chew. 'Too pregnant, perhaps,' he said between mouthfuls. 'Or maybe she has those moppets to subdue.'

The general volume of the room rose as spiced wine was poured and the joints carved and shared. Chel looked up from his own food to see Tarfel looking quite cheerful, his cheeks pink and lips purpled with drink. On his far side, Spider was fixated on his platter at the exclusion of all else, so the young prince had attempted to engage Palo in conversation. His reedy voice carried over the din.

'I was beginning to worry it would be old bread and dried goat forever!' the prince exclaimed.

The big woman put down her cup and nodded to him, then resumed her meal.

'So what is this place, anyway? There are high-period Taneru ruins here, if I'm not mistaken. Was it an old sea-fort? A watchtower?'

Palo once more put down her food and turned to the prince. 'I'm afraid I don't know, your highness.'

Undaunted, Tarfel ploughed on. 'And who's the liege around here? I didn't see any pennant on the way in, is that tolerated?'

'Wavecrest has no liege, highness, beyond Erdi and her family.'

'Oh. Who's her family? I should know all the primary branches.'

'Her family are my family, highness. We are cousins.'

'Oh, she's a Palo, too? It's funny, I'm sure I've heard your name before but I can't place it.'

Palo placed her knife carefully beside her platter.

'If you wish to place it, try Farashan.'

Tarfel frowned, his stained lips moving as he navigated his memories. Chel became aware that the room had quietened, as if all present were listening in. Rennic was staring straight ahead, unseeing, his cup tight in his hand.

'Farashan? You're a long way from home, that's on the other side of the kingdom.'

'Indeed. This would have been nearly a quarter of a century ago. Before it was part of the kingdom.'

Even Chel could pick up the cues of a dangerous conversation. Tarfel was either too drunk or too ignorant.

'Oh! That was one of the big sieges, right? In the Liberation?'

'It was the first.'

'Did your family ride with my father against the heretics?'

'No.'

'With another liege of the Hallowed Union? As emissaries of the Church?'

'No.'

'I don't understand.'

'Of that I am aware.' Palo shifted in her chair. She'd removed her mail and travelling leathers, but she remained physically imposing, wide-shouldered and powerful. Her knife still rested beside the platter on the table before them, and she didn't look directly at the prince. 'Perhaps you would recognize my name's original form: Oktepalo.'

'But . . . that's the name of the godless villain that my father rescued my mother from . . .'

Chel saw the moment that Tarfel's brain caught up with the conversation. The colour drained from his face, rendering him a dark-lipped ghost in the torchlight. Before he could respond, Palo continued.

'Farashan was my family's seat for seven generations. When my cousin surrendered the city, it was on the condition that its populace – and his family – be spared. He alone would atone for whatever sins Vassad had laid at his feet. These terms were agreed.'

Tarfel swallowed hard.

Palo turned and fixed him with her gaze. Her face, like her tone, was flat, expressionless, her eyes dark pools that drank in the light. 'Do you know what happened then? Did your tutors tell you? Do they teach it at the Academy? Perhaps your father sang you the tale as he bounced you on his knee?'

The prince shook his head. Sweat shone from his forehead.

'Do you know what it means, to be crossed? For a family to be crossed?'

'To be . . . betrayed?'

'I'm talking about the . . .' she paused. '*Righteous punishment.*'

Tarfel was visibly shrinking down.

'It's where they, uh . . .'

'It's where they mark a person, then traverse their family tree. Across. Up. And down. Sisters and brothers. Mother or father, whichever carried the name. The grandparent, great-grandparent, if they still live.' Palo's eyes were still locked to Tarfel's. His eyes were slick in the torchlight, from horror, terror or both, Chel couldn't tell.

'And, of course, the children.'

Tarfel nodded, his movements spasmodic.

'And then they are executed, one by one, top to bottom. To send the message that the Shepherd is just and loving and wants only what is best for us all.'

She broke her gaze and returned to her food, biting and chewing with no great emotion.

Tarfel sat for a moment, clammy and trembling, and Chel thought he might faint. He reached out an unsteady hand and took another swig of wine, then sat a little straighter and made to speak.

'If it were up to me,' Palo said, her eyes still on her platter and the knife in her hand, 'I would have killed you the moment I saw you. I would have blinded you, castrated you, separated your limbs from your torso. At this moment, nothing would please me more than driving this knife into your body until you were empty of blood and innards. I would tan your skin for my saddle. I would make pipes of your bones.'

She set the knife down again and met his gaze.

'Be grateful that it is not up to me, your highness.'

Tarfel nodded again, cowed, silent. This time Chel was sure he was crying. Palo signalled to Dalim's erstwhile henchmen. 'Our guest has finished his meal. Please escort him to his quarters and see that he remains there comfortably.'

The two men hauled Tarfel to his feet and bustled him from the room. Before his cup had settled on the table, Palo herself stood and nodded to the remaining diners.

'I must bid you a good night, but please stay and finish at your leisure. Beds have been laid for you, and there's plenty more wine at least.' She took a deep breath, and for a moment Chel thought he saw true emotion dart across her face. Then she leaned forward, hands on the table, addressing the members of the mercenary company. 'You've done well, very well. You've surprised us. I've sent word ahead. This will be the start of something.'

She left through the other door, while Chel wondered who 'us' referred to. Dalim followed a pace behind, mouth twisted in petulant resentment. He kept sniffing his hands. Spider made a show of finishing the food on his platter, wiping his mouth, and exiting the room at a leisurely pace in the other direction.

For a moment, all was still, then the clink of wine jug on cup echoed around the room.

'Popular fellow, princey's dad, eh?' Lemon chuckled.

Rennic's scowl lingered only from habit. 'He doesn't know the half of it.'

He's not the only one, Chel thought to himself, and reached for his mug.

***

They stayed up drinking until the wine was gone, then Loveless and Whisper went to find more. Even the lanky scout was in her cups, her normally sure steps a touch unsteady, her speaking gestures more expansive, less precise. She certainly smiled more than the others. Even drunk, the rest of Rennic's crew seemed to keep their mirth internal, expressed only as barbs at each other's expense. Through the haze of wine, Chel wondered if Whisper escaped the cycle of sniping only because she lacked a tongue to lash. Foss remained gentle in his humour, Lemon perverse, Loveless contentious. Rennic was darkest of all, but as he refilled his cup for what must have been the thirtieth time, the sharp corners of his mouth were tweaked upward, his voice loud and incautious.

'Training starts tomorrow, fuckers. Remember that!'

Lemon's head was resting on the table, but she raised

her cup in acknowledgement. 'Aye, right, you mentioned.'

Chel turned his head one way, then back again, marvelling at the gap between the movement and the lurch of his consciousness. 'So, what's happening tomorrow? Is the job finished? Someone said it was finished.'

Rennic gazed at him across the table, his black eyes, for once, no longer burning with checked rage. 'Aye, it's done. Tomorrow is payday, boy. Tomorrow we get what we're owed.'

'And then what?'

'I'm buying some shiny new armour.'

'And after that?'

'Then? The future. The unwritten. The great expanse.' He waved both hands through the air, summing up the majesty of existence.

'But—'

'Why do you run?' He was leaning forward now, one elbow on the table, finger pointing. 'Did you. Why did you run?'

'I—'

Rennic slapped the table in front of Foss, who was dozing, his head on his ample chest. 'Hoy! Did you know that? Fossy? This fucker ran every morning, rain or shine. Not that you see much beyond shine in Denirnas. But up he went, off round the walls at dawn, fast as his little legs could carry him. Every fucking day for weeks.'

Foss nodded, eyes still shut. 'Mmm-hmm,' he said.

'I saw you drink a skinful of that wretched port-wine they have up there, and still you were bouncing along the following day. The fuck did you do it?'

Chel sat dumbfounded. 'How long were you watching me? Why were you watching me?'

Rennic's eyes narrowed. 'I asked you a question, boy.'

'And I asked you in return. Answers for answers, Gar Rennic. Spear of the South. Eastern Eagle.' He trotted out the names Dalim had used, trying to recapture some of their barb, and felt himself flushing as he did so.

Whatever history lay there, it got a reaction: Rennic bristled, his mighty nostrils flaring. 'Dangerous choice, boy.'

Chel held his gaze, cheeks burning. 'So is calling me boy. Last fellow who did that fell to his death in flames.'

Rennic sat back, one eyebrow raised in sceptical appraisal. 'You killed him? Didn't strike me as the slaughtering type, Chel the Andriz.'

'Well, I . . . I was beside him when he fell.'

Rennic's smile returned, wolfish, hungry. 'You're a well of surprises, aren't you, little man?'

Chel shrugged. His shoulders felt heavy. Whisper and Loveless had been gone a long time, and he was beginning to wonder if they'd gone to bed already. 'I'm only me.'

'So why do you run, only Chel?'

'Answers for answers.'

'Nine fucking hells, boy, fine. Answers for answers.'

'You first. Why were you watching me? How long for?'

'That's two, but I'm a generous soul. Lemon will tell you.' Rennic nudged Lemon beside him, who remained face-down on the table. Up came the cup in agreement. 'We watched you for as long as you were in Denirnas. We watched you because you were in Denirnas. We were watching everyone in Denirnas.'

'Why?'

'Now, now, my turn. Why the running?'

'I was usually late for—'

'Yet you took the long way around the walls. Truth. Now.'

Chel squirmed in his chair. He felt hot and tired, and his shoulder ached. 'My father.'

'What about him?'

'That's another—'

'Don't fuck about. My patience for this game is strictly fucking limited.'

Chel put up a hand. 'He used to. Run. Every day at dawn. He'd go off round the manor, look in on the settlements.'

'I'd have expected a mount, even for a little manor.'

'Father always said the tenants shouldn't have to look up to see their liege. Guards had to run to keep up. I tried to keep up, but I never could . . .'

Rennic nodded. 'When did he die?'

Chel blinked at the question's bluntness. 'How did you know—'

'Give me some credit.'

Chel recovered some poise. 'Then it's my turn. Why were you watching Denirnas?'

Rennic looked away, tutting in exasperation. 'You want this to be your question?'

'Wait, right . . . Because that was the job. For Palo.'

A sarcastic thumbs up.

'But who does Palo work for? One of the Names? The Great Powers? Outside instigators?'

His brows came down like a portcullis. 'Ask something else.'

'Wh—'

'Something. Else.'

Chel chewed, his tongue thick and furry with departed wine. 'Why did you trip me? That was you, wasn't it?'

'Ha!' The grin returned. 'Simple enough. I wanted to see what you'd do.'

'What I'd do? How about fall the fuck over?'

'Then hypothesis proven.' His dark eyes were keen in the low light.

'Ever pull the legs off an insect to see what it would do? You seem the type.'

'Are you an insect, Chel the Andriz?'

'You've not pulled my legs off yet, old man.'

'How is the arm?'

'Healing. Back to its best in no time.'

'Good to hear. You should take care of it. You never know when you might need both hands.' He flipped his knife up from the table, landing its grip on the back of his hand. His eyes still fixed on Chel, he flicked it up, rolling it around then on to the back of the other hand, before spinning it over and snatching it from the air. He drove the tip into the table's wood with a thud.

'That's nice. Almost as good as when Spider does it.'

Instead of the anger he'd expected, Rennic's face broke into a broad grin, one that reached the corners of his eyes. 'You'll do, Chel the Andriz. You'll do.' He paused. 'So explain the name. Why does an Andriz family have a name from the south-east?'

'My parents . . . They took local names, when they moved down, gave me and my sisters local names.' Chel put his chin on his hand. His throat was very dry, and his head was beginning to pulse with great foreboding. 'Did you mean what you said earlier? To the others. About me having saved you all.'

Rennic tilted his head to the side. 'Maybe.'

Heat suffused Chel's cheeks and his ears were glowing. Hot from wine, hot from pride. Hot from the feeling of Rennic weighing his value. 'Why did you bring me?'

'Pretty sure it's my turn. When did your father die?'

'When I was eight. Eleven years ago.'

'Battle?'

'Plague.'

Rennic sucked air through his teeth. 'Rest of the family?'

'Untouched. Quarantined himself.' *The black door, the heavy door, the cries beyond but never opened.*

'Good of him.'

Chel didn't respond. His teeth were grinding in his jaw, his breath coming heavy.

'Great news, degenerate booze-fiends of the world!' Loveless came striding into the room, a dark cask under her arm. 'While we found no more wine, our benevolent creator saw fit to bestow this magnificent bran—' Her eyes fell on the knife, still quivering in the table-top. 'Fuck's going on in here?'

Rennic didn't look up. 'The boy and I are getting acquainted.'

A great rumbling snore echoed around the room, Foss at its epicentre. Lemon's cup went up once more.

'I'm not a boy.'

'He's not a boy,' Rennic said with an exaggerated head-shake.

Loveless stood in the doorway, uncertain. 'Do I need to come back, or something? Is this man-time?'

'I'm a man.'

'He's a man.'

She nodded, her smile crooked. 'Fuck it then. Here's your brandy.' She dumped the cask on the table beside them. 'Good night, men. Don't forget to put Lemon away.'

'Fffuck your horsssess,' came the reply from beneath Lemon's mound of hair, as Loveless left the room.

Chel was aware of the sudden quiet in the room, as drunk as he was. Rennic had one casual hand on the brandy cask but was staring at him with sudden intensity.

'That night on the mountain, at the trapper's hut,' he said. 'You were outside.' He closed his eyes, took a long breath through his nose, but the gaze was no less fierce when it resumed. 'Is there anything I should know?'

Chel blinked and looked away, glancing first at the slumped form of Lemon, then the empty chair where Spider had sat.

He swallowed.

'No.'

Rennic nodded, then stood, hands on the table to steady himself. 'Going to need some water,' he muttered.

'Wait,' Chel said, grasping hand outstretched. 'We're not finished.'

'We're finished all right, boy.'

'Man.'

'We're finished all right, little man. Know when it's over.'

'Why did you bring me?'

'What?'

'Why bring me? Why drag me out of the palace, all the way down to the river?'

'I fancied a change of luck.'

'Be serious. Why?'

'Fine.' Rennic took a long breath, one hand on the door

frame. 'I saw you, down in the plaza. Again in the palace. Reminded me of someone. And you'd have died in that fire if we'd left you. Now, I'm going to bed.'

'Wait! Who?'

'Get some sleep, little man. Tomorrow, we get paid.'

'Wait!'

He was already gone.

TWENTY

Chel awoke to the barking of dogs in the yard, the cries of gulls over the rustle of the wind through the grove, and the pounding of a battering ram against the front of his skull. He found himself face-down in bitter drool on a pallet, stripped to his underclothes and covered with a rough blanket. His clothes and a pitcher of water lay beside the pallet, and jovial voices drifted in through the open shutters.

He dressed and struggled into the courtyard, pulling the blanket tight around his aching shoulders to find the stockade swathed in mist. Cooking smells wafted from a glimmer of fire close to the stables, along with familiar chatter.

'Would you rather be an eagle with no wings, or a fangless snake?'

'Hmm. The snake. At least if you kept your mouth shut, no one would know you were harmless. Hoy there, friend!' Foss grinned at him over the sizzling iron. 'You look as good as the orange one smells.'

'Piss off, Fossy, smell better than you raising a sweat.'

Lemon and Foss huddled over the cooking fire. Whisper sat to one side, running a sharp-stone over the edges of a frightening array of knives and bladed weaponry. She gave him a nod of acknowledgement.

Chel rubbed at his temples. He wished he'd brought the water with him. 'No formal dining room this morning?'

Lemon barked with laughter. 'Aye, right. No chance, chum – think we ran our hospitality dry when the household folk turfed us into bed in the wee hours.'

Foss's grin subsided. 'They might have left us there if you hadn't started singing.'

'Ah, balls to 'em, those kids woke themselves up. Who doesn't love a sing-song?'

'You weren't singing "The Ballad of the White Widow" then?'

Foss and Lemon stiffened, their smiles vanished.

'What's the problem with that song? Why doesn't Rennic like it?'

Foss's eyes were serious. 'He's never said why. But if one of the company has an issue with a thing, then all in the company do. That's how it works, my friend.' His smile returned. 'Now! Enjoy some mystery trail-meat with us, care of our hosts. Then, if you wish, we can go through your exercises together.'

Chel lowered himself down beside them, feeling every ache of weeks on foot, and took a grateful bite of Foss's offering. 'Everyone else up? I can't be the only one feeling like the back end of a dog.'

Whisper smirked, indicating Lemon with a twirl of the sharp-stone. Lemon blew hair from her eyes. 'Aye, right, fine, maybe I've lost one breakfast already today. I'm on the mend, though.'

Foss flipped another slab of the mystery meat on the iron. 'Our good company has survived the night, indeed. The boss is off with Lady Palo, Spider at his back no doubt.'

'Loveless?'

Foss blinked, then nodded past his shoulder. 'You walked past her, friend.'

Chel turned, finding the mist thinned behind him. Loveless was ten paces away, out in the courtyard, arcing through forms with her scabbarded blade in hand. She moved in silence, pivoting and stretching with poise and precision. Chel recognized a couple of the positions, but her movements between them were so fast and fluid and controlled that the whole practice seemed wholly alien.

Lemon grunted. 'Bit bloody keen if you ask me. I'm sure the boss didn't mean *dawn* dawn.'

Chel watched, entranced, bobbing his head as nuggets of mist drifted between them. 'She moves like a dancer.'

'Like that's any bleeding surprise.'

'What do you mean?'

Lemon gave him an even look. 'Are you yanking my plank? You're as bad as Prince Dick-head.'

'Hey, wh— Wait, where is the prince?'

The mercenaries exchanged a look. 'Lady Palo took him,' Foss said.

'Took him where?'

'Down to the jetty, I think.'

'The jetty? What's there?'

Lemon gave him a considered look. 'Boats?'

Chel was on his feet. 'Why? What's going to happen?'

Whisper's hands moved in a calming gesture, followed by a short string of motions. *It's out of our hands*. Foss nodded. 'Our bit's done now, friend. Your prince will be well looked after. Lady Palo has more honour than a sackful of lords and churchmen.'

'She said she wanted to kill him!'

'Yes. But she won't.'

'Which way is the jetty?'

Lemon stood up beside him. 'Easy, wee bear. Listen, we're down a man or two, and always looking to expand. Even the boss has said you'd be an, uh, adequate hire.'

Whisper gestured. *He said more than that.*

'Aye, right, but point stands. You could kick along with us from here. No bugger would think any less of you, except maybe Dalim, and he's a pox-riddled prick. You've already gone way farther than anyone else would.'

Chel's jaw was set. 'I swore an oath.'

Foss stood too. 'So did we all, once upon a time.'

'Which way is the fucking jetty?'

With a sigh, Foss pointed. 'Mind the path, it'll be a bastard if the mist clings.'

Chel was already racing away, the blanket left in the mud.

'Didn't even hesitate. I'm a bit offended by that,' Lemon muttered.

'Keep your wits!' Foss called after him.

Lemon tossed a dismissive hand. 'Too late for that, Fossy. Far, far too late.'

***

The steps were carved straight into the cliff-side, smooth with age, slick with cooled mist and streaked with gull-shit. Chel bounded down them as quickly as he dared, arms extended for balance, the pain in his shoulder dull but persistent. He heard Rennic's voice rumble out of the mist as he approached the cliff's foot, the only visible shapes before him a run of greasy timber and a looming dark pillar that might have been a mast.

'What in hells? What about the rest?'

'It's exactly what you agreed with my comrade.' Palo's voice, steady, compassionate.

'Yeah, for a sit-and-squint. We've brought you a fucking prince!'

'And we're beyond grateful. This is a turning point for our campaign.'

Chel slowed his pace, boots slipping on the last of the wide steps.

'So, where's the material aspect of your gratitude? I've half my gear in hock and a company that's owed. We could have brought you nothing but a report of his death!'

'I understand your company has dwindled. That should mean more to go around.'

'That's low—'

'Please, Master Rennic, you know as well as any that we are neither kingdom nor church. Every copper must be accounted for. Can't it be enough to know that, for once, you will be on the winning side?'

Chel crept along the jetty, the incessant crash of the waves around them covering the creaking of the boards beneath. Man-shapes materialized at the jetty's end, Rennic's bullish form looming and stiff.

'I'm on no one's side, Palo. What am I to tell my crew?'

'Whatever you would have told them if you'd done the job you originally took. Perhaps they'd all still be with you, and you'd be less out of pocket. Who's to say? We're grateful for the windfall, but the coffers are empty.'

Rennic took a step forward. 'Perhaps I'll take my prince back, then. He's bleated plenty about his worth in ransom.'

Chel heard a whimper from Rennic's feet and realized with astonishment that Tarfel was crouched between them, wrapped in a cloak and shivering.

Palo's head tilted. 'Come, come. We both know there's no ransom to be had. Tarfel Merimonsun of Vistirlar is dead, murdered by Norts at Denirnas. The kingdom mourns.' She looked down at the huddled form at her feet. 'Your value is not in ransom, young man. But rest assured, you remain valuable.'

Chel thought he heard a muffled 'thank you' from within the cloak.

'Now, on your feet, please. The tide is slipping. My thanks again, Master Rennic, for your efforts and your sacrifice. You will be remembered, irrespective of "sides". You have my word.'

'Your word is shit to me, Palo – can I sell it? Burn it to stave off winter cold?'

Palo ignored him, turning with the risen Tarfel toward the gang of the narrow boat behind them. They were taking him aboard. Chel bounded forward.

'Hoy! Wait!'

Those on the jetty turned. Something sprang from behind Palo, a lithe figure, and Chel skidded to a stop as the blade of Dalim's glaive whipped up through the mist, halting inches from his chest.

Dalim curled his lip. His nose was still swollen, marring his easy looks. 'Chel the Andriz. You're in the wrong place.'

Chel looked beyond him, to Palo, as she stood with one foot on the gang.

'Where are you taking him?'

He could make out her face now. Her expression was guarded, but not angry. Curious, perhaps, her gaze even. 'Master Rennic, this is one of yours.'

Rennic strode over, slapping Dalim's glaive aside, his voice a growl. 'The rodent-rapist is right, boy, you're in the wrong place.'

'Lady Palo, where are you taking him?'

Palo hadn't moved any further. 'What concern is it of yours, Master Andriz?'

'I'm sworn to him, Lady Palo. At his brother's behest. I cannot leave him, nor allow harm to befall him. I'll be coming too.'

One eyebrow raised, Palo turned her gaze to Rennic. The big man shot Chel an exasperated glare, then turned to meet her.

'Interesting company you're keeping, if you'll forgive the pun,' she said.

Rennic's eyes narrowed in sardonic acknowledgement. 'He's new.'

'Is he lying?'

'No.'

She nodded to herself, then turned back to Chel. 'I'm taking your liege to a safe place, away from assassins and prying eyes. We're going to meet someone very special. And we're going to change the tide of history.'

Chel stepped forward, away from Rennic, past the snarling Dalim.

'Who? Who is *your* liege, Lady Palo?'

She offered him a sad smile. 'We have no lieges, Master Andriz. Our oaths are sworn to duty, not people.'

'That sounds confusing.'

'We make it work.'

'Then who is at the other end of the boat ride?'

She stood in silence for a moment, lips pursed, then nodded again. 'You will have to see that for yourself.'

She waved him onward, then turned and escorted the shuffling prince up the gang and onto the boat. Rennic surged after her, shunting Chel aside.

'Now wait one moment, that's my thrice-damned prince! You're going to take my prize, and the boy, and leave me here pissing in the mist? I don't fucking think so.'

Palo turned her head as she steered Tarfel aboard. 'You wish to join us, Master Rennic? I can't promise you a sympathetic audience at our destination.'

Rennic spat into the churning grey waters. 'More than I'll get here. Hold fast while I gather the crew and some supplies.'

'No time for that. We're leaving with the tide, and the tide is impatient, Master Rennic. Come aboard now or not at all.'

Chel had already started back toward the steps. He and Rennic exchanged a glance, his uneasy, Rennic's intent. 'Fuck it then. Send a runner to tell them we'll be back . . . When?'

Palo was ushering Dalim and his henchmen up the gang. 'Before long. Now or never, Black Hawk Company.'

Rennic thumped his splintered staff against the pitted boards of the jetty. 'You heard the lady, man-boy. Move your Andriz arse.'

TWENTY-ONE

The mist was no thinner away from the shore. Grey waves rolled and foamed against the hull of the narrow vessel, blurring into the curtains of mist that enveloped them. The dark tombstone cliffs were swiftly lost from view, and soon Chel heard nothing beyond the creaking of the timbers and the whispering rush of the water beneath. Even the miserable gulls seemed to have abandoned them.

He stood with his hands on the rail, breathing hard and fighting down the boiling sickness in his gut that lurched with the vessel's every rolling thrust. The pulsing in his head was diminished, but perhaps only by comparison. He took great gulps of briny air, trying to appreciate the drifting spray cooling on his clammy skin. He should have brought the blanket.

'Fuck's wrong with you?'

Rennic appeared at his elbow. He'd found something to eat, possibly a portion of the same mystery meat Foss had offered. Chel realized he'd left his own breakfast behind.

'Fresh air must not agree with me.'

'Not after a skinful of the upstairs' finest grape, I'll bet.' He took another bite, tearing off a great strip of grey meat and chewing noisily. 'Shepherd's tits, boy, pull yourself together. No such thing as a hangover at your age.'

Chel shivered at the echo of Heali's words. He swallowed with great purpose, then said, 'Where are we going?'

'Fuck knows.'

'Who does Lady Palo work for?'

'Someone with coin, God willing.'

Chel turned, his sickness fading. 'How can you not know? You must have an inkling, at least?'

Rennic turned, his eyes dark.

'Plenty of inkling, no shortage thereof. But I'm not one for making claims of knowledge I don't possess. So, I'll be keeping my counsel for now, and we'll see what our prayers bring us.'

Chel stared at him, uncertain, and he tossed his head toward the back of the boat.

'Go on, go tend to your whimpering liege.'

***

He found Tarfel at the back of the boat, huddled beneath his cloak, semi-disguised as a sack of grain. Dalim stood over him in haughty guard, maintaining perfect poise against the deck's roll, his leather-wrapped glaive held steady across his shoulders. He looked away as Chel approached, but made no move to depart. Chel steered around him, good hand against the rail, then lowered himself down beside the prince.

'Are you all right, highness?'

Tarfel's gaze was hesitant, brimming with mournful resentment.

'Oh, you.'

'Of course me, highness. I wasn't going to let them take you.'

'They seem to have taken both of us instead.'

Chel shifted against the deck. 'I don't know where they're taking us, but I stand by my oath. My life for yours.'

The prince snorted, a gentle puff of air that set his stringy fringe dancing.

'I thought you'd forgotten.'

Chel couldn't tell if he meant it as a rebuke. The prince sat staring into the drifting wall of grey beyond the rail, his head rocking with the boat's roll. His eyes were red-rimmed and glassy, but for now his tears had passed.

'You know, Vedren,' he said after a contemplative pause, 'I don't think I'm going to be ransomed. I think I'm being sold. This is the worst thing to happen since . . . since the Month of Sorrows.'

Chel wasn't sure if he was supposed to interject. 'Was that . . .?'

'Yes, when Corvel died and Father fell ill – well, he'd been a bit unsteady for a while before that, I remember, but that was when he was struck down and bedridden. Corvel died, Mendel was left horribly scarred, then Father collapsed in grief and nothing was the same. I was off to Denirnas within weeks, ward of Duke Reysel, for my own safety, and enrolled in the Academy within the year. I was only thirteen, Vedren, a little boy. Who wanted nothing more than to play games with his big brother, who'd turned overnight into a wounded, brooding soul who craved only isolation.' Tarfel waved a hand. 'He's better now, of course – you saw, he's got his humour back. But now he's the heir he has no time for games any more, I've barely seen him since I was sent away. I miss Corvel. He might have been a ruthless bastard but he was still my . . . brother . . .'

The prince's eyes were pooling again, and a single tear wandered discreetly down one pale cheek.

'I never asked for this, Vedren. I never asked to be chattel.'

'No one ever does, highness.'

Tarfel sniffed and wiped at his eye. 'I've not forgotten our bargain. Deliver me safely from what follows, I'll see you released. From everything.'

Chel nodded, jaw set. 'On my oath, highness.'

A cry turned them to the bow. Chel had little idea of how long they'd been on the water, or even how far from the shore they'd strayed, but at last the mist was shifting. Drifting grey chunks thinned and split, and patches of weak, watery sunlight shone through, the sky a mottled rose behind. The surface clouds fell away before them, and the island hove into view. It jutted from the seething water, a towering pillar of stark, chunky granite, buttressed by hollow arches, ringed by sharp little rock teeth, poking up from the foam.

At its summit, hewn directly from the island's rock, stood a structure. Small, dark squares of window travelled its walls in a spiral, while at its fringes lumpen stacks of granite had been carved into towers, topped with pale stone domes. Flat, grey walls abutted bloated formations of natural rock, following their curve and climb, and at the peak of its central dome, flanked by hazy pennants, stood a proud, giant crook.

'What in hells is that?' Chel stood, his eyes fixed on the towering icon. 'Is that a church?'

Rennic was ahead of him, knuckles white around his

staff, breathing harsh and nasal. He spun around, his whole body bristling like a startled cat. 'What fuckery is this, Palo? Are you handing us to the fucking Rose?'

Palo was at the mast, her expression unconcerned. 'Not every sacred building is a church, Master Rennic, and not every church is in Primarch Vassad's clutches.' Rennic growled, and she took a step closer. 'You'll find friends here, be at peace.' She turned and began calling commands, preparing the boat for their arrival.

'Are you armed, sand-crab?' Rennic's eyes were still on Palo's back.

Chel patted at his empty belt. 'No.'

'Then we'd better hope they're friendly as fuck up there,' Rennic said in a low voice. 'As we've got a busted staff and a skinning knife between us.'

'Chin up, shit-heads.' One of the hooded figures that had accompanied Dalim aboard was standing beside them, eyes fixed on the approaching rock-pile. 'Never seen the Silent Sepulchre before?'

Rennic's hand shot out, seized the man by the shoulder, spun him around. He jerked back the man's hood.

'Spider. The fuck are you doing here?'

Spider's bald head glimmered with spray. He snarled, unrepentant. 'Same as you. Protecting my investment. If you're chiselling extra coin for Prince Shitehawk, I'll see my half.'

Chel puffed out his chest. 'Half? You were one of seven on the job.'

Spider's glance was withering. 'And who do you think brought Beaky the job, rat-bear?' He swept an arm across the boat. 'These are my people, not his, and not yours. You are not among friends. So how about you keep your head down and your mouth shut, and you let the Spider do his work.'

He flicked the hood back over his head and stalked away.

'Prick,' Rennic muttered after him.

'He telling the truth?' Chel said. 'He's not one of your company?'

Rennic grunted. 'We go back a long way, Spider and me. Always had our separate concerns.'

'So he's the one who works for Palo, brought you the job?'

Rennic wheeled on him. 'You'd best be following his advice and all, boy. Head down, mouth shut.' He turned back toward the great column of rock and stone that drew ever closer. Flocks of pale birds wheeled and swooped around the building, burnished in the feeble light. It did not look welcoming.

***

To Chel's surprise, their boat swept wide of the island, carving a path around the savage rock teeth that enclosed it and revealing a chain of irregular, interlocking pillars in its far shadow. The island was in fact the tip of a thickening peninsular, the barren land stretching off into the receding mist toward some distant coastline. Some of the arches below the rocky formations stood overhung and lightless, no easy passage through to the sea beyond. It was toward one of these sea caves that the boat aimed.

The cave swallowed them, and as they tossed their way into darkness, Chel thought for a moment that the rock meant to consume them, to dash them against its mouth of stone teeth and devour them into a watery pit. Then torches spluttered in the darkness, and the hull bumped against netted barrels on the side of a stone jetty.

Shadowy figures on the dockside called out in a dialect Chel didn't understand, to be answered by one of Palo's men in what he assumed was the same tongue. The gangway was thrown, and a moment later their crew was disembarking into the gloom.

Rennic clubbed him on the shoulder. 'Move your Andriz arse, boy. They're hauling off our golden calf.'

Palo was leading Tarfel unprotesting down the gang, his head hung low. Dalim followed too close behind, full of superfluous swaggering menace, his glaive a balancing bar. Chel and Rennic scrambled after them, and moments later the boat was deserted, bobbing softly in the darkness beneath the Silent Sepulchre.

***

They descended into chilly darkness, the slap of the waves on the dock giving way to the plop of unseen drips from the rock that surrounded them. Chel followed in Rennic's hulking shadow, the distant light of their escort's torches glistening from the walls ahead.

'Is this a smuggler's dock?' His voice echoed strange and uncomfortable from the cold black stone. 'Where are the steps up? Are the Sisters smugglers?'

Rennic turned his head then bumped into the low ceiling before him. His enraged hiss carried down the passage, and the bobbing torches paused for a moment. 'Fucksake, boy, not now!'

They stumbled on, eyes straining, always chasing the receding light. Other passages split and disappeared into the rock, some lit by torches or candles, none apparently occupied. No stairs presented themselves. For every upward step, another downward followed.

Over the echo of their jangling footsteps came a growing hiss, like the sizzle of hot fat on an iron. It was quiet at first, but louder with every step, until the torches guttered out ahead of them and the passage widened into a wide stone chamber, its entire far wall open to the grey sea beyond.

The group fanned out in the gloom. Rennic took a step to one side and bumped his head on the low stone ceiling.

'God's bollocks! What kind of prick lives in a rocky piss-hole like this?'

A throat cleared in the darkness, a rumbling, wet gargle, slick rocks rattling in a pool.

'That would be me, Gar Rennic of the Black Hawk Company.'

Chel squinted against the haze. A large block at the cave's centre, something he'd originally taken for a rock formation, had moved.

Rennic, to Chel's surprise, did not back down. 'And who are you, Man-Sitting-In-Slimy-Darkness? You seem to have the better of me, and that's bad manners for a host.'

The shape chuckled.

'Perhaps you should all come and sit down.'

TWENTY-TWO

It wasn't until the cloaked escorts had drawn thick coverings over most of the opening to the sea and lit candles around the cave that Chel could register the surroundings, and it wasn't until two iron braziers were aflame in the cave's edges that he felt the numbing cold and concomitant anxiety ease.

The light revealed a stack of dovecotes along the far wall, beside the great window out to the sea, the occasional coo or flutter from within. Still their host lay wreathed in shadow, the candle at his desk dim and futile. He wore a thick, dark cloak, his face hooded, and on the desk before him lay no papers, only small slabs of wood, some coated with wax on one side, as well as a collection of small bells of varying dimensions.

'Please forgive the draught. I do enjoy the feeling of the sea air sometimes.'

The escorts laid out low chairs, then withdrew to the cave's fringes, leaving the party standing before the desk. Tarfel almost hung from Palo's resting grip, his face expressionless, eyes vacant and downcast. Dalim stood close behind with his men, the glaive resting against one foot, his damaged face trying to betray no curiosity. Rennic and Chel stood the other side of Spider, uneasy but unbowed.

'Please, take a seat. Ayla, why don't you tell me who you've brought. Let me hear how you sound.'

Chel frowned as he seated himself behind the others. He found the hooded man's manner disconcerting. Palo sat, then leaned forward, almost dragging Tarfel with her. 'You received my message?'

The hooded man's fingers traced over one of the wax-covered boards before him.

'Indeed.'

'Then you know who sits before you.'

The hooded figure sat back in his chair. It was high-backed, almost regal, carved from dark wood and shining with moisture. Chel guessed it was lacquered, some measure of protection from airborne seawater.

'Let me hear it from him.'

Dalim reached forward and jabbed Tarfel with a finger. 'Tell him who you are, worm.'

Tarfel looked up, then around, as if waking from a dream. Dalim jabbed him again, repeating the instruction.

Tarfel told him.

The man grinned, his smile gleaming from the darkness beneath the hood.

'Truly, it is you. The lost prince of Vistirlar is among us.' He clapped his hands together. 'This is wonderful, wonderful!'

Rennic leaned forward, jaw set. 'Now that we've established we're not brimming with horseshit, how about you return us the favour?'

The man nodded. 'By all means, Master Rennic, by all means.' He stood, one hand on the desk, revealing a stocky, portly figure, probably an inch or two below Chel's height. He reached up and drew back the hood, revealing a wide, jowly face, thinning hair and pitted skin. His eye sockets were completely empty.

'My name is Raeden Torht, although you will know me by other names. You can guess which.'

Spider began to chuckle, becoming a reckless, uncontrolled laugh that echoed around the cave. 'He's blind. The Watcher in the Wind, the Grey Owl of Freemen, He Who Sees. . . you're blind!'

Torht nodded, his empty eyes pools of utter black. He seemed unruffled by the outburst.

'The Rau Rel welcome you, your highness.'

***

The shadowy servants brought out food while Palo gave a full report to Torht, the man in the high-backed chair. The platters laid before them were surprisingly rich, fine pastries and grilled meats, and once again Chel's thoughts went to the great holy building that stood somewhere above them, and its relationship with those in the dark caverns below.

Torht ate and listened in silence, his fingers reaching for dishes without hesitation, as if everything was simply where he expected it to be. He gave no indication that anything Palo told him was either news or familiar, letting her speak uninterrupted, his rubbery mouth working in constant chewing procession.

'. . . we allowed an evening of recovery at Wavecrest, then sailed with the morning tide today. The prince's sworn insisted in coming with us, as did Master Rennic, who believes his company's efforts have been insufficiently rewarded.'

Palo sat back, her report completed. She hadn't yet touched any of the food. Chel flicked a glance to Rennic beside him. The big man's eyes were narrow, but he made no move to speak.

Torht finished chewing, wiped grease from his lips and steepled his fingers. He swept his sightless gaze across the group, and Chel felt himself flinch away as it passed over him.

'Who, apart from those here present,' the so-called Watcher said, 'knows that Prince Tarfel is alive?'

Palo looked to Rennic.

'The remainder of my company. The lady there, and her people.'

'And those you encountered in your journey here?'

Chel thought back to everyone they'd seen since the Nort attack on Denirnas, and the massacre at the winter palace. The men who'd boarded the riverboat, the last of whom Foss had thrown overboard; the boat's crew, slaughtered and scuttled. The Fly had been murdered by Hurkel and the Mawn, whom in turn they'd ambushed in the mountains. The Nanaki hunters, dead and burned to ash, and the runner left for the buzzards. Things had not gone well for those whose path Prince Tarfel had crossed.

'In theory, the grand duke's son, Esen, the slippery shit, and whoever sent that meat-stack Hurkel after us.'

'And what became of Brother Hurkel?'

'The boy here broke his knees, and another of our number took his hand. Wolves got the rest of him.'

'I see. Anyone else?'

Figures loomed in Chel's mind. The Mawn. What had been the woman's name? Grassi. Grassi of the Mawn.

Rennic's eyes glittered dark in the candlelight.

'No one.'

Torht stood, and Chel caught himself flinching backward. The blind man turned to address Tarfel directly. The prince was staring at his boots, his eyes rheumy, his posture a compound slump.

'Prince Tarfel, you are a dead man.'

Tarfel stirred, blinking but long-inured to new terrors.

Torht spread his hands wide. 'And this, your highness, is the best thing to happen to you in a long while.'

Tarfel's chin lifted, a frown creasing his pallid brow.

'It is an open secret that something rots at the heart of our kingdom, your highness, and I'm sure you know it better than most. The provinces have been riven by plague and warfare, nigh without interruption, for more than two decades. The loss, the destruction, the wasted lives, all incalculable.' Torht began a slow walk around the wide table, one hand tracing its edge. 'And to what end? Who has profited from all this suffering? Certainly not the common man, who has seen armies rampage criss-cross over his lands, scouring food and populace. Not the local liege, who is crushed for tithe and forces while her sworn wither and die among the plague-borne.'

Torht came to rest before the prince, who watched him with undisguised curiosity.

'Not even the Names, the great lords and ladies, whose promised plunder from new conquest has given way to ever more demands for service and manpower, who are driven from their grand homes on unending campaigns against former brothers, sisters, cousins, from the blood-crazed redoubts of the savages of the far south to the ruthless stone-holds of the northern reaches. Whose sons murder their own fathers in a power-play, in the hope of winning the favour of those one rung up this greasy ladder of horrors. Who profits? Who sits at the apex of misery?'

Tarfel only blinked. Chel wasn't sure himself if the question was rhetorical, but he was pretty sure he knew who the Watcher meant: Primarch Lo Vassad and his Order of the Rose.

Torht's smile returned, pulling at the glistening corners of his mouth as he spoke. 'I suspect you know very well the answer, highness, when you set your mind to truth. For now, let me assure you that you have not been taken for ransom. You have been spirited to safety by the only group who truly care about you, and who truly care for the fate of the kingdom. For restoring peace and prosperity to all.'

Chel glanced at Rennic. The big man's bushy eyebrows were raised, a sceptical lip curled.

'Let us acknowledge,' Torht said, 'that were it not for the efforts of those around you, you would truly be as dead as the Church's proclamations claim. It is our collective good fortune that you are not. Which brings us to this young man.'

Torht leaned back against the table and turned his sightless gaze on Chel. Chel started, then swallowed. The others were looking at him.

'Hello?' he said.

'Chel, isn't it? Vedren.'

Chel nodded, then remembered to add words. 'Yes. Do you know me?'

'Eldest of Justina and the late Antonin Chel of Barva,

Andriz inheritors. Usurped as heir by remarriage to Amiran Dalimil.'

Chel felt his cheeks flushing. 'Do you mind? That's intimate.'

Torht smiled his unpleasant smile again. 'Nothing is intimate to me, Vedren Chel. The Watcher sees all.' He waved a hand. 'In a manner of speaking.'

'Well, you don't have to say everything out in public then,' Chel said, his jaw set. The sudden attention was making him petulant; he found something irksome about the man's manner. 'Is there anything you need to tell me?'

Torht's mouth narrowed. 'Only that your efforts are appreciated, and we hope the prince is grateful for the sacrifices you have made for him.'

Chel nodded. 'Oh. Thanks.'

'So what now?' Rennic was sitting forward again, his dark eyes shining in the torchlight. 'What are you planning? And what's your budget for company work?'

Torht's grin returned, as wide as his face.

'Now, Gar Rennic, we save the kingdom.'

'How?'

Torht pointed one chubby finger in Tarfel's direction.

'With him.'

TWENTY-THREE

'Preparations are underway,' Torht said, satisfied hands resting on his stout belly. He felt around for a desk bell and gave it a sharp ring, and a moment later a silent companion appeared at his elbow, one hand on the Watcher's arm, the other carrying a torch. 'Please, follow me.'

Torht pulled the hood back over his head and strode off into the darkness, steered by the figure at his arm. Palo stood and followed without question, the hand she kept on the prince's shoulder bringing him smartly alongside. Chel and Rennic exchanged a glance, then hurried after them into the dim tunnel beyond.

Torht held forth as he walked, his voice echoing down the clammy passageway. Two more of the hooded figures had joined them from somewhere, walking in silent lockstep. 'To lift the shadow that haunts our land, we must strike at corruption's heart. We must excise the tumour, as a surgeon might say. And that tumour sits behind walls of stone and steel, for he knows full well his sins. How could he not? Lo Vassad has corrupted the sacred office beyond redemption, and none knows sin better than a primarch.'

Torchlight ahead revealed a widening of the passageway, then a carved spiral of wide stone steps twisting upward through the granite. At last, Chel thought, stairs. Already the air seemed to smell a little fresher.

'You've heard the stories, no doubt. The Primarch never leaves the tower of Black Rock. The Primarch travels incognito, sending doubles in his stead. The Primarch sees only the king and has him carried into his chambers on his sickbed. The Primarch rules the kingdom, and not your father, highness.' Tarfel stiffened at this, but Torht continued as they began to climb the stairs.

'He is protected by a legion of red confessors, who taste his food, purify his water, let none catch even a glimpse of their charge.' He chuckled, then waved his free hand. He was already slightly out of breath. 'Each of these stories carries, at its heart, a kernel of truth. Our adversary lives a life of jealous fear, terrified that at any moment the people will see him for what he truly is, and rise up!'

The air warmed as they climbed, until the stairs finished at a sturdy door of dark wood. Torht's companion paused and fished for a key from a ring at his belt, then unlocked the door with an echoing clank. Two more bolts followed before the door opened. He ushered Torht through into the darkness beyond, and the others followed. The two other hooded figures moved ahead of them, rummaging in the gloom until a shaft of cold grey daylight broke through, then widened and flooded their surroundings.

They stood in the annexe of a store-room, piled with boxes and crates, a narrow gap opened from a wall of loose stones. Sounds of activity echoed from an open archway beyond. As they were hurried into the room itself, Chel marvelled at the efforts put into disguising the door and its vestibule. The two hooded figures remained in the darkness, replacing the loose stones, and when the last slotted into place there was no longer anything to suggest that there had ever been anything there but blank, coarse wall.

Torht cleared his throat. He was wheezing a bit. His attendant had stowed his torch in a sconce.

'Please, this way.'

They passed openings as they walked, store-rooms and kitchens, where hooded figures toiled. All were absolutely silent, bar the clatter and clank of their activities. Chel saw elements of fine craftsmanship in the stonework and throughout the hallways.

As they approached a large open space, Palo called Spider, Dalim and his two henchmen to her; a moment later the four marched to the hallway's end and disappeared from view. Torht had stopped at a door. After a quick rummage with a key, he entered, the attendant steering his steps.

Inside were a simple desk and chair, rolls of pressed paper and a heavy smell of ink. Torht shuffled over beside the desk, and indicated that the prince should sit. 'There is, however, one other person permitted access to the Primarch's chambers.'

'Who?' Tarfel asked, obeying without thought. Chel and Rennic squeezed into the office, and Palo pulled the door closed behind them.

The Watcher rested one hand on the desk. To Chel's eye, he was struggling to keep down a smirk. 'The only remaining embodiment of royal power in the kingdom, highness. Your brother.'

Tarfel's expression danced through a series of emotions,

arriving finally at suspicion. 'Meaning what? That he's the Primarch's man?'

'No, no, quite the opposite. Highness, you have come to us at a crucial juncture.'

'I didn't come to you, I—'

'Your highness, we must tread carefully. Your brother is surrounded by overwhelming force at all times, ostensibly his to command, but in truth the engine of Vassad's shadow state. But his actions and proclamations are dictated by Vassad's vicious proxies. Our Primarch's vile plot has a weakness, however, a critical flaw: the power of the state must still be seen to rest with the crown, lest suspicions be aroused and light be cast upon the corruption he has wrought.'

'Meaning what?'

'Meaning, your highness, that if your brother commands, he must be seen to be obeyed. He lacks only the understanding of the wheels that turn against him, against your royal family, the kingdom and its people. He lacks only the knowledge of what he must command. And this is where you come in. Prince Mendel is the key to unlocking Vassad's stranglehold, and you are the key to his rescue.'

'I am?'

'We must be swift and judicious. There is now a window to reach your brother, to alert him of your survival and collective peril, and move to rescue your father before we are discovered. We must secure Mendel before Vassad realizes our intentions, for I dread to consider what he might do should he become aware of the noose that tightens around him. As you found yourself, highness, once Primarch Vassad deems you disposable, prince or no, a knife in the dark soon follows.'

'But, but . . . surely he wouldn't dare try to kill Mendel? He's the crown prince!'

'If he realizes he is cornered, I doubt he would hesitate for an instant. He's tried before, after all . . . Or do you still believe that bandits killed his elder twin, your highness?'

Tarfel paled. He placed trembling hands on the desk, visible sweat on his brow. 'You're lying!'

'Consider, highness. The time of year, the location of the ambush, for ambush it was. Two dozen highly trained, well-equipped "brigands" set upon your brothers, enough to overpower their guard, enough to leave no survivors. It is a testament to your brothers that one should give his life that the other might live, even scarred.'

'It *was* brigands! They—'

'You have seen it for yourself, highness. The men who tried to murder you in the winter palace, were they not confessors disguised as Norts? Vassad has his favoured tricks.'

Tears were leaking down Tarfel's wan cheeks. 'You're lying,' he said in a sad, small voice.

Torht nodded, and tapped the attendant's hand. 'Founin.'

The attendant reached into his robe and produced a slim tube. From the tube slid a narrow scroll, which he unfurled onto the desk before the prince. Parts of it were stained very dark.

'This is the order, highness. This is the order that Vassad gave to his agents, five years ago, commanding your brothers' deaths. Look closely, and you will see the imprint of his signet upon it. I'm told.'

Tarfel stared. The room was too cramped for Chel to feel like he could offer any comfort. Rennic was staring at the ceiling, where a narrow-bodied spider bustled over an expansive web.

Torht reached out a hand to Tarfel's shoulder. 'Vassad killed your eldest brother, your highness, and has tried to kill you. Repeatedly. Mendel is not safe while he rules.'

Tarfel swallowed, then looked up, blinking tears from his watery eyes. 'What must I do?'

'Simply write a letter.'

'Eh?'

'Winter is nearly upon us,' Torht said, his smile growing, 'but before the great and good withdraw to their palaces for the feasting season, the Star Court will gather for one last grand occasion: the King's Hunt in Talis. Your brother will attend; indeed, he will be expected to lead the hunt in your father's absence. Scattered in the dark woods, away from the eyes of the confessors, here we may finally reach him. All he needs is a message, signed and sealed by his dear little brother, telling him that you are alive and are coming to free him. We can guide him to an arranged meeting point, and there spirit him away before Vassad's thugs are any the wiser. You still have your signet?'

'Will I be going to Talis?'

'Do you wish to see your brother?'

Tarfel looked up and over and met Chel's eye. He seemed to be looking for comfort, or confirmation. Chel offered him a nod.

The prince steeled himself, wet-eyed. 'I do. What should I write?'

'Hey, hey. Wait.' Rennic was looking around the cluttered room, at each of the faces in turn, his eyes searching. 'You can't take my prince anywhere. I've not been paid yet.'

Torht raised his head from Tarfel's ear. 'You wanted greater payment, Master Rennic? Ensure that this endeavour is a success, and it can be yours.'

'Now hold on,' Rennic said. 'This "endeavour" is, what, ride out into the woods and hope princeling's brother shows? What if he doesn't? Or what if he does, and Vassad's fucking murder-boys are with him?'

'The wording in the letter will be most specific. Once Mendel is separated from his minders, he will be ours. And our party, in turn, will not be defenceless. For this journey, we will open our coffers. If, that is, Master Rennic, you are still interested in paying work?'

Rennic paused, swallowed, cleared his throat. 'If I say yes, I want a proper contract this time. In writing. And back-pay for bringing the prince.'

'You shall have it.'

'My people are back at Wavecrest, no doubt honing their skills with each passing moment—'

'They can catch us later. We must depart immediately, we daren't delay.'

'If I don't like what's in the contract—'

'Yes, yes, of course. Now please excuse me, I must help his highness with his words.'

Rennic looked decidedly unconvinced. He shot Chel a challenging look. 'I assume you'll be following your man on this mad little jaunt.'

Chel's eyes were still on Tarfel. On my oath, he thought. He nodded, and Rennic rolled his eyes. 'You realize, if you're going as his sworn man, you don't qualify for a share of the job's take? Is he even paying you? What does a sworn man make these days?'

Palo moved to open the door. Rennic caught her arm. 'You going along with this, too, Palo?'

She shook him off without a look and pulled the door open. 'Death to tyrants,' she said, and marched out.

'Fucking partisans,' Rennic muttered. 'Well, it's not like I can let you go on your own, is it?' he said to Chel. 'You two could drown in a puddle.'

***

A line of wagons stood in the courtyard, each bearing the colours or pennant of the Merciful Sisters. Many were loaded, some with ale barrels, some with medical supplies, and a few with both. Torht and his attendant walked to the vehicle at the end of the wagon line, a great wooden hospital wagon painted in the Sisters' colours, lashed to four thick-bodied oxen. Sisters milled around it. One of them moved with an evident strut, a long pole with a leather-wrapped end resting over one shoulder. Chel nudged Rennic.

'Is that Dalim?'

The big man nodded, brows drawn. 'And friends.'

Chel looked again at the figures and realized that Spider and Dalim's two henchmen made up the wagon's crew, all robed as Sisters. This mission of mercy travelled beneath a false flag.

'So that's where they went.'

Rennic grunted. 'Our friend the Watcher seems to have banked on your prince's assent.'

Torht and his attendant led Tarfel to the wagon's rear while Palo climbed up to the driver's bench. Tarfel was looking anxiously at the vehicle, almost recoiling from its bulk.

'We're travelling right away?'

'Indeed,' came Torht's reply.

'In this?'

'Rest assured, it is more comfortable inside than it looks. I'm told.'

Dalim's henchmen led out a string of pack mules, two spare for Chel and Rennic. Rennic eyed the mules with distaste. They did not look even-tempered. Rennic breathed deep through his nose, shook his head and wandered over.

A flutter of wings from above announced the flight of a dozen doves, soaring into the silver sky from somewhere deep beneath the Sepulchre. They wheeled and split, disappearing over the walls and out of sight in a dozen different directions. Chel watched them, wondering if each of them carried a different message, and to where. The partisans must have agents all over the kingdom. Everywhere . . .

Torht was beside him, his eyeless face beatific. 'You hear the doves, Founin? Great wheels have begun to turn.'

'How are you getting the message to Prince Mendel?' Chel kept his voice low, mindful of potential eavesdroppers.

Torht turned, dragging his attendant back half a pace. 'Yes, Vedren Chel?'

'If he's watched by the Thorn at all times, how are you going to get Prince Tarfel's message to him?'

Torht smiled. It was not a pleasant smile.

'The crown prince escapes their notice on special occasions. For example, when he pays a moonlit visit to his betrothed, the confessors will maintain a safe distance, lest their sacred vows be tested.'

Chel frowned. The mention of Latifah, Mendel's intended, had raised the hairs on his neck. *People call her Latifah the Dim, sometimes to her face, poor lamb.*

'If,' Torht continued, 'we had, for example, an agent in the young lady's retinue, I imagine it would be only too easy to slip a message into the prince's belongings while he was otherwise occupied.'

Chel swallowed. *You know, bit of this, bit of that. Making friends, keeping my eyes open.*

'Do you have such an agent?'

Torht's smile affected insincere uncertainty. 'Perhaps.'

I'm not a duckling, Bear.

'And what would be her name?'

'Dear Master Chel, I think you already know.'

PART IV

TWENTY-FOUR

The mule's blanket saddle chafed against Chel's raw thighs. Streaks of mud splattered the beast's legs and flanks, and Chel's boots were caked. The woods around them glistened beneath dark clouds, already thick with the promise of another storm. Chel was cold, he was sore, and he was angry.

'How in five hells did I get here?' he muttered. He glared at the great hospital wagon that rumbled on ahead of them, its iron-rimmed wheels leaving thick ruts in the squelching road. Dalim's men rode either side of it, their robes hanging heavy in the damp. A glimmer of warm light spilled from within, and Chel shivered at the sight.

'Hunted by red confessors,' he grumbled, 'almost blown up by witchfire. My shoulder ruined. Locked in a boat, shot at by Mawn, bitten by wolves. Nearly devoured by fucking cannibals!'

Rennic ignored him. His face and beard were spotted with a fine mist of mud, his knuckles on the rein rope cracked and filthy. He'd offered little conversation on their journey, lost in his own sour reverie.

'And then this guy? This Watcher. He made it sound like we should have heard of him.'

'Plenty have heard of the Watcher in the Wind.'

'Not his title. His name. Did you know him?'

Rennic sighed but didn't answer.

'It sounded made-up. I don't trust him.'

Rennic grunted, adjusting the roll of blankets that constituted his saddle. His mule flicked an ear in irritation as her feet splashed through a shining puddle. 'This is still about your sister, isn't it?'

'Is it fuck. He's basically kidnapped the prince, dragged him into some scheme against the Church, and for all we know old Watcher is planning to kill both him and his brainless brother out in the woods and blame the wolves.' He paused. 'Are there wolves out here?'

'There are wolves everywhere.'

'Right. Like I said then.'

Rennic sighed again. Chel found the sighing irritating. He wondered if this was how Rennic felt most of the time. 'You don't even know for certain that it's—'

'Of course it's my fucking sister! How else would he know who I was? About my family?' Thoughts of Sabina were uppermost in his mind, bubbling up to the exclusion of all else. For the duration of the journey he'd stewed, caught between simmering resentment toward those who'd use his sister for their political ends and his own hot shame at being so excluded. *He* should be the one putting himself in danger, not her . . .

Chel took a breath, tried to blink mud from his eyelashes. 'I swore an oath, remember? Remember those? Dalim had plenty to say about your history with keeping pledges. Said you'd broken more vows than a rutting nun.'

The anger returned to Rennic's eyes in an instant, his gaze fierce as a flash fire. 'Watch yourself, little man. You don't know a thrice-damned thing about me.'

Chel felt himself shrink back, and he coughed. 'Yeah, well, whose fault is that?' His shoulder was aching in the cold, as Lemon had said it might. 'All I'm saying is we don't know who this Watcher is.'

Rennic glared at him a moment longer, then up at Dalim, who sat hunched against the cold in Sisters' robes at the wagon's bench. 'Fuck Dalim, the fur-palmed tool. The fuck would he know about swearing service? All he does is attach himself to whatever cause he thinks will get wenches mewling. Fat chance of that.' He sat back for a moment, and the rage left him. 'As far as we're concerned, little man, that there Watcher is our client. He's paying the fee, so we do the bidding.'

'I'm not a mercenary, I'm—'

'Yes, yes, you swore an oath. Save me from another anguished repetition. But you heard him, no harm will come to your precious princes. He needs them for his grand scheme, whatever the fuck that is.'

A flight of migrating birds went cawing overhead, bellies pale, on their northward journey.

'Swear it, then.'

Rennic wiped his grubby face with his equally grubby hand, leaving grimy stripes like war-paint. 'What?'

'Swear that no harm will come to the princes.'

'I'm not the fucking Shepherd, little man. The absolute power of life and death eludes me yet, despite my tireless questing.'

Chel gave him the most level stare he could manage, given the wobbling gait of the mules along the rutted mire of the road. 'Then swear you'll protect them, if it comes to that.'

'Shepherd's cleft, you're serious.'

Rennic was quiet for a while, staring straight ahead.

'Very well. I give my oath as a man of the north that I will let no harm fall to your dear princes, should it fall within my power so to do. Happy?'

'You're from the north?'

'You don't get a nose like this by accident, man-boy. Now be quiet.'

Rennic was upright in the saddle, alert, eyes darting around the trail. All Chel heard was the slushing of the wagon's wheels, the creak and jingle of its structure, the squelching plod of the mules' hooves.

'You think it's bandits?'

'No shortage of arseholes in these parts, but in this case, no.'

Something white fluttered out of the slate-coloured sky, wheeling around the wagon before settling on the perch behind the driver's bench. Palo's robed form scooped up the bird, then banged on the wagon-side.

'Good news, little man,' Rennic said with a bitter grin. 'This eternal mule-ride may yet have an end.' He rubbed at his face again, the fresh rain loosening some of the surface mud. 'Lemon and co had better be right behind us, or they're going to miss all the fun.'

***

'This is a bit much, isn't it? He'll be on his own, that's the whole point.' Chel cast a suspicious eye over the arms and armour Dalim was distributing to his men from the barrels they'd carried up the hill on the mules' flanks.

Rennic leaned over and rummaged in the nearest barrel. 'Maybe. Hope for the best, plan for the worst. Where the fuck is Lemon? She's got all our tools.' He pulled out a rusty mail shirt and a battered-looking short sword, then pushed them into Chel's arms. 'You'll be needing these.'

Rays of weak sunlight had fought their way through the clouds, casting the hilltop fort in pale yellow light. They'd left the road at dawn, Torht and the heavy wagon with them, and travelled into the woods in the company of a local tracker and two companions. For the day's first hours their guide steered them through thicket and cloying, sodden brush, until they reached a sparsely wooded hill, proud of the surrounding woodland and the curtain of grave-grey peaks that lurked at the horizon. At the hill's cleft summit stood a ruined fort, its rugged stonework battered and dilapidated by the elements but still intact on three sides. A slender sister tower, twisted and leaning, jutted from the hill's second crest, connected to the main structure by a narrow gantry on chipped pillars.

Rennic looked up at the horizon, squinting in the hazy glare. Behind them, Spider shrugged his robe into the mud and set to work climbing the pitted exterior toward the tower-top, while the three local archers clambered up the ruined stairway inside. Dalim and his men were already taking up positions in the ruined courtyard at the tower's base.

'Let's hope the Watcher got Tarfel's message to his brother in time for the hunt,' Chel said, staring out over the woods. 'Or we're going to spend a whole day sitting around in this crumbling crap-heap for a whole lot of nothing.'

'At least it's a good day for hunting,' Rennic murmured. His eyes were distant, and Chel felt a sudden and growing sense of isolation. Had the whole court travelled to Talis? Would his sister be among them? Would she have some part in the hunt?

'Why haven't the others caught us up? It's not like that wagon was a racer.'

'Because we went halfway down the coast in the boat, little man, then four days inland from there. Give them a chance. Now collect your princeling from Palo and get him up that tower. Keep him out of sight until she signals it's time to come down, and keep an eye out for the others while you're up there.'

'You really think they can find us?'

'Whisper's with them. She could find you underwater.'

Above their heads, the pennant of the Merciful Sisters unfurled from the battlements.

TWENTY-FIVE

'Why do we need all these people?' Tarfel fidgeted with irritation and anxiety, peering over the rutted crenellations. 'And why are they all so armed? Mendel will be on his own, I was very clear in my letter.'

'I'm sure he'll try, highness,' Chel said. The mail felt heavy and constricting and smelled of damp and rotting iron. The short sword was no better; it was cold, heavy, and dull as a sermon, and set his shoulder throbbing whenever he tried to raise it to a semblance of a fighting posture.

'What if one of them shoots him? What if he sees all the weapons and turns tail? Then what?'

Chel considered a calming hand on the prince's shoulder, then decided against. 'Everyone is out of sight bar Palo and Dalim, and they're in Sisters' robes. Nothing alarming here.'

Tarfel did not look mollified. 'Do you think he's coming? Are you sure he got the message? He never sent a reply.'

'I think that might have—'

'What if he can't get away? What if one of the bloody

lords insists on riding with him and he can't shake him? What if—'

'Highness! Please. Try not to fret. Hope for the best, plan for the worst, right?'

The feeble sun drifted through maudlin cloud, but the rain held off. Chel did his best to keep the prince focused while they waited, fearing a downward spiral in the prince's thinking if too long unattended.

'What did you and our friend the Watcher talk about on the road?'

'Hmm? Oh, nothing really, this and that, politics, history. I'll say it was nice to have someone telling me what's going on for a change, though. He's an odd fellow, no doubt, but he seems trustworthy.'

Chel managed an insincere smile in return. His underlying unease toward the Watcher and his nebulous plans remained, but as he reminded himself, he was here for Tarfel. The sooner this meeting was resolved, the sooner he could find out where his sister was.

It didn't make him any less relieved that Rennic had agreed his extended contract after all.

It was mid-morning when they heard the first horn, echoing around the woods from the direction of Talis Castle. A further chorus followed in short order, and the distant yipping of hounds came and went. Chel's heart started to beat faster.

The group made ready. Rennic stood in the broken shadow of the fort, pressed against the old stone, his hair tied back and breathing steady.

Chel scanned the carpet of treetops that stretched around them in all directions. Even the roads, the shallow rivers they'd forded, were lost somewhere in the undulating spread of vegetation, dark and dewy in the skewbald sunlight. Despite Rennic's words, he began to doubt that Whisper and the rest of the crew would be able to follow them. He began to doubt that Prince Mendel would be able to find his way to them, alone or with company.

The horns moved on, growing fainter, and Chel's hope went with them.

A flock of birds burst from trees beyond the foot of the hill, and Chel realized that he could hear hoof-beats over the thump of his own pulse. He strained forward, pressed against the stone of the gantry, forgetting his tacit admonition to the prince.

Two riders had emerged from the trees, the first on a gleaming grey horse festooned with sparkling adornments. The rider carried a long spear in his free hand, a gilded sword belted to his saddle, and his breastplate and helmet glittered with filigree. As he urged the champing horse up the hillside, the rider looked every part the prince they had been expecting.

Chel remembered himself and ducked. Tarfel remained upright, peering over the wall.

'It's him! It's Mendel! He's come for me!'

'Highness, get down!'

The second rider was a bulky figure in tan and green, riding a stocky roan devoid of the first's finery, a brace of short spears bouncing in their fixings at the saddle, a long, curved sword strapped to the rider's back. The helm was dark, the guard down. The second rider stayed very close to the first.

The two riders crested the rise, horses picking their way over the overgrown rubble that marked the fort's former outer wall. Tucking his spear, the first reached up and removed his helmet, a cascade of golden hair billowing from within. The watery sun chose that moment to pierce the clouds, and for a moment the prince glowed in a shaft of honeyed light.

'Good Sisters,' he said, voice carrying easily over the battlements, 'is this the hill of the raven?'

Palo, still robed and hooded as any sister, nodded, her gaze low. Beyond the mules, Chel saw Dalim's men shifting their hunched stances, keeping the animals between themselves and the prince. Dalim himself, to his credit, had stayed where he was, beside the lump of stone that hid his glaive.

'Is this a field hospital? I'm to meet someone, you see – anyone else out here with you?' Mendel said with a friendly grin. He stowed the spear and rested his fancy helmet across the pommel of his saddle.

Palo had edged closer, keeping her hood forward, her gaze low. 'You were to come alone,' she said. 'We should kill your brother immediately.'

Chel shot a look at Tarfel, who had blanched.

'I take it this means I have the right people, as well as the right place.' Mendel frowned, his handsome features crumpled in perplexity.

'Alone.'

He spread his hands, helpless. 'Oh, come now, I could hardly leave my first sworn behind. It was struggle enough to escape the rest of the party – *"Oh look, a boar!" Whoosh!* – but they'll fret less if they know I have someone keeping an eye on me.'

The second rider flicked up the helmet's guard. The face beneath was black-eyed and malevolent and gave the surroundings a look of deep suspicion.

'Balise da Loran,' Chel groaned, as Tarfel sagged beside him.

Mendel's first sworn geed her mount a step toward Palo, unfastening one of the short spears at her saddle. Her voice was still as rough as pumice. 'Who are you, false sister? Do you have breath left to repent your lies?'

Mendel raised an arm. 'Now, now, Balise, we're here because – I hope, at least – my little brother is alive and well after all. Is that something, perhaps, that we could address before we go too far down another road?'

Before Palo could signal, Tarfel was on his feet, waving from the narrow rampart. 'Mendel! Brother! I'm here! I'm alive!'

Mendel's grin lit the hillside. 'Tarfel! What a relief! Come down here, let me embrace you.'

Tarfel was already scurrying. Chel scrambled after him, grabbing his shoulder. 'Highness, wait!'

Da Loran's spear was in her hand, held ready to throw. She looked like she knew how. She fixed her dark gaze on Palo. 'Bring him down and tell your vagrants to stand down if you want to keep your guts on the inside.'

Palo made no move.

'Very well,' da Loran said with a snarl.

Mendel was speaking very fast. 'Hold on, hold on, there's no need—'

A howl echoed from the woods below, unnerving and murderous. Another followed, then a chorus, odd-pitched and malign.

Hunkered at the edge of the gantry with the younger prince held firm, Chel exchanged a glance with the archer crouched in the shade of the upper floor. 'The fuck is that? Wolves?'

She shrugged, no less nervous. Chel found he wanted to stay close to her and her arrows. He looked for Rennic in the ruins below, but the big man was out of sight from their new position.

'Well, wolves are everywhere,' Tarfel said from beneath his grip.

The howls repeated, this time accompanied by shrieks and screams, echoing faint and protracted from around the woods. Occasional barks, growls and yelps joined them, the sound of dogs in fear.

Da Loran wheeled her horse around, spear still clenched in her fist. 'What is that? What vile trickery is this?'

Palo shook her head. 'Not us. Not us.'

Mendel looked alarmed, his earnest calm dissolved. 'What's happening?'

Rennic's head appeared through the wrecked floor beside Chel and Tarfel. 'Gird your gonads, boys and girls, looks like someone had the same idea we did.' He began to duck back below.

'Wait, what do you mean?'

'Someone's ambushing the hunting party. Get that fucking sword arm warmed up.' Then he was gone. Chel pressed himself back to the rampart's edge, peering down into the remains of the courtyard.

'Enough of this!' Da Loran rode to the edge of the hill and waved her spear in an arc, then swung around with a satisfied smile. From the woods behind her, a dozen new riders appeared, mail-clad, their shields bearing the sigil of Talis.

Chel gasped. Mendel had betrayed them, brought a heavy guard after all. His gaze snapped to the crown prince. Mendel was caught between confusion and panic, wheeling his horse in a circle. 'Balise! Balise, what's happening?'

No, Chel thought. This wasn't Mendel. This was Balise. This was the Rose.

The howling came again, much closer. It seemed to be coming from all around them. Palo dropped her arm, and Dalim dived for his glaive. Around the ruin, the archers nocked arrows.

'Highness, to me!' da Loran cried, flashing the spear to her off hand and drawing her sword, steering her horse with her knees.

'What are they doing?' Tarfel said, his voice a nervous whine. 'Don't let them hurt my brother!'

The royal guardsmen were almost clear of the trees at the foot of the hill when the first horse stumbled and fell with a scream, throwing its rider to the mud below. A second rider jerked to the side, then slid from his mount, his helm split by a vicious-bladed axe. As the other riders faltered their charge in confusion, a figure leapt from the trees, a wild-haired thing with pale, pale skin, a double-headed axe in its grip.

'Shepherd's mercy,' Chel said. 'It's Lemon!'

Two more pale figures leapt from the woods, howling and screeching as they came, manes of ash and flaxen hair flowing behind them. The three of them hurled themselves at the confused riders, falling on them with razor-edged savagery.

Chel's throat felt thick, a cold feeling in his gut flooding out the hope that had bloomed. 'That's not Lemon.'

One of the regulars on the tower's far side gave the shout. 'Horvaun!' A gurgling scream followed from the same direction, and Chel realized with horror that pale figures were already at their back. He lumbered, thick-footed, to the gantry's far side. Pale-skins flooded up the escarpment, maybe a dozen, circling the hilltop beneath the gantry. A handful were already scaling the fort's broken-edged wall, questing hands finding easy holds in the crumbled stonework.

Rennic's head reappeared from below. Before he could speak, Chel almost shrieked at him. 'What in hells are Horvaun reavers doing here? We're in the fucking midlands!'

Rennic's eyes were wide, his nostrils flared. 'Agonize later, little man. Looks like they've come after the hunt, and golden boy's trick with the guards has led them right to us. They're our problem now. When it comes to slaughter, Horvaun don't discriminate.'

'What do I do?' Chel's teeth were chattering, rattling in his skull.

Rennic locked gaze with him. 'Same old. Keep the prince alive. Don't die.' Then he dropped back through the hole in the floor, leaving Chel dry-mouthed on the gantry with the prince at his feet.

He looked up, to the tower-top, and flinched at the sight of one of the regulars lolling over the battlements above, half his skull gone and an expression of limitless surprise still plastered to his face. Dark liquid flowed down from his body, a black flood staining a channel down the grey stone. A moment later, one of the Horvaun reavers staggered into view, hands clutching at something Chel couldn't see. Flashes of movement followed, then the reaver was over the edge, arcing through the air, as limp as pudding. The body whistled past the gantry, clipping a foot in a sickly indifferent fashion, before thumping into the rubble below and rolling to a stop.

'Fucking have that!'

Spider stood at the tower's edge, arms spread wide, a

slick curved blade gleaming in each fist. For a moment, he met Chel's shocked gaze with a vicious grin, then vanished back over the roof in the direction of the climbing reavers. Chel glanced back down at the bloodied shape below. Its white skin was riddled with scars and tattoos, black, blues and reds, so much so it was hard to separate bodily damage from decoration. The reaver's face, half-covered by thick plaits of wild hair, had been painted like a skull, smeared with ash and charcoal, hollow-eyed and grinning. The reaver was not grinning now.

More were climbing the fort. Chel grabbed Tarfel's shoulder, jabbing his finger toward the twisted watchtower at the gantry's end, away from the main keep. 'Highness, we need to move. Go, go, go!'

In the courtyard below, Palo had thrown off her robes, revealing gleaming mail beneath. She waved a heavy, long-bladed sword toward the fort. 'Fall back inside!' Reavers were already breaching the courtyard through its broken walls, the archers in the tower loosing off arrow after arrow.

'Highness!'

Balise da Loran was upright in her stirrups, javelin poised to throw, eyes fixed on the hillside. The riders from the wood had made it no further. Their surviving horses milled in panic, unsure of which way lay safety in the face of the howling, snarling reavers that had capered in their midst, hacking at the bodies of the downed riders. Now the reavers were halfway up the hill, blood-sprayed and shrieking, the lead runner a giant of a man with a short axe in each hand.

'Highness, behind me!'

Da Loran twisted and hurled the javelin. It streaked from her hand, ripping through the air and straight through the lead reaver, emerging a full two feet from his back. His howls turned to gurgles as he reeled and collapsed, but his comrades continued. Da Loran swung around to see where Mendel was, snatching up her second javelin. She saw the prince backing his horse away from an injured reaver, two arrows jutting from the Horvaun's blood-streaked body, his axe swinging with mindless fury. Mendel's hunting spear was gone, smashed from his hand by an axe-swing. Without hesitation, da Loran flung the second javelin, lancing the gasping reaver for a third time, driving him to his knees. She brandished her sword and urged her mount forward, racing across to carve a gaping wound in the stricken reaver's neck.

More Horvaun had reached the hilltop, scrambling up the cleft beneath Chel's gantry. The group split, most heading for the fort's ruined opening, others going for Mendel and da Loran. An arrow flashed from the fort's lower interior, whistling high and wide, and one of the reavers flung an axe in return. Something inside made a wet crunching sound and began to whimper.

The reavers were almost inside when Dalim erupted from the darkness, his glaive whirling around his head. The reavers' attacks were repulsed in a whirl of steel, until two lunged for him simultaneously. He danced backward, up the rubble-pile, his breathing heavy, the glaive beginning to slow in his hands. Cut and furious, the reavers scented blood.

Rennic surged out from behind them, bursting from his hiding place among the rubble piles. He smashed his splintered staff into the reavers as Dalim danced forward, the glaive once more a blur. Palo appeared at his shoulder, her long sword held up more in defence than assault, guarding Dalim's open flank. Dalim pirouetted and slashed, sending sprays of arterial fluid in great arcs. Rennic was less ostentatious, but no less effective. He drove a reaver to his knees with the staff, then followed up with a fatal slice from the skinning knife at his belt.

Something clunked beside Chel, a loose piece of stone clattering to the rough floor by his foot. He turned, slower than ever in the tight mail, to see a pale hand crest the edge of the gantry, quickly joined by another.

'Highness, get behind me.' He was already regretting dragging Tarfel to the gantry's far end.

Tarfel was shrieking. 'Vedren, do something! Kill it!'

Chel hefted the short sword. His shoulder throbbed incessantly, the bone never at peace in its socket. As a head crested the parapet, he swung.

He missed. The dull blade of the heavy sword clunked against the grimy stone, spraying powdery flakes but doing no harm to the clambering reaver. Before he could drag up the sword again, the skull-face filled his vision. The reaver swung over the gantry wall, lunging forward with both hands, long, inhuman fingers wrapping his throat. His breath caught, his eyes bulging, a sudden burst of pain spreading out across his body.

Something flickered in the corner of his vision and the grip weakened. The reaver staggered sideways with a grunt, and Chel saw the arrow protruding from her thigh. The dark-eyed archer stood at the gantry's far end, her face locked in concentration, fishing for another arrow from her quiver. It stood empty, and she met Chel's gaze in panic.

Tarfel cracked a large chunk of stone over the reaver's head, and she dropped.

Chel collapsed against the wall, gasping, hands probing

his battered gullet. Unable even to summon the breath to thank the prince, he looked out over the courtyard. The reavers at the fort's opening lay curled and bleeding, but those who had come from the wood had cornered da Loran at the courtyard's far side. She was on foot, her horse fled or dragged away, facing off against three surviving reavers with her curved sword. Blood leaked from half a dozen shallow slashes on her arms. Mendel stood at her back, his helmet gone, his gilded sword held unsteady before him. He looked dazed.

One slashed at da Loran, and, as she turned to block, another stung across the backs of her legs with a thin blade. She looked like she had moments left before she fell, and then the reavers would be on Mendel.

Chel found his voice.

'Rennic! Rennic!'

The big man looked up, and Chel gestured frantically toward Mendel and da Loran.

He looked across, then back. He was breathing heavily and streaked with blood, Chel had no idea whose. 'What?' he bellowed.

'Save him!'

The dark brows dropped. Palo stepped to his elbow, gaze distant. Chel struggled to make out her words. 'Let them have him,' he imagined her say.

'Rennic! You swore!'

Palo's hand was on Rennic's arm, and this time Chel heard her urgent voice. 'Let him die! We need only the crown, not the man.'

Tarfel was shrieking, screaming both Chel's name and his brother's. Chel's voice cracked as he bellowed over the prince's squeals.

'For fuck's sake, you old bastard, keep an oath for once in your life!'

The big man bared his teeth, then pushed away from Palo. He was across the courtyard in a heartbeat, flying on giant strides, arriving with a great crack to the spine of the nearest reaver from his staff. He swivelled and brought it down on the collapsing man's back, and the splintered staff finally split, disintegrating in his grip. Rennic dropped its remains and grabbed the skinning knife, rolling over the fallen man as his comrade swung at him with an axe. Rennic's arm flashed out, once, twice, first to the groin, then the abdomen, and this time the reaver's shrieks were of agony and horror. He staggered back, ripping the skinning knife from Rennic's hand, still lodged in his gut.

Rennic rolled again to dodge a slash from the final Horvaun, who advanced on him with a desperate ferocity. He scrabbled for a weapon in the mud but found nothing, and after two more rolls he lurched to his feet. This time, when the axe came swinging around, he stepped inside the attack and grabbed the weapon's haft. The reaver stared at him, her immobile axe, then back to Rennic. He smashed his forehead against her nose, slammed an elbow against her temple then punched her throat as she wobbled.

The reaver pitched forward into the mud as Rennic walked back to retrieve his knife, then without visible emotion he cut the throats of all three Horvaun as they lay prone. Chel felt his stomach turn at the efficiency of his actions.

Da Loran knelt in the churned mud, leaning on her sword, her breath coming hard. 'I'd thank you,' she said as he approached, 'but you're doomed and damned to nine flaming hells no matter your actions. None in the Church will speak your names.'

Rennic looked at her for a moment. 'Fuck off,' he said, and walked away.

Tarfel was off, scampering along the gantry toward the rubble ramp, crying his brother's name. The dark-eyed archer was coming the other way, her bow slung, expression grave. She'd retrieved a couple of arrows, at least. She leaned aside to let the young prince pass, then fished a knife from her belt. The Horvaun at his feet was stirring, moaning and pawing at the bleeding gash on her skull. The archer approached, knife drawn.

'Wait,' Chel said, stepping in front. His voice was still ragged. 'Stop.'

The archer paused, confused. She gestured with the knife at the stunned reaver, then mimed drawing the knife across her throat.

Chel nodded. 'I know, I know. But there's been enough killing. I'm not about to murder a helpless woman.'

The archer frowned, uncomprehending. Chel couldn't tell if language or concept was the cause. He motioned knot-tying. 'Do you have any rope? Anything we can bind her with?'

The archer nodded, blank, then fished a reel of spare bowstring from a pouch. Chel took it with thanks, and bound the reaver's wrists with as much firmness as he could muster. He tried not to chafe the skin beneath; that seemed insult to injury.

'Little man! Get down here!'

He nodded to the archer, who gave him a look of deep uncertainty. 'Stay here, watch her.' He mimed pointing the bow at their prisoner, and she nodded, stowing the knife and unslinging her bow. Chel gave her a grin. 'Maybe she'll have something useful to offer, eh?'

He'd gone only three paces when he heard it, just at the edge of his hearing, as the wind lulled through the trees. The gentle clatter of wood on stone. A falling bow hitting the gantry floor.

He turned to see the archer slumping, the half-crouched reaver before her, the knife in her bloodied grip. Chel stood motionless, then with a scream he charged her, bodily throwing the reaver to the ground, her still-bound hands releasing their grip on the weapon as she fell. They flailed at each other, rolling on the stone, until Chel forced her beneath, thumping at her skull-face with a wild fist while he struggled to keep her sinewy hands from his throat. He scrabbled with his knees, his feet, finding the broken shaft that jutted from her thigh and jabbing it. She hissed and spat, snarling as she tore away his grip on her arms and thumped him sideways on the counterstroke.

Chel's vision blurred, something purple exploding before his eyes, leaving a high-pitched squeal that lingered somewhere at the back of his head. He rolled, boots scraping the gantry wall, blindly avoiding the crunch of heavy stone aimed at his head. He found himself next to the fallen knife.

Another kick to the damaged thigh brought the reaver crashing down, and he was on her again, numb fingers grasping for her bound wrists, weak hand gripping the knife to stab. He forced an opening, pressing the small blade to her throat. He pressed it hard enough to draw blood.

'Yield!' His voice was a raw mess. 'Yield!'

The reaver spat. She wrapped her arms around his weak hand and twisted, throwing him off-balance and to the ground, leaving a shallow groove scored in her neck. Then she was on him, both hands pressed to his throat, her delirious, black-ringed eyes an inch from his. Sweat and blood and saliva dripped from her chin, her mouth drawn back in a horrifying grin. Chel scrabbled and struggled, his arms dead from the elbows, his fingers too weak to prise her off. The incredible pain returned, his body locked with spasms, his movements impossible to control. His vision was dimming.

The reaver's head jerked backward, her eyes wide in shock. Something lifted her bodily off him, hauled her backward by the braided hair. Chel gasped as her choking fingers were dragged from his neck, the savage pain lingering despite their absence. A dark fist punched the reaver once, twice, then slammed her down into the gantry wall. The weakened stone crumbled, and the upper chunk of wall slid from view. For a moment, the reaver was there, her sagging body pressed against the yielding stone, and then she was gone, vanished through a spreading hole in the rampart. Something crunched among the tumble of blocks below.

Rennic's face filled his vision.

'Nine hells, boy, it's like you're doing it for a bet.'

TWENTY-SIX

Chel sat and nursed his battered throat while the remaining Rau Rel piled bodies in the shadow of the ruined fort. Rennic stood at the foot of the ramp, crusted with dried sweat and ribbons of blood. He was wiping down the skinning knife, the ruins of his staff at his feet.

Chel shot a look to the young prince, who was embracing his brother out in the courtyard, a discreet distance from where Dalim's surviving confederate and Palo were slinging corpses. Aside from the reavers, one of Dalim's men joined the pile, as did two of the archers. Chel tried to tune out the piercing wails of the narrow-faced guide.

The dark-eyed archer had been his daughter.

Chel clenched his eyes and knocked his head back against the stone, but it was no good. Nothing was different.

'Gonna ask us to bury them, rat-bear? Better get digging.'

Spider stood by the corpse-pile, little eyes glittering. He was slick with blood and looking very pleased with himself. Chel though he saw a fresh gold ring at his finger.

'Lay off him, Spider. Shepherd knows you've had enough off-days in your time,' Rennic retorted. He looked drained.

Spider's smile shifted to a sneer. 'Never sat about crying after one.'

'Maybe some quiet reflection would do you good.'

Spider made a gesture, then turned and slunk away. Rennic leaned back against the stone next to Chel.

'You all right, little man? Anything broken?'

Chel shook his head. His throat would be purple for a few days, but he'd had worse. Above, the crows wheeled.

'Actual Horvaun reavers. I've only ever heard stories . . .' What if they'd slaughtered the rest of the hunt? What if Sabina had been with them?

'I'm sure our pal the Watcher can shed some light on the why and how. Come on, I need your help shifting something.'

Chel forced himself to his feet. His shoulder was on fire again. 'Not much good at lifting for now,' he said, trying to remember Foss's exercises.

Rennic walked back around the wall, then dragged something heavy through the mud and into view. There, in the churned and blood-soaked mud, bound hand, foot, waist and mouth, and staring up at him with hate-filled eyes, lay the reaver. One of her arms was lashed against her body. It was not bending the right way.

'The fuck is this?' Chel was numb. 'Are you mocking me?'

'Get over yourself, little man. You might be criminally unable to hitch a captive, but your instincts weren't wrong. Now help me get this venomous shit-heap down the hill.'

***

Mendel had taken some convincing that his best move was to accompany them, but given the slaughter of his escort and the likelihood of more Horvaun roaming the woods between the fort and Talis Castle, Palo talked him round. Despite the elder prince's expectation that his little brother would have been accompanying him back, Tarfel surprised everyone by impressing upon his brother the importance of hearing his escorts out. Thus, the two princes descended the hill with Dalim, Spider and their remaining regulars, as Palo assured them she would retrieve a horse or mule on which to transport the stricken da Loran.

Da Loran was sitting in the mud, binding her wounds with torn strips of cloth, when Rennic and Chel dragged the reaver past her on their way toward the wood. She paid them no attention whatsoever. Palo approached her, leading one of the recaptured mules.

'About fucking time, peasant. I'm going to flay you all for this, you realize that? You think you'll survive this little outing? As soon as the prince and I are back in Black Rock, I will scour this land. I will find you, and I will take the skin from you, piece by piece. I'll show it to you, fucker. Each shred, dangling in front of your eyes. Maybe I'll make you eat it. Ha, maybe I will.'

Palo stopped before her with a heavy sigh. 'Balise da Loran.'

'Don't even speak my name, you godless bitch.'

Palo removed a small scroll and unrolled it. 'You have been found guilty of treason of the highest order, the betrayal of the common people of Vistirlar and its provinces.'

'What?' Da Loran was laughing. 'What the fuck are you babbling about?'

'As you were tried in absentia, you may make a mitigating statement before sentencing. Have you anything to say?'

'Shut your mouth and help me up. I assume that mule is for me? Stop talking. Stop talking!'

Palo nodded. 'Your statement is noted. Your sentence is unchanged.'

'Shut up! Stop talking!' Da Loran was looking around now, her eyes wild, her laughter stilled. Mendel had gone with the others. The hilltop was deserted, but for Rennic and Chel dragging their reaver.

'You! Peasants!' she called after them. 'Attend me. Your Church commands you. Now!'

Palo's voice was quiet and even, her face impassive. 'I believe you know the sentence. Do you have anything further to add?'

Da Loran pitched forward in the dirt, scrabbling on crippled legs back to where her curved sword jutted from the ground. Palo was there first, removing the sword and holding it with a steady hand.

Da Loran threw up a hand. 'No! No!'

Palo stepped to the side and swept the blade down. Still expressionless, she placed one foot and jerked the sword free, then swung it down again. Da Loran made no sound as the life left her.

Rennic yanked on the reaver, and Chel felt himself pulled along.

'What the f—'

Rennic shook his head. 'Stay on the right side of the people's court.'

They continued in silence.

TWENTY-SEVEN

Chel watched the flicker of the fire through glazed eyes, arms wrapped around his knees, his back against the wagon. It had taken them the best part of the day to retrace their steps, diminished as they were, and the evening was deep and cold by the time they reached their camp clearing. Chel had done little more than sit and watch the fire since they arrived. The screaming of his joints and wounds was distant, as if another man's. Images flashed and floated before his eyes, and at one point he choked off a sob.

Rennic levered himself down beside him. He'd got some ale from somewhere; not all of the barrels had been decoys, after all. He offered Chel a mug. Chel took it but did not drink.

'You coping, little man?'

Chel said nothing. On the far side of the clearing, the two princes were sitting side by side, tucking into whatever Founin had prepared in their absence. Tarfel, his adrenaline spent, was shaking and grinning uncontrollably. Mendel simply looked vacant, but seemed compliant enough, especially beneath Spider's watchful eye.

'Don't fret overmuch for our former colleagues. They knew what they were into. Maybe not reavers, sure, but the principle at least. And they got silver for the risk, which is more than some of us.' This with a meaningful look toward Torht, who was loitering behind the wagon, awaiting Palo's arrival.

'Does this mean nothing to you? This death? This suffering? This . . .' Chel tailed off.

Rennic took in a long breath through his nose, then sipped his ale. His expression suggested it wasn't great stuff.

'No, it's not meaningless. But I'll tell you a secret. Those who died today, they weren't friends of mine. I didn't know them. There. That's it. If I look like I'm smiling, it's because I'm alive, and so – bluntly – are the people who matter.'

'How can you say that?'

'Because it's the truth. Want my best advice? Don't make friends. Don't get close. Make sure you can cope with the loss of a fellow traveller. Because fuck knows none of us live forever.'

Chel gritted his teeth. 'And how's that approach working out for you?'

Rennic sat back. 'Not that well.'

They sat in silence for a while.

'You need to teach me to fight,' Chel said at length.

'I need to teach you to tie a fucking knot.'

'I'm serious. You said it yourself.' He turned to face the other man, grey eyes gleaming in the firelight. 'What kind of sworn can I be if I can't defend my liege?'

'You've defended him just fine so far,' Rennic said with a nod to the young prince, who sat on a barrel, beaming at his brother. 'He's healthy, like you said, and he's none to thank more than you.'

Chel's glance slid to the reaver, who now lay curled and chained to the wagon's front axle. She moaned occasionally, sometimes retching, sometimes snarling, never able to break her bonds. Beneath the skull-paint, she looked very pale and very ill.

'She nearly killed me today,' Chel said, eyes fixed on the bound and shivering form. 'Twice. Tarfel saved me the first time, and you did the second.'

'And you've saved princeling's hide a dozen times already, and – perhaps – mine, once or twice. That's how it goes. That's why we keep each other around, fuck's sake. It's certainly not for the stimulating conversation.'

'And what about the next time? What if no one's around to drag a reaver off my throat?'

Rennic pursed his lips in irritation. 'I thought you weren't a born killer?'

'Don't need to be a killer to fight. Just need to . . . not . . . get killed.'

The reaver shivered and retched again, her broken spasm ending in a low whimper. Chel shivered along with her, his loathing for her undercut by her visible suffering. 'What's wrong with her?'

'Comedown. These Horvaun berserkers, they chew something, or, I dunno, swallow it or something. Makes them, well, like you saw. Gives them the blood-rage.' He spat into the fire. 'Supposed to make them impossible to kill, give them superhuman strength. All in service to the blood-gods, of course. I say, fuck it, it addles their minds and makes them a doddle to read. Idiots.'

'So . . . So did she know what she was doing out there?'

Rennic sat back and looked at Chel, his eyes narrow. 'Aye. She knew. She knew enough.'

Chel nodded. He was quiet for a moment, then said, 'So will you teach me?'

Rennic rubbed his eyes. 'Hells, boy, we're too far gone for this now. We're maybe a week from Roniaman, less if we ramp it – and I suspect we will. How much do you think you can learn in that time?'

'More than I know now.'

***

Torht beckoned for Palo the moment she reappeared, his attendant Founin guiding him to the edge of the firelight at the wagon's rear. She was the last to arrive, leading the last of the mules down into the clearing.

'Ayla, Dalim claims to have slaughtered an entire war-band.'

Palo was stone-faced as ever. 'Maybe three dozen Horvaun attacked.' She set about tying the mule's halter to the back of the wagon. 'Despite our prince's claims, Balise da Loran came with him, and she brought a dozen guardsmen with her. The reavers set about them before they reached us at the fort.' Palo turned to the Watcher, the faintest signs of strain pulling at her features. 'How did a war-band from the southern seacoast get this far without warning, Raeden? Could the south-west be so riven by plague that they could sneak through undetected?'

Torht's hollow sockets were narrow. 'There were whispers, hints, but nothing solid enough to believe . . .'

Rennic stood with a cough. 'Uh, the boy and I, we kept one. Alive. She had this on her.' He held out a rolled scrap of jagged hide. Chel looked up, blinking. This was news.

The Watcher's expression was sharp. 'What is that, Master Rennic? Ayla, describe it.'

Palo unrolled the hide and stared at it for a long time. 'I believe it's a map. These markings are Talis Castle, these the woods. And here is a rendering of the day's moon-phase. They were targeting the hunt. The same hunt as us.'

Torht growled. 'Then there are two possibilities: the reavers were dispatched by someone with knowledge of the court's social calendar, or someone with knowledge of our intentions. I do not care for either.' He turned his sightless eyes to Palo. 'We are so close. We cannot fail, for the sake of the kingdom. Either someone is intercepting our messages, Ayla, or we have a traitor among us. We must find out.'

Palo looked back at the map, then over to where the stricken reaver lay. 'I will vouch for those present. That woman knows more. We should try asking her.' Her eyes were steady, her voice level, but Chel shivered at her words. Palo took a step toward the reaver.

Rennic coughed again. 'Already tried. We need an interpreter. We need Lemon.'

Palo's frown swung in his direction. 'She's Horvaun?'

'No, but she grew up next door. Speaks it like a native.' He turned to the Watcher. 'Where are my team? They're meant to join us.'

Torht nodded. 'And they will. Until they do, we bring the reaver with us.' He gestured to his attendant. 'Founin, ready the black doves. We must depart tonight. But first, there is the matter of our new arrival.'

***

'Your royal highnesses.'

Mendel appeared to register Torht for the first time, a new, eyeless face among his captors. His golden visage shifted to surprise, then indignation, and he jumped to his feet. 'Who are you?' he demanded. 'What do you want from us?'

Torht smiled. 'My name is Raeden Torht, your highness, but you may know me as the Watcher in the Wind. You find yourself a guest of the Rau Rel.'

Mendel's brows lowered. 'So you really are partisans. You people are a real . . . a real . . .' He tailed off, his gaze drifting.

'Voice for the downtrodden? Shield of the oppressed?' Torht offered, one hairless eyebrow raised.

Mendel nodded, scratching at his scar. 'Mmm, yes, perhaps that was it. What do you want from me? Why are you holding me and my brother?'

'All will be explained shortly, your highness. All this has been a long time coming. We shall depart very soon.'

Mendel blinked, his mane of golden hair glowing in the firelight. 'Well, we can't go anywhere without Balise. Where is Balise?'

Chel and Rennic looked at Palo.

'She is dead.'

For the first time, Mendel's composure cracked. His mouth opened and closed, his eyes unfocused. 'But . . . Her wounds . . . They weren't mortal, I thought . . .'

Tarfel jumped up beside his brother, concern etched on his young face. Chel glanced back at Palo, wondering whether she'd let the prince believe his first sworn had died of her injuries.

'I executed her.'

'WHAT? Who do you think you are? You can't go executing my sworn! I'm . . . *I'm the fucking crown prince!*'

His pale skin was boiling red in the light. Tarfel took a step back in shock.

Palo was unmoved. 'She was convicted of treason against the people of these lands by the people's court. She was in the pocket of the Church and steeped in its rank corruption. She was guilty of the murders of countless innocents. For this, and more, I executed her.'

'How fucking dare you! Are you going to execute me next?'

'It is true that you have also been tried by the court.'

'*What?*'

'Your sentence remains suspended. Your cooperation in the coming endeavour will go a long way toward its commutation.'

Mendel stood, open-mouthed, clenching and releasing his fists. Tarfel edged forward and placed one cautious hand on his shoulder. 'Perhaps it's for the best, brother.'

Abruptly, the ire left the crown prince. 'No, no, indeed. You may be right, little brother. Forgive my outburst. Long day.' He scratched at the scar again. 'Sometimes I just . . . I just . . .'

Palo walked to the mule and returned with a heavy sack, which she held out to Mendel. It dripped.

'What's this?'

'The head of your first sworn, for proper disposal or interment.'

Mendel's face curdled, but to his credit he swallowed back his reaction. 'I'd be much obliged if you'd put it with my horse.'

Palo walked away. Mendel put his arm around his brother and sagged. Chel was surprised to see Tarfel bending to support his brother. The younger prince was taller than he'd realized.

'Perhaps,' the Watcher said, 'you might feel better after a drink of this, your highness.' He produced a drinking gourd from within his robes. 'It's quite safe, I assure you – at worst it may trigger a little gas.' Torht unstoppered the gourd and took a drink himself, belched and proffered it to Mendel.

'What is it?' The crown prince looked shaken, as if the reality of his capture had hit him all at once. He did not take the gourd.

'A mere precaution, I assure you. There is a rare herb extract, perhaps a compound, I regret that I lack the alchemy to name it, that in sufficient and regular dose elicits in its subject a compliance, a pliancy. In combination with patterns of suggestion, especially delivered by those in a position of trust, the subject can be persuaded, nay, *compelled* to act in a manner of another's choosing.'

Mendel's golden brows lowered. 'You mean to . . . to . . . dose me?'

'Quite the reverse, your highness. While my agents have occasionally had cause to employ this substance on individuals of strategic importance – in service to the cause of the salvation of every subject of this great kingdom – each keeps one principle paramount: the dosage must be short-term, and carefully managed. Failure to adhere to this risks the permanent health of the subject, leading to degradation of both body and mind, and no doubt in cases of reckless disregard, death.'

Mendel had one hand halfway to his scar.

'Exactly what are you talking about? Are you saying my brother has been drugged?' asked Tarfel, his shocked face a mirror of his brother's.

'Not just your brother, your highness. A report of one

particular case reached me some time ago: a nobleman in a position of great power, once celebrated for his vigour and good health now left stricken in the prime of life, unable to rise from his bedchamber. His sworn must come before him for judgement and guidance, and his voice is so weak that his will can be expressed only through the twitches of his hands. Those in his presence complain of a curious, alchemical smell—'

'You can't mean . . . How dare you?' Mendel was crimson. Tarfel was staring at the ground, shaking his head. 'Our father is ill, not poisoned! Not . . . Not . . .'

'Coerced,' Tarfel muttered.

'Coerced!' Mendel finished.

Torht's hairless brows lifted.

'Are you so certain, your highness? Have his recent rulings not favoured the Church, most exclusively?'

'This . . . This is absurd. The Orders love our father.'

'They love his compliance, highness! The judgements, the orders you receive in your father's name are the will of the Primarch. Vassad has been dosing and controlling your father, and the kingdom with him, for almost as long as these wars have been raging. Do you know who Vassad was when your father first ascended the throne, before the Hallowed Union's wars of "Liberation"?'

Mendel shook his head. 'Who?'

'An itinerant preacher. A wandering prophet, a soothsayer. A nothing, the kind of man who goes from village to village hoping to tell fortunes for fish-heads.'

'Can't imagine fish-heads have much fortune,' Tarfel said.

Chel heard Rennic snort, but Torht clapped his hands together in anger. In the silence that followed, his voice was low and dangerous.

'By cosmic accident, highness, you and your brother were born into positions of great favour, and greater peril. Have you not felt your thoughts slipping, your mind writhing with ideas that were not your own? And your brother has been dodging Vassad's assassins since Denirnas.'

'God's breath,' Mendel murmured, flopping back down to the grass. 'Can it be true? Our father poisoned, the throne . . . the throne . . .' He frowned in concentration, scratching at the scar.

'Usurped?' Tarfel suggested.

'Usurped, exactly,' Mendel said. He sat forward, head in his hands.

'It's a lot to take in, isn't it?' Tarfel said, putting one hand on his brother's shoulder.

'Am I poisoned, Tarf?' Mendel croaked. 'Am I in their thrall? I have such trouble . . . remembering . . .'

Prince Mendel started to cry.

'Be not afraid, your highness. The draught contains sufficient remedy to begin to flush any poison from your mind and body. By the time we reach Roniaman, you will be as hale and hearty as ever.'

Mendel looked up with tearful eyes, took the gourd, and drank deeply.

A moment later, a great flapping mass issued from the wagon, and a phalanx of black-feathered doves fluttered up into the evening sky. They circled and stretched, then separated, dissipating in all directions and out of sight over the forest.

Torht felt his way to the wagon's door.

'Let us go. The wind rises and our revolution has begun!'

TWENTY-EIGHT

'If we're going to do this, we're going to do it properly.' Rennic stripped off his coat and draped it over a dangling branch, slapping his bare arms against the chill. His breath came in plumes as the last red light of the sun lit the new camp beside the soft river, its numbers already swelled with both regulars and Rau Rel partisans. Smoke from the cooking fires drifted across them.

Chel tried to stretch hours of mule-ride from his aching legs. 'What do you mean?'

'I mean I'm going to hurt you.'

'What?'

'You want to learn fast, right? Fast lessons are hard lessons, and none will come harder than this.'

Chel opened his mouth to say something about harder lessons, but something thumped into his chest and drove him backward into the mud. He sat up spluttering. 'The fuck? I wasn't ready!'

Rennic swept around him. 'Think the red confessors will ask you if you're ready? Get on your feet!' He slammed his heel down and Chel scrambled backward, stumbling into a crouch. Already his shoulder throbbed.

'Good. That's lesson four. Keep your feet. Unless you've no alternative.'

'Four? What about the others?'

Rennic tutted. 'Hells, boy, you're as bad as the Foss.' He walked round in a slow circle, and Chel shuffled with him, no longer trusting the big man's motives.

'Here's lesson one of fighting, then, although no doubt it'll be wasted on you. Ready? Good boy. Lesson one: don't fight.'

'Come on—'

'. . . unless you've no alternative.'

Chel wondered how much that phrase would punctuate Rennic's teachings. He raised an eyebrow.

'Never start a fight you can't win. And if you know a fight is coming, and you can't get away from it, you make thrice-damned sure it's over before it starts, and you're the one walking away.'

'B—'

'You hear me, boy? This isn't a fucking game we're talking about here. This is desperate people, scrapping for their lives. Unpredictable people, vicious people. You want to prance around with an antique knife on a stick, talk to that toss-pot Dalim. You want a shimmering dance of bladesmanship, I'm sure Loveless will be delighted to take you through the forms, if she can spare fifteen years to teach you. You stick with me, assuming you can, you learn to stay alive. If you're lucky. Are you lucky, boy?'

Rennic was beside him, and suddenly his foot was in front of Chel's legs, a beefy arm shunting him in the back and down into the mud once more. 'There's lesson three:

keep your fucking eyes open, and know where everyone is, and where others might be. Stay alert!'

Chel pushed himself up, ready to protest, but instinct sent him rolling to one side as Rennic's boot came smashing down again. 'Better!' came the cry as he bounced back to his feet a safe distance away.

He brushed the mud from his hands. 'What's lesson two?'

'There's no dignity in dying, no matter how nobly you do it. The most honourable warrior giving his life in sacrifice still shits his breeches the same as any peasant on a pitchfork.'

'So . . .?'

'So *don't die*.'

'Huh, Lemon said the same thing once.'

That drew a smirk from Rennic. 'Who do you think she learned from?' He crouched down and picked up a twig, then began to draw lines in the mud.

'What I mean, little man, is that the ambush is your friend. Always ambush, always surprise, put them on the ground – remember lesson four? – and finish them. Never fight fair, never spare a killing blow, never consider for a moment that what's on the other end of your blade is another living, thinking, dreaming, human being. Your enemy is your enemy, understand? You start playing the wondering game, someone *will kill you*.'

'That's . . . grim.'

'That's life, fuck-o. Deal with it or let it go.'

'Huh. What's lesson five, then?'

Rennic launched himself up from the ground and was on Chel before he could move out of the way. The big man's massive bodyweight bore him to the ground, driving the air from his lungs, one bulging inked arm crushing his own limbs against him. The other held the muddy end of the twig to his throat.

'Know your distances,' Rennic said with a grin. He smelled of sweat, of mule and dust. He drew the twig over Chel's throat, making the sound effect himself, then sat up on his knees, keeping Chel pinned beneath him.

'And that, little man, was five lessons in one. Here ends the teaching. You've got a lot to think about.'

Chel sucked air into his bruised lungs. 'That's . . . horse-shit. What about . . . techniques? What about, I don't know, how to swing a sword, hold a shield, use a knife?' He tried to sit up but Rennic's thick thighs kept him prone.

'Haven't you been listening, boy? Learn the fucking lessons and you won't need "techniques". Just your fucking brain and the will to do what's necessary.' He chuckled. 'Although a good knife saves time.'

'God's bollocks, boys, you've not been on the road that long, have you?' Loveless's tinkly laughter followed her voice along the river bank.

Rennic bounded to his feet, looking both self-conscious and pleased. Chel struggled up after him. 'We're not all any-port-in-a-storm-ers at this camp,' the big man said, a grin splitting his black thicket of beard. 'Unlike some.'

'Oh, get fucked. Or was that the idea?'

They embraced, and Chel felt a forgotten but familiar surge of hot jealousy. He tried to look away, but his mind wouldn't let him. Even so, he still couldn't tell if their hug was amorous or amicable. When at last he tore his gaze away, he found himself staring at Lemon, who was dragging more sacks than usual behind her. Foss and Whisper followed, leading a pair of well-laden mules. Chel was delighted to see them all, and the realization both surprised and pleased him.

Lemon waggled her eyebrows. 'What's up, fuckers? Miss me?'

'Like a treasured tapeworm,' came the reply.

***

'Ah, what did you tell them that for?' Lemon scratched at her mound of hair. 'Do all we fucken pale-skins look the same to you, is that it? Speak Horvaun like a native, aye, right!'

Rennic put down his mug with deliberate care. 'I needed to make sure you lot joined us at your earliest convenience. This seemed an excellent opportunity to align our employers' goals with ours.'

'Why didn't you ask Prince Fuck-stick or Prince Block-head? They're basically related to the fucken tribals down there.'

Loveless arched an eyebrow. 'Now who's sailing on the good ship generalization?'

'Aye, no, I'm serious. Their mam was a tribal, came north in the quiet years, before the war, part of some noble-marriage alliance bollocks. Sad thing is, fella she married was first off the wall come the old "Wars of Unity". But lucky lass she was, good King Lubel swept her off her feet in the aftermath and the rest is history. He's a fucken tribal himself and all, second-generation, mind.'

'That was the cousin Lady Palo mentioned?' Chel sat forward, enjoying the fire's warmth, his mug cradled in both hands. 'How do you know all this?'

'Mercy, do you have no scholarship in the provinces?

Sometimes I think I'm the only fucker in this kingdom who ever read a word.'

A peal of merry laughter carried over the rumbling camp, the unbridled delight of the elder prince. He seemed greatly restored by the effect of Torht's gourd. The firelight cast his golden features with a mellow glow, and once again, he shone.

'So that's the White Lion of Merimonsun,' Loveless said, as if chewing something delectable. 'Comely.'

The prince laughed again, too hard, too long. Beside him, Tarfel looked almost embarrassed.

'You can see why he did it, eh, Vassad? Offed the other one.' Lemon was staring at the crown prince, her lip curled.

Loveless nodded. 'Corvel was the heir, the schemer; some called him Shrewd. I wonder if dear Primarch Vassad felt the sands slipping away as the young prince stepped from his father's shadow. Couldn't have kept him at arm's length for long.' She sighed. 'Makes you wonder how things might be, had he survived.'

Lemon sniffed. 'He'd have made a better fist of crown princing than dingus over there.'

Rennic cleared his throat with measured menace. 'If our idiot princes can speak tribal Horvaun, they kept it to themselves. Lemon, are you saying you can't talk to our busted reaver after all?'

'Well, I've still my education of course, I'm not devoid of linguistic acumen.'

'Is that a yes?'

'Aye, but do we have to do it now? Fossy's cooking up a shank!'

Chel looked over. 'Where did he find mutton out here?'

'Who said it was mutton?' she replied with a wink.

'Please don't joke about meat, Lemon. Too soon.'

***

Lemon and Chel stood in the evening's fresh chill as Rennic stepped away to retrieve the reaver. Chel drew the woollen blanket tight around him, grateful that it wasn't raining again.

Lemon gave him a sidelong look. 'Oh, but look at your neck, wee bear! Are you sure you want to be here for this?'

He nodded, dragging the blanket up over his throat. 'I want to hear why she was there.'

Rennic reappeared, dragging a bulky mass after him. It was wrapped with rope and a length of chain, and occasionally it jerked or growled.

'Aye, fuck, that's an ugly mess.'

Rennic released the bundle at Lemon's feet. 'Yeah, we had to gag her to stop her biting the mules. Lemon, meet Breckikuristaja.'

'Brecki . . . Brecki the Strangler?' Lemon shot another sideways look at Chel's neck. 'Now there's a name with no fucken mystery to it.'

The bundle growled.

After a few minutes of fruitless, broken questioning met by snarls and grunts, Lemon threw up her hands. 'Language barrier or no, boys, I'm getting no joy from this wanker. Doubt we ever will.'

The skinning knife was already in Rennic's hand. 'Then let's put an end to this sorry chapter now.'

'Master Rennic, please stay your hand.'

Palo was behind them. Chel had no idea how long she'd been there. Lemon spun around. 'Aye, fuck, where'd you come from?'

Palo ignored her. 'She deserves a trial, as does every freeman of these lands.'

'Oh, aye, right, course she does.'

Rennic raised his eyebrows. 'A trial? For a Horvaun reaver? Palo, we watched her kin commit murder as savage as any I've ever seen.'

Palo gave him an even stare. 'I did not say that she would be acquitted.'

'Well, can we do it now?'

Palo frowned sharply, as if the question was so absurd it caused her pain to hear it. 'There is nothing like a people's quorum here. She can wait until we reach Roniaman and resolve matters there. There will be much to settle in the days that follow.'

'Seems like we'd be saving ourselves a lot of trouble—'

'No, Master Rennic. Not in the name of the free people.'

'Then what the fuck do we do with her until then? Keep feeding her? Wash her? She was none too fragrant when we met her, and she's only gone downhill since.'

Palo turned and stared off into the darkness in the direction of the river's babble.

'I'm sure you will do as your conscience directs.' With that, she strode off toward the big tents.

Rennic stared after her.

'Well, what the fuck does that mean? Who's going to risk their fingers trying to keep this wretch alive?'

Chel stared down at the battered, broken woman, the ruins of her war-paint now indistinguishable from the streaks of road-grime that coated her. Brecki was indeed none too fragrant. She'd murdered the dark-eyed archer, she'd tried to murder him too. Twice. He put one hand to the bruises on his neck and closed his eyes. Palo's words echoed in his head.

'I'll do it,' he said.

TWENTY-NINE

'Do we ride with an army now, boss?' Foss was carrying almost as much on his back as one of the mules, and easily keeping pace. He looked out over their expanded column, over Chel's head, taking in the fluttering pennants that marked the latest arrivals as they joined the rear, slogging through the churned ruins of road in the early morning drizzle.

Beyond Chel, Rennic jerked the rope on his mule, yanking its questing head from a verdant roadside bush. 'Hardly call this bunch an army. Maybe a contingent. Seems our Watcher has been calling in some favours. As long as we keep ahead . . .'

'Been a long time since we fought beneath a pennant.'

'You shit-heads better keep away from anything with a flag on it, yeah? Wouldn't want to lose one!' Dalim was jogging past them, his leather-wrapped glaive flexing against his shoulder, his step light despite the mud.

'Jog on, pickle-tickler,' Rennic said, without any particular emotion. Dalim flicked a hand-signal and continued his progress toward the wagon at the column's head, where Torht travelled in comfort with the princes.

Chel leaned forward. 'What's he talking about?'

Rennic spat into the mud, but Foss turned his head to reply. He looked pained. 'The boss and I once had an . . . unfortunate outcome to a contract. You know what a Company of Death is?'

'They guard a . . . standard?'

'Among other things.'

'And . . .' He paused, reflecting on Dalim's words. 'They defend it with their lives?'

Foss gave a sad nod. 'Yet here we are.'

'That's why he keeps calling you failures?'

'Well, that other mess at Lauwei did our reputation no favours. Nor did that dropped charge against the western breach at Paradeh.'

'Just those, then?'

Foss looked uncomfortable. 'Those . . . and perhaps some other things.'

Rennic snorted, not in mirth, but as a horse might. 'None of which we could be blamed for. Not by anyone who knew shit about shit. A contract man can't help his orders; you do the job or the job does you. And if those other company wankers think themselves too precious to work with us, well, that's their fucking issue.' He turned his head, animated now. 'And who's to say there'll be fighting this time, anyway?'

Foss looked out over the woodside, drenched and glistening grey. 'This many marching folk, the fighting will find us,' he said, so quiet it must just have been to himself.

'We've got a contract, Fossy. In writing. The pricks are going to honour it, one way or another.'

Foss looked unconvinced, running an absent hand over

his bundle of braids. 'Roads are too empty, even for this close to winter.'

Rennic nodded with a soft grunt. 'Looks like the lands are waiting to see how this one falls.'

'. . . and a kingdom holds its breath,' Foss intoned, although Chel didn't recognize the reference.

'Any news from the north?'

'Garbled. Norts departed, Norts invaded, Norts unchanged. Riots and unrest, whispers of another famine.'

'The port still blocked?'

'Heard from more than one that the new grand duke, that weaselly friend of yours, celebrated his ascension by ordering an assault on the visitors in the bay.'

'Yeah? How did that go?'

'About as well as you'd expect. He's abandoned Denirnas, fled south with his surviving household to Roniaman. Left the winter palace for the birds.'

Chel had never liked the peacocks.

A horse thundered past, throwing clumps of squelching earth from its hooves. The rider reined in at the wagon, throwing back the hood of his cloak to reveal Spider's glistening dome beneath. He exchanged low words with Palo on the driver's bench, far from Chel's hearing.

'The road was full of ill tidings,' Foss said, his eyes on the new arrival, 'sad tales. You hear about Grigol of Koba?'

Rennic grunted. 'Dead?'

'Someone carved him up in his sleep. And his wife, children, half a dozen servants, twelve hells, even the dog.'

Between them, Chel recoiled. 'The fuck they do that for?'

'Stop it barking,' Rennic said automatically. 'Thought he'd have been off the road, this time of year.'

'He was,' Foss said. 'Household back at Koronur.'

'Serious? Were they besieged?'

Foss shook his head. 'Assassins scaled the walls, scaled the keep, came in through the roof. Left the same way. Guards never raised the alarm.'

Chel followed his gaze. It was fixed on Spider, who was grinning at the unsmiling Palo.

'How far is that from here?' he said.

'Couple of days' ride, maybe, less if you weren't minded to spare the horses.'

Rennic jerked his mule onward again, then spat in irritation into the verge. 'Evil days,' he said.

'Evil days, boss.'

They plodded on in soggy silence for a while, until Foss spoke again. 'Bad time to be a member of the Executive Council, it seems.'

Rennic took a long breath in through his nose but said nothing. When it became clear he wasn't going to speak, Chel said, 'Why do you say that?'

'Two gone in a week.'

'Who was the other? Was it bad?'

'Asa Keshani. Ate something that disagreed with her at Qish Baymul.'

'She died?'

'Retched out her organs, heard it told. They were turning to jelly as they came out. Course, you can never believe everything you hear, but she's passed over, no doubt. Right in front of the local worthies.'

'Poison?'

Foss raised an eyebrow, his gaze still on Spider. 'And how would I be knowing anything about that?'

Chel gave a rueful nod. 'Evil days,' he said.
'Evil days, friend.'

***

'D'you ever feel like, I dunno, the world lost something . . . irreplaceable . . . when the empire collapsed?' Lemon said, staring across the sloping valley at the ruined bridge that marked the official bounds of Roniaman city. Beneath them the wide sweep of the Roni glittered in the rosy light of the diminishing sunset, the air already crisp and misting. The great towers of the Ronilartsei bridge itself stood proud and solitary along its broken span, huge, sinuous spirals of bone-pale stone, glowing like coral in the dying light. Behind them, the final camp bustled. When the sun rose again, they would enter the city.

'Bollocks,' Loveless said, fishing around for her wine-skin. 'The Taneru enslaved half a continent and drove it to ruin before they fucked and drank themselves into oblivion.'

'Aye, right. Thought you'd have approved of that?'

Loveless stood and took a long swig. 'Oh sure, I'm a big fan of drinking and fucking. Not at the same time, mind, tends to lead to spillage. But those Taneru arseholes mixed it all up with a shit-load of gods and *divine provenance*, while expecting their serf class to take their word for their lot in life.' She gestured with the skin at the ruined bridge. 'Who do you think built those beautiful spires? Sure as sow-shit wasn't any clean-fingered imperial citizen. No wonder the slaves buggered them all to death.'

Chel almost dropped his cup. 'That's . . . not . . . what I was taught.'

Loveless grinned. 'I like to think that's what happened.

And if you believe in something enough – and tell enough people like it's true – isn't that the real truth?'

'Er, no.'

'Well, I say it is. Hence proved.' She took another drink.

Shaking his head, Chel turned back to the valley, to the city beyond it. He thought again of Sabina, of her role in all this, of her current whereabouts. Was she somewhere within the capital, awaiting them? Was she safe? Chel had tried, several times, to confront the Watcher and demand information on his sister, but for a blind man Torht had an excellent instinct for avoiding him.

The last, low rays of the red sun slid across the landscape, slipping beneath the hard cover of black cloud overhead. They threw the far bank of the river into relief, stretching long shadows from dark bumps and bundles that rippled the terrain. The dark covering stretched for miles, all the way to the pale walls of the city itself on the distant hilltop.

'What's that?' he said to Loveless. 'On the far bank.'

'You never been to Roniaman before, cub?'

He shook his head.

'Those are the Shanties.'

***

Chel squatted before Brecki with his now-customary pitcher of water and hunks of trail-meat. She glowered up at him, the firelight reflected in her pale eyes like a manifestation of her hatred. She still flinched from his attempts to wash her, trying to bite him through the gag.

'Come on,' he muttered, waving a piece of overcooked meat in front of her. 'You need to eat.'

She glared at him, then allowed him to slide down the

gag. She immediately bit the food from his hand and set about chewing, staring into his eyes the whole time. It was hard to shake the feeling that she was visualizing chewing through him.

He stood, breaking the gaze, and the rage in her eyes faded. A moment later, she was simply chewing.

'What brought you this far north?' he murmured, too quiet for her to hear. 'Can you even show contrition for what you did? Can a reaver learn remorse?'

The lights of Roniaman twinkled across the valley. It looked pretty and peaceful, but somehow the sight set something burning in his chest.

'I'll be back for you, Brecki, when our mission is complete. You're my responsibility.'

You're my mistake, his brain added. My penance. To be kept clean and healthy, right up until her trial and execution. He thought of his father, his pronouncements on 'doing the right thing'. He thought again of the young archer, dying on the stones with a rent in her gut.

'How can it ever be wrong to do the right thing?'

Brecki was looking past him, to where Torht and the princes were talking. She was smiling.

***

Torht summoned them before dawn. Several figures loitered by the wagon in the gloom, figures wearing mail and tabards, figures with gleaming gear and clean pennants. Their band had attracted some followers with budget. The Black Hawk Company regarded the newcomers with suspicion tinged with envy.

Mendel and Torht appeared from beyond the wagon, the

crown prince dangling from the Watcher's arm in rapt attention. Founin, the attendant, slouched behind. Mendel seemed to have become utterly enamoured of his blind companion in their days together, hanging on his words with the wonder of a child. To Chel's eyes, with Balise gone Mendel had taken the Watcher as his new controller, desperate to have someone to keep his thoughts aligned.

'But how would the Names have known to send contingents?' he asked, breathless. 'We only crossed paths a few days ago.'

Torht smiled, his empty sockets crinkling beneath his cowl. 'We have a network of, you might say, like-minded folk, highness. Fellow travellers on the road to a Vistirlar free of Rose-control. I merely gave word of our situation, our progress.'

'And which Names have sent help?'

'Founin can give you a list.'

Chel sensed movement at his elbow, and turned sharply to find Rennic standing dew-slick beside him, the plume of his breath merging with the mist. He offered a mirthless grin. 'Hells, would you look at all these posh pricks, there's some coin been dropped on this one. We should *double* our fee.'

Torht stepped away from Mendel with a nod and turned to face the gathered crowd. 'Today, my friends, we will make history. Today we will reclaim our fair kingdom, our homeland, from the pernicious forces that have choked it for too long. For more than two decades, Vassad and his snarling Rose have squatted like poisonous reptiles at the heart of our state, spreading misery, disease and death. Today that ends!'

Chel found himself nodding along. Images of the past

floated unbidden into his mind, and he clenched his eyes and shook his head to try to shake them away. If Rennic noticed, he said nothing. He was watching the proceedings with one eyebrow raised, idly chewing at a nail.

'I can only thank you for the sacrifice and dedication that has brought us together here today.' Torht continued. 'Truly, we stand at the cusp of something momentous. And we would not be here without Prince Mendel's devotion to his kingdom and his people, and his desire to see justice done at last!'

To a chorus of cheers, Torht reached out a hand and ushered Mendel forward, urging him to speak. The handsome young prince bounded forward, bright eyes wide, narrow silver band shining at his brow.

'My subjects,' he began, then paused. 'My *friends*. I have learned *so much* in the last few days that my head is spinning. I have learned of the crimes of Primarch Vassad, more heinous than I could have ever supposed. I have learned that five years ago, when my beloved brother Corvel and I were attacked by brigands and he gave his life for mine, when my father Lubel was struck down by grief on the news of Corvel's death . . .' He paused to wipe at one beautiful eye. 'I have learned that those brigands were agents of the Rose, and that my father fell to Vassad's alchemy. I have learned that Lo Vassad murdered my brother and poisoned my father. And I am so glad that today is the day that we rid the kingdom of an ungodly stain!'

He stood back, beaming, to another round of cheers. Tarfel gazed at his big brother, enraptured.

Rennic spat out a sliver of nail. 'We should *triple* our fee.'

***

Lemon found them as they were repacking the mules. She was dragging one of the sacks. 'Got something for you, boss,' she said with a grin, and tossed the sack to Rennic.

He opened it and dug inside, then cried in triumph. 'About fucking time! How'd you swing that? Here, little man, give me a hand with the lacing.'

Lemon smiled. 'Took a detour on the way over. Palo's cousin, or whoever she was, she really came through, sorted us out with some bonus silver for the Denirnas job. Thought you wouldn't mind if we spent a bit.'

Rennic unbundled a great leather carapace from the sack, trailing laces and straps, its body composed of hard, overlapping scales. It looked finely made, if very battered.

'Wait . . . Where's the fucking helmet?'

Lemon coughed. 'Well, fella said prices had gone up, what with the Nort blockade and all, and your share didn't—'

'There's no helmet? What the fuck am I supposed to do now?'

Loveless stuck her head over a mule.

'Try not to get hit on the head, maybe?'

Rennic cast his eyes skyward. 'Thrice-damn you. I leave you alone for a moment, and this—'

'Hey.' Loveless's tone was fierce. 'Be grateful. Thank the lady.'

Rennic paused, then turned slowly to Lemon.

'Thanks, you cloth-eared fuck-stool.'

'My pleasure, you reeking piss-wizard.'

The big man sighed. 'Come on, little man, help me get this on. You can call it another learning opportunity.'

Loveless popped her head up again. 'How's you in armour going to help the poor lad's training? He's getting a mud-breakfast either way.'

Rennic grinned, dark and sharp. 'Little man knows the drill. His beatings continue until he lands a mark on me. Maybe this old gear will slow me down a touch, eh, little man?'

Chel's own grin was weak, half-formed. He was not enjoying his training.

***

Chel arrived late to Palo's briefing, appalled to find Rennic already standing at the back of the mail-clad ring of partisans, mercenaries and seconded house-guards, each craning to see where she carved lines in the cold mud with a spear-tip. Others milled and drilled in the background.

'You could have—'

Rennic hushed him with a glare, then returned his gaze to where Palo stood in the dawn light. Chel went up on his tiptoes in an attempt to match.

'. . . cannot risk alerting those within the citadel before we are ready to strike,' Palo continued. 'They must have no idea that the prince both lives and is at their threshold until it is too late to intercept him. Our subterfuge will keep them off-balance, rob them of the chance to run for answers to our enemy in his tower.'

She moved around, drawing lines in the black earth that were lost to Chel through the thicket of legs. 'The advance party will infiltrate the city by way of the Shanties, avoiding the checks at the Pauper's Gate. The guards at the Widow's Gate are unloved and easily bought.' She scraped two more invisible grooves. 'From there we must pass into the Cityheart via the Queen's Gate. It is here we shall trigger the diversions we discussed. The confusion should allow the remaining force to enter the Newtown while the advance party attains the citadel gates. Here we shall reveal the prince, and then we shall have them.'

She stood back with a grim smile. 'Those at the citadel gates will be forced to assume that the prince's arrival is Vassad's wish. Only he and his inner circle will know otherwise, and once we are inside the citadel it will be too late. We need only a handful of agents to enter the keep, and but one to climb the tower. Vassad is blind to our approach. He is unprepared. One hand of our strike shall attend to the king, the other shall see to the Primarch. With the king secured and the Primarch in chains, we give the signal and dig in at the citadel. Before any red-robed churchman thinks to act rashly, the rest of our forces, the vast bulk of you that wait without the walls, take the city. We emerge from the tower, our nation's rightful rule restored, and the Church will bow or be cast down as traitors. The people will hang them from the citadel walls.

'Does each of us understand her role? Good. You two, remain. I have your alchemical devices.'

The group dispersed, heading for mules and gear. Chel was surprised to see Tarfel had been front and centre of the briefing. He met Chel's eye with a nervous smile.

'Exciting, eh, Vedren?' It was the first words they'd exchanged for some time, and Chel reflected on their renewed separation since they had encountered the Watcher: Tarfel was once again a confirmed prince, and Chel was once again his servant.

'Yes, highness. How are you feeling?'

'Oh, well, I suppose. Wonderful to be with Mendel again. We've seen so little of each other since I was sent north. And of course he's changed, we both have, and he's had his injury, and the pressures of heirdom, and the alchemy of course, so some differences are to be expected . . .'

'Of course, highness.'

'You know, Vedren,' the prince said, watching the preparations around them with nervous eyes, 'the Watcher told me and Mendel the strangest tale last night. Remember Farashan, the first great siege of Father's wars?'

'Ah. Palo's cousin?'

The prince swallowed, recalling their dinner conversation, and nodded. 'You remember that my mother Irja – she died birthing me, of course you knew – was married to said cousin, prior to the siege? The Watcher told us that they had a secret son, who escaped the executions that Palo mentioned, although at the expense of a terrible maiming. That would make him my half-brother, Vedren! Imagine! Apparently, he's still out there somewhere. Father will know more. We can ask him once he's safe.'

Chel nodded and smiled, but his mind lingered on a maimed half-brother, and the blind man who'd told the princes his tale. There was more at play here than he'd been told, of that he was certain. He looked around for Torht, but his view was obscured by the marshalling forces that swirled around them. A small force to infiltrate, the rest to sweep in once the citadel was taken. Hammer and anvil. What could go wrong?

'Our bargain still holds, doesn't it, Vedren? Deliver me through what comes, and you'll be released.'

'That sounds . . . good, highness. Really good.'

'Wonderful. We'd best away and prepare, Vedren. Today we rescue my father, and the kingdom with him!'

THIRTY

An odd, tingling feeling fluttered through Chel as he led Tarfel's mule along the muddy road, a pace behind the mules bearing Mendel and Torht, who had Palo at the lead-rope. The riders were robed as Merciful Sisters, while Chel and the marchers were a mixture of apparent sisters and their fur-clad retainers. Unease, perhaps even dread, simmered within him, but also tremulous hope, the consideration that if the wheels turned the way the Watcher had schemed, the kingdom could be forever changed.

So much had happened since he'd arrived at Denirnas with his step-uncle; by now, he'd wager none of his family had the first idea of what had become of him. Apart, perhaps from his sister . . .

Mendel was cured: he seemed clearer, more vital by the day. If anything, their arrival at the capital had energized him; he seemed raring to breach the gates of Black Rock and free his father likewise. Chel's stomach rose at the thought. Could an end to the desolation of their country be at hand?

His gaze slipped back to Tarfel, who lacked his brother's visible energy. If anything, the prince looked physically sick.

'Are you feeling all right, highness?'

Tarfel looked up, his eyes taking a moment to alight on Chel. 'Hmm? Oh, yes, yes, Vedren. It's all very, well, big, isn't it?'

'It is, highness.'

The prince lowered his voice. 'Vedren, I'm scared. I've been so oblivious.' He shook his head, sighed, then sat up straighter. 'But Father needs me, and Mendel is brave enough for us both. We're going to do it, Vedren. We're going to save the kingdom.'

'We are, highness.'

On they trudged, down from the woods and on to the muddy road, while the bruised winter sky prickled with the promise of snow. They crossed the river at the new bridge, a low, jumbled construction of wood and uneven stone that squatted self-conscious in the shadow of the magnificent ruin upriver. Chel suspected that the bridge had creaked and juddered even when fresh-built. On the far bank, they entered the Shanties.

However much the lean-to slums beyond the walls of Denirnas had shocked him, the Shanties were something else. They stretched for miles; from the fringes at the river bank, the city's walls were a distant haze. Narrow trails and roads-by-convention criss-crossed them, riddled with shallow streams and channels of dirty water spanned by driftwood trestles, and Chel was grateful that someone else was responsible for their navigation.

Dogs barked unseen, while lean alley cats watched their passage with the same casual indifference as the denizens they passed, hollow-eyed and hollow-backed folk who paused their daily activities to follow the clandestine procession with joyless eyes. Everywhere there was coughing, and the stench of disease suffused the air.

'A sand-flower!' At the cry his heart sank. The songs followed.

'Where the Shepherd wandered, so the chosen came . . .'

Rennic glanced over in irritation at the youthful chorus, his restored armour creaking beneath his matted furs. 'What have you done, boy?'

Chel's own borrowed mail was cold and heavy as ever beneath his furs. He cast his gaze downward at the brittle mud crust beneath his boots. 'Nothing. Kids.'

'Adorable.'

The songs and calls followed them as they trudged on.

'Will you bring us luck, sand-flower?'

'Yes, will you share your luck with us?'

'Will we be princesses?'

'Will we have fine dresses?'

Chel kept his gaze low. 'Let's hope so,' he said, only to himself. 'That would make a pleasant change.'

***

Squat, dark outer walls filled their view, piles of ugly grey stone from the northern quarries. The Shanties ended abruptly a couple of hundred paces from the walls, and with them went the children's singing. A few hunched figures tried to follow as they crossed the blasted ground, but were hissed back by the guards at the Widow's Gate, their spears gripped tight at the sight of the approaching column, eyes narrowed in pre-emptive hostility.

The liveried gate captain raised a hand as they approached.

'No entry here, Sisters. You'll need to go via the free way, Pauper's Gate.' She jerked a thumb around the curve of the walls toward a wide, clear path that travelled away downslope, carved through the Shanties like a scar. Scant traffic moved along it, picking its way around the charred and broken debris that littered it like the area before the wall. Rennic noticed Chel's frown at the scorched, cracked earth.

'Won't let them build too close,' he said in a low voice. 'Burn them back if necessary.'

'Not that I'd put my breakfast on you getting in there,' the captain went on. 'You'll need to be quarantined now after crossing that mess.' A nod toward the Shanties, which from here seemed to stew beneath a soggy film. 'Any one of you could have been touched, and Shepherd save us from the Sickness within the walls. You'll be in stockade for a good couple of weeks. King's orders.'

Mendel threw back his hood. Even in the wintry light, his silver band gleamed on his golden brow. 'Is that so, captain? Perhaps I might ask my father himself.' He presented a dazzling grin. Chel saw Torht put his head in his hands.

The captain wobbled on her feet, eyes goggling, then dropped to one knee. She looked at serious risk of an aneurysm. 'Your . . . your highness!'

Mendel raised an airy hand. 'My thanks, captain, we'll take it from here. Have your men there crack the gate and let's be away, shall we?'

'But . . . But . . . the risk of plague, the quarantine . . . What if you were touched?'

Mendel laughed, light and silvery, the utter confidence of the bold or highly stupid. 'We are the righteous, captain, on a mission of mercy. The Shepherd wouldn't let a divine mission suffer the ravages of white plague, eh?' Chel wondered if he believed it.

Torht and Palo exchanged urgent whispers, then Palo stepped toward the captain and her guards, who took half a step back themselves. 'Your loyalty to your prince will be noted, and rewarded,' she said, her gaze serious as ever. The stress on the word reward brought the captain back to her feet, and a moment later the Widow's Gate creaked open wide enough to admit the mules.

'You're doing God's work, my soldiers,' Mendel called as he rocked past. 'Tell your comrades, tell one and all: Prince Mendel has returned!'

Palo held their gaze. 'Tell nobody of this.' She exchanged a quick look with Spider, then tugged on her mule's rope and set off after the prince. 'My comrade sister will have your reward.'

Chel and the others followed after the mules, squeezing through the narrow, rotten-smelling gate and into the gatehouse gloom. An arced slice of silver light at its end announced the city beyond. Spider hadn't yet followed, lingering near the expectant guards.

'Please, your highness,' he heard Torht call to Mendel as his mule pulled alongside. 'We're attempting to remain undiscovered, remember? Do try to keep your identity hidden.'

'Ah, overcooked it a bit, did I? My apologies. Won't happen again.'

Chel looked over his shoulder as they reached the inner gate. Spider was taking his time.

***

Low, rugged grey buildings, hewn from the same stone as the walls, stretched away either side as the city rose before them, but it was the twin hills that filled their view, surging up around the ash-walled Cityheart. Along one peak lay the ruins of the imperial palace, broken columns like the bleached bones of some long-dead animal; hacked into the other, the fearsome citadel, the city within the city: Black Rock. It glowered in the weak light, its lone, barbed tower an angry finger of condemnation.

From everywhere came the sounds and smells of a city in transition, the hammering bellow of dispersed construction, of packed workshops, the scents of metallurgy and masonry mixed. Fumes and stone-dust hung in the misty morning air, while overhead mingled the drifting smoke of a thousand chimneys. The ground crunched beneath Chel's boots.

'Artisans' quarter,' Rennic said in answer to Chel's expression. 'Easy to hide in all this.'

They merged with the traffic of what Chel took to be the city's main road, carts and wagons two abreast, mules, donkeys and the occasional rider battling for space around each other. Several low-backed wagons rolled past them, piled high with quarried white stone, their fat wheels leaving deep ruts in the churned earth. Rennic watched them pass with a sneer. 'Still hauling the pale stuff halfway across the kingdom. Pricks must think they're born-again Taneru.'

Twice Chel saw flashes of crimson robes in their periphery, swaggering patrols inspecting the shop-fronts that lined the boulevard. He kept his head down, hood forward.

'Five hells,' Chel said as they trudged past churches, markets, looming crofts and prayer towers, the city's sprawl unfathomable. The citizens seemed busy but guarded, almost fearful. He was not alone in keeping his gaze low. 'Just how big is this place?'

'Big,' Rennic said. 'Bigger than anything in . . . Where are you from?'

'Barva.'

'Bigger than anything in Barva. You've never been?'

'No.' He stared at the great white walls looming ahead, nestled between the curves of the peaks. 'But my father lived here for a while.'

'Lucky him.'

***

At the inner wall, beneath a magnificent gatehouse of crumbling pale stone that Rennic identified as the Queen's Gate, Torht bade the column pause. The liveried guards at the gate were restless, their idle attentions drawn back to the robed group and their laden mules with increasing frequency.

'Where's this distraction, then?' Rennic said, his voice an angry hiss as they congregated. 'The fucking guards are taking an interest.'

Torht's hand was up. 'A moment's patience, please, Master Rennic.'

Chel caught a whiff of something on the breeze, a jarring scent that sent him back to the attack on Denirnas. Alchemy. Somewhere a bell began to ring, then another. Shouts lifted over the outer city's general hubbub, cries of surprise and alarm.

'What's happening?' Chel said.

'I believe our moment is at hand. Prepare to move on, my friends.'

The shouts were increasingly interwoven with screams.

A great din rose from the direction of the Pauper's Gate at the free way's distant far end. The bells tolled with urgent frequency. A moment later, a runner in livery pelted past them, tearing up chunks of soft earth with his boots. He screeched to a halt at the gate, before gasping, 'The Shanties are burning! The vermin are fleeing, trying to flood into the city!'

The guards exchanged panicked looks. 'What do we do?'

The runner raised his arms in exasperation. 'Come and push them back out! Summon everyone!'

He took a great gulp of air, then resumed his run, through the gate and into the inner city. The guards looked at one another, hesitant, then hoisted their pole-arms and set off for the outer walls at a jog. A moment later, another dozen guards came through at a run, heading in the same direction, and disappeared into the city.

The gate stood deserted. Torht cocked his head. 'Sounds like it is time.'

'Wait,' Chel said, looking around them. One of the party was still missing. 'Where's Spider?'

'Oh, no doubt he'll catch us up.'

***

The pale constructions of the Cityheart crowded around them, their walls blocking and overlapping each other on the steady rise toward the double-peaked hill that towered over the city. Rennic stirred, squinting up against the day's dull glare.

'Huh. That's new.'

Chel looked up at the wooden scaffolding that wrapped the ruined palace. 'What's that? Are they rebuilding it?'

'It's part of the Restoration,' Tarfel said from his mule. 'Asa Keshani said it would . . . I suppose it was the Primarch's idea.'

'Have you spent much time here, highness?'

'Oh, not in the last few years, Vedren. I've only been back a handful of times since I was sent to stay with Duke Reysel.'

'You've not seen much of your father?'

The prince scratched at his chin. 'No, not as such, a few audiences only, as part of a wider delegation. We've exchanged letters, of course — that is, I've sent a lot, and he's sent a few.' He sat back on the mule with a sigh. 'Of course, now I know Vassad was pulling the strings, it explains why they were so anodyne. And literate, for that matter.'

The streets had emptied, the sounds of panic and screaming from the outer city driving the citizens either out of or deep within their homes. Shutters and doors slammed shut as they passed, and the guards that jangled past them at speed were far less concerned with a Merciful Sisters mule-train than they were with the inferno-induced riots at the outer wall. Chel wondered how long it would take them to think to close the inner gate.

The Watcher had been vague on how they'd cross the Cityheart to the citadel, and now he knew why. He wondered where Spider had set the fire (assuming it had been Spider, and he was certain that it had), and with a sudden cold shock he thought of the children in the artificial forest of driftwood and jetsam, the singing, calling children who had asked him for some of his luck. Would Spider have set the fire in a sparse corner, raised the alarm early to allow those on their route to escape? He pictured the children, lost amid smoke and flames, calling out, coughing . . . His hands started to tremble, his breath caught in his throat.

Rennic had moved beside him and now nudged him. 'Look sharp, piss-cheeks, here comes the citadel.'

***

A half-circle of confessors ringed the foot of the wide, winding steps that led up to the citadel gate. Over their blood-hued tunics, their breastplates shimmered in the day's chill glare, their breath rising in fat wads of vapour. Long maces hung from their belts or dangled from loose grips.

Palo halted them just out of sight, in the faint shadow of a decaying wall. 'As expected,' Torht said, 'the confessors are unmoved by the plight of others. Highness, this is your moment.'

Mendel blinked. His energy had waned since they had entered the city proper, almost as if he was losing focus again. Perhaps he had been spooked by the fire in the Shanties, too. The prince stared at Torht a moment, as if deciding something, then the zeal returned to his eyes.

'What must I do?'

Torht smiled, empty sockets creasing in the shade of his cowl. 'It is time to reveal your royal magnificence.'

Mendel nodded with increasing vigour. 'It shall be so.'

Torht turned to the rest of them. 'Strip away the trappings of the Sisterhood!'

Robes were removed, some turned inside out. The mules' packs were emptied of weapons, the animals set loose. Mendel threw off his robe. His burnished hunting armour gleamed beneath, the circlet at his brow completing the ensemble.

Palo led, Mendel bounding in her footsteps. Dalim took over steering the Watcher. Chel realized with a start that Spider had rejoined them. He smelled strongly of smoke. He caught Chel's glance.

'Off we trot, rat-bear. The Spider's never killed a ruler before, and his blades are thirsty.'

Chel shifted instinctively toward Tarfel, but he held Spider's gaze. We're square, he told himself. The Nanaki squared us.

The rest of the group followed Palo and Mendel, marching as retainers.

'Who approaches the sacred sanctum?'

Palo told them, her voice devoid of inflection or swagger. Her hands lingered at her belt, fingers close to her sword's hilt, then Mendel sprang from her shadow, his golden face lit with a broad grin.

The confessors bowed and shuffled apart.

As they climbed the wide, worn steps, Torht said between breaths, 'We are almost there, my friends. They won't know what hit them.'

'There are a *lot* of confessors here,' Foss muttered as they climbed above the lower, outer walls and looked down into the courtyards behind. Red-robed figures lounged and drilled in each, in plentiful dozens.

'Wars create orphans,' Rennic growled back. 'Looks like a swathe found their way here.'

'But why would there be this many, boss? How much spiritual guidance do the provinces need?'

'Guessing the wee bastards doing blade drills down there aren't overly concerned with matters spiritual, Fossy.'

'Do you think we have enough troops outside to subdue all these, boss?'

'Do our bit right, it won't matter.'

'Tell you one thing Vassad's got right,' said a voice from beside Chel. Loveless was climbing next to him, her sudden presence as unnerving as it was welcome. 'If you're going to build a private army, make it from young men.'

Chel blinked.

'Know why all the confessors are young men nowadays?' she went on. 'Youth and stupidity are easily harnessed. No simpler bunch to incite to a duplicitous cause than young men of low status, especially those with what you might call limited romantic prospects. Promise them meaning, promise them power and promise them sex. They'll do what they're told.' She gave a grim smile. 'The late Brother Hurkel being a notable exponent.'

Chel frowned after her. 'Should I be offended at that?'

A flash of warmth lit her smile. 'Depends how limited you consider your prospects, cub.'

A wide, circular courtyard lay behind the ugly gatehouse. It buzzed with activity, the air thick with shouts and calls and the barking of unseen hounds. Carts and wagons stood along one wall, reminding Chel of their departure from the Sepulchre.

'The court of confession,' Palo said, her voice low, 'has seen its last spectacle.'

Chel wrapped himself in her words like a cloak.

A breathless seneschal intercepted them as they reached the keep's outer door. A grand, fussy woman, she looked like she'd been caught midway through breakfast.

'Your highness! Blessings upon you, your presence honours us. We've been in such confusion here – the most dreadful reports we received, of Talis, the hunting party set upon by savage tribals? So shocking, that they might range this far north. So few survivors made it back to the castle, we heard you and your guard lost, but we are delighted to see you healthy, most gracious highness. Are, by chance, the rest of your household with you?'

Mendel laughed, hearty and confident. Chel wondered if the tension was getting to him. He reassured the seneschal that he was very much alive and well, and that he was returning as summoned post-haste for his audience with Primarch Vassad. The seneschal confided that the Primarch seemed most upset by the news of his potential loss; he'd barely touched his food in the days since, nor issued new decrees to the staff within the citadel. Mendel assured her that he would put the old boy's mind at rest in short order. Chel was impressed at how readily his amiability could be applied to misdirection.

'I'll detain you no longer, highness,' the seneschal said with another benediction, her grand robes sweeping around her like layered curtains. 'Your retainers, in the kitchens or by the stables, wait while you attend within. Blessings upon you.' She fussed away, beaming.

Left alone on the keep steps, Torht and Palo exchanged murmurs, then Palo spoke to the rest of the group in a low voice. 'You know your duties, comrades.'

Only a handful of them could enter the keep without arousing suspicion. The rest were to secure the courtyard, and the gatehouse with it, standing ready to hold the gates open when the moment came and the outer force descended on the citadel. Chel took a long breath. He would be Tarfel's vizier, Torht Mendel's. Dalim and Palo would impersonate the crown prince's sworn, Rennic and Spider for the young prince. The others were staying outside. He stared into the yawning darkness of the keep interior and felt a deep disquiet, a tingling finger pushing into his guts, making him shiver.

'You all right, little man?'

'Fine.'

'Ready to save a kingdom?'

'Always was, old man. Your knees up to this?'

Rennic almost managed a smile, then he wheeled on the other members of the Black Hawk Company. He kept his voice as low as Palo's. 'Right, fuckers, this has got "dark turn" written all over it. Get to the corners, stay alert, and watch for what happens next. Stay close to that gate. If this goes to shit, don't try and hold the gatehouse – I want you out of here. Regroup at the campsite; failing that, fall all the way back to the Sepulchre.'

Loveless stepped forward, eyes at full glare. 'Horseshit,' she hissed. 'If it goes tits-up in there, we're not leaving you.' Chel felt another hot surge of jealousy. Her words were not directed at him.

Rennic looked away, his eyes rolling. 'Whisp! Explain this to her. The little man and I have work to do.'

Whisper nodded, stretching a lean arm around Loveless's shoulders and drawing her away. Her other hand moved in front, throwing out a firm series of gestures. Chel nudged Foss before he could move away.

'What's she saying?'

The big man offered a rueful smile. 'Only that by the time we are aware of any troubles that have befallen you within, it will be long past our time to intervene.'

'She said all that?'

'I paraphrase. Be careful in there, my friend. There are a *lot* of confessors here. Shepherd's grace go with you.'

'Uh, yeah, you too.'

Lemon reached out a hand. To his surprise he found one of her hammers in it. 'You still unarmed, wee bear?'

He patted his belt where Rennic's skinning knife nestled, his prize for landing a hit at last when they were sparring. 'Thanks, but Rennic saw to it. I've got a good knife at last.'

She smiled. It was a nice smile. 'Good lad. See you on the other side.'

Rennic cut in with a hiss. 'Can we terminate this tearful fuckery? Our friends in red are starting to wonder why we're exchanging vows of eternal devotion when we'll all be seeing each other very soon. Yes?'

'Aye, right. See you soon.'

Chel and Rennic hurried into the darkness after the others.

THIRTY-ONE

The lower floor of the keep matched its austere exterior, the flagstones wide and sunken, the walls solid blocks of dark, battered rock. Pennants and tapestries hung between dim sconces, displaying what Chel took to be Rose-approved imagery. The sign of the rose and its forms bloomed prominently. Fires crackled from wide, deep hearths, but their heat seemed swallowed by the oppressive, implacable cold of the mass of dark stone. At every corner steel-and-crimson-draped guards watched the royal party with hostile eyes.

Torht, steered by Mendel at his elbow, halted them at the base of a giant, carved staircase, great grey slabs piled up one on top of the other, climbing in a wide, slow spiral out of sight.

'And here we split once more. Prince Tarfel, it is time to attend to your father. Once he is secured, Vassad will have no hold over you, even should he somehow elude us today. Surprise will be your biggest asset. You understand?'

Palo nodded. 'We will see to King Lubel.'

'Prince Mendel and I will begin the climb. Vassad sits

snug in his lair, by now expecting an audience with the crown prince.'

Mendel nodded and patted the sword at his belt. 'I shall cleave my enemy's head from his shoulders.'

Torht smiled indulgently, then continued. 'Once Vassad is subdued or slain, we will give our signal. You will know what to do.'

'I will. Shepherd guide your hand.'

'And yours, Ayla.' Torht was already scaling the lower steps, Mendel at his elbow, his progress laboured.

Palo looked at the rest of them. 'Prince Tarfel, you had best lead the way.'

***

Thick furs, bear and wolf, covered the flagstones of the royal wing. Statues and engravings stood in contrast to the staid weavings of the main keep, none of whom Chel recognized. One particular statue showed a giant of a man, one foot on a bear's head, a huge stone axe hefted over one shoulder.

Tarfel noticed his glance. 'Akko Merimonsun, the first of our line,' he said. 'My grandfather.'

They looked up at the huge stone man, who would have towered over them even without his chunky plinth.

'Is he to scale?'

Palo hissed through her teeth at them, and they hurried on.

Four confessors stood at the fine-wrought door to the audience chamber, clearly wearing mail beneath their rust-coloured robes. All had swords, full-length and well-made, strapped at their waists, and long spears resting against their shoulders.

'What happened to the Church's Articles on bearing arms?' Chel muttered to Rennic.

'Perhaps they were amended.'

Palo urged Tarfel forward. One of the confessors looked up in surly surprise, then blocked his path with a meaty arm.

'Where do you think you're going?'

Tarfel summoned all of his regal bluster. 'Unhand me! I am Tarfel Merimonsun, Prince of Vistirlar, and I am here to see my father.'

The confessors exchanged a look.

'You what?' one said. 'Prince Tarfel's dead.'

'I am anything but, I assure you. I am, uh, hale and hearty. Bend your knee.' With that Tarfel flung his ringed hand at the guards.

'But . . . the king's not receiving visitors.'

'Do you hear me, wh— whelp? I am a prince!'

The confessors exchanged another look. 'We need to check. No one's allowed in without a prelate. Wait here, your, uh, highness.'

Palo leaned in close to Tarfel's ear. 'Please take a step back, highness.'

Tarfel did so.

The movement was a blur. Palo, Spider and Dalim stepped forward as a trio, knives in their hands from nowhere. The three confessors at the door had no time to grapple their spears around or draw their swords, their arms flailing as quick blades dug into their throats and bore them to the ground in jingling, gurgling heaps.

The last confessor was three paces further on. Rennic's knife had slipped from his grasp and clattered on the flagstones. The confessor's eyes were wide, and he turned to run.

Rennic was flailing in the gloom for his knife. 'Little man! Get him!'

Chel ran.

He pounded after the confessor, blood thumping in his ears, as the bigger man sprinted away. The royal wing had been deserted, but the main keep was thick with traffic. He would be there in moments. Chel forced his legs faster, teeth clenched, breath coming in hard gasps, every pace bringing him inches closer to his armoured quarry.

As they hared around the last corner, he was almost close enough to reach out and touch the man's fleeing back or catch a pumping elbow, their feet slapping down half a second apart. It dawned on him that he had no idea what he was going to do if he caught him. He hesitated, breath catching, and the confessor turned his head.

A door opened in front of them, directly in the confessor's path. The man crashed into it at full tilt, slamming it back and out again, whereupon it struck him a second time as he reeled. He staggered back, hood flattened. A deep line in his forehead was placid for a moment, then a steady trickle of blood began to flow. He sat down, breath harsh and halting, then his eyes rolled closed and he leaned slowly against the wall.

A robed head appeared around the battered door. 'What in God's name was that?'

Chel stood over the stricken confessor, gasping fresh air back into his burning lungs, one hand up as a plea for indulgence. His brain worked as hard as he could force it. 'We were . . . racing . . . Wager.' He swallowed, then corrected himself. 'No . . . coin . . . of course.'

'You bloody fools! I should have you stripped. Look at

my door!' He heard a sniff of disgust. 'Your friend looks unwell. I suggest, perhaps, a visit to the chapel of healing?'

Chel nodded, still bent double. 'Yes, absolutely.'

'Yes, absolutely, what?'

He raised his gaze. There was something familiar about the voice. The robes covering the feet before him were not rust-coloured but plain white, edged with delicate vermilion stitching. He'd seem that shade before.

'Wait,' said the woman's voice. 'Who are you? Why are you dressed like that?'

'Better get to the chapel,' he said, trying to hide the burning of his cheeks and neck as exertion. He reached under the confessor's armpits and began to drag him away, ignoring the groan from his weak shoulder.

'Where are you going?' the woman called after him. 'The chapel is that way.'

Chel ignored her, picking up the pace of his drag. The confessor's leaking head lolled as Chel scuttled backward at top speed. As he reached the corner, he risked a quick look up.

Sister Vashenda was looking straight at him. Her eyes widened in recognition. 'I know you,' she said. 'The sand-crab! Hey! Hey, come back!'

She began to trot after him. She was not yet running.

Rennic was waiting around the corner. Without acknowledgement, he grabbed one of the confessor's limp arms and dragged beside Chel, and they tore down the hallway, Vashenda's footsteps and cries echoing after them.

'Who the fuck's that?' Rennic said as they cleared the next corner. They were leaving a splattered trail in their wake.

'The fucking executive prelate of Denirnas.'

'What's she doing here?'

'No idea. Maybe she's being punished for something.'

'And why does she know you?'

Over his shoulder Chel saw the royal chamber's gilded door approaching.

'Oh, I'm quite the popular fellow.'

* * *

'Bar the door. Our sand-crab has attracted some unwanted attention.'

'Hey, I'm not the one who dropped my fucking knife!'

'And where *was* your knife back there? I didn't give it to you for—'

'Quiet!' Palo's eyes blazed in the gloom as the door swung closed behind them. Three former confessors lay piled beside the ornate arch, swiftly joined by their fellow. Spider delivered a perfunctory coup de grâce, but Chel suspected that Vashenda's door had done the heavy lifting. Dalim had liberated one of the spears and draped it across his shoulders in familiar fashion. Swords were distributed. There were not enough for Chel to get one.

Tarfel stood alone before the heavy curtain that stretched across the chamber, dividing the rows of banked wooden benches on their side from what lay beyond. The room was cold and dark: a few low candles flickered in alcoves along the walls, but the hearths were empty, and the slit windows, high on the wall, offered only narrow slices of grizzly light, far overhead.

'My father's rooms should be beyond the curtain, through the audience chamber. There . . . there may be more guards.'

Palo put a hand on Chel's shoulder and nodded at the prince. 'Keep him out of the way.'

She approached the curtain and pulled it slowly aside, revealing a wood and woven-rush screen behind. Chel stuck close to Tarfel as the prince edged closer. Through the screen a few candles glimmered, their light feeble in the tall chamber's pressing gloom. No fire burned on either side of the screen, and their breath misted before them. Chel felt the sharp cold against his skin, despite the acerbic heat in his muscles and the thumping of his blood in his ears.

A shape loomed beyond the screen, more obscured than visible through the woven slats. A mound or pyramid, something altogether more massive above it. Before it, the vague outline of an intercessor's lectern. Nothing moved but Palo, taking one careful step after another as she crept along the wooden barrier, pulling the curtain as she went. The room was very quiet, and an odd smell tickled at Chel's nostrils. The alchemical taint that Torht had mentioned, no doubt.

Palo found a door to one side of the screen. It opened with the merest creak, and she slipped through and into the darkness beyond. Tarfel made to go after her, but Chel stepped in front. 'Highness, wait here a moment.'

'My father's chambers are through there, Vedren. Let me through!' His voice echoed around the cold stone.

'Just— Just let me go first.'

If anything, the air beyond the screen was colder than before. At the room's centre, posed directly before the screen upon a dais, stood a huge, elevated bed, inclined to allow any occupant a view through the screen. Behind and over it stood another great stone statue: a crowned giant in hunter's garb, a greatsword hefted in a two-handed grip, towering and muscular. If that was supposed to be Lubel Merimonsun, it seemed a little insensitive to have his invalid daybed directly beneath it. To one side, a stout door led elsewhere into the keep, presumably to the king's private chambers. Palo tried it. It was locked. She made to draw her weapon on it, then stopped, looking back at the elevated bed at the chamber's heart.

The bed was occupied.

Its covers and furs were rucked and tented over a figure, dwarfed by the grand scale of its furnishings. Colourless hair spilled out from the darkness of the pillows, flat and sallow. Palo, Chel and the prince advanced on it, none speaking. The alchemical smell was stronger here, far stronger, and Chel felt his eyes beginning to water.

Palo had reached the dais and was climbing up beside the bed. Something glittered in her hand in the stumbling candlelight. Chel's heart beat faster, his stomach lurching, his head light from more than the room's unsettling smell. Tarfel was only a couple of paces behind him.

He rounded the intercessor's lectern and leapt up beside Palo, feeling a jolt of complaint from his shoulder as he gripped the side of the dais. If Palo noticed him, she gave no sign. The knife was in her hand, gripped ready to plunge, and as he reached her she whispered.

'*Death to tyrants*.'

'Nine rancid, sheep-fucking hells,' came Rennic's voice from across the dais. His head appeared at the bed's headboard, level with the mounded pillows.

Chel couldn't yet reach Palo's knife hand, but she was holding where she was.

'What?'

'Princeling. Uh, bad news, I'm afraid.'

Tarfel had reached the foot of the dais.

'What? What is it? Father! Father!'

'I'm sorry, but your dad, he, uh, ain't breathing.'

'What? What?'

'He's dead. Look, no breath.' Rennic swept a hand toward the pile at the bed's head. No telltale plume rose in the frigid air.

'And from the look of it,' Rennic continued, reaching out and drawing back the covering furs, 'he's been that way for quite a long time.'

The mummified face of Lubel Merimonsun stared sightlessly at them from silken pillows, white-gold tresses splayed around him like a classical halo. The body was hopelessly shrunken, shrivelled back to taut grey skin over the bones beneath.

'That's what that smell is.' Rennic shook his head, more baffled than angry. 'Not herbal manipulation. He's been fucking embalmed.'

'Father! No, no!' Tarfel began to sob. Rennic gave Chel a look that strongly suggested he look after the grieving prince, but Chel felt no pressing inclination.

'*The king is dead, and we shall all of us burn.*'

Beside him, Palo stirred.

'What? What did you say?'

'Nothing. Just . . . something I heard once.'

Below the dais, Tarfel was raging. 'That bastard, that shit-pig-bastard! He killed Father. He killed his king. And he covered it up. My own father is dead . . . and I didn't know. I didn't know!' He began to kick the side of the intercessor's lectern, knocking over a candlestick.

Rennic cleared his throat and nodded in the prince's direction again for Chel's benefit. Still, Chel didn't move. Something had caught his eye as the candlestick rolled, a glimmering line through the air, rising up from the back of the bed and up toward the statue.

'What's that?'

The door to the chamber rattled, then rattled again. Everyone froze, even Tarfel mid-kick.

'Who's in there? Sand-flower, is that you?' Vashenda's voice came muffled and alarmed through the thick wood. 'Open this door! Where are the guards!'

The door bucked against the bundled spears barring it shut, twice, three times. 'Open this fucking door in the name of the Primarch!'

Rennic gave Palo a sharp and hungry glance.

'We need to leave. Now, before she gathers more.'

Palo shook her head. Her face remained as expressionless as ever.

'Our mission ends within this chamber.'

Vashenda's voice shrieked from outside. 'Alarm! Sound the alarm! Guards, guards!' Her cries receded as she disappeared back into the keep. Back toward legions of mail-clad red confessors.

'Don't give up on me, Palo. We can fight our way out if we move fast. Even Prince Ding-dong there.'

Tarfel gave them a look of tear-streaked defiance.

'Absolutely. I'm absolutely ready to kill something. Just give me a sword.'

Palo was unmoved.

'Our job is done. Done for us, in fact,' she said, her voice almost a whisper. Louder, she said, 'We must keep them from the tower, to give Raeden the best chance of reaching Vassad. We must draw them here and delay them as long as possible.'

'You mean dying valiantly, yes?' Rennic said. 'Fuck. That. Little man, get the prince and get to the door to the king's chambers. We'll bust it open.'

Tarfel shook his head. 'The private chambers are a dead end. There's only one connecting door from this wing to the main keep.'

'What about elsewhere? Other doors to the outside?'

The prince shrugged, sniffing angry tears. 'We're halfway up a hill, built into the rock. Where would they go?'

'Fuck. Fuck!'

Chel had followed the line of light, fingers tracing the slender thread. It passed through a loop at the edge of the wooden headboard, then travelled straight up the body of the statue into the darkness above. He gave the thread a gentle tug.

Beneath the covers, the dead king's hand twitched.

'So that's how they manage the audiences,' he said, tugging the thread again. He scanned the headboard and spotted four more tiny rings, barely perceptible threads running through each. 'A strong smell, no voice, only gestures and twitches,' he recited as he clambered onto the statue's plinth, eyes fixed on the path of the tiny threads up and over the stonework.

'Little man, what the fuck are you doing?'

'There's something here. They were controlling the king like a puppet.' He paused. 'Apologies, your highness.'

Tarfel waved a hand, past caring. Rennic was less serene.

'Fascinating. And that helps us because . . .'

Chel followed the threads through a single ring, barely visible, hammered into the statue's shoulder, then out and across the far side. Very thin slits were visible between the stone blocks in the wall behind the statue.

'I think there's—'

Something crashed against the chamber door, rocking it inward. The spears creaked.

'Sand-flower! Open the door and receive the Shepherd's mercy!'

Rennic was beside him. 'What? What is there? Hurry now!'

Chel grabbed one of the feeble candles and held it toward the wall. 'There's something here. They made the king move with threads from behind here. Made it look like he was moving.'

'Who did?'

'Fuck knows, Vassad, his minions, who cares now? Someone had to be back here, though.'

'And you think there's a way out?'

'I think it's possible.'

The door crashed again, then again a moment later. The thumps against it picked up a sickening rhythm. The bundled spears began to splinter. All the while, Vashenda called through what she no doubt considered to be reassurance.

'Open the door, sand-flower. We care only for the health of the king. Surrender now and receive only the Shepherd's mercy!'

Chel cocked an eyebrow. 'Doesn't she know about the king?'

Rennic grunted, indifferent. 'If she does, would she tell?'

Palo and Dalim were back at the screen door, watching. Waiting. Spider was closer to Chel and Rennic than to them.

'What's rat-boy found?'

'Fuck off, Spider, let him work.'

'There!'

A concealed hinge lay in the wooden panelling that lined the far wall. Chel dug at it with his good knife, tracing the outline of a small door. He snagged the catch as the spears began to split.

'Here! Everyone! Here!'

Spider was inside before he could get the thing all the way open. Rennic ran back to grab the prince and drag him through. Only when Dalim bolted and it seemed she'd be left completely alone did Palo follow.

Chel pulled the door closed and jammed his knife through its latch as darkness swallowed them. Slivers of wan yellow light from the chamber lent precious little illumination to their new surroundings.

'What now?' Dalim whispered and was immediately shushed. Chel crept along the cold stone and pressed his eye to one of the slits.

The royal chamber's door slammed open, ripping apart the spears that had barred it in a burst of splintering wood. Vashenda strode into the room, as furious and haughty as the day he'd first seen her in Denirnas, even as a mashed blur of colour through the screen. 'Sand-flower!' she roared as she entered the chamber, flanked by a dozen or more red-robed shapes. They fanned out, spreading across the chamber, but came to a halt when they reached the screen. They seemed unwilling to go any further.

'Sand-flower? Come out now, surrender yourself and end this farce. Stop being a thrice-damned fool.' Vashenda waited, angry breath steaming in the pallid light, then she snarled. 'Very well. You lot, get in there. Now!'

The confessors' reluctance broke against her fury, and

they were through the screen a moment later, fanning out into the audience chamber. Vashenda's pace and confidence slowed as they did, her certainty replaced by confusion. 'Sand-flower,' she said again, but this time her rage was undercut by suspicion. 'Where are you hiding?'

Tarfel tugged Chel's elbow.

'What if she knows about the little door?' he said as quiet as he could.

Cold panic bloomed in Chel's guts. He swung his gaze around the darkness of the puppeteer's enclosure, but his eyes were not yet adjusted. A gentle creaking from the corner drew his attention. Spider had found a ladder.

The others quickly followed, movements furtive, but Chel risked another look through the wall-slit. Vashenda had made no move toward the hidden door. She stood, hesitant, in the shadow of the raised bed and its giant statue. Her confessors milled around, poking at the room's periphery. One confirmed that the door to the royal chambers was locked.

'She doesn't know,' he whispered.

Another confessor called from the corner, having stumbled over the stacked corpses of his former colleagues. Vashenda scowled. 'He had company. Who did he come in with? Where did they go? Who has the keys to the royal chambers? We must attend to the king.'

'She doesn't know.'

A soft twang by his head drew his glance. Rennic had cut the threads. They floated gently into the darkness behind the statue, and the last clue to their location removed.

'Uh, the king is here, Sister,' one of the confessors said, nodding to the bed.

Vashenda swivelled, mortified. 'Your majesty! My apologies – are you hurt?'

A confessor climbed aboard the bed.

'He's . . . He's dead.'

Vashenda's jaw clacked shut in rage, her knuckles tight. 'I knew it. Shepherd damn that Andriz bastard.'

'Uh, he's been dead a while, Sister.'

She paused. 'How long is a while?'

'I'm not sure, Sister. He's been embalmed.'

Rennic put a hand on Chel's arm and pulled him away with gentle insistence. Vashenda's disbelieving roars covered the sound of their climb.

THIRTY-TWO

A rough, rocky passage, tunnelled straight from the hillside from its unfinished appearance, led away from the ladder's rest, curling around and upward. Spider led the way, a fat candlestick in hand, half-invisible in the darkness. The air within was cold and stale, but free, at least, of the embalming stench.

Tarfel walked alone, half sobbing, half muttering. As the sound of Vashenda's inchoate rage fell away behind them, Chel risked a word.

'I'm sorry about your father, highness.'

Tarfel sniffed and nodded.

'When did you last see him?'

The prince's eyes were glossy pools in the low light. 'See him? Ha. A few months ago. I made my presentations, as ever, and was rewarded with a nod and a gesture. A nod and a gesture! But I was grateful, you see. Grateful for the acknowledgement. Because he was so very . . . ill . . .'

He spluttered into another choking sob, then wiped away the tears with his sleeve.

'But it was puppetry! My father a primarch's marionette!' He swallowed, loud and wet, then cleared his throat. 'My father, my sole parent, one third of what remains of my family, has been dead all this time, and I've been played for a *fool*!'

His voice was loud enough to echo down the tunnel, and heads turned ahead of them, but nobody said anything. The prince turned on Rennic, who looked like he wanted no part of the conversation. He was already hunched against the tunnel's low ceiling.

'How long? You saw him. How long has my father been dead?'

Rennic prevaricated. 'Hard to say, uh, your highness.'

'How long *could* he have been dead? Months?'

Rennic nodded to himself, as if he'd expected the question.

'Years.'

'How many?'

'Four or five, maybe more. Less than ten, I'd guess, but I'm no practitioner. This tunnel is only a few years old, I can tell you that much. My guess is you'd find its diggers entombed in here if you had a proper rummage.'

Tarfel's eyes glazed as they shuffled on through the gloom.

'It was five years ago that bandits attacked my brothers' caravan. They killed my brother Corvel, and left Mendel the only survivor – gravely wounded, forever changed.'

Chel pictured the crown prince, his bright, shining eyes, the jagged scar down his cheek, his earnest compliance.

'I remember.'

'I mean, Corvel could be cruel and devious, but he was our blood, and we loved him. At his loss, my father became bedridden. Struck down by grief, they told me. Of course, I was much younger then.'

'Of course.'

'And thanks to Master Torht, our Watcher, I know that Vassad himself was behind my brother's murder.' He turned back to Rennic, gaze hard. 'But what if there's more to it? What if we have events backward?'

Rennic offered only a blank look.

'Did Vassad kill my father first? Tried to control him with alchemy, poisoned him by accident or design, then decided to kill my brothers before they could ascend, to cement his hold on the kingdom?'

Rennic's hands were spread. He could offer no answers in the echoing dark.

'And that's why Mendel still lives now.' Tarfel's voice fell away. 'Because he was hurt, because he's . . . he's pliable. Am *I* pliable?'

Rennic looked to Chel in pleading.

'I'm pliable, aren't I? Aren't I, Vedren?'

Chel swallowed. 'You can't be that pliable, highness. Look where you are now.'

Tarfel laughed, surprising himself.

'No, no, indeed. Ha. Maybe that's what happened at Denirnas, eh? Maybe the old bastard saw something like this coming?'

Chel offered half a nod, unconvinced.

'Let's hope not.'

***

Palo held open the sturdy door at the tunnel's far end. Spider and Dalim between them had burst the lock, using

Dalim's pilfered spear as a lever. The door opened into a crate-filled store-room, and Chel thought immediately of the room in the depths of the Silent Sepulchre, the secret wall, the smugglers' caves beneath. He thought of Torht and Mendel, their laborious journey up the tower's great spiral. They would have reached the top by now. They must have done. Unless they'd also been caught up in the confessors' violent response.

Rennic tilted his head, tracing what looked a well-worn path through the crates to a curtain-covered opening on the far side. 'Well, I'm going to check every store-room I come across for hidden doors in future.'

Spider was already at the curtain, peeping around, curved knife in his hand. Palo joined him.

'Where are we?'

Spider turned with a leering smirk.

'We're in the tower. Close to the meat.'

An empty office lay beyond, the quills, ink and rolls of paper suggesting a senior church clerk's. Chel wondered if such a clerk existed, and whether that clerk was in on the puppet-king conspiracy. How far did the tendrils reach?

They crept through a narrow set of interconnecting rooms, each seemingly empty, then the passageway opened to reveal the great stone spiral at the tower's heart. Palo cocked an ear at its edge.

'Activity below, but doesn't sound like it's coming our way. They may still believe we are hidden in the royal wing.' She turned and looked upward.

Dalim stepped beside her.

'Anything?'

She shook her head. 'Perhaps they have already succeeded.

Perhaps the pennant of the free peoples is unfurling as we speak.'

Dalim nodded, cradling the spear in his arms. His habitual assurance had deserted him.

'Yeah. Maybe.'

'Then let us finish our climb and find out for ourselves.'

***

The upper reaches of the tower were devoted to the Primarch's private chambers. The spiral stair curled around with a final, wide flourish, pitching them before a giant set of gold-inlaid doors at the tower-top's inner edge. Above, the ceiling climbed in a gleaming dome, similarly golden, emblazoned with the figures of the sanctified and hierarchs past, drawn against a backdrop of swirling stars. From somewhere came a strange rumbling sound, and the distant clatter of rolling chain.

'Well, this is grand as fuck,' Rennic muttered as the ceiling came into view. 'What happened to all that shit about charity and bestowing all the good stuff on the meek?'

Chel offered a sardonic smile. 'Not exactly meek, are you?'

'Fuck off, I'm meek. I'm meek as anyone.'

'Hey,' a voice said from above. 'Stop there. Stop right there.'

Two confessors stood before the doors, their garb grander than those below. Their robes were finely layered and embroidered, a cut above the rough, rust-coloured fabric of their comrades. Gleaming, ornate maces hung from their belts, but they seemed otherwise unarmed and unarmoured. Braziers burned to either side of the grand door, casting the confessors in a warm, fiery glow.

Palo came to a halt at the top of the grand stairs. Tall windows, inlaid with multi-coloured glass in sacred patterns, cast crisp winter light across her. The whole floor reeked of incense.

'Tell me, brother,' she said. 'Has the crown prince come this way?'

'Who are you?' the first said, expression uneasy. 'You shouldn't be up here.' His colleague looked only bored, although this was in danger of being the first interesting thing that had happened on their watch.

Palo spread her hands, her inherent lack of visible emotion going some way to reassuring the confessor. 'We are his retainers. He asked us to complete a task for him, but we have been unable. Is he in consultation with the blessed Primarch?'

The confessor nodded, and Chel felt something unclench within him.

Palo smiled. It looked wrong on her face. The confessor's look of suspicion returned.

'Why are you armed? Weapons aren't allowed in the tower.'

His colleague stirred, as if the thought had only just occurred. 'Those are blessed blades!'

They looked at each other, then to the engraved silver bell that hung from a frame beside the stairs.

Palo's smile faded. She dropped her hands. As the confessors lunged toward the bell, Spider and Dalim surged past her up the stairs and onto the landing. Dalim's spear transfixed the first confessor, punching through his midriff and driving him backward toward the door, his legs flailing and buckling. Spider leapt upon the second, carrying him sideways past the bell-frame, driving him down against the cold stone floor. The two barely managed a cry between them before they were silenced.

Rennic shot Chel a look that said, are you taking notes?

Tarfel peeped a miserable face up from the staircase, frowning at the stricken confessors. 'Did we have to . . . Wasn't there another way?'

Rennic tilted his head, one thick eyebrow raised. 'I doubt we could have won them over with strength of argument alone.'

'But couldn't we just have tied them up?'

'You got a great spool of secret rope hidden somewhere in your pantaloons, princeling?'

Chel sighed. 'It would take too long to secure them properly,' he heard himself say. The image of the archer floated across his mind, her nervous smile, her slumped form at the feet of the strangling reaver. 'And someone would need to keep watch on them. Even that would be no guarantee. This is just . . . safer.'

Something in his chest withered. Should we simply have killed Brecki? he wondered. Would that have been . . . better? Would it have been right?

Tarfel wiped at his nose with a sleeve. 'So much . . . killing, so much death. And for what? I doubt these two were even in robes when my father died.'

Palo turned from the top of the stairs and fixed the young prince with a gimlet stare.

'They are complicit,' she said. She walked toward the grand doors as Dalim dug the spear from the first confessor. He lay crumpled at the wall's foot, breath coming in short gasps, a dark puddle spreading beneath his robes. He tried to speak, but he couldn't force out a word. Palo looked down at him for a moment, expressionless once more.

'You know,' she said, 'when I was a girl, long ago now, before the wars, before the schism, before the New Church and its rancid corruption, we had a confessor in our keep. Just the one: a gentle, patient man. His divine calling was to listen, to hear the confessions of the keep's people and provide guidance, and perhaps even absolution. The confessions he heard were freely given, not extracted!' Anger rose in her voice. 'A confessor is a keeper of a sacred duty. Not a red-clad thug, a tormentor of the helpless.'

She breathed deeply, and the anger left her again.

'May your god forgive you, for mine will not.'

She reached down and cut the man's throat, wiped her blade on the shoulder of his fine robe, and threw open the doors.

THIRTY-THREE

A short, dark passage of new-looking chunky stone led to a thick metal gate. A low rumbling emanated from somewhere beneath their feet, a sound that suggested something heavy was moving nearby. As they neared the gate, Chel realized that it was moving. The thick, crossed bars were sliding sideways, a new vertical pillar appearing in the doorway as the last one disappeared from view.

'The fuck is this?' Spider said, prodding the metal with a knife. Dalim reached out and grabbed the bars, trying to slow or stop the metal's movement. He whipped his hands away just before the doorway's stone edge would have crushed them.

'Shit-pipes!'

Palo stood before the sliding wall, unmoved. 'This is the gate to Vassad. That it moves is good. We need only wait.'

Chel and Rennic exchanged uncertain glances, but her confidence quelled dissent. They waited, peering through the gaps in the bars. Beyond lay a wide, stone-floored chamber, mostly in darkness, its far side promising a door-shaped sliver of silvery daylight, half-obscured by heavy curtains. Chel imagined he saw thin bars moving across the distant slice of light, but the glare made it hard to be sure.

'Ah,' Palo said, and took a step forward. 'Quickly now.'

A gap opened in the bars, a framed space that widened as the wall slid. Palo stepped through, and Dalim and Spider followed. By the time Chel and Rennic reached the doorway, the gap's far edge had already appeared. The doorway began to close on them.

'Highness, this way!'

Tarfel wasn't moving, his gaze fixed on the narrowing doorway. 'There's . . . There's not enough time . . .'

Rennic grabbed his arm and yanked him forward.

'Like fuck there isn't.'

He shoved Chel through the doorway ahead of him, then wrapped his arms around the prince and bundled him through. The rolling wall slid closed as they fell to the smooth stone flagstones beyond, almost slicing Rennic's boot-heel as he kicked free.

'God's bollocks, princeling,' Rennic said, pushing himself upright and checking his scuffed boot. 'You know how to make a meal of things, don't you?'

Dalim offered them a disdainful sneer, then turned to Palo. 'What now?'

They stood in a circular space, two dozen paces wide, in darkness but for the narrow light from the curtain-wrapped far doorway. The ceiling rose in a high dome overhead, continuing the same gilded motif as the outer hall, the serene faces of church figures past beaming down at them with a dull golden gleam, the bejewelled stars at their backs doing little to light the gloom. The rumbling beneath their feet was louder, joined by a ticking clank of thick chains in whatever mechanism drove the rotating cage wall.

Palo nodded at the empty metal door-frame, now grinding slowly over a wall of blank stone at the chamber's edge, then at the dull grey light beyond. 'We wait. Our friends should be on the other side.'

'What is this room?' Chel said, as Spider leapt at the ceiling, arm extended, trying to prise out one of the dome's embedded gemstones. He fell short, and looked to Dalim for the use of his spear.

Rennic squinted in the gloom. 'Plenty of scuff marks, old fireplace over there. Looks like a receiving chamber. Once.'

'And now?'

Rennic looked at the circular cage wall that surrounded them, its single doorway rolling steadily toward their presumed exit. 'A holding pen.'

Chel shivered. 'This is . . . very strange.'

Rennic scratched at his beard. 'This is the kind of construction someone might build if they wanted to keep all visitors at arm's length, control their comings and goings while observing them from safety. Look at it, one entrance, one exit, only one can open at a time, controlled by a mechanism which I'm guessing is behind those cage bars and curtains over there. It's a paranoid's paradise. We should probably check there aren't spring-mounted spikes in the ceiling.'

Tarfel had made his way to the far side, keeping a nervous pace back from the moving bars. The edge of the door-frame was approaching the far doorway. The prince peered through the sliding metal into the light beyond, then started and took a step forward.

'Mendel? Mendel!'

His shriek brought the others running, but he was already pushing at the narrow gap, his nervousness forgotten. He slipped through before anyone could reach him, despite Palo's shouts and Rennic's lunge.

Something clanked beneath their feet, and the wall stopped moving with a judder. Tarfel hesitated, then pushed on, running into the watery glare, bellowing his brother's name and throwing the curtains aside. Rennic tried to squeeze after him, but the gap was too narrow. He huffed and swore while Palo snapped at him, then pulled back, enraged.

'Little man! You're dinky enough, get in there.'

Chel had his bad arm and shoulder through when the floor clanked again. The metal wall trembled. For a moment, Chel was relieved: he'd no longer have to scrape himself through after the skinny prince. Then the wall began to move.

Backward.

His screams alerted the others, and Rennic and Dalim between them dragged him free, hauling him back into the circular chamber, coughing and sweating and desperately afraid. He sat on the floor, arms cradled against his body, shivering and gasping, unable to forget the cold metal against his skin, the crushing sensation against his chest.

Rennic nudged him with a boot. 'Get up. Wall's stopped again. Get your prince to open it.'

The room was silent, but for a murmur from beyond. Chel forced himself back to the doorway, now blocked with thick bars of cold steel. His heart was thumping in his chest, his breath shallow and head fuzzy, but he could hear Tarfel's voice. He pushed his face as close to the bars as he dared. The curtains that had covered the archway were thrown open, and finally he could see what had sent the young prince running.

The Primarch's opulent chambers stretched away on either side, rich decor and fine furnishings, thick furs on the floor and beautiful tapestries festooning the walls, to Chel's utter unsurprise. Mendel sat, slumped, in a tall-backed wooden chair, surrounded by a halo of weak daylight from the open balcony behind. He was covered in blood. Tarfel knelt at his side, whimpering and gabbling, his hands roving his brother's armoured body as he searched for his wounds.

'Brother, oh brother, what's happened? Where's the Watcher? Where's Primarch Vassad? Oh brother, come back to me, please! Father is dead! You're all I have!'

Mendel stirred, raising his head as if from a doze. 'T— Tarfel? You made it.' He offered a weak, generous smile. Blood flecked his teeth. 'Where are your friends?'

'They're in the . . . The cage room.' Tarfel gestured, and Chel tried to catch his attention. He saw no sign of Torht, nor of any guards, let alone their quarry. His focus was only on escaping the receiving chamber, but he didn't fancy marching straight into whatever had done that to Mendel.

'Highness,' he hissed. 'Prince Tarfel!'

Tarfel looked back, bleary-eyed and choked with emotion. 'What?'

'Find the mechanism! Get us out of here.'

Tarfel stood to look around, but Mendel put a gentle, bloodied hand on his arm. 'Tarfel,' he said, his voice weak. 'Tarfel, I'm so glad. I'm so glad you made it all the way up here.'

Palo jostled Chel aside, gripping the bars until her knuckles whitened. 'Mendel!' she called. 'Where is Vassad? Where is the Watcher?'

Mendel turned his head toward them. His beautiful face was criss-crossed with blood splatter, but still he seemed serene, beatific. He smiled, wide and genuine and gory.

'Oh, he'll be right along. He's just around the corner.'

'Who will?'

A cackle filled the chambers, an eerie sound like the shrieking of an evil mimic bird. Mendel swivelled his gore-streaked head. 'Here he comes now.'

A white-clad figure danced into view. It was not Torht, not by any stretch of the imagination. The man was tall, long of hair and beard, now more silver than black. His posture was stooped, his limbs spindly, but he moved with great freedom, skipping around the two princes in his simple white robe. Light spots of blood dotted the robe like the gentle patter of rain.

'You see, you see,' the new figure said. 'Room goes round, round and around, then back around, round and around, yes. The world is round, round and around. You see? You see?' It was unclear to whom this was addressed.

Chel peered over Palo's shoulder. 'Who is that?'

Palo was rigid.

'Lo Vassad.'

The white-robed figure stooped to pick up something Chel couldn't see, then held it to his ear, nodding as if it spoke to him. He turned and uncupped his hands with great tenderness, as if he'd been cradling a precious butterfly, then waved into the empty air beyond the open balcony. He swivelled on one foot, nimble as a veil-dancer, then sashayed over to the barred doorway.

'Faces! Faces in the world room. Friends or foes, friends or foes? Friendly faces are fool's foils, firmly.' He tittered to himself, then walked back to the princes with wild, exaggerated strides.

Chel's jaw hung loose. He could feel Rennic's breath over his shoulder, the others crowded in around him and Palo. 'He's . . . He's fucking mad.'

Rennic sounded no less confused. 'I'll say. I've seen saner box-preachers.'

Palo said nothing.

'But . . .' Chel's head was spinning, faster than the chamber walls ever had, 'how can he command the Rose? Write their orders?'

Mendel stretched out his legs, then bounced to his feet. His smile was no less wide, no less generous, but somehow the light in his eyes was no longer warm. Despite the blood coating him, he moved easily. Tarfel took an involuntary step back at his brother's sudden rise and looked from the chattering Primarch to his brother and back.

'Mendel? Wha—?'

'You know,' said the crown prince, reaching down to pick something up from beside the chair, 'I didn't think you'd get all the way up here. I wasn't sure, truth be told, that I wanted you to. But in the end, I'm glad. I wanted you to see it all.'

He hefted a sack that hung heavy and sodden.

'See all what?' Tarfel said. 'Whose blood is that? What's in the bag?'

Mendel turned toward the barred door. Behind him, Vassad crouched to listen intently to the conversation of two passing mice, who, he announced, knew a great many secrets, but were bound by oaths of sharpest discretion.

'I wanted you to see my work, brother. I wanted you to see that I have already won.'

'What do you mean?'

Mendel took a deep breath. 'Tarfel, the greatest villain ever to stalk our kingdom is now, for want of a better term, my pet.'

Chel's brain caught up with his eyes. Of course. Alchemy. The malicious herb.

'What? But . . . but how? Are you saying you control the Primarch?'

'I'm saying this shambling husk here,' Mendel gestured at the robed figure, who had seated himself on the room's other chair and was listening intently, 'became so paranoid, so jealous of his power, that he walled himself off from the world. He created an engine of control, a shadow state, its levers at his sole command, and I . . . I took it from him.' Mendel patted his chest. 'Once I had his seal, the kingdom was mine. They were all accustomed to taking his orders from me. They still take orders from me. They know no different.'

'I don't understand. Did he kill Father? Did . . . Did you?'

Mendel looked genuinely offended. 'Fuck off, Tarf! Of course he did! Your pal Torht had it right, just not all the way. Vassad drugged Father for a decade, pushed it too far and poisoned him, then tried to clear the board in a panic.' Mendel laughed, an oddly bitter sound from his golden countenance.

Tarfel was paler than Chel had ever seen him.

Mendel began to walk around the chair, the sack dangling from his hand. 'He was going to keep Father "alive", if you will, for as long as it took to cement his own claim.

Didn't want to risk the whole thing turning into a war of succession. But Brave Prince Mendel had suffered a terrible injury and wasn't quite the same upstairs any more. Music to this malignant arsehole's ears.'

'How do you know this?'

'He told me. You know, before he, ah, lost it all upstairs himself. When he thought I was his. I cut my own face, did you know that?' He ran one finger along the scar on his cheek. 'It was that or wait for the knife in my back.' He sighed.

'He never drugged you?'

'Oh, he tried, of course – didn't want to risk me forming my own ideas. But I knew his game. And once he thought it was working . . .' All levity left his voice. 'I returned the favour. He's still in there somewhere, you know? Blood in the air gets him all fired up, gets him clanking the mechanism round and round until he calms down. That was him trying to crush your man there.' Mendel winked toward the door. 'Hello again, sand-flower. Sorry about laying that mess at Denirnas at your feet, but it's always easier to scapegoat an outsider, eh?'

Tarfel stared for a moment, speechless. 'But why is he still alive?'

Mendel pursed his lips. 'Someone needs to be up here. Eat the food, defile the privy, keep the servants entertained.' He smiled. 'Ha, you know, there's a place somewhere in the deep east where it's a fairly quotidian punishment to tweak out someone's tongue? God knows where, but the transgressors make for the most discreet help, especially when you throw in the language barrier.'

Chel thought of Whisper and shivered.

'Why not end this? Why not reveal all?' Tarfel was leaning

forward, one hand on the chair. He seemed weak, desperately pale.

'Are you familiar with those metal rods that crowned the tallest spires in the old cities? They ran all the way down the sides, all the way to the ground. Most are rusted away to nothing now, of course, but I'm told you can still see the grooves in the stone. Do you know what they were for?'

Tarfel shook his head, dumbfounded.

'They were storm-catchers, channellers of tempestuous fury. Our Taneru forebears used them to draw lightning from the sky.'

'But why?'

'Because if you choose where the lightning will strike, you also choose where it won't.'

'I don't understand.'

'Our shuffling ex-Primarch is my storm-catcher, brother. The great jutting villain that looms dark over the provinces. His shadow leaves a lot of room to operate.'

'To what end, brother?'

'To draw out our secret foes! The so-called nations that crowd our diminished borders have no wish to see a unified Vistirlar, the rebellious territories and breakaway cities reunited at last. They do not want their meddling and profiteering disrupted, Tarfel. They fund their wars and their courts with credit and favour, they whisper and scheme and sow division and dissension, and it is time to cut off their grasping fingers. Those nations were our vassals in the time of the empire, they were thralls to the Imperial Throne. They need a reminder from history.'

Tarfel said nothing, merely watching his brother with wide, wet eyes.

'Where is the Watcher?' Palo said from the doorway. Her hands gripped the bars, knuckles white.

'Ah.' Mendel turned to her. 'Here. You'll be wanting this.' He slung the sack toward the door. It bounced twice before sliding to a halt at the foot of the bars.

'Where is the Watcher?' Palo said. Her voice was like cold lead. Chel realized he was shaking.

'I think you should open the bag.'

Palo made no move, but Dalim reached down through the bars and snatched at the sack. He rolled it open far enough to reveal the sightless sockets of the severed head within, then staggered back with a howl.

'He put up sod-all fight as well,' Mendel said, his tone conversational. 'Witless dolt. Never saw it coming.' He blinked, then laughed. 'Ha, never saw it coming, Tarf. Ha!'

Tarfel stood frozen, framed by the gallery beyond. 'You killed him? Why?'

Mendel started as if catching a foul odour. 'He and his ghastly minions have been a persistent irritant for far too long.' He waved a hand toward the prisoners in the audience chamber. 'Using the Merciful Sisters as cover, though, I should have spotted that. Oh, the Sisters are due a reckoning for their treachery. But don't worry, they'll be in good company.'

'Why kill him? You know everything, you've seen everything! He only wanted to root out the corruption of the Church! To bring peace to the kingdom! Why did we all come here today?'

'Oh, Tarfel,' Mendel said, head tilted, his expression weighted with compassion. 'Don't be thick. They came here to kill us – all of us. You, me and Father. He was carrying a little vial of poison, presumably to off me once the heavy lifting was done. He was convinced that he was our mother's secret son, that we were half-brothers. That sightless pederast thought he had a claim, thought he'd clear out his rivals then scoop up Vassad's reins. Well, someone beat him to it.'

'But—'

'No. Sit down and be quiet. I've been very patient with you, little brother, but I think we've wasted rather too much time laying things out for the proles. Here ends the lesson.'

Tarfel moved to speak again, and Mendel's hand jumped to the sword at his waist.

'Enough, Tarfel.'

The young prince took a step back, eyes burning with emotion. For a moment, his gaze met Chel's, then his gaze dropped. His old shoulder-slump returned, and he began to shuffle toward the chair. Behind them, Vassad had made his way to the chilly balcony, burbling at a cluster of congregating pigeons.

'And now,' Mendel said, turning back toward the barred doorway, 'as for what to do with—'

The knife whipped through the air, flashing between the two princes and ruffling Mendel's hair. Mendel ducked down behind the chair, Tarfel stood dazed, unsure of what had happened.

'Cheeky!' Mendel said, peering up from behind the chair. 'Was that you, Palo? Pity you're a rotten throw.'

'Am I?' Palo said from the door, her voice razor blades.

They turned. At the balcony, Vassad wavered, wide-eyed, a dark red stain flooding down one arm of his brilliant robe. The knife jutted from his shoulder. He wasn't screaming or crying, but he certainly looked perturbed.

Mendel's gaze snapped back. 'Fucking hells. Tarfel, grab

him and get him back to his chamber. We'll need to staunch that. Lady Palo, you and I are going to have a long talk before you depart this mortal realm.'

Tarfel blinked but made no move.

'Tarfel, go and get him. Move your useless arse!'

'The attack at Denirnas,' Tarfel said. 'The false-Norts, the counts who tried to kill me, the confessors who hunted me after we escaped. Was that you? Did you order that, as him?'

Mendel paused just a little too long. 'No. Don't be absurd. I can't control every shit-wipe of a nobleman, especially when they're nasty little social climbers. Those confessors just wanted to bring you back to me.'

'I see.'

'Now get him back in before he does something unpredictable.' Mendel was still hunched behind the chair. Tarfel began to walk toward the balcony, unhurried, unbent.

'He killed my father,' he said softly as he walked. 'He killed my brother. He tried to poison and enslave the last of my family.' His voice rose as he approached the Primarch, whose face was almost as pale as the unstained parts of his robe.

The distant eyes settled on his.

'Faces in darkness,' Lo Vassad said in his faraway, sing-song voice. 'Friend or foe?'

'You don't deserve to live,' Tarfel Merimonsun replied, and shoved the man with both hands.

'No!' Mendel roared as the white robe fluttered over the balcony and out of sight. 'No! What have you done?'

Tarfel turned, eyes blazing. 'What you should have done when you had the chance. I'm ending this!'

'You're ending nothing, you stupid boy!' Mendel cried,

and launched himself at his brother. He smashed a mailed fist against Tarfel's jaw, and the young prince dropped to the flagstones.

Mendel turned with a snarl as the first cries drifted up from below, shrieks, shouts and screams, the sound of alarm, of outrage, and then the clash of steel. A bell began to toll.

'Well,' the crown prince said through gritted teeth, 'that answers the question of what to do with you all. Our red-robed friends will be with us shortly to take your confession.' He cocked an ear. 'And it sounds like your comrades in the courtyard are making their acquaintance, too.'

Chel thought of Lemon, Foss and the others below, and felt sweat-palmed queasiness churn within him. Maybe the rest of the Rau Rel forces would cross the city and reach the citadel in time. There were *a lot* of confessors down there.

'Five years,' Mendel growled toward his groaning brother. 'Five years of patience, of sacrifice, of acting Prince Moron the Fuck-wit. You see, little brother, as I was lying, blood-soaked, beneath my dear, dutiful twin, who gave his own stupid life for mine, I had something of an epiphany. Only one man could have ordered the attempt on my life, and only from panic. I was no threat, not yet ascended to manhood, and Father was in the prime of life. I knew in that moment that Father was dead, and that it was vital that Vassad believe that his desperate plan had succeeded. That Corvel the Wise, heir of Vistirlar, was dead. Mendel the Fair could live on, scarred and cracked, pliant to his new master's bidding. For a time, at least.'

The snarl returned. 'For five years I tolerated that

revolting bastard's existence. If I could do it, so could you, you stupid. Little. Bastard!'

Tarfel pushed himself up on one elbow. Already his jaw was swelling, blood welling from a dozen mail-scrapes. Mendel loomed over him, despite his diminutive stature.

'God's breath,' Tarfel said in a tiny, broken voice. 'You're . . . not . . .'

A wild smile lit the elder prince's face. 'Oh bravo, little brother, you got there in the end. Perhaps you're a little more like me after all.'

Chel watched transfixed from the doorway.

I cut my own face, did you know that?

Chel felt his throat closing. 'It's Corvel,' he breathed.

***

Corvel Merimonsun, called Corvel the Wise, snapped his hands together and blasted out a long breath. The bells outside were proliferating, the drifting shouts and screams from below now part of the background. 'You know why they called dear, dead bro "the Fair"? Everyone assumes it was his looks, but let me clue you in – we were *fucking twins*. Perhaps not identical, but good as, eh? No, it was because he was *equitable*. He was fair-minded. He was dutiful. And that's why he had to die.'

'*You* killed him?'

'Oh, rest assured, he'd probably have died from his wounds eventually. But I had a narrow window to make my play, and make it I did. The only way for our family to triumph was for there to be a single survivor, and for that survivor to be me. I had to become Prince Mendel, which meant there couldn't really be another Prince Mendel coughing and croaking around, eh? I did what was necessary, and I will not hesitate to do so again, little brother.

'Perhaps there is an upside to this mess after all,' the prince continued. 'It's time for a change in the Church, I think, a clean slate. And thanks to the sterling efforts of our friends the Rau Rel, the most insidious and pernicious elements of the Executive have already been removed, along with a couple of problematic Names. Care of the bitter scheming of your late Watcher, nobody with a power base of any significance remains.'

Chel looked around their group. Spider and Palo were immobile, eyes fixed on the scene beyond. Dalim knelt, bereft, one hand through the bars still gripping the sack that contained Torht's head. Rennic had edged away, eyes scanning the great circular room. His gaze met Chel's and offered nothing but defeat.

'You know, it's funny,' Corvel said. 'I thought we were sunk when the Norts came sailing into Denirnas, hell of an overreaction on their part. Of course, turns out they were just putting on a show for their own, but we weren't to know. You see, we'd taken something from them, something we thought that perhaps they wouldn't miss. Can't be right all the time, eh?

'But the strangest thing happened: the greyhairs of Omundi were suddenly concerned. "What if the Norts attack?" they said. So I saw to it that they did. Half the ducal family, and my own brother, wiped out by invaders. Ghastly business. Had to be a bloodbath to sell it, though, so needs must. And you know what? Those daft old buggers folded at a stroke. The others followed. The north has never been so united in the face of foreign aggression.'

He tipped his head forward, staring into the dark of the

cage. 'That's when I saw it, what Vassad himself had seen. The lesson of the Taneru. Common purpose, common identity, common enemies. That's how you build something to last. And the best part?' He grinned and raised his eyebrows. 'I got to keep my stolen prize. I foresee the unrest in the south will soon be over.'

'We should have let you die at Raven-Hill,' Palo snarled through the gate. 'Should have let the Horvaun tear you to strips.'

Corvel nodded, considering. 'Yes, I daresay you should. It's unlikely you'd be in this position now.'

'You will burn for what you've done.'

'I doubt it. Certainly, your little movement is at an end. I have your leadership, your support, your backers, and not before time. But do me a favour, will you? When the confessors come, don't put up a fight. I'd love to hear your public confession. Oh, that reminds me.'

He disappeared from view, keeping Palo in sight as long as he could. A moment later, the floor clanked, and the wall began to rotate once more. Back the way they'd come. Back toward the outer door. With a whimper, Dalim released the bloody sack. Corvel reappeared, hopping back behind the chair.

'You know, I still owe you for Balise. What you did was unforgivable. You can consider the bag a down-payment on that.'

'She got what she deserved,' Tarfel said from the floor. Blood dripped from his chin, and his entire cheek had swollen. 'Balise was vile.'

'Balise was angry and full of hate and *very* easy to control!' Corvel said. 'She was an excellent first. Where in twelve hells am I going to find a replacement?'

The outer door buckled, then burst inward. Light flooded the narrow passageway beyond the circular cage. Those in the audience chamber swivelled, hands fumbling for weapons. All except Palo, who stood immobile at the gate.

'Well, it's about fucking time,' Corvel snapped. 'It's a good thing we weren't in real trouble. Tarfel, look upset. Perfect!' He dropped to his knees, throwing his arms over his head. 'Shepherd help us!' he cried. 'They killed him, Shepherd's grace, they killed him! They threw the Primarch from the balcony! Save us, please!'

Shapes blotted the passageway light. The grinding of the wall brought the door-frame around, inching ever closer to the empty archway. A lumbering shape hove into view, filling the passage, waiting for the door to arrive; a grotesque figure of gleaming steel limbs, a great wolf's head upon its hulking shoulders. It roared with a distinctly human voice, rattling the cage bars with one pink hand, pulling at them, trying to drag the doorway around. The clanking quickened.

'Whatever that is, it ain't friendly.' Rennic pulled his sword from its once-blessed scabbard. Dalim was back on his feet, the spear fast in his hands, his arms spinning in familiar alternation. Spider's curved blades glinted in his fists.

'God's bollocks,' Rennic whispered. 'There are hundreds of the fuckers.'

Chel scampered back to the gate, squeezing past Palo to press his face to the sliding bars. 'Highness,' he hissed. 'Prince Tarfel!'

Tarfel lay in the balcony's shadow, eyes glazed, blood now pooling from his damaged chin on the flags below.

Chel hissed again, and he looked up. His watery blue gaze offered only fear and helplessness.

'The mechanism,' Chel called. 'Reverse the mechanism! Please!'

The young prince blinked a couple of times, as if the words were meaningless, but as Chel prepared to cry again, Tarfel moved. He struggled to his feet, one hand wobbling against the flags, and looked around for his target. He'd already taken a step when Corvel lashed him with a sharp kick, knocking him sprawling. His drive recovered, Tarfel scrabbled forward, making for the hidden levers, but his brother was on him. Another kick knocked him to his back, and before he could pull away Corvel's sword was out, its point resting on his chest. He'd cleaned it, but badly, since beheading the Watcher; gory streaks darkened its otherwise gleaming length.

'No, Tarfel,' Corvel said, breathing hard but voice level. 'No. You're my brother and I'm not going to kill you, but I'll cheerfully take a fucking hand if you move again. You fancy being Prince Stumpy for the rest of your days, you go right ahead.'

Tarfel looked up at him, then back to Chel, tear-filled and pleading, then he slumped back against the cold stone, crying. Behind Chel, the steel doorway ground over the stone edge of the outer passage's archway. The cries of the confessors reached fever-pitch, and the giant roared again. Corvel stepped from view, ready to halt the cage's movement.

'Come on then, you red bastards,' Rennic said. 'Who wants to see your afterlife?'

The doorway opened.

The giant was too big to squeeze through at first, and a

smaller confessor slid in, mace gripped tight. Another followed, a tuft-headed man carrying a length of heavy chain. Those behind them jostled and cried, and some had begun a ritual chant.

Dalim met the first man head-on, faking one way with the spear before slapping it back and around, slamming the point against the man's cheek. As he reeled, Spider passed him, slicing hot cuts across his neck and back as he swirled around. Rennic watched the chain-bearer approach, sword loose in his hand, stepping back from the man's wild swings. Chel guessed he was not a fighting confessor, more an enthusiastic amateur, but that made his whirling chain no less dangerous. Rennic watched him all the way, then dropped to one knee and drove the sword into the man's midriff. The confessor collapsed, gasping, and as Rennic stood he slashed the sword across the man's face.

Already two more confessors were inside, and the doorway was now wide enough for the great metal giant to enter. He stooped and scraped inside with another gleeful roar, the white fur of the wolf's head brushing the gilded edge of the dome above, and a moment later the floor clanked and the wall stilled.

Chel turned to Palo, who remained motionless, facing away. 'Palo! We need to fight! We need to get out!'

She said nothing, her mouth a thin line, her brow creased.

'Fine, give me your fucking sword then.' He reached, but her hand was fast on the pommel. She wouldn't budge. Still she said nothing. Behind them, Dalim had impaled one of the new confessors and Spider and Rennic between them had sliced the second, but the giant was closing and they were falling back against a red tide.

'Five fucking hells!'

Chel darted away, stooping low to avoid the swish of a sword stroke, and snatched up the trailing edge of the chain the second confessor had dropped. He ducked again as a spear whistled past, then scuttled back to avoid a mace-strike from a confessor who'd spotted him. Now the man filled his vision, his face snarling with righteous fury as he thrashed at Chel with the mace. *He does think we killed his Primarch*, Chel thought as he scrambled backward on all fours. *No wonder he's angry.*

A sword blade hacked at the man's arm, and as he turned in rage a second slash cut him across the legs. He pitched forward with a cry, and the blade slammed into the top of his head.

'Palo?'

Rennic looked up as he tried to dig his sword from the confessor's skull. 'What?'

'Nothi— Behind!'

Rennic ducked instinctively, and a great sweep of a metal arm passed over his head. He abandoned the sword and rolled away as another blow swung back, a length of blunt steel whistling over him as he dodged. The giant turned and noticed Chel, and a great, guttural laugh spilled from within the white wolf's head.

'Sand-crab! This is the Shepherd's will!'

Chel backed away. The cold metal of the bars pressed into his back. 'What is?'

'That we should meet again!'

Chel blinked and looked again. The huge figure was clad in armour unlike any he'd ever seen, plates of steel wrapped around each limb, articulated joints blended without visible mailed seam. It looked impenetrable. The only uncovered parts were the head and hands, the former covered in a giant wolf's head, its white hide draped over the massive shoulders and back, the latter—

One hand. The right wrist ended in a simple metal fork, a two-pronged piece of steel.

No.

He looked again at the legs. The knees were heavy, reinforced, the legs braced with extra lengths of metal. The giant's gait was slow, lumbering. Painful.

'Brother Hurkel?'

'Best pray for the Shepherd's mercy, sand-crab! You'll be seeing her soon!'

A mace slammed against the giant's back and he turned in irritation.

'Didn't we already kill you once, fuck-stick?' Rennic said, flinging another discarded mace at the armoured figure. Dalim danced into view, spear still in his hands despite the close surroundings, its tip glossy in the low light. He whipped the weapon around, driving the blade against the steel torso faster than the giant could slap it away. It left only a small nick on the carapace.

Hurkel laughed again.

Something bright bloomed in the gloom of the circular chamber, something hot and fearsome, fierce enough to blind those closest and throw a cloud of choking black smoke into the passageway and upward into the dome. Confessors reeled, coughing and hacking, those at the end of the passageway scrambling back into the open space beyond, gasping.

'The fuck was that?' Chel said, muffled through the arm pressed over his nose and mouth.

At the chamber's exit, Spider stood triumphant, rivers running from the curved blades in his hands. 'Like a bit of fucking alchemy, do you?' he bawled at the fleeing confessors, catching one with a vicious slash as he staggered past. Even Hurkel seemed stunned by the sudden burst of flame and its choking aftermath, spinning on stiff, ponderous legs, pawing at the miasma with his fork-hand.

Chel reacted fastest. He lashed out with the chain, whipping it out and around the giant's tree-like shin. The chain wrapped around as Hurkel twisted, looking from his blinkered wolf-view for the source of constriction.

'Yes, little man!' Rennic had grabbed another mace from somewhere and ducked beneath Hurkel's swing to slam it against his armoured chest. This time, the armour dented, just enough for the bump to show. Rennic fell back, calling toward Spider, who stood surrounded by a heap of stricken confessors at the chamber door.

'Spider, let's finish this fucker!'

Spider looked up, across the chamber at the steel giant and the handful of confessors still standing. Then his gaze swung to the empty passageway beyond.

Rennic dodged back from another of Hurkel's swings. He was running out of room, even as Chel strained against the chain, trying to keep the giant in place.

'Spider!'

Spider nodded, an odd, twitching gesture. 'Cheerio, pricks.' He fled down the passageway, past the blinded and choking confessors. A moment later, they heard the sound of breaking glass, and then nothing.

Chel stared after him in disbelief. 'What in hells . . . What's he—?'

'Spider only cares about one thing, little man,' Rennic growled back. 'Spider.'

'After him!'

Rennic jumped back again, jarring an elbow against the wall behind. 'Can you climb like he can? Because I fucking c— Ah!'

Hurkel dragged his leg forward, wrenching Chel's ruined shoulder and throwing him sideways to the flagstone floor. He caught Rennic with another blow, knocking him back against the wall, the mace clattering from his hand.

Three sharp bangs echoed against the steel of Hurkel's armour, and he lumbered around to find Dalim stabbing at his back. Dalim swivelled and flowed, a sinuous human weapon, two confessors mortally wounded in his wake.

'Time to die, shit-head,' Dalim said, eyes aflame. He half stepped one way, then pirouetted back, spinning the spear around and driving it toward the great wolf's head.

Hurkel's fork-hand trapped the spear, snatching the shaft from the air and twisting it sideways. His good hand seized the lead arm that held it, grasping Dalim's wrist and wrenching it around. Dalim screamed. As the spear dropped, Hurkel's good hand clamped down over Dalim's head, crushing at the skull beneath, a jubilant gurgle issuing from the bobbing wolf's head.

'Enough!'

Palo's voice carried clear across the smoke-filled chamber. She stood at the gate, sword finally in her hand, blade extended, unwavering.

Hurkel turned, flinging Dalim against the wall with horrible ease. Palo stared at him, into the darkness of the white wolf's jaws, then let the sword fall. Its clatter on the flagstones seemed to echo for an age.

'We yield.'

Hurkel paused. 'You yield?'

'We yield.'

'Do we . . . fuck,' said Rennic, from the floor. His face was bloodied and one arm hung limp. Chel had managed to crouch, but his landing on the flagstones had been unforgiving.

'We yield,' Palo repeated. 'It is over.'

'Coward,' Rennic said, voice cracked with blood and smoke.

'It is over,' Palo said again.

From the chambers beyond came Corvel's voice. 'Take them alive, good brothers! They must confess! The people must hear of their crimes!'

Chel had barely made it to his feet before the confessors bore them to the ground.

THIRTY-FOUR

Chel watched the drip form, watched the water congregate and swell, marking the heartbeats until it fell. His estimation was improving.

'What are you counting?' Rennic glowered from his straw-covered pallet in the cell's opposite corner. His jaw was still swollen, but he could see through both eyes again now.

'Nothing.'

An icy wind blew from the grille at the top of the cell wall, carrying a few drifting snowflakes from the courtyard beyond with the shouts and clatter of activity. The scaffold was being prepared again. From down the cell-block came the perpetual sounds of captive misery, the shuffling, whimpering aimlessness of multitudes held against their will. More had come, over the days that followed; the bulk of the Rau Rel force, the regulars and mercenaries, even some of the minor nobles who had lent their arms, then anyone who could be identified, however hazily, beyond that. The scaffold had gone up pretty promptly afterward.

Chel pondered, between the drips. He thought of the tower-top. He thought of the princes. He thought of Brecki the reaver's smile as she'd watched them in the camp.

Footsteps echoed on the stairway, the clanking, juddering steps of an armoured company approaching. Torchlight flared against the walls beyond the cell's screen of bars, lighting the grim stone with an almost cosy warmth it did not deserve. The monstrous gaoler stirred in her chair, shifting in discomfort at the arrival of someone of presumed importance.

Corvel marched straight past them to the cell beyond. He didn't even turn his head to look in as he passed. The thin band of gold at his temple gleamed as he walked, his bearing regal, his rich cloak the colour of cream edged with crimson. A silver brooch in the shape of a familiar flower shone from his throat. Chel wondered if he was still pretending to be stupid. A phalanx of armoured confessors followed him down the steps, the massive form of Brother Hurkel at their head.

'Who else, Palo?'

No reply came from the next cell.

'I know the late Watcher was your blood. What about the rest of your family? Who are they? Where are they? You have to tell me something. You know people are suffering. You're supposed to care about the people, remember? That was the whole point.'

No answer again. Corvel leaned back against the wall, into Chel's eyeline.

'This is all very noble, but you're only making things worse.'

Silence.

'Very well.' The prince made a quick signal with his

hand. Armoured footsteps sounded, and a familiar, urgent terror gripped Chel until he heard one of the cells at the block's dank end opened with an ominous groan, its occupants dragged struggling and screaming from within: two more of the regulars sent by the Names. Still no sign of Lemon, Foss, Loveless or Whisper. Perhaps they'd done as Rennic ordered and escaped the citadel after all. He dearly hoped so.

'I shall be king soon,' Corvel said, quite conversational, as the men were dragged away. 'Word's out about Father, and, well, Primarch Vassad's end was rather public, wasn't it? Strangest thing, it turns out he took the trouble to name me successor to both his estates and sacred duties, even though I'm not even a man of the cloth! So now I have to organize a coronation. We can wait for spring, I think, get a good turnout on the free way, grubby little hands waving in the sun. Perhaps I'll strike a new coin. The plebs love a new coin, don't they?'

Corvel grinned. His smile was nothing like the amiable jollity Chel had witnessed when he was Mendel.

'I shall miss our chats, Ayla. Until next time.'

He turned and swept from the cells, the red-robed battalion in pursuit after Hurkel's lumbering steps. Chel avoided the big man's gaze as he departed. One of the guards lingered, hesitating before their cell, a flickering torch in hand. A narrow figure, small for a confessor, hood pulled forward over the head. Chel leaned forward, squinting into the hood's darkness.

A pair of silver-grey eyes looked back, tearful but burning with purpose.

'Don't give up, Brother Bear. I'm going to get you out of here.'

Then Sabina was gone, footsteps echoing from the cold stone of the under-cells, her torchlight fading from the harsh, ugly walls.

Heart thumping in his chest, fingers tingling, Chel shuffled back on the creaking bench, stared up at where a new drip was forming, and dared to hope.

Acknowledgements

This book would not exist without the support, hard work, and enthusiasm of a great many people, and I would like to use this space to distribute a plethora of vast and resonant Thank Yous. First and tallest, to my literary agent Harry Illingworth, who leapt on the manuscript with the tenacity of some kind of small Yorkshire dog and dragged it into the publishing world by his teeth. Harry's youthful vigour has served as an inspiration to a jaded and disintegrating husk like me. Cheers, boss.

To my editor, the peerless Natasha Bardon, who carved a bloodier and more commanding swathe through the text than the Black Hawk Company ever managed; to Jack Renninson (who picked a far better title and wrote much better copy than I ever managed) and Vicky Leech; to the wise and measured Caroline Knight; to superlative cover artist Richard Anderson (hot DAMN is he good); and to all the production staff at HarperVoyager: you have made the book, in some cases literally. Thanks to the bally lot of you. (Any lingering typos and mistakes are, of course, all mine.)

To Francesca Haig, who donated her time and energies to the Authors for Grenfell auction* and who, when I was lucky enough to win her lot, went far, far beyond the norm in her level of review, feedback, enthusiasm, and absolute loveliness: I cannot thank you enough. (And anyone reading this should rush out to buy Francesca's magnificent books.) To Kat Howard, for most excellent editorial feedback (Kat's books are also stellar).

To my advance readers, cultural companions, sounding-boards, and suggesters-in-chief: Adam Iley, James G Smith and Laz Roberts. Thanks, chaps, couldn't have done it without you. You'll get yours.

To everyone who suffered through my early work and provided feedback and encouragement (or insufficient discouragement to stop me): Adam King, Bambos Xiouros, CP Grisold, Claire Gavin, DBF, Damian Francis, Dan Williams, David Winchurch, Ed Sayers, Jon 'Global Head' Brierly, Lexie Harrison-Cripps, Lisa Perry, Paul Bridges, Paul Fallon, Paul McEwan, and Paul Restall. Your mental and emotional sacrifices were not in vain.

To my colleagues, past and present, sadly too numerous to name (although a special shout-out to Steph Brown and Jon Atkins for inspiring parts of Foss and Lemon's travel banter): I wonder what it was about working with you lot that led me to write about a bunch of shiftless, morally ambiguous mercenaries devoid of loyalty and compassion and perennially doomed to fail? We may never know. And no, none of you is Lemon.

To my parents, and my teachers, who razed me and tort me to rite gud. To my remaining friends and family, for maintaining an appropriate level of polite interest. To my daughters, for eventually going to sleep and giving me a chance to write anything at all.

Finally, and most wholeheartedly, to my wife Sarah, to whom this book is dedicated. For encouraging me, supporting me (always emotionally, often financially, occasionally physically), gracefully handling both my absences and my presences, and for shouldering so many burdens; for being the person who told me to stop wittering on about maybe writing a book and get on with it; for being my absolute rock, and the greatest source of fun I've ever known: thank you. You are the single best thing in the world. MWAH.

* A portion of the advance for this book was donated to Family Action's campaign to help those affected by the Grenfell Tower fire. You can find out more at:
https://www.family-action.org.uk/what-we-do/grants/grenfell-response/